GERMANIA

Book five of the Veteran of Rome series
By: William Kelso

Visit the author's website **http://www.williamkelso.co.uk/**
William Kelso is the author of:
The Shield of Rome
The Fortune of Carthage
Devotio: The House of Mus
Caledonia - Book One of the Veteran of Rome series
Hibernia - Book Two of the Veteran of Rome series
Britannia – Book Three of the Veteran of Rome series
Hyperborea – Book Four of the Veteran of Rome series

Published in 2016 by FeedARead.com Publishing – Arts Council funded

To: Grandma and Granddad Kelso and Johnson, the greatest generation

About the author

My name is William Kelso and I am a British author specialising in ancient Roman and classical historical fiction. My interest in history and in military history started at a very young age when I was lucky enough to hear my grandfather describing his experiences of serving in the RAF in North Africa and Italy during WW2. Recently my family have discovered that one of my Scottish and Northern Irish ancestors fought under Wellington at the battle of Waterloo in 1815.

I have always wanted to be a writer. It was my childhood dream, that and being a pilot, a Royal Marine and a Jedi knight. I grew up in the Netherlands in the 1970's and 80's in a wonderfully liberal place with a great passion for football.

As a child growing up just north of Eindhoven it was impossible to get away from the reminders of World War 2. The town where I grew up, Son en Breugel, straddled Hells Highway, the main road that was used by the allies during Operation Market Garden in September 1944. Indeed, the US 101st Airborne had dropped in on the fields where I often played football. The Dutch are very thankful for that liberation. They commemorate it everywhere, in street names, square names, names of bridges, liberation day (5th May) and through memorials, one of which, the Joe Mann memorial was close to where I lived.

My love affair with ancient Rome began when I read Rosemary Sutcliffe's 'The Eagle of the Ninth' and Alfred Duggan's 'Winter Quarters.' These two writers had a huge influence on me and after seeing the majestic ruins of the ancient Forum in Rome I knew that this was the period I wanted to write about. I have not looked back. Now, the more I learn about ancient Rome, the more I see her influence reflected in modern life; from law to language; place and country names; to the football stadiums of today. The soundness of many Roman ideas and concepts has stood the test of time and we should respect the ancients for what they achieved. The Greeks may have been thinkers but the Romans were doers! The Romans were an immensely proud people but they were always happy to copy and adopt other people's good ideas. It is this quality that makes them so likeable and so enduring. The Romans would have had no problems adapting automobiles for military use. God forbid what they would have done with a mobile phone.

I didn't end up becoming a Marine or a Jedi Knight. After leaving Holland in 1991 for a place at Lancaster University in the UK, I decided to use my summer and Christmas holidays to hitchhike around Europe and bring medicines to the UNHCR in Zagreb, which was then embroiled in civil war. I still vividly remember sitting in my small tent on the hills just outside the city and seeing the anti-aircraft gunners celebrating the start of the New Year. After my idealistic phase had run into that great barrier, i.e. lack of money, I decided to get a job and joined a financial publishing house as a conference salesman and organizer and had a ball of a time.

I live in London, one of the greatest cities on the planet, a town the Romans would be proud of, if only they could see what their once humble port has become.

William Kelso, London, November 2016

Germania
(Book Five of the Veteran of Rome)

Chapter One – The Cave

(Late spring AD 105, the North of Britannia)

Fergus stifled a yawn and glanced up at the night sky. Dawn was not far away. Nearly time to wake Aledus and change the watch he thought. Then at last he would be able to get some sleep. He lay stretched out on his stomach on the rocky ground of the forest, hidden amongst the tangled undergrowth, a brown woollen army blanket carefully covering his back. The hood of his cloak was drawn over his head, hiding his red hair and preventing the moonlight from reflecting on his body armour and revealing his position. The night was peaceful and surprisingly warm and the only noise was made by the rustle of the branches and leaves in the gentle, western breeze. Over his head the sharp tops of the tall, conifer trees pointed at the twinkling stars, like a dense phalanx of spears. Bored, Fergus turned his attention back in the direction of the cave mouth, eighty paces away, across the open, barren, boulder- strewn ground. In the darkness he could not make out the entrance to the cave but it didn't matter. The cave wasn't going anywhere, he thought grimly. For two days and now this night, he and the five legionaries in his squad had been staked out in the forest, watching the cave. And during that time, they had seen nothing but a single lost-looking sheep. But Titus, the Company Centurion had ordered them to watch the remote cave, for the villagers in the valley had revealed that it had sometimes been used by Arvirargus and his band of fugitives. For weeks now, the twelve infantry companies of the Second and Sixth Cohorts of the Twentieth Legion had been combing the mountain valleys, hunting for the famous Briton fugitive and last of the rebel leaders. Fergus sighed wearily and peered into the darkness. The Centurion had forbidden them from starting a fire and since their watch had begun, they'd had nothing to eat but

4

stale, cold bread, cheese and water. The boredom was beginning to get to them and there was still another day to go before they would be relieved.

In the undergrowth a twig suddenly cracked and Fergus turned sharply to glare into the darkness behind him. Something was moving amongst the trees, slithering slowly towards him.

'Fergus, are you awake,' a voice whispered.

It was Aledus, Fergus's Londinium-born mess mate and friend.

'Of course,' Fergus whispered in an irritated voice, 'I don't fall asleep on watch.'

A moment later, Aledus, clad in a brown cloak, appeared out of the darkness and crawled up to his side. In the gloom Fergus missed the cheeky grin on his comrade's face.

'What's the matter,' Fergus whispered. 'You are not on for another hour.'

'I can't sleep, Aledus muttered. 'Seen anything,' he added jutting his chin in the direction of the cave.

'No, nothing at all. There is no one up here but us,' Fergus growled in disappointment.

For a while the two young legionaries were silent as they lay in the undergrowth, peering out into the darkness in the direction of the cave.

'When we get back to Deva,' Aledus whispered at last as he licked his lips, 'the first thing I am going to do is buy myself some lovely, piping hot lamb-stew and stuff my face. And after that,' he paused savouring the moment; 'after that I am going to the baths for a good scrub. There is nothing better than a good scrub and scratch, after having been out in the field for as long as we have.'

Fergus said nothing as he peered into the night. It had been eighteen months since he, Aledus, Catinius and Vittius had all joined the Twentieth Legion together as new recruits. The four of them had formed a close-knit friendship, that had grown stronger after Fergus had been promoted to Decanus, Corporal, and leader of his eight-man Contubernium, tent group. Fergus's promotion had however not gone uncontested and had earned him the violent, implacable hatred of Fronto. He was another of the Company's squad leaders, whose ambition to be promoted to Tesserarius, third in command of the company, Fergus had helped thwart. At the thought of Fronto, Fergus's face darkened. The man had tried to murder him a year ago in the Lucky Legionary tavern and Fronto and his mates had beaten Aledus up so badly, that he'd spent six weeks in the military hospital. There was a score still waiting to be settled with that man.

'Do you think Arvirargus and his men are going to show up?' Aledus whispered.

Fergus shrugged. At his side, Aledus turned to glance at his friend.

'Is it true what they say, that it was your father who killed Arvirargus's brother, at the start of the Brigantian rebellion," Aledus muttered. 'They say your Dad put him up on a cross, outside the fort at Luguvalium, and left him to die, right in front of his tribesmen.'

Fergus frowned as he peered into the darkness and, for a moment, he didn't reply.

'It's true,' he murmured at last.

'Don't worry,' Aledus whispered with a cheeky smile, 'I won't tell Arvirargus. But best not let him capture you or you may end up like that Christian god, Jesus.'

Suddenly Fergus no longer felt tired. The thought of his father had the same sobering effect as a bucket of ice-cold water being poured over his head. He had not seen Marcus, his father, since he'd paid him a visit at the legionary base at Deva Victrix, more than a year ago. There, his father had handed him Corbulo's old sword. In her letters to him, Kyna, his mother, had written that Marcus had left Londinium, in spring of last year, on a ship bound for Hyperborea, wherever that might be. His father had set out to try and retrieve Corbulo's mortal remains and carry out his grandfather's final instructions; to be buried amongst his comrades on the battlefield where he'd fought against Boudicca, the Barbarian Queen. But there had been no news from Marcus in well over a year now and the family back on the Isle of Vectis had begun to fear the worst. Tensely, Fergus reached down to touch the pommel of Corbulo's old sword that hung from his belt. The touch of the cold steel felt reassuring, as if his grandfather Corbulo was standing beside him, encouraging him, and as he gripped the sword, a fierce wave of pride suddenly coursed through him. Three generations of his family had served in the Roman army. Forty-four years ago, his grandfather Corbulo had fought in the decisive battle that had destroyed Boudicca's rebellion. His father Marcus had risen to the rank of Prefect of the Second Batavian Auxiliary Cohort and had saved the whole unit from annihilation at Luguvalium, during the start of the Brigantian uprising. And now it was his turn. Now it was his turn to uphold the honour of the family and make the spirits of his ancestor's brim with pride. For one day, he would have to explain himself to them.

***

Fergus was woken by a rough hand shaking him awake. Instantly he sat up, his hand already reaching for his sword.

Aledus was crouched beside him. The young man's face was flushed with excitement.

'We have company Fergus,' Aledus hissed, 'A dozen or so warriors just arrived. They entered the cave.'

Fergus blinked as he stared at Aledus in stunned silence. It was dawn and in the morning light, he saw the other four men of his squad, lying curled up asleep on the ground, wrapped in their brown army blankets. Quickly, Fergus rose to his feet and turned to stare in the direction of the cave. The dense forest and undergrowth however, blocked his view.

'What do you want to do,' Aledus whispered.

'Are you sure of what you saw.' Fergus muttered turning to give Aledus a sharp look. 'You didn't fall asleep and dream this up?'

'I swear, Aledus protested and from the look on his friend's face Fergus instantly knew that he was speaking the truth.

'I mean,' Aledus stammered, 'I don't know if Arvirargus is with them, I didn't get a proper look but they definitely didn't look like a bunch of farmers or hunters seeking a nice spot to make a camp. The men I saw were armed to the teeth. They looked like proper fighters.'

Fergus did not seem to be listening. Hastily he strode up to the sleeping figures on the ground and gave each man a kick.

'Wake up, all of you,' Fergus hissed, 'we have company.'

Without a word, the others stumbled to their feet and hastily grabbed their spears and large, rectangular legionary shields emblazoned with thunder-bolts. Bleary-eyed and subdued, they turned to look at Fergus.

'Catinius,' Fergus gestured to his comrade, 'run back to the main camp and tell the Centurion that we have made contact. Tell him that we have seen a dozen or so heavily armed men enter the cave. Be quick and make sure that you are not seen.'

Catinius nodded that he had understood and without a word he dumped his shield onto the ground, turned and sped away through the trees.

'The rest of you stay here. Stay alert. Aledus with me,' Fergus snapped as he pulled his army blanket over his shoulders and set off through the undergrowth. As he neared the edge of the forest he got down on his stomach and started to crawl through the tangled bushes and over the sharp rocks. At his side Aledus did the same. As they reached their observation post, Fergus stopped moving and lay still. The morning light was growing stronger and across the open, barren, grey slate-covered mountain slope, he had a clear view of the dark, gaping cave-mouth, eighty paces away. There was no sign of anyone. The cave-mouth looked just like it had looked yesterday and the day before.

'A dozen men you say,' Fergus whispered. 'No horses, no dogs?'

Aledus shook his head.

'They came on foot, from over that ridge over there,' he murmured.

Fergus grunted and peered at the dark cave-mouth. The grey slate-covered slope offered very little cover. Anyone leaving the forest would be instantly spotted from the cave. Tensely Fergus bit his lower lip. The men Aledus had seen could be Arvirargus and his war band or it could be a group of complete strangers. There was no way of knowing. Back at the legionary fortress at Deva the army briefing and descriptions of what Arvirargus actually looked like had been vague and confusing leaving

Fergus in little doubt that few Romans actually knew what the famous rebel leader looked like.

'If he is really in there,' Aledus whispered in a voice that trembled with excitement, 'we're going to be fucking famous Fergus. How long has Arvirargus been on the run? Sixteen years? And it was me who spotted him. The whores are going to give me a free one for just that alone.'

'His name is more powerful than the man himself,' Fergus whispered, not taking his eyes off the dark, cave entrance, 'As long as he is free and he lives, the north will never be fully at peace. He offered the tribes hope. That is why he is so dangerous. I heard the officers talking about the importance of destroying his name. They want him alive.'

'Why?' Aledus frowned. 'If we kill him then he is gone, isn't he?'

'They want to put him on trial,' Fergus murmured. 'They want to show how no one is above the law. They want to make an example out of him. Then they will execute him in public and let everyone see what happens to the enemies of Rome. That way the Brigantes will lose hope and give up their resistance to Rome.'

Aledus muttered something under his breath as he stared at the cave.

'Well the man is a prick,' Aledus whispered at last. 'The Brigantian rebellion was crushed many years ago. He didn't need to keep on fighting.'

Fergus didn't reply as he stared at the cave. The main company camp was two miles away down in the valley. It would take Catinius twenty or so minutes to reach it. An hour or so before he would be back with Titus's orders. Tensely he clenched his hand into a fist and pushed it against the rocky ground. An hour. If the men in the cave decided to leave before then, there was precious little he would be able to do about it with just five soldiers.

***

'Fergus,' a voice whispered suddenly from the thick, tangled undergrowth. Stiffly Fergus turned to look behind him and recognised Vittius. The man was lying flat on his stomach, clad in his army cloak and clutching his spear.

'What is it?' Fergus hissed.

'Titus is here,' Vittius murmured. 'He has brought the whole company. He wants to speak to you.'

Leaving Aledus behind, Fergus carefully backed out of the observation post and crawled through the undergrowth until he was a safe distance inside the wood. Vittius gave him a quick, excited glance.

'Do you think he is in there', he asked as the two of them got to their feet and strode through the trees back to their camp.

'Maybe,' Fergus grunted.

Their small forest camp had been transformed by the arrival of the full company of eighty heavily-armed legionaries. The men were spread out amongst the trees, kneeling on one knee, as they clutched their large, rectangular legionary shields and throwing-spears. They looked tense. The soldiers were fully armed and clad in their fine, segmented, body-armour and helmets with wide, cheek-guards. Lucullus, the grey-haired company Optio and second in command, stood behind his men, clutching his long wooden staff. He was in his forties and his eyes narrowed suspiciously as Fergus and Vittius appeared.

Titus, the company Centurion, was easily recognisable from his magnificent red-plumed helmet and the vine stick, which he kept slapping against his thigh. The veteran officer stood waiting

11

calmly, in the centre of the small forest camp, together with the signifer, clad in his wolf skin cloak and holding up the company standard. Fergus strode straight up to Titus and saluted smartly.

'Sir,' Fergus snapped.
'Are they still in the cave?', Titus said quickly, watching Fergus carefully.

'Yes,' Fergus replied. 'One of my men is watching the cave mouth right now. He says he counted about a dozen men. Warriors, Sir. They were armed to the teeth.'

Titus said nothing, as he glanced past Fergus in the direction of the cave. Then silently he raised his hand and beckoned for Lucullus, the Optio, and Furius, his third in command, to approach.

'Good man,' the Centurion said, patting Fergus's shoulder.

Fergus said nothing as he strode back to where Vittius and Catinius and two other men of his squad were waiting. It was rare for Titus, the company Centurion to show public emotion towards his men. The prospect of capturing Arvirargus must have even got their commander excited. Titus had a reputation for being a first-class soldier, stoic, calm and competent, who did not abuse his position and always made sure that his men were well looked after. That was the unspoken contract that Titus had with his company. In return for unquestioned loyalty and obedience, the soldiers knew that their commander would always do his best to look after them. But woe to the man who broke the contract, the man who disobeyed an order, or crossed Titus. The vine staff which he carried had only one purpose and that was to be used to beat legionary backs to bloody pulp.

Tensely, Fergus picked up his shield and Vittius handed him his spear and helmet. As he pulled his helmet over his red hair, Fergus glanced at his commander. Titus was conversing in a low voice with Lucullus and Furius. As he watched the officers,

Fergus suddenly noticed Fronto, staring at him from amongst the trees. Fronto was down on one knee and surrounded by the eight men of his squad. There was a contemptuous sneer on the Decanus's face as he glared at Fergus.

'He didn't like that acknowledgment Titus just gave you,' Vittius murmured softly leaning in towards Fergus.

Fergus grunted as for a few moments he coolly held Fronto's gaze, before turning to look away. Fronto might be a few years older than him and the more experienced soldier, but the two squad leaders were both the same rank, which was the problem. Fronto blamed Fergus for thwarting his promotion to Tesserarius, a position, which had gone to Furius, Fergus's old squad leader.

'That murderous swine will get a knife in his back one of these days,' Catinius whispered behind Fergus. 'I will do it myself.'

'Quiet,' Fergus hissed as he adjusted his helmet.

The officers had finished their discussion and were moving apart. Lucullus, the grey-haired Optio, clutching his long staff, was coming towards Fergus.

'Fergus, with me,' the officer snapped, 'The company will advance in line at a walk. Your men will be on the extreme left. None of those bastards in that cave are to escape. If Arvirargus is with them, he is to be taken alive.'

***

The legionaries emerged from the forest and slowly started to walk up the slate-covered slope towards the cave entrance. The men were spread out in a long, thin line, holding up their large rectangular shields to protect themselves and menacingly pointing their spears at the cave entrance. Fergus tightened his grip on his shield, as he warily studied, the dark cave-mouth. The Britons must have seen them by now, but there was no

13

reaction. All remained quiet. Lucullus, the Optio, clasping his long staff in both hands, strode along a few paces behind the men and, in the centre of the Roman line, Fergus could see Titus leading his men straight towards the cave. On the right flank Furius, the Tesserarius, was doing the same. Steadily the Romans converged on the cave mouth and still there was no reaction. Tensely, Fergus exhaled. The rebels had left it too late. There was no way they were going to be able to escape now.

When he was a dozen paces from the cave-mouth Titus, the Centurion, raised his arm and around him the legionaries came to a halt, crouching down behind their large shields, their spears raised and ready to be flung at anything that came out of the cave. Fergus glanced at the men of his troop. They were all staring at the dark cave entrance, their faces taught, nervous and excited. For a moment the mountain slope remained silent, except for the gentle whine of the western breeze.

'You, in the cave, come on out and throw down your weapons,' the signifer clutching the company standard, suddenly cried out in the Briton language, 'If you surrender, we will spare your lives.'

From the cave there was no reply.

As the silence lengthened Titus turned and gestured to the small rear guard of legionaries, clustered behind him. Instead of their shields these men were holding tree branches, which they had cut from the forest and two of the men were also clasping burning torches. Hastily the soldiers surged forwards and flung their branches into a heap just in front of the cave entrance, before hurriedly retreating. Within a few seconds the men carrying the torches had set the pile of branches alight. Thick, dark smoke belched upwards into the air as the flames spread, crackling and devouring the wood and soon the breeze was blowing the smoke straight into the cave. Outside in the morning light, the legionaries crouched and waited.

14

They did not have long to wait. From within the cave, Fergus suddenly heard an enraged bellow, like that of an injured bull. Moments later, a single spear came flying straight out of the cave and caught the Optio in his shoulder, sending him spinning and tumbling to the ground. The spear was followed, a split second later, by a group of men, who came charging and leaping through the wall of flames and thick smoke, as if they were immune to heat and suffocation. The warriors were screaming and roaring, their fierce faces painted with blue woad or covered in tattoos and they were armed. They were met by a merciless hail of spears that killed half the group before they had barely cleared the fire. Fergus cried out in warning as close by a huge warrior launched himself at Vittius, crashing into his shield with such force that his friend was knocked clean of his feet and onto his back. The huge warrior, clutching a spiked club, was accompanied by an older companion with a handsome face and long black hair, holding a spear in one hand and a Roman gladius in the other. The men slashed and hacked at the Romans around them, as they desperately sought to break through the Roman line. But it was an unequal fight. Without thinking, Fergus sprang forwards, his shield catching the smaller warrior in his side and knocking him to the ground. At the same time Aledus, and one of the other legionaries attacked the huge warrior, stabbing him from behind and in the side and kicking him to the ground. Close by, the older warrior was grimacing in pain. The man had lost his spear, but as Fergus approached, he slashed out at Fergus's ankles with his sword. Fergus sprang back just in time. Wildly he raised his spear to finish the man off. On the ground the warrior, seeing that all was lost, suddenly raised his head to look up at Fergus and as he did, his fury faded and a calm, resigned look appeared on his face.

'You will never defeat us Roman,' the man hissed in the Briton language, 'Another will take my place when I am dead. You cannot destroy freedom.'

'We need them alive,' a Roman voice roared across the smoke-filled and corpse strewn slope.

Fergus hesitated. From the corner of his eye he saw several of his men approaching the fallen warrior, their swords stained with blood, their faces filled with wild murderous intent. Then before he could act, the warrior on the ground grimaced, bared his exposed neck and slit his own throat with his sword.

'Fuck,' Fergus cursed as he dropped his shield and hastily wrenched the sword from the dying man's hand. But it was too late. The blood was welling up and gushing down the warrior's chest. With a last flicker of his eyes, the man gurgled and stared up at Fergus. Then he died and his head rolled to one side.

Fergus swore again, as he knelt over the fallen warrior. But there was nothing he could do. Around him the legionaries were gathering, their heavy laboured breathing mingling with the roar and crackle of the fire. Moments later a figure pushed his way up to Fergus and crouched down beside him. It was Titus. The Centurion was looking down at the corpse, his chest heaving with exertion.

'Is that him? Is that Arvirargus Sir?' Fergus exclaimed.

Titus did not reply. He was staring down at the fallen warrior with an anxious frown.

Fergus steadied his breathing and then repeated to the Centurion what the warrior had said to him and as he did the frown on Titus's face darkened.

'Furius, have a section search the cave,' the Centurion cried out as he rose to his feet ignoring Fergus completely. 'And I want these bodies placed on stretchers. We will take the corpses with us to the Tribune's camp. If he is amongst the dead, there are family members of Arvirargus there, who will be able to identify him. And I want a runner to go on ahead to warn the surgeons that we have wounded.'

Without another word the Centurion hastened up the slope towards the spot where Lucullus had fallen. He was closely followed by the signifer clad in his wolf skin cloak and clutching the company standard. Slowly Fergus got to his feet and as he did he caught Furius's eye. The Tesserarius and third in command of the company gave him a disapproving, questioning look but Fergus shook his head and raised his shoulders in a defensive gesture. This time it really wasn't his fault that the warrior had managed to elude capture.

Chapter Two – The Promise

As the column of Roman legionaries, a thousand or so strong, approached the gates of the Legionary Fortress at Deva Victrix, a solitary trumpet call rang out to welcome them home - from up on the stone walls. The column was led by a solitary tribune on horseback and the standard bearer, proudly holding up the vexillation standard of the Twentieth Legion. Along the side of the road, the civilian inhabitants of the town, that had sprung up around the huge fortress, had gathered to stare at the returning legionaries. The monotonous tramp and crunch of the soldiers' hobnailed boots on the stone road was, however, drowned out by another noise. Bringing up the very rear of the otherwise silent marching column, Fergus and the eighty men of the Second Company of the Second Cohort were in full and lusty-throated song, as they came on towards the fortress gates, their armour, weapons and shields glinting in the noon sun. Led by Titus, their Centurion and the signifer, clutching the unit banner, the company were singing with gusto, belting out their favourite marching song - a bawdy, rude song about the Legate's love life. Fergus, his head held high, his voice lost amongst those of his comrades, felt the hairs on his back stand up with pride as the town's folk stared at the company. A few days earlier, at the Tribune's HQ in the mountain valley, Arvirargus's relatives had confirmed that the man with the long black hair had indeed been their kinsman. The news had sent ripples of excitement coursing through the whole counter insurgency task-force and in recognition of their role in killing the last fugitive rebel leader, the Tribune had granted Titus and his whole company the honour of being the only company in the taskforce that would be allowed to sing upon their return to the Legionary base.

As the vanguard of the column started to enter the fortress, Fergus suddenly saw that the walls of the army base were lined with legionaries. All of them were eagerly staring at the Second Company. At the sight of his comrades, up on the wall, a flush appeared on Fergus's face. The whole Legion and indeed the whole province would soon know, that it had been his company that had finally managed to catch up with the famous Briton rebel. That was an honour that would not soon be forgotten. Ahead, the gates loomed up and, as he drew closer, Fergus caught sight of the envious faces of the men staring down at him from the walls. There would not be a single soldier up there, Fergus thought, who wouldn't be wishing he was down with us right now.

Belting out their song, the company was the last to pass through the gates and into the camp. Ahead of them the other infantry companies were beginning to disperse to their quarters amongst the long lines of dreary-looking barrack blocks. Then at last, Titus's deep booming voice, brought the company to a halt.

'Second Company, stand to attention,' Titus roared as the singing abruptly ceased. In the middle of the street that led towards the Principia in the centre of the camp the whole company smartly, and smoothly, straightened-up in ten rows of eight men, as if they belonged to a single, living-organism. Fergus, staring straight ahead, suppressed the urge to laugh. The company was performing its parade-ground drill in the middle of the street, in full view of the whole camp. There was no need to do that. The Centurion was showing off. Titus may be a stoic, but he must be enjoying this moment every bit as much as the rank and file.

'Men,' Titus bellowed, staring at the rigid legionaries standing before him. 'The Tribune has granted you all a free afternoon. All of you are released from regular duties until dawn tomorrow. Make the most of it.'

Amongst the eighty legionaries, standing stiffly to attention before their commanding officer, not a man moved or made a sound. Fergus bit his lip. From experience, the whole company knew that their Centurion was only finished with them when he uttered his immortal words of dismissal, for which he had become known in the Legion.

'Furius and all squad leaders however, will report to my quarters in an hour,' Titus cried out, his face stern and streaked with dust and sweat.

From the corner of his eye Fergus noticed Aledus's mouth, working on a silently spoken sentence, as if he was anticipating what Titus was about to say next. Seeing Fergus's disapproving frown, Aledus replied with a cheeky smile.

'That's all,' Titus bellowed, 'Rome conquers all.'

As if released from a magic spell, the company relaxed and broke up, as the men started to head towards their barrack's block.

'Rome conquers all,' Catinius repeated quietly as, with a grin, he, Aledus, Vittius and the other members of the squad clustered around Fergus. Fergus shook his head with a little smile of his own. Then he adjusted the focale, the white neck scarf that was tied around his neck to stop his armour from chafing on his skin.

'Well you heard him, make the best of your free afternoon. I will see you all back in the tent before nightfall,' Fergus said, giving them all a nod.

The five men in his squad, however, did not move and gazed at him with a twinkle of humour in their eyes as if they were waiting for something.

'I am not going to say it,' Fergus blurted out with an embarrassed grin, as he suddenly realised what they waiting for. The men were baiting him, trying to get him to dismiss them in the same way in which Titus did.

With a chuckle the men turned and strode away, leaving Fergus standing alone in the middle of the muddy street. Fergus watched them go and then slowly shook his head. At only nineteen he was young to have been promoted to Decanus. He knew that. It had initially been hard for him to exercise authority over the men of his squad, who were, all older and more experienced, but he had managed it. He had managed to gain the respect of his comrades and that was quite something, he thought, as he turned and started to head in the direction of his barrack's block.

***

The Centurion's quarters were at the end of the Company barrack's block and they were far more spacious and luxurious than the cramped, two-room squad-quarters, which Fergus shared with his men and their equipment. Titus, still clad in his body armour, was splashing water from a bowl onto his face and over his short, grey hair, as the ten, silent, company squad-leaders stood motionless in line before him, their hands clasped behind their backs. Fergus stood, staring fixedly across the room at the far wall, on which hung a bronze diploma. The writing was however, too small for him to be able to read what it said. There was no sign of Lydia, the Centurion's young wife. It was one of the privileges of his rank, that Titus was officially allowed to marry. Furius and the signifer, both with their helmets smartly tucked under their arms, stood to one side waiting patiently for Titus to speak. Taking his time, the Centurion wiped his face on a cloth, scratched his head and then turned to stare at his NCO's and, as he did, Fergus saw that the old man looked troubled.

'Right,' Titus muttered glancing at Furius, 'I will get straight to the point. Lucullus is wounded. The good news is that the surgeons say that he will live. The bad news is that he is going to be out of action for a long time. He's been transferred to the base hospital.'

Titus paused and, for a moment he studied the line of men standing before him, as if trying to guess what they were thinking.

'I can't be without an Optio,' he said at last. 'So with immediate affect I have promoted Furius to fill Lucullus's position. Furius will be acting, second in command until Lucullus has fully recovered. That though, means that the position of Tesserarius is once again vacant.'

Fergus stiffened and ever so slightly, he turned to glance at Fronto. His arch rival gave no indication that he'd noticed Fergus's glance, and continued to stare straight ahead at the far wall. The position of watch-commander, Tesserarius, keeper of the daily password, third in command of the company was the highest rank his grandfather Corbulo had ever attained, Fergus thought. Was Titus about to announce another promotion? It was a position every ambitious squad leader aspired to and it came with extra pay.

'In this company,' Titus said, turning to stare at his NCO's, 'I expect, demand that every one of my squad leaders should aspire to becoming my watch commander. It is a privilege to hold this rank. We are the best company in the whole Legion and I will not tolerate weak leaders. So, I have made my decision.'

Fergus tensed, swallowing nervously. If Fronto was given the job, the man would become his superior and the only thing he could expect from Fronto, would be an endless stream of shit, abuse and pain.

'The position will remain vacant,' Titus said sharply, 'It will be filled by the best and ablest man for the job. You all will compete for the position. Only the best one of you will be promoted. Is that clear?'

The ten NCO's remained silent as they stared fixedly ahead. Fergus could barely breath. What was this? Titus was leaving the position open. He hadn't been expecting that.

'The position will stay vacant until I have made up my mind which one of you deserves it,' Titus growled. 'This could be weeks or months. In the mean-time each one of you will prove to me how good you are. I want this company to excel at everything. I want the Legate himself to see how fucking good we are. Hell, I want the gods themselves to take an interest in us. I want you all to inspire your men to be the best. You think you did well out there in the mountains. Our orders were to take Arvirargus alive and we failed. We failed! The Tribune and his staff may not really care whether we caught him alive or dead, but I do,' Titus barked.

The room fell silent as the Centurion glared at his junior officers.

'So starting from tomorrow,' Titus growled, 'we will be drilling and training the men every day for an hour longer than the other companies.'

Titus paused and rubbed his hand across the grey-stubble on his chin. Inside the room not a man made a noise.

'And there is something else,' Titus muttered, 'something I have just been made aware of. There is news. Whilst we were away in the mountains, a dispatch arrived all the way from Rome. It seems that war has broken out again between us and the Dacians on the Danube frontier. King Decebalus has attacked our garrisons along and beyond the river. The Emperor is said to be organising an expeditionary force. The despatch we received contained orders. The Twentieth Legion is to send a vexillatio to the Danube to take part in the war. The Legate will decide shortly which units will be going. That's all I know.'

The room fell silent, suddenly pregnant with excitement.

'Do you think they will be sending us Sir' one of the squad leaders piped up, unable to hide his excitement.

'I fucking well hope so,' Titus growled.

23

***

The Lucky Legionary Tavern stood a short distance from the fortress walls, in the sprawling, civilian town that had grown up around the army base. Fergus, clad in his simple, white army-tunic, boots and a belt from which hung Corbulo's old sword, pushed his way down the crowded street towards the tavern with its modern, red Roman-style roof tiles. It was early evening and it was starting to get cold. Around him, the town's shop-keepers were crying out, advertising their wares and services in brash, confident and loud voices. The long and narrow, terraced strip-houses lined the street; the front rooms acting as shops and workshops, whilst the inhabitants lived in the middle and back rooms. A bewildering array of signs, price boards, graffiti and bawdy, humorous adverts were plastered on every available inch of wall. The shop fronts were lined with endless examples of merchandise; leather shoes; chunks of meat; dried fish; roots; herbs; tunics and fine iron-tools. The smell of stale-urine and pig shit mingled with that of unwashed-bodies and wood-smoke. Ignoring the street hawkers, Fergus paused beside a flower shop and bought a bunch of pretty looking flowers. As he turned he caught sight of the large, welcoming sign, hanging above the entrance to the tavern.

He was indeed the lucky legionary, Fergus thought, as a smile of anticipation slowly appeared on his lips. The 'Lucky' as it was known amongst the legionaries was run by Galena and her father, Taran - both local Britons. It was here in this very building, during one of the occasional soldiers' brawls, that in a drunken rage, Fronto had tried to murder him. It was here too, whilst hiding out with Galena and Taran in the cellar, that he'd discovered that Taran had been there with his grandfather on his last day and had seen Corbulo die. But that was all in the past. Galena was his woman now. She was seventeen and the most beautiful and sexy woman he'd ever known. It had taken him some time to work up the courage to ask her out, but when she'd said yes, it had been one of the greatest moments of his young life. And now that she was his woman, she had woken something in him. A fierce, insatiable lust and hunger for sex. It was all consuming and at night, in the barracks block he shared with his mess mates, he'd spent long hours thinking of nothing else. Galena and he had done it everywhere and on every occasion they'd met, going at it often more than once. They had humped in the loft of the tavern, in the cellar, down by the river, in the forest and, on one memorable summer occasion, at night against the walls of the Legionary fortress. He'd been insatiable and there had been many a time when she'd begged him for a rest. Fergus grinned, as clutching the pretty flowers, he approached the entrance to the tavern. He'd been out in the mountains with his company for a long time, but tonight he was going to get some pay back.

The tavern was nearly empty. A few, older locals were reclining on chairs around a table in the corner beside the empty hearth, but it was too early for any off-duty legionaries. Most of the young civilians did not visit the tavern, for this was known to be an army, drinking hole. Taran was standing behind the bar, counting coins that had spilled from a leather pouch. He was a big man with a grey beard and a belly that sagged a little too much over his belt. As Fergus approached, nodding a greeting, Taran acknowledged him with a strange, sympathetic look.

'She's around the back, cleaning the jars,' Taran muttered gesturing at the door around the back of the bar. 'Good luck.'

Fergus nodded again and frowned as he turned towards the doorway. That was odd. Taran was alright and seemed to approve of him, but he was fiercely protective of his daughter and not usually in the habit of giving him a sympathetic look. What was going on?

As he stepped out through the back door, he saw Galena. She was bent over a large ceramic amphora, cleaning the inside of the container with a sponge. As she saw him she straightened up. Her fine, beautiful, long, blond hair was tied back in a ponytail, and she was wearing a heavy stained, leather, work-apron. Seeing the flowers, her lips twisted into a smile. Then she dropped the sponge and hurried towards him, wrapping her arms around him and pressing her head against his chest.

'The company just came back today. I came as soon as I could,' Fergus said as he ran his fingers through her hair and felt her breasts pushing against his chest. 'I have got a couple of hours before I have to be back.'

She broke free from his embrace and looked up at him with her sharp, intelligent eyes and, as she did, he marvelled at how stunningly, beautiful she looked.

'There is rumour going around that some of the soldiers are going to be sent away to fight in a distant, foreign war. Is it true?' she exclaimed.

Fergus shrugged and smiled.

'Maybe, I don't know, I don't get to make those decisions.'

'Maybe you and your company will be going,' Galena said, staring up at him. 'They say that the soldiers will be gone for a few years, some may not return at all.'

'It's possible,' Fergus shrugged and then playfully reached out and placed his hand on her bum but she quickly reached out and removed his hand.

'When will you know?' she said sharply.

'When the Centurion tells us. But the chances are that they will send some other Cohort. Don't worry.'

Galena was silent for a moment. Then she looked away and Fergus suddenly saw the tension and raw emotion on her face.

'Remember what I said to you, that night when you stood up and told the whole tavern about your grandfather,' Galena said looking up at him. 'Look at me, Fergus. What did I tell you?'

'You said that if I wanted you to be my woman, it should be forever and it should only be you,' Fergus said with mounting unease.

Galena nodded and gazed up at him and, as she did, she suddenly gasped.

'I am pregnant Fergus,' she whispered, 'It's been three months. The doctor confirmed it last week.'

Fergus stared down at her in shock. Nervously he swallowed and for a moment, he seemed unable to speak and, as he gazed at her, he suddenly realised why Taran had given him that sympathetic look.

'That's fantastic,' he blurted out. Then he gasped as the full realisation that he was going to be a father sank in. Quickly he raised a hand to his mouth and, as he did, a little tear started to make its way down Galena's cheeks. She smiled up at him through her tears.

'I want to be married before you go,' she whispered clasping hold of his chin and forcing him to look at her.

'I can't get married,' Fergus sighed trying to avoid her gaze.

'The army doesn't let men like me marry. You know this. It's not legally possible.'

'I know,' Galena said hoarsely, 'but we are going to do it anyway. We will do it in secret and the ceremony will be in the manner of my forefathers. No one except us needs to know. But I want this Fergus. I want us to be married before you go.'

'They haven't decided which units are going to be sent,' Fergus stammered.

But Galena shook her head and the tears streaming down her cheeks could not wash away the determination that was clearly written across her face. 'They will send you, I know they will,' she whispered. 'I want us to be properly married and I want you to make a soldier's will. I told you Fergus, I am no harlot, no man shall have me except you, even if you don't come back. I gave myself to you and I will be yours until the day we die. Now promise me that you will do these things.'

Chapter Three – A Roll of the Dice

The solid, stone walls of the huge Legionary Fortress were protected by a muddy, deep, V shaped ditch and, at the rounded corners of the playing-card shaped base, watch towers rose up. Along the ramparts sentries were patrolling. Fergus however did not notice the impressive fortifications. He looked stunned. Staring down at the ground, lost in thought, he strode back towards the camp, completely oblivious to his surroundings. It was getting dark and along the street, the shop keepers were closing for the day. He was going to be a father. He was going to have a child. In a few days' time, he was going to get married - in secret. It was all happening so suddenly. The heavy burden of responsibility suddenly weighed on his shoulders. He'd given Galena his word and now he was going to have to support her and the baby and he also had to make a will. He took a deep breath and exhaled, trying to calm his nerves. He was going to have a son or daughter. He had never thought about children and if he was honest, he didn't know whether to feel happy or worried. But it was happening and there were things he needed to do. No one could know about the secret wedding. The army would force him to divorce if they found out, and making a will was going to be problematic, not because the army objected, but because legally it was Marcus, his father who owned everything. Fergus had no legal right to leave any of his family's possessions to anyone, not until he was head of his family. But no one had heard from Marcus in over a year. Maybe Marcus had perished. Maybe he, Fergus was already the legal head of his family? But who determined that, when his father was still missing? Wearily, he shook his head. And at some point, he would have to let Kyna and Efa back on Vectis know what was happening.

Distracted and without looking up, he stomped through the gates of the Fortress giving the guards the day's password and thus he was oblivious to the three men loitering near the gate.

'Heh,' a familiar voice suddenly cried out, as Fergus was struck by a pebble.

Annoyed, Fergus halted and looked up. Fronto and two of his mess mates were approaching. Fronto's lips curled in contempt as he sized Fergus up.

'What,' Fergus hissed in an annoyed voice, as he turned to face his rival. And, as he did, his hand dropped to rest on the pommel of his sword.

'There is no fucking way that you are going to become the next Tesserarius,' Fronto growled aggressively jabbing a finger at Fergus. 'That position belongs to me. The whole company knows that. So here is some advice for you, pretty boy. Don't get in my way. Don't compete with me and don't try to bribe your way to the top, for if I hear you are trying something, me and the boys will have to come around and teach you a lesson. Got that.'

'Did you really need to have two of your goons with you to tell me that,' Fergus retorted. 'Not man enough to come and tell me that on your own.'

Fronto's face darkened in suppressed rage. 'Just remember what I said,' he hissed. 'There is a lot of trouble coming your way if you don't.'

And with that, he gestured to his mates and strode away.

Fergus watched him go, his chest heaving with a mixture of nerves and disgust. Fronto was the worst of the worst. A bully, a thug and petty criminal, with a strong sense of entitlement, whose violence was feared and loathed by the men in the company. But he was also a good soldier and smart enough never to cross the officers and get himself into trouble. Tensely, Fergus bit his lip. He had to be careful. Fronto's words were no idle threats. The man had already tried to murder him once and he was perfectly capable of trying again. It would be difficult whilst Fergus had his men around him and the officers were watching, but there were always times when he would find himself alone, vulnerable and unprepared. And there was not much he could do about it for he had no Patron's amongst the senior officers of the Legion, who would protect him and there was no police force to which he could report the threats. And Titus the Centurion would only care if the disturbance affected the performance and standing of his company. Anything else was fair game. The Legion and its Fortress, brimming with five and a half thousand highly-trained professional killers, was a dangerous, violent place. The only thing that stopped the legionaries from running riot, looting and settling scores, was the severe and harsh, army discipline with its beatings, capital punishment and court martials.

***

Sighing impatiently, the signifer of the Second Company of the Second Cohort sat down behind his desk and began to sift through the pile of small, wooden tablets. Fergus stood before him, his hands clasped behind his back, staring down at the neat writing and numbers that covered the hundreds of thin, wooden tablets. The small, office annex inside the Principia, the Legionary HQ that served as the company's administrative office, was cluttered with a vast bureaucracy of wooden tablets, receipts, accounts, lists, army records, letters and blank, bronze diplomas.

'Fergus, Fergus, Fergus,' the signifer muttered to himself as he thumbed through the army personnel records. 'Ah here we go.'

The signifer pulled out a wooden tablet and sighed again, as he stared at the writing. Then, in an impatient voice, he started to read out aloud, summarizing as he went.

'Joined us eighteen months ago; father sent a letter of recommendation; confirmed citizen; age upon joining - 18; in good health; passed the physical examination. No distinguishing body marks. No homosexual behaviour. Pay grade is the standard legionary rate; promoted to Decanus; no disciplinary remarks; funds in account as of 1st January of the year 857 since the founding of Rome 300 denarii. Standard pay 300 denarii per annum; no bonus granted; account supplemented by two quarterly payments each of 75 denarii; withdrew 110 denarii at the start of this year for food and equipment, twenty denarii were transferred to his pension, plus on January 20 withdrew 50 denarii; on February 14 withdrew another 60 denarii; on March 6, 60 denarii and on April 7 another 135 denarii, leaving us with the grand sum of 15 denarii remaining until the next pay day.'

The signifer looked up at Fergus. 'That's it,' he growled. 'You have 15 denarii left in your account. I am in a hurry, so do you want the money or not?'

Fergus cleared his throat and stared down at the thin wooden tablet that contained all his army personnel details. Fifteen denarii! Was that all he had left from his account. It was a sad state of affairs and the year was barely half-way through. Half-heartedly he raised his hand in the air.

'What would be the best way for me to invest the remaining money?' he muttered.

The signifer glared at him, as if he had just said the stupidest thing. 'My job is to look after the company's records and the soldier's pay but I don't hand out investment advice,' he growled. 'Now do you want the fifteen Denarii or not? I haven't got all day.'

Fergus stared down at the jumble of personnel records, strewn across the desk. Then he nodded and with a relieved look, the signifer turned towards the iron, pay-chest in which the whole Company's pay was kept. Fitting a large key into the lock, he unlocked it and peered inside.

Fergus looked down at his feet. A few days had passed since Galena had told him that she was pregnant and he'd thought it prudent to ask the company signifer to check, on how much money he still had in his account. With a baby on the way and a new wife, he would be needing money. But fifteen denarii for the rest of the quarter. That was shocking. Looking guilty, he studied his army boots as the signifer counted out the coins, carefully placing each one on the desk for him to see. There was a reason why his finances were in such dire straits. A reason which he'd kept from Galena, for he didn't have the courage to tell her that he'd lost three hundred and five Denarii he'd withdrawn throughout the year to gambling. Three hundred and five Denarii! It was over a year's salary. Gone for good with nothing to show for it. He had not told her about his gambling habit. It was a stupid habit, he knew that, but he couldn't help himself. The lure of the cup and the roll of the dice was simply irresistible and now he was paying the price for his addiction.

'What about credit?' Fergus muttered lifting his head and looking at the signifer.

The Standard Bearer paused and glanced up at Fergus. Then his eyes narrowed. 'The army doesn't give credit,' he murmured, 'But if you are desperate there are always the money lenders in town. But I would not advice it boy. They charge a phenomenal amount of interest. If you are short, then borrow from your mates. But getting into debt is never worth it. Stay away from debt if you ask me, it's dangerous.'

Fergus looked away as the Standard Bearer closed the pay chest and locked it. But he couldn't live off fifteen denarii for the rest of the quarter, Fergus thought. That was impossible. He would have to find a way to increase the amount. Signing a wooden receipt with his own hand, he scooped up the coins, counted them and then slipped them into a pocket, before turning for the doorway.

Outside he blinked in the afternoon sunlight. The spacious courtyard of the Principia, the Legionary HQ at the centre of the Fortress, was surrounded on three sides by the administrative offices and storerooms of the Legion and, close by too, were the personal quarters of the Legionary Legate and his family. The open, sandy square, used sometimes as a parade ground, was today empty except for a few men hurrying towards the entrance into the fine stone basilica, the great hall, that towered over the courtyard. Fergus, looking glum, headed back towards his company's barracks. What was he going to do? The army wouldn't give him any credit. Asking his mess mates for money would be a humiliating experience and he didn't like the thought of going to the money lenders in town. That left him with the unappealing option of writing to Kyna, his mother and asking her to send him some funds. Fergus groaned. That would not go down well on Vectis, and his mother, would be furious with him. But what could he do? He needed more than fifteen denarii for the next three months.

As he approached his barracks block he suddenly paused and thoughtfully rubbed his fingers across his forehead. Then he sighed and looked down at the ground. There was just one thing for it. Tensely he turned and headed back towards the barracks block of the Third Company. Right at the end of the block, closest to the outer wall and furthest from the main street, was the Cohort's premier gambling den. The small, twin rooms that housed this particular eight-man squad, were well known and it was here that he'd lost a fortune playing dice.

***

The two legionary's grinned at Fergus as he reached for the throwing cup and carefully examined the three, six-sided tesserae dice. It was not unknown for the dice to be loaded, but these looked alright. He sat cross-legged on the floor of the small barracks block, which looked exactly like his own. On the ground, in between him and the two legionaries lay a pile of gleaming coins, including his fifteen denarii.

34

'Feeling lucky,' one of the men said showing a mouth which was missing several teeth.

'Like Venus,' Fergus muttered as he wrenched his eyes away from the dice and stared down at the pile of money. There was enough there, to make things manageable for the next few months and, as he gazed at the coins, the money glinted and urged him on. So close. Nearly his. He had to do this. There was no other way. He couldn't let Galena down.

Across from him one of the legionaries casually drew his pugio, army knife from his belt and laid it purposefully on the floor in front of him. His friend, the one with the missing teeth, jutted his chin at Fergus.

'Now we're not going to have any trouble with you when you lose,' he said in a hard, unfriendly tone. 'We don't take kindly to losers who refuse to accept the outcome of an honest throw.'

'I won't be any trouble,' Fergus growled. 'And I am not going to lose.'

'Alright let's do this then,' the other soldier hissed, his eyes suddenly gleaming with greed as he looked down at the pile of money.

Resolutely Fergus dropped the three dice into the cup, held it up, gave it a good shake, said a silent prayer and sent the dice rolling onto the ground. A six, a three and a four. Not bad. Anxiously he looked on, as the first of his fellow gamblers grabbed the dice and dropped them into the cup. As he threw them onto the ground, Fergus twisted his fingers and his lips worked on another silent prayer. Across from him the man cursed. A two, a three and another two, lay on the ground. Fergus felt a flutter of excitement.

'Nearly a dog,' the soldier with the missing teeth laughed. as he caught the disappointed look on his comrade's face.

Swiftly the legionary picked up the dice, dropped them into the cup, gave them a shake and quickly rolled them onto the ground. Fergus groaned and his face went pale. A six, a five and another six. The legionary who'd thrown the dice, whooped in delight. Fergus closed his eyes in dismay. He'd lost. He'd lost every last coin of disposable income he had. It should not have been like this. What had he been thinking? This was a disaster. Across from him the man with the missing teeth was scooping up his winnings, with a huge grin.

'That's the closest to Venus you will ever get,' the legionary exclaimed, looking up at Fergus with a big taunting grin.

Chapter Four – The Letter

The company had been standing to attention in the burning noon sun without moving for over three hours now, and still Titus refused to dismiss them. The eighty or so legionaries, clad in their full, body armour, wearing helmets and clutching their large rectangular shields and heavy throwing, Pila, stood motionless, in ten ranks of eight. The men were staring straight ahead into space, sweat trickling down their faces. Not a man moved and the company were silent, for each man knew that to move but an inch, was to invite a fierce beating from the Centurion's vine staff. Around them, the legionary parade and exercise area had long ago emptied, and now the only spectators were a few off-duty soldiers lounging around in the shade of one of engineering workshops. Titus, clad in his plumed-helmet and grasping his vine staff, stood a few paces beyond his men facing them, his eyes flicking from one man to the next. There was a tough, harsh look on his face. The Centurion, even though he was over twice as old as most of his legionaries, had himself not moved or said a word in over three hours, as if he was daring his men to try to think that they were tougher than him. At the rear of the company Furius, holding the Optio's long, wooden staff, also stood ready to beat the first man, who dared fall out of formation.

Fergus closed his eyes, as he felt a trickle of salty sweat run down his cheek. The gods were always on the side of the officers, he thought, for today, of all days, the sun had decided to come out at its fiercest and hottest. What luck. A day had passed since his latest gambling disaster and the tough physical exercises and constant training, that Titus had put his men through, was not making him feel any better. There had been no time to see Galena. Would she provide him with a dowry? The thought had crossed his mind, but she and her father were not wealthy people. But it didn't matter he thought. She was his girl and he loved her. He knew that deep down. And in the end, that was all that would matter. He was going to be a father and he would find the money from somewhere. He was going to make her proud to be his woman.

'Company,' Titus roared suddenly, his deep, booming voice filling the parade ground, 'Company, will stand easy.'

An audible sigh of relief swept through the ranks, as the legionaries relaxed and raised their hands to wipe away sweat and scratch at their cheeks, ears and chins. Titus glared at his men, but there was no malice in his eyes and, for an instant, Fergus thought he caught a glimpse of concern, on the grey-haired veteran's face.

'You think you are tough,' the Centurion roared. 'You think you can handle a barbarian charge. None of you have ever witnessed one. None of you have ever stood in the line and stood up to such an assault. You are all going to piss yourselves when you do. The peoples beyond the Empire's borders are bigger and taller than us. They are physically strong and they are fierce. They are not afraid of death. I have seen them and I know what they can do. But there is one thing that they do not have, and that is discipline. They do not have our Roman discipline. They do not have the patience or character to stand in the heat for hours, and wait for the right moment, and because they lack our discipline that is why we are going to defeat them. That's why we are going to slaughter them, when they have the misfortune to run into the Second Company of the Second Cohort of the Twentieth Legion. I want you all to remember that.'

Titus glared at his men as he paused to take breath.

'Rome conquers all,' he cried.

***

Fergus and his mess mates had just returned to their barrack rooms, when at the doorway to their block, a slave boy

38

appeared, clutching a leather despatch case. Nervously the boy eyed the tired, sweat-soaked legionaries.

'What do you want, Vittius snapped at the slave. 'Well?'

'Fergus,' the slave stammered in a thick Briton accent, 'I am to deliver this to Fergus. They told me that this was the block.'

Fergus wiped his forehead with the back of his hand as he stepped towards the boy. 'I am Fergus,' he said. 'What have you got for me?'

In reply the slave fished into his satchel and quickly handed Fergus a small, brown, double-hinged, wooden tablet; the size of a hand. The tablet looked exactly like the ones which Fergus had seen, stacked up in the company's administrative office inside the Principia.

'A letter,' Fergus exclaimed with sudden excitement, as a little colour shot into his cheeks. Turning towards his mess mates, he held up the hinged, wooden-tablet. In the barrack room his comrades stirred, with a mix of curiosity and sudden envy. Receiving letters from home was a rare event at the base, and the further away or the poorer a soldier's family were, the rarer they became. Fergus smiled and turned to look at the brown, wooden-tablet. Instantly he recognised the scratched handwriting on the outside. It was from his mother, Kyna, on the Isle of Vectis. Without another word, Fergus strode out through the doorway of the barracks room and headed for the communal latrines, for if a man wanted to be left alone in the crowded fortress, that was by far the best place to go.

The long, line of holes cut into the wooden plank, stretched from wall to wall. Fergus sat over one of the holes, his under garments at his ankles, as he carefully studied the letter, turning it over in his hands. For the moment, he was the only occupant of the toilet block. Sending letters was an expensive business, for there was no organised postal service, and the sender had to rely on merchants, travellers and friends to pass on messages to their loved ones, and often the letters took ages before they arrived, and sometimes they did not arrive at all. So, they were precious, for news from home was always precious and had to be savoured, read and re-read again and again. Why had she written? Had there been news from Marcus, his father? With a resigned sigh Fergus broke the wax seal and opened the tablet and started to read the lines of tiny, neat hand writing.

Kyna, to her Fergus, greetings.
I hope you are well and keeping healthy my son. I am afraid that I write to you with sad news. The winter has been hard and cruel on us here on Vectis, and it is with great sadness that we have had to say our final farewell to Quintus, who died on the seventh day of March. He was not well as you will remember, but I take comfort in the fact that we gave him a good home in which to spend his final few years. Petrus is overcome with grief and refuses to eat at our table, and the whole family is much affected by our loss, as I am sure are you. Efa and Dylis send you their greetings. We buried Quintus in the place where he fought against the Barbarian Queen, as per his final wishes, the same spot where your grandfather Corbulo wishes to be laid to rest. There has still been no news from your father and every day now, Efa and I go out to pray beside the sea and give offerings for his safe return. I do not know whether the Gods are listening. Dylis thinks that her brother will not be coming home, but I do not accept her despair, for I believe that your father is not dead, a sentiment which I hope you share. Recently a letter arrived from the bank in Londinium. It was deposited there by your father before he set out on his voyage and addressed to me, to be opened only if he had not returned within a year. The letter still rests on my table, for I have made up my mind to refuse to read its contents. We must be strong and hope for the best. That is what your father has taught me, and that is what I intend to do.

There is further troubling news, my dearest son. We have received word from our agent and partners in Noviomagus Reginorum, that there have been complaints made to the local magistrates about our ownership of our land and the villa here on Vectis. A wealthy, equestrian Lord by the name of Priscinus, is laying claim to our land. In his complaint, he is claiming that the land, farm and villa were promised to him by Agricola and he says that he will produce evidence of this in due course. He is trying to take away our property and livelihood. Efa believes that we shall have to go to court to defend ourselves. I feel bad, my son, to lay these heavy tidings at your feet, for I am sure that you have enough to do in Deva, but it is right that you should know about the evils that afflict us. We are all thinking about you here in Vectis and praying that the gods protect you, and that the rigours of army life are not too heavy. Write to me when you can, and let us know how you are faring. Farewell, my boy, dearest soul, as I hope to prosper and hail. To Fergus, son of Marcus, from Kyna his mother.

With a troubled look, Fergus lowered the letter, sighed and stared down at the ground as he tried to picture Quintus in his mind. The news that old Quintus, Corbulo's army comrade and fellow veteran of the Twentieth Legion had died, was a crushing if not unexpected blow. When he had still been a boy, growing up on Vectis, he had spent many days accompanying Quintus around the farm, and listening to the veteran's war stories and stories about Corbulo, his grandfather. He and Quintus had formed a close bond. Quintus had inspired him. He had written the letter of recommendation that had gotten him into the Twentieth Legion and, he had pretended to be his father when Marcus had been absent with his Cohort. Despondently Fergus raised the letter and read it again and, as he did so, his sadness gave way to anger. Who the fuck was this arrogant prick who was trying to take away his family's home? How dare this Priscinus, this equestrian lord, suggest that his grandfather's land did not rightfully belong to his descendants. The more he stared at the letter, the angrier he became.

'Fergus, Fergus, are you in there,' a voice interrupted.

'I am here,' Fergus growled, annoyed at the sudden intrusion.

'What's up?'

A moment later, Catinius appeared in the doorway to the latrine block. His face was flush with excitement. He grinned as he caught sight of Fergus sitting on the toilet.

'There is news,' Catinius exclaimed in an excited voice, 'They are sending us to the Danube frontier, Fergus. We are going to war. The Legate has just made the announcement. We are heading to Dacia to kick the shit out of King Decebalus. They are sending the whole Cohort and the Sixth as well. Titus has just been called to a conference. They are saying that we will be leaving within a week.'

Chapter Five – Farewell

The forest grove was overrun with huge numbers of colourful, spring flowers that grew amongst the long and lush, green grass. The flowers were bursting with life, their scent filling the grove and attracting a horde of eager bees and fluttering butterflies. In the trees, the birds were coming and going, rustling amongst the leaves and undergrowth. Rays of sunlight cut through the tall, thick oak and pine trees of the forest that surrounded the grove, bathing it in a strange, warm light. In the June sunlight, the place looked magnificent and hauntingly beautiful. A little way through, the trees the peaceful river flowed along on its eternal and silent passage towards the sea.

Fergus and Galena stood in the centre of the grove, facing one another. They were smiling at each other. Galena's long, free-flowing, blond hair was crowned with a circle of interwoven, white flowers and she was clad in fine long, flowing, white robes, whilst Fergus was wearing a smart army tunic, made of black wool. The two of them were each holding the end of a small tree branch. Taran and two of his female relatives, older women with shawls draped over their heads, stood a few paces away bearing witness to the wedding ceremony.

As he finished saying his vows, Fergus grinned at his new wife and in response, a little tear appeared in Galena's eye. Hastily she wiped it away and turned to smile at her father and kin, who broke out into loud clapping.

'The contract has been made,' one of the female relatives said dipping her head respectfully at the newly married couple. Then she turned and silently and respectfully bowed to the grove.

Ignoring the witnesses, Fergus stepped forwards and kissed his wife.

'There is one final thing we must do,' Galena said with a radiant face and eyes that sparkled with happiness. 'Keep hold of the branch,' she whispered. 'Don't let go for it will bring bad luck.'

Without another word, she led him through the trees towards the river's edge. As they reached the riverbank, both still clutching the branch, she paused and stared at the placid, peaceful water.

'The river is eternal,' she said, the look on her face calm and distant. 'It's water will still flow long after all trace of us has vanished. But the spirits of my ancestors and the spirits who live here in the rocks, trees, flowers and water; they will remember us. They will know who we were, and they are witness to the promises we have made here today.' She paused and took a deep breath. 'Now we must throw this piece of wood into the river. We must do this together, so that we will begin our journey into the world together and drift on its currents for all eternity.'

She turned to look up at him and gave him a smile and, as she did, Fergus felt his heart melt, and in that instance, he knew he had done the right thing in marrying her.

Together they dropped the branch into the river and watched it drift away on the current, until it vanished from view. Then Galena turned to him and reached up to run her fingers lightly across his cheek.

'You have made me the happiest woman in the land,' she whispered; her eyes twinkling, as she studied him in her calm, intelligent way, 'I know you must go. I know you must leave, but I want you to know that I and our child will be here waiting for you to return. I will come back to this place every month on this day, and I shall lay a stone beside the river, for every month you are gone. And when our child is born, I will bring him or her here. Because this grove, Fergus, this is where I will be closest to you.'

Fergus swallowed and, unable to think of anything to say, he clasped hold of her and pulled her against him, running his fingers through her hair.

'Of course I will come back,' he muttered at last as he stared at the river.

She broke free from his embrace and stared up at him, with searching eyes and suddenly she looked vulnerable.

'I will have no other but you Fergus,' she said, with a note of pride in her voice. 'You are a good man. I know you. I know who you are and I want to give you something. Something that will protect you from the dangers that lie ahead. Something that will bring you back to me and our child.'

From her dress, she drew forth a fine-looking, iron amulet and pressed it into his hand. The amulet was circular and fastened to a fine and delicate-looking iron linked-chain. The intricate and beautifully worked, high quality, metal work, seemed to represent a maze, bordered by woven Celtic knots.

'It will protect you and show you the way out,' she whispered, staring up at him. 'Even when you have lost all hope. It belonged to my grandmother and it has powerful magic.'

Fergus nodded and slowly slipped the chain over his head, so that the amulet lay pressed against his chest.

'It will remind me of you,' he said, trying to smile.

She nodded and held his gaze, her eyes boring into him, as if they were searching for his very soul.

'The child will be born on the first day of the New Year,' she murmured. 'I have counted the days and she will be on time. I know she will be.'

'She,' he said shaking his head.

'It's going to be a girl,' Galena smiled back. 'And I want you to give me her name.'

Fergus sighed and looked away, and for a while he was silent.

'Alright,' he murmured at last, 'We shall call her Briana, for she will be a strong girl and she shall have her mother's beautiful, blond hair and she shall fear nothing.'

Galena smiled and looked away, but he could see that she was pleased. Then before he could stop her, she had grabbed his groin and pulled him close, her eyes staring up at him with sudden determination.

'I know you Fergus, soldier of Rome; I know your desires; I know what you like to do with this thing of yours, but when you are away fighting your war, you had better get used to using your right hand. Stay away from those town whores and pretty temptresses for none of them will ever be me. None of them will ever give you what I will give you.'

***

The thousand or so legionaries stood crammed into the parade ground, packed in close together, as they listened to the young Tribune. It was morning and the grey, dull sky was heavily overcast. The senior officer was standing on top of a box, as he addressed the troops, clad in his fine, muscle-cuirassed armour and red cloak. At his side Fergus could see the Legion's Legate and a cluster of senior officers, together with the standard bearers, proudly holding up the gleaming standards of the Twentieth Legion. Fergus stood at the back of the crowd, craning his neck to get a glimpse of the young Tribune, who had been appointed to lead the Vexillatio. The officer was speaking in a loud voice, but Fergus was too far away to properly hear what he was saying. Around him, he sensed the soldiers' excitement. Competition to be included in the Vexillatio that was being sent to the Danube frontier had been fierce, for the war offered not only a taste of action, but also the prospect of promotion and serious looting. A soldier could return a rich man from a successful war and there was, not a single legionary in the Legion who didn't expect Rome to win. And now the Legate had decided to send the Second and Sixth Cohorts, a total of a thousand legionaries. The rumour that had spread through the ranks, was that the Legate was keen to send younger soldiers and leave the older men behind at Deva. Fergus sighed. Galena had been right; they were sending him half way across the Empire; a two-thousand-mile journey, to fight in the coming Dacian campaign. A resigned look appeared on Fergus's face. He had never even left the province of Britannia and now he was leaving his pregnant wife behind. Galena had managed the farewell in a stoic fashion, but he knew she was desperately worried. No one knew how long the Dacian war would last and he could easily be gone for years. It was going to be hard on her. But he had made a will just like he had promised, and he had deposited it with the signifer in the office, where all the company records were kept. The will hadn't been much, just a simple statement that he left all his earthly belongings to his wife, not that they amounted to much. And now that everything had been taken care of, he was worried, for he would not be there at Galena's side when his baby was born. Childbirth was a daunting challenge for any woman and there was a significant chance that Galena would die during the ordeal. Nervously he fingered the iron maze amulet that she had given him. He needed to be strong and not think about such things. Turning to look away from the Tribune standing on his box, Fergus noticed that the Legionary workshops were a hive of activity, as the army engineers swarmed over dozens of wagons and carts, preparing them for the long, journey ahead. The word in the company was that they would be leaving Deva within a week. Fergus sighed again and looked down at his feet. It was time to tell Titus about his plan and he was fairly certain that the Centurion was not going to like it.

'He will see you now,' Titus's slave said quietly as he opened the door leading into the Centurion's quarters. Stiffly, Fergus rose from the small bench outside the door where he had been waiting. Titus was wealthy enough to own two slaves who lived with him in the barracks. That Titus could afford such luxuries, did not surprise Fergus, for the Centurion had been a soldier for over twenty-two years, and the rumour in the company was that his pay was over eight times that, which a normal legionary received.

The slave silently closed the door behind him. Lydia, Titus's young wife was reclining on a couch against the far wall, idly dropping grapes into her mouth. She was a pretty, fit looking young woman of around twenty; twice as young as her husband. She gave Fergus a friendly wink as he stepped into the room. Titus, clad in white army tunic was sitting behind a desk, resting his head on his elbow as he stared at the huge pile of documents that lay on the table. Wearily he looked up.

'What is it?' he said sharply.

Fergus turned, took a step towards Titus and saluted smartly.

'Sorry to disturb you Sir,' he said quickly. 'I was wondering whether I could have a word with you Sir. It's important.'

'Speak,' Titus said, turning to look down at the pile of documents on his desk. 'Get to the point Fergus, I don't have all day.'

'I want to ask your permission for some leave, Sir. I have had news from my family on Vectis; bad news Sir. I would like your permission to go and see them before we ship out.'

'You want a holiday,' Titus exclaimed in a surprised voice, as he leant back in his chair and stared up at Fergus.

'Not a holiday Sir,' Fergus muttered. He was committed now. There was no going back. 'There has been a death and I need to see my family. There are some matters that need taking care of. Please Sir, we are going to be gone for a long time. This is my last chance to say goodbye. And I promise that I will report back to the company before we set sail for Gaul. You have my word.'

Titus's eyes narrowed as he stared at Fergus and for a long moment, the room was silent.

'You ask for permission to take leave and visit your family just before the company is about to embark on a journey, half way across the Empire,' Titus said slowly. 'Were you not present when I spoke to all NCO's about the importance of inspiring their men? Were you not there when I said that I only wanted the best man to be my Tesserarius? I need you here Fergus, there are a lot of preparations to take care of and if I let you go the others will soon be demanding the same privilege.'

'Please Sir,' Fergus muttered staring straight ahead into space, 'There are matters that I must take care of that cannot wait. Legal matters Sir. My father is absent.'

'Oh let the poor boy go, Titus,' Lydia called from her couch, 'The boys are not going to see their families for a long time. He has already promised he will report back before we sail.'

Titus's face itched with sudden annoyance but he did nothing to scold his wife for interrupting. Instead he tapped his fingers on the wooden table and thoughtfully looked down at the documents that lay strewn across it.

'This is unexpected Fergus,' he said at last in a disappointed voice. 'And I cannot say that I am pleased. You are asking for a lot and your timing is shit.'

Titus looked up sharply and Fergus could see that he was indeed not pleased. 'We embark for Gaul from the port at Rutupiae. I shall expect you to report back to me there on the last day of June. If you are late or do not show up I will report you as having deserted.' The expression on Titus's face hardened. 'You know the penalty for desertion, you know what the consequences are.'

'Yes Sir, but I am no deserter,' Fergus replied. 'I will be there on the appointed day. I will not let you down Sir and thank you.'

'Alright,' Titus said raising his hand in a dismissive gesture. 'You had better get going.'

Fergus saluted, turned smartly and headed for the exit and, as he did, from her couch, Lydia gave him another wink. Just as he reached the doorway and the slave waiting outside, Titus called out.

'I am only doing this out of respect for your grandfather, Corbulo.'

***

The horse trotted down the straight Roman road, its hooves clattering on the stone, paving stones and gravel. It was early evening and the road was deserted. Already the Legionary Fortress of Deva Victrix had nearly vanished from view. Fergus, clad in a long, dark cloak with a hood drawn over his head, paused and slowly turned the horse around and gazed back at the army base. He was leaving Galena behind. He was leaving his unborn baby behind, and for a split second it felt as if he was running away. Tensely he gazed at the distant buildings. But Kyna and Efa needed him. His family on Vectis were in trouble. They needed a man to sort out the danger that was circling the family home. That was why Kyna had written to him. His mother would never admit it of course, but it was there, the unspoken words in her letter. She needed his help. He wouldn't have much time, but he would do what he could. Anxiously he raised his hand and scratched the stubble on his cheek. He had not forgotten what Marcus had told him over a year ago.

'Do your duty, honour your family and the gods and you will be a man, son,' Fergus muttered to himself, repeating the exact words that his father had spoken. 'If you can do that, you have nothing to fear in this life or the next. Look after yourself and remember that one day, you will inherit the farm and our land on Vectis and that you will be responsible for all our people there.'

Kyna, Efa, Dylis and the others were in trouble. They were his people and in his father's absence he was the head of his family. So, he was going home to help them. He would do what he could.

***

As he started off again down the road, heading south, Fergus was oblivious to the eagle that soared high above his head. The hunting bird drifted on the air currents, its talons extended and its sharp eyes and curved beak taking in the solitary rider. Then with a high-pitched shriek, the hunter effortlessly wheeled away towards the distant sea. As it glided over the coastline, the bird was lifted by a stream of warm-air, which sent it shooting upwards into the darkening gloom. Drifting on the choppy, upward drafts, the eagle turned gracefully, its sharp, beady eyes watching the water. And as it did it caught sight of a small battered Roman merchant vessel stubbornly ploughing through the waves. It opened its mouth and cried out again; its piercing cry lost amongst the whine of the wind. Far below the hunter, the ship's red square sail was bulging outwards and from the top of the mast the proud pennant depicting Hermes fluttered in the wind as the vessel headed straight for the wide river mouth that led upstream to the Roman Fortress of Deva Victrix.

Chapter Six – The Old Man

The Hermes plunged and rose through the waves sending gusts of salty spray flying and spattering over the deck. Marcus stood on top of the deck house, steadying himself against the ship's railing as he gazed at the grey coastline, his head and body covered by a rough, seal-skin hood and cloak. He looked tired and his pale, weather-beaten face and emaciated body had shrunk, turning him into an old man, something his long grey beard and seal skin clothes could not hide. His eyes however betrayed no emotion, except for a certain grim satisfaction. In his right hand he was clutching a Hyperborean pipe, which he now and then raised to his lips, exhaling and sending little puffs of smoke drifting away on the fresh, sea breeze. At his side clutching the tiller, Alexandros too was staring at the distant coastline, a black, eye-patch covering one eye. The two men were silent as the Hermes headed towards the wide, river estuary. Amidships, the new and rough Hyperborean mast towered up into the sky and the patched, red-square sail bulged in the wind and the ropes that held it in place, creaked and groaned.

Idly Marcus raised his head and squinted up at the sky, as he swore that he heard a bird's high-pitched cry, but amongst the heavy clouds he could see nothing. Not long now he thought. Not long now before their long and epic sea voyage would come to an end. At the thought, sadness appeared on his tough, emaciated face. It would be a sad moment when the crew finally said goodbye to each other. What things they had seen on their fifteen-month long journey; what things they had experienced together; what an adventure they had shared. As if reading his thoughts, Alexandros turned his head towards Marcus. The Greek captain nodded and a little weary smile appeared on his lips. There was no need to explain, Marcus thought, Alexandros understood. The whole crew had formed a tight-knit bond, welded together by the shared need and desire to survive, and which allowed them to read each other without saying a word.

'The river will lead us to the Legionary Fortress,' Marcus called out, gesturing at the estuary. 'Fergus is based there. It's not far. Tonight, we shall sleep on land.'

Alexandros nodded but said nothing. Instead, with his one good eye, he was watching his daughter Calista who stood at the bow of the ship together with Jodoc. In her arms Calista was holding a baby, heavily wrapped in bundles of cloth against the cold, sea spray and fierce breeze. She smiled as Jodoc placed his arm around her and pointed at something on the coast. A flicker of contentment appeared on Marcus's face, as he stared at the young couple and their new-born daughter. Then he took another drag from his pipe and blew the smoke from his mouth, and as he did so, he remembered the sullen and angry young man he'd dragged back onto the Hermes, all those months ago, when they had managed to escape from the Hyperborean's on the beach beside the ruined druid trading post. Having Calista, and becoming a father, had changed Jodoc for the better. He had found happiness with his new family and it had helped him come to terms with his father's death. He had also consoled himself with the thought that his father's book, the History of the Tribes of Britannia, was safely hidden somewhere in Hyperborea.

The contented look on Marcus's face vanished abruptly, as beneath his feet he heard a loud groan. A moment later Cora, Alexandros's wife, appeared from the deck house and turned to look up at the two men standing on the roof. Her hard, weather beaten face creased with concern.

'He's asking for you,' Cora said sharply, as she looked up at Marcus. 'You had better come down and talk to him.'

Without saying a word, Marcus emptied the remnants of his tobacco pipe over the ship's side and started to climb down the ladder. As he landed on the deck, Cora caught hold of Marcus's sleeve. She looked anxious.

'I have tried everything I know,' she said quietly in a resigned voice. 'But he is not getting any better. If I knew what was wrong with him, then maybe I could do something about it. But I have never seen an illness like this one before. If the legionary doctors don't know what to do, then he is going to die and die soon. There is not much time. He is getting weaker.'

Marcus did not reply as he stepped into the dark and dank cabin. Cunomoltus lay stretched out on the floor on a bed made from seal and moose skins. A large, brown bear-skin covered his body and his head lay propped up against a pillow of beaver hide. His eyes were closed and he was groaning. On the rolling and pitching deck around him, lay an assortment of cooking pots and iron utensils. Carefully Marcus knelt beside his brother and touched Cunomoltus's forehead with the two remaining fingers of his left hand. He was burning up with fever. With a sigh, Marcus sat back. The illness had struck on the fourteenth day after they had last sighted land. Cunomoltus had complained of fatigue and then, one day his body was covered in spots and his skin had started to turn yellow. It had been followed by teeth loss and blood in his shit, and the longer it had gone on, the weaker he'd become.

'I am here,' Marcus said quietly. 'I am here, brother.'

In his bed, Cunomoltus groaned and slowly opened his eyes. His face seemed to have shrunk and now resembled little more than skin over bone.

'Marcus,' Cunomoltus wheezed as he tried to smile. 'Marcus, I think I know why this is happening to me.'

'You need to rest,' Marcus said firmly. 'You are going to survive. We have sighted the coast. We should make Deva Victrix before nightfall. We are nearly home, brother. Just a few more hours. You have to remain strong.'

Weakly Cunomoltus shook his head. 'No, listen to me brother,' he murmured. 'I know why this illness has taken me. The Gods are punishing me. This is my punishment for leaving Alawa behind. We should have brought her with us, Marcus. I should not have left her behind. Now I must pay for my sins.'

Marcus sighed and looked away. Alawa had been a Hyperborean girl; a girl with whom Cunomoltus had fallen in love with during the harsh cold winter. His brother should have known better, for there had been no chance of her coming with them across the ocean. Her tribe would never have allowed it and so, when spring had finally come and the Hermes had set out on its long, sea voyage back home, Cunomoltus had been forced to leave his pregnant sweetheart behind. It had very nearly broken his heart and for days, he had not spoken a word to anyone. And now this. Annoyed, Marcus shook his head.

'You will stay alive brother,' Marcus said. 'We have not just crossed the ocean and faced all its perils for you to die within sight of home. Don't you dare. You are going to survive.'

Stiffly Marcus got to his feet as in his bed, Cunomoltus groaned and looked up at him.

'I mean it,' Marcus snapped harshly. 'If you die now, I am going to be so fucking pissed off, I will give you a burial at sea, just like we did with Matunaagd, without the proper rites. There are still things that need to be done. Or have you forgotten that we are still obliged to fulfil our father's final instruction. Corbulo is waiting to have his mortal remains buried on the battlefield, where he fought against Boudicca and that is what we are going to do, together.'

***

Marcus strode across the pitching deck towards the forward cargo hatch. He had long ago stopped feeling the sway and roll of the sea. Up ahead, the coast was drawing closer. Without a glance at the young couple standing by the prow, he heaved open the cargo hatch and disappeared into the dark hold. In the gloom, it took a few moments before his eyes adjusted to the light. Bales of moose, beaver, bear, seal and wolf skins, lay packed along the bulkheads, and further along, he could make out sacks of Hyperborean fruits, roots, plants and a single, bone-headed harpoon. The harpoon had belonged to Matunaagd, a native whom they had befriended during the long winter and who had volunteered to come with them back across the ocean. But during the crossing the Hyperborean had grown sick and had died and they had been forced to bury him at sea. Marcus grunted as he stooped and began to search for something amongst the bales and sacks. It had taken Alexandros and Cora the whole long, dark and freezing winter to collect everything which they had done through hunting and bartering with the natives. Ignoring the supplies, they'd picked up when they had first sighted the Hibernian coast, Marcus rummaged around in the semi-dark, until at last he found what he was looking for. He'd developed a strong liking for the Hyperborean smoking herbs, which had a strange calming effect on him, and on the long voyage home he'd become addicted to his pipe. Stuffing some of the herbs into his pocket, he turned and climbed back up onto the deck and into the day light.

As he strode back towards the deck house filling his pipe, Alexandros called out to him.

'We will never be able to sail up that river,' the Greek captain cried, pointing at the estuary. 'Not without rowers. The wind is slackening.'

Marcus turned to stare in the direction of the wide bay. Then he nodded. Alexandros was right.

'Alright,' Marcus cried out in reply. 'Sail her into the estuary as far as we can go and anchor along the north shore. Jodoc and I will go on foot from there. Deva Victrix is only about 6 miles inland along the river, if I remember correctly. It should take us half a day to get there and back, at a brisk walk. Stay with the ship until we are back.'

From his position on top of the deck house, Alexandros nodded. 'Bring me back some wine,' Alexandros boomed in his deep voice. 'It's been so long since I last had a drop, that I have nearly forgotten what the stuff tastes like. And I don't care what you all think, I am getting drunk tonight.'

Marcus did not reply, as he paused beside the ship's side and finally managed to light his pipe, using two, small flint-stones. As he took a long and satisfying draw and blew the smoke from his mouth, he turned to study the green meadows and dark forests that were now only half a mile away. He was nearly home and his long and epic journey was nearly done. Now that he was so close, his sadness at knowing their journey was coming to an end, was beginning to fade and a long repressed, powerful, excitement was taking hold. He could deny it no longer. He missed his family. It would be good to see Fergus; it would be good to see Kyna, his wife and Efa, Dylis and the others. For too long he had resisted the temptation of thinking about them, for fear that it would tip him into melancholy, restlessness and despair. He had been away for too long, and when he returned to Vectis he would keep his promise; a promise he'd made the day that Alexandros had rescued him from the ruined trading post; a promise to never leave Vectis, and his family again. He was done with travelling and adventure; he was done with fighting and hardship. The time had come to spend his remaining energies on the welfare and prosperity of his family. That was the least he could do to make up for all the times he'd been absent. Idly he reached up to touch the small canister that hung from around his neck and which contained Corbulo's ashes and as he did Marcus smiled revealing a couple of missing teeth.

'Look, you bastard,' he whispered, jutting his chin at the green landscape. 'I brought you home and soon you will rest beside your comrades. I did this.' Marcus took another draw from his pipe and glanced up at the sky. 'I did this,' he said quietly. 'So now we are even, old man.'

***

The path along the river was deserted. Away from the water, the green, pleasant meadows were covered with lush, green-grass, colourful June-flowers and interspersed with small groups of trees. Buzzing bees and fluttering butterflies flew around in the strong warm sun. Birds were everywhere and out across the sluggish river, the sunlight reflected from the water and insects darted across the surface. Marcus and Jodoc strode along the path at a brisk pace. They said nothing as they looked around them in wonder, as if they had never seen a summer's day quite like it. The firm, steady earth beneath his feet felt strange to Marcus after having spent so long on board the Hermes and he could see that Jodoc was having the same experience. Apart from a brief few days off the western coast of Hibernia, to take on much needed supplies, the two of them had not set foot on land for over forty-three days. But now everything was a delight and they revelled in the scents, the sight of familiar trees and plants, and the thought that soon they would be back in a proper Roman town.

'What will you do now,' Marcus said at last, glancing sideways at Jodoc.

The young man shrugged and kept his eyes on the path ahead.

'I will get married to Calista, in the proper legal way,' Jodoc replied. 'Alexandros has given me his consent. My father is dead and I do not have any other kin, so I guess I will go with Calista and her parents to Rome. I don't really care where I go.' Jodoc shrugged again. 'I will work and I will provide. Maybe I will become a sailor like Alexandros. It doesn't matter. As long as I am with Calista and my daughter, I will have everything I need.'

Marcus nodded. He was relieved that the young man had managed to find a sense of purpose again. It had not always been so. Marcus looked down at the earth beneath his feet and bit his lip, as he remembered the wounded and despairing young man they had found lying along the river bank in Hyperborea. Jodoc had very nearly ruined everything and the only reason Marcus had kept him alive, was because they had needed him to help crew the Hermes back home. But that was all in the past now, and Jodoc did not need to know. The two of them were never going to be friends, but neither were they going to part as enemies.

Sharply Marcus looked up as he struggled to contain his mounting excitement. Fergus, his son was based at Deva. As he strode along the path, Marcus tried to picture what Fergus looked like. The boy's red hair was his own, that was true, but his son seemed to worship his grandfather, Corbulo, even though he had never known him. Marcus sighed. The boy would no doubt be surprised to see him, maybe even happy. But the fact remained that he and Fergus barely knew each other. And that was his fault. He had been away too many times. But now, he was going to put that right. He had resolved to get to know the boy. Fergus needed to know who his father was and that meant spending time with him. For there was something else, something Marcus could feel in his bones, something he had only slowly become aware of; he was getting old. The strain of the long, epic voyage to Hyperborea had aged him beyond his forty-two years. Idly he reached up to touch the canister that hung from around his neck. Yes, he needed to spend some time with his son. He would start by telling the boy about his adventures in Hyperborea. He would show him the canister, containing Corbulo's ashes, and he would let him hold Corbulo's skull and, with luck, he would be able to convince the boy's commanding officer to grant him leave, so that he could attend Corbulo's burial. The boy would like that. And so would I, Marcus thought. But he would have to resist the temptation to go and find Fergus a little longer, for first he had to find a doctor, who would be able to help and treat Cunomoltus. His brother needed a doctor urgently.

The civilian town was filled with noise and bustling with activity, and as Marcus and Jodoc strode past the river harbour, Marcus gasped as he suddenly remembered that this was the spot where, nineteen years earlier, he and the Second Batavian Auxiliary Cohort had embarked for Hibernia. As they penetrated deeper into the town, Marcus became aware of just how many people crowded around the tightly-packed strip houses and in the market places, streets and shops. In Hyperborea the native settlements had often consisted of no more than a dozen people or a single extended family, living quietly in the forest or beside a river, but here in Deva Victrix there had to be thousands and they were all living on top of each other. Quietly Marcus exchanged glances with Jodoc. The young man too, seemed taken aback by the noise and scale of activity. They had forgotten. After their long isolation, they had forgotten what a Roman town felt and looked like. Warily the two of them pushed on into the settlement towards the vast legionary base and as they did, Marcus became aware of the curious looks and glances from the townsfolk, as if the people sensed that there was something strange and different about the two newcomers. The street hawkers and merchants advertising cries faded in volume, as they caught sight of Marcus, and here and there, people stopped what they were doing to stare at them, whilst others hastily stepped aside to let them pass. Marcus kept his eyes stubbornly on the street ahead. It felt uncomfortable, having all these eyes on him, but no one stopped them or spoke to them.

'It's our clothes,' Jodoc muttered. 'The seal skins and Hyperborean shoes. They stand out. No one has ever seen them before. That's why they are staring at us.'

Marcus did not reply. Down a side street he paused beside a large barn. Inside, six or seven horses stood quietly in their stables, looking out over the street. For a long moment Marcus stared at the beasts, marvelling at their strong, gracious bodies and taking in their peculiar smell. He'd spent most of his army career in close proximity to horses, but in Hyperborea he'd seen none.

'I want to buy two of your best horses,' he said, turning to the dealer who was reclining on a bench before the stables.

The dealer raised his eyebrows and studied Marcus with a frown.

'How will you pay me,' the man replied.

'I will pay you in gold and I need them right away - your best,' Marcus said quickly as he undid a small leather pouch from around his belt and showed the dealer several gleaming coins.

'That should do it,' the dealer grunted, staring respectfully at the gold.

'Can you recommend any good, quiet taverns in town,' Marcus added, glancing at the horse merchant. 'One of my friends is ill. He needs a good, comfortable bed.'

"Well, there is the Trajan near the harbour or the Lucky Legionary, but that's not always quiet; an army tavern if you know what I mean,' the man said as he headed into the stables.

'And a doctor,' Marcus called out. 'Who is the finest surgeon in town? I am willing to pay good money.'

***

Cunomoltus, wrapped in moose hides, lay stretched out on the ship's deck in the warm sunshine. He was staring up at the sky with feverish eyes, his drawn and emaciated face covered in spots and sores. The doctor, a balding man of around fifty, was kneeling beside him, muttering to himself as he examined his patient. Close by, Marcus and Cora stood looking down at Cunomoltus, their arms folded across their chests, their faces emotionless. The Hermes lay at anchor in the river mouth and, on the bank Jodoc was busying himself, looking after the two newly purchased horses.

'Is he going to live?' Marcus said in a harsh voice.

The doctor did not immediately reply as he examined Cunomoltus. Then at last, with a frown, the man rose to his feet. He looked perplexed.

'You say that there is blood in his excrement,' the doctor muttered.

Marcus nodded. 'He has been losing teeth as well. They just fall out of his mouth. It's all rotten. So, is he going to live?'

The doctor stroked his chin as he looked down at Cunomoltus. Then slowly he shook his head. 'I have only seen these symptoms once before, and that was with a man who had been forced to eat nothing but wild fowl, for weeks on end. The good news is that the disease is not infectious and recovery is rapid, if he gets a lot of rest, and most importantly, he gets fed a balanced diet.' The doctor turned to look at Marcus with a grave, serious expression. 'You need to feed him roots, fruits, blackberries, onion's, vegetables, beans and peas, those sorts of things. Your brother has been deprived of these foods. That is why he is sick. If you make sure he gets this diet, his recovery will be rapid and yes, he will survive.'

Marcus sighed with relief, and nodding his gratitude he silently handed the doctor a single gold coin, which the man smoothly slipped into his pocket.

'If you have all been eating the same food as your brother,' the doctor said, 'then all of you must take the same diet for the disease can strike down anyone.'

Puzzled the doctor turned to stare at Marcus, then at Cora and finally around the deck of the ship.

'What I don't understand is how you could not eat these things for such a long time,' the doctor said with a perplexed look.

'Your brother is not sick because he picked up a disease. He is sick because of neglect. It's almost as if he has been starving. Vegetables and fruit are hardly exotic goods. Many of them grow wild in the forest.' The man's puzzled look deepened. 'And those clothes you are wearing, I have never seen anything like it and those hides; they are not from around here.' The doctor's eyes narrowed suspiciously as he turned to look at Marcus. 'Where have you people been?'

Marcus raised his head and quickly glanced up at Alexandros who was watching them from the roof of the deckhouse, a cup of wine in his hand and a happy, contented smile on his lips.

'Nowhere,' Marcus replied with a shrug as he caught hold of the doctor's sleeve and started to guide him back to the raft that lay alongside the Hermes.

Chapter Seven – Separate Ways

The fire crackled, spat and roared, it's flames sending showers of sparks shooting up into the black, moonless night. Out on the peaceful river the water lapped against the tall reeds that covered the bank, and in the darkness beyond, Marcus could just make out the faint outline of the Hermes, lying at anchor. A little way off, the two horses stood motionless, tethered to a tree and somewhere in the distant forest a fox was barking. The six crew members of the Hermes sat around the fire silently sharing the flask of wine which Marcus had brought back from Deva. Cunomoltus lay stretched out in the grass, wrapped in moose pelts, his lips and mouth stained with the juices from forest fruits, which Calista had collected for him that evening. His eyes were closed and now and then he groaned. Marcus raised his cup of wine to his mouth and poured the contents down his throat in one go. Alexandros was right he thought, tonight he was going to get drunk. And as he looked around the fire at his companions, he could see that they too were out to get drunk. The silence around the camp fire was heavy with a strange sadness. Tomorrow the crew were going to go their separate ways. Tonight, would be their last night together.

Marcus turned to glance in the direction of the horses as he poured himself some more wine from the flask. Tomorrow he would take the horses and Cunomoltus, and head into Deva. He would find himself a tavern where his brother would be able to recover, and then he would go and seek out Fergus. And when Cunomoltus was capable and ready to travel, the two of them would head south, for he was growing keen to reach Vectis and his family. And after that he would make the journey to the battlefield, where he would finally lay Corbulo to rest beside his comrades. Slowly Marcus raised his head and turned to look across the fire at Alexandros. The Greek captain was staring moodily into the flames, his hand clenched tightly around his wooden cup, as if he was still at the helm of the Hermes in the midst of a storm. At his side Cora was picking at her finger nails, her red cheeks glowing in the fire-light, and beside Marcus,

Jodoc had his arm wrapped around Calista, who was holding her new-born in her lap. The two youngsters were staring sombrely into space, their minds seemingly, on things far away.

'Are you still determined to go to Rome?' Marcus said turning to look at Alexandros.

Across from Marcus the captain and owner of the Hermes stirred and wrenched his gaze away from the fire.

'Yes,' Alexandros replied in a determined voice. 'All the way to Rome. I will get my audience with the Empress even if I have to crawl on my belly to her rooms in the Imperial Palace.'

Marcus looked away. On the many days and nights that the two of them had stood together on the roof of the deckhouse out in the endless ocean, Alexandros had never tired of telling him what he was going to do, when they finally got back home. The Captain had not stopped talking about the rich ladies of Rome and their desire for eastern silk and other luxuries and so he, Alexandros, great sea captain, was going to take the Hermes and his family to Rome. He was going to petition the Empress, wife of Trajan, himself, for permission to lead a fleet of Roman ships back across the ocean to explore the coasts of Hyperborea and, if possible, to establish trading posts. And to back up his petition, Cora had kept a detailed written account of everything that had happened to them in the past fifteen months. She had enriched her account with dozens of beautiful drawings of the strange landscapes, animals, people, plants and objects that the crew had seen on their long voyage. And if that was not enough, Alexandros had taken care to amass a veritable mountain of physical evidence of their journey, all of which, hides, skins, Hyperborean weapons, fruits, bone amulets, herbs and plants had been carefully stowed into the cargo hold of the Hermes. The whole lot, Alexandros had told him, would be his gift to the Empress. How could she possibly say 'no' to his petition, the captain had argued, with supreme confidence. And as he remembered their conversations, Marcus slowly shook his head in bewilderment and reached for his Hyperborean pipe. Cora however, had not seemed too sure that the Empress would be willing to listen, but like the good team they were, she had not undermined her husband in front of him.

'Would you have given Matunaagd to the Empress if he had lived? Was that why you wanted to bring him back with us? An exotic Hyperborean slave for the mistress of the world,' Marcus said quietly glancing at Alexandros, as he filled his pipe with the Hyperborean smoking herbs.

The Captain did not reply as he turned to stare into the flames. Then he raised his cup to his lips and downed the wine in one go.

'He died, that's all there is to it,' Alexandros growled sullenly.

'You will need a couple of deck hands to help you sail the Hermes to Rome. It's a long voyage and you can't do with just the four of you,' Marcus muttered as he took a drag at his pipe.

'I will come with you into town tomorrow,' Alexandros grunted. 'I am sure to find a couple of willing sailors at the docks.'

Marcus nodded. That made sense. Sending a satisfying cloud of smoke drifting upwards into the darkness, he turned to look at Cunomoltus. His brother's eyes were open and he was staring up at the night sky.

'So we are all agreed then,' Marcus said. 'The tale of our voyage will be kept secret until Alexandros has had a chance to present his petition and evidence to the empress in Rome.'

As he looked around the fire, each member of the crew nodded in solemn agreement. They had discussed it at length just after they first sighted the western coast of Hibernia, and had decided it best if they kept their epic journey a secret for now. Cora, Jodoc and Calista had feared ridicule and disbelief, but Marcus had been more concerned about news of their journey reaching the druids. For the druid's would be wondering what had happened to their little trading post in Hyperborea and he did not want them coming to him and his family for answers and revenge.

'My brother and I shall return to our home on the Isle of Vectis,' Marcus said. 'I want you all to know that you are welcome, if you decide to pay us a visit. There will always be space for you.'

Across the fire from him, Cora suddenly raised her cup in the air and glanced around at her companions.

'To us,' she called out quietly.

Around the crackling fire the cups were slowly raised.

'To my father, who we had to leave behind; may his spirit find peace,' Jodoc said in a grim, taught voice.

'To my daughter, born in Hyperborea,' Calista called out with a happy smile.

'To the Hermes,' Marcus said decisively, 'for that little ship never let us down.'

All of them fell silent as they lowered their cups to their lips and drank. Then from across the fire, Alexandros stirred, glanced up at the night sky and slowly opened his mouth and started to sing. His deep, mournful and melancholic voice drifted away into the darkness and as he sang they all joined in, singing the beautiful and tragic Hyperborean song they had all learned, during the long and harsh winter they'd spent in the New World.

Chapter Eight – A Legion of Troubles

The sweltering July sun beat down on the two riders as they walked their horses down the rutted, unpaved country lane. It was afternoon and Marcus's horse was lathered in sweat and desperate for a drink, but Marcus kept the beast firmly on the path. There was not far to go now before they were home. An old and stained focale, an army neck scarf, was tied around his neck, soaking up the sweat. Sternly Marcus glanced sideways at Cunomoltus. His brother's head was covered by a wide brimmed hat and he was squinting up at the sun. Cunomoltus looked much better now. His skin had returned to its normal colour and the spots had vanished and although he had lost several teeth, no more had fallen out since he'd gone onto his fruit and vegetable diet. The bleeding from his rectum had also ceased. The doctor had been right, Marcus thought. Recovery had been rapid and after ten days of enforced rest in one of the town's tavern's, the two of them had been able to set off southwards, homeward bound at last. But not rapid enough, Marcus thought with a pang of disappointment, for at the Legionary camp he had learned that Fergus had already left for Vectis, only a day ahead of them. Cunomoltus's condition had however, prevented them from following immediately and now it was unlikely that Fergus would still be on Vectis when they arrived, for Fergus, Marcus had learnt, was bound for the Dacian frontier with a vexillation from the Twentieth. What luck, Marcus thought grimly, to have missed his son twice by just a few days.

Noticing Marcus, Cunomoltus turned to him with an unsettled look.

'Now that we are nearly home,' Cunomoltus murmured, 'I feel more nervous than when I was on the Hermes. What happens if all we find is disaster, death and ruin. We have been away for a long time, Marcus. Anything could have happened.'

Marcus grunted and turned to look down the lane and then across the gently rolling fields and copses.

'Yes we have been away for a long time,' he muttered sternly. 'But don't be so despondent. Disaster, death and ruin do not change the fact that this is our home and that I am the head of my family.'

'Well you sound confident,' Cunomoltus said sourly.

'This is not the first time that I have come home after a long absence,' Marcus growled. 'And after a while you realise that you have spent your life worrying about things that never happen.'

At his side, Cunomoltus did not reply. Marcus however, was no longer paying attention to his brother. He had come to a halt in the middle of the track. In the distance he had caught sight of the smart, red roof tiles and neat, white-washed walls of a large Roman villa. The farm-house and its complex of outhouses, granaries, storerooms, agricultural buildings and barns, enclosed a courtyard. Smoke was rising from a chimney and a sturdy, wooden fence demarked his property. Out around the back of the villa the fields were covered in acres of glorious, golden wheat and a single field of barley. As Marcus stared at the villa a dog started to bark.

Cunomoltus turned and grinned at him. The farm looked the epitome of prosperity and well-maintained order. Someone clearly had taken great pride in their home and refused to let the farm fall apart. Without a word, Marcus started out towards the front gate and as he did, he remembered the last time he'd come home, on a bitterly cold winter's day, eighteen months ago, to find his wife had given birth to another man's child. As they approached the front gate, a sleek hunting dog came bounding towards them, barking loudly. The dog was followed a few moments later by three children who came running up to the gate. The boy and two girls looked between eight and five years old, and all three came to an abrupt halt, as they caught sight of him. Then one of the girls turned and shouted something towards the villa.

Marcus and Cunomoltus paused in the lane, clutching their horses' reins. The children were clad in smart little summer tunics and they looked in rude health. For a moment, they eyed the two strangers warily. Then, as they caught sight of Cunomoltus, their faces lit up in sudden recognition and to Marcus's astonishment they came running towards him with loud, shrill, excited cries.

'Cunomoltus, its Cunomoltus; he's come back,' the children shrieked in delight. And, as Dylis's children reached him, Cunomoltus roared in laughter and flung open his arms and grasped hold of the three children in playful delight. Slowly Marcus shook his head in bewilderment. He had forgotten how popular Cunomoltus had managed to make himself with his half-sister's children, when he had first arrived at the villa. All three children were babbling at once and too fast, for his brother to answer the growing mountain of questions. Suddenly however, a heartfelt female shriek rent the hot, sweltering afternoon and Marcus turned to see a woman running towards him. He gasped. It was Kyna, his wife. There were tears streaming down her face, as she rushed towards him and flung her arms around him. Staggering backwards he grasped hold of her, as she buried her face into his neck, sobs of joy shaking her whole body.

'It's alright, it's alright,' he whispered soothingly as Kyna clung to him.

Dimly he was aware of more activity beyond the gate, as more people appeared from the farm buildings. Then Kyna was looking at him, a massive smile stretched across her tear-soaked cheeks.

'I knew you would come back,' she said, in a hoarse voice. 'I knew you would. Nothing will ever stop you Marcus. That's what I told everyone.'

'Kyna,' he said quietly as he ran his fingers through her long hair, 'I have come back for good this time. I will not be leaving you again. That is a promise.'

She said nothing as she buried her face into his neck. Then slowly Kyna released her grip, turned and slipped her arm around her man's waist and gently and happily laid her head against his shoulder. Marcus suddenly spotted Dylis staring at him in disbelief, her arms folded across her chest. She was in her mid-twenties, a good ten years younger than Kyna, and to Marcus's shock she had changed. Gone was the happy aura that had always seemed to surround his half-sister and instead, Dylis's face looked creased with worry and strain. Slowly his sister shook her head, recovered from her surprise, and calmly came up to him, to give him a little, cold embrace.

'Welcome back brother,' she whispered. 'Welcome home, Marcus.'

Efa stood beside the gate and at her side was Petrus, a small, wooden cross dangling from his neck. Efa looked every inch the stern, old family matriarch. Her white hair had been done up in an impeccable manner and her fingers were adorned with glittering rings. She was clad in fine clothes and was staring at him with a shrewd, pleased expression. As Marcus caught sight of her, she respectfully dipped her head.

'You found him, didn't you,' Efa said her voice barely louder than a whisper. 'You have brought my Corbulo back to me?'

Marcus looked down at the ground and for a moment he did not reply. Then he looked up at Efa and nodded. 'I did,' he said resolutely.

For a moment, no one spoke. Then slowly and with infinite grace, Efa stepped forwards, reached out to grasp Marcus's hand and gently kissed it.

***

The dining room was filled with loud, happy and excited chatter and good natured banter. It was evening and Marcus sat at the head of the table, his forearms resting on the solid oak, as he watched his family eating and drinking. He had ordered the kitchen slaves to use the finest of everything and they had duly cooked up a feast that covered the table leaving, on Efa's instructions, just one single, empty plate, set aside for Corbulo's spirit. As he took a sip of wine, Marcus silently glanced around the long rectangular table. They were all here, Efa, Corbulo's aging widow; Dylis, his younger half-sister; Jowan her husband; their three, cheeky confident children who had greeted him at the front gate; Kyna; Petrus, the Christian boy whom Corbulo had rescued from certain death in Londinium, nearly twenty years earlier; Cunomoltus and, sitting quietly between them the two newcomers, Elsa and Armin, Lucius's orphaned children. They were all here except for Quintus, Ahern and Fergus. Quintus had died during the winter and had been buried on the battlefield, where he and Corbulo had fought against the Barbarian Queen, forty-four years earlier. And Fergus, Marcus sighed, for as he had expected, he had missed his son by only a few days. Fergus had already left to report to his unit at Rutupiae, prior to embarkation for Gaul. Kyna had told him that the boy had come to Vectis, with the intention of trying to help her before his brief leave was over. He'd not achieved much in the short time he'd stayed, but Fergus's action had nevertheless pleased Marcus, for his son had clearly remembered what he'd told him the last time they had seen each other. And now Fergus was destined for the Dacian frontier, just like he, Marcus had once been, many years ago. Marcus lowered his eyes with sudden sadness. It could be years before Fergus returned, if indeed he ever did. At his side, noticing his changed mood,

Kyna reached out and laid her hand over his, and smiled at her husband.

'You haven't asked about Ahern,' Kyna whispered, as she leant against Marcus. Without allowing him the chance to answer she continued; 'last year Dylis and I managed to arrange for him to attend Maximus's Ludus in Londinium. That is where he is now, in Londinium. The school is an elite institution. It has the best teachers and Ahern was smart enough to gain entrance.' Kyna's face grew flushed. 'The teachers say he is a very gifted and talented boy. He is going to grow up amongst the young sons of the richest, and most powerful families in the province. Isn't that something?'

Slowly Marcus nodded, as he digested the news. He had refused to accept Kyna's son by another man as his own and instead had forced Jowan and Dylis to adopt Ahern. But the news that the boy had been accepted into such a prestigious school was pleasing even though Ahern would never legally inherit anything that belonged to him. The boy should count himself lucky that he had been spared.

'That must have cost us a lot of money,' Marcus replied quietly, as he placed his arm around his wife's shoulders.

'It did,' Kyna replied. 'But the farm is doing well, we are prospering. Dylis has been managing our affairs and she is doing an amazing job. She has a head for money and business. You should honour her for that, Marcus?'

Marcus grunted as he turned to glance at his half-sister. Dylis was listening to her children talking in loud, excited voices, but she clearly looked tired and stress had left its mark on her face.

'Children, quiet now,' Marcus said sharply. Obediently the youngsters fell silent as, around the table all eyes turned to look at him. Marcus cleared his throat. 'Now that we have eaten and drunk our fill,' he declared in a quieter, tired voice, 'it is time that

I told you about our journey across the sea. But before I do, you will join me in a toast, a toast to us, a strong family, Corbulo's family, for this is who we are and without him we would be nothing. He dines with us tonight.'

Marcus rose to his feet and raised his cup and around the dinner table the others did the same, some of them glancing at the empty plate. Having completed the toast, Marcus gestured at Cunomoltus, who retrieved a small leather bag that hung from his belt.

'We have been across the ocean to Hyperborea,' Marcus said quietly looking down at the table. 'It was a long, hazardous voyage into the unknown, but now we have returned and we have come home with Corbulo's mortal remains. He will be buried as per his final wish and his spirit will finally find peace.'

'You have made us all proud Marcus,' Efa replied.

Ignoring Efa, Marcus gestured once more at Cunomoltus, who began to empty the contents of the pouch out onto the table. And as he did, a murmur arose around the table as everyone stared at the colourful stone and bead necklaces, Hyperborean pendants, armbands, plain rings and bone earrings.

As the pile of gifts began to get shared out around the table, Marcus began to speak slowly, recounting their journey on the Hermes across the ocean and their adventures in Hyperborea and as he did, the table gradually fell silent in stunned disbelief and fascination.

'So Captain Alexandros arrived just in time to save us from the Hyperborean war band,' Marcus said, pausing to take a sip of wine. 'But the Hermes was in no state to make the journey back across the ocean. We needed time to make proper repairs to the ship and Jodoc's wounds needed to heal, so we headed north along the coast until we reached a small island at the mouth of a river. The island was deserted, rocky and heavily wooded, and it made an ideal spot on which to carry out our repairs. During our stay we made contact with the natives, a tribe called the MicMac and with them we established friendly relations, bartering and trading for food, clothes and other essential goods. By the time the repairs to the mast and hull had been made and Jodoc's wounds had healed, the summer was over and the winter storms were upon us. Under such conditions it would have been madness to try and cross the ocean, for we were by now fully aware of her power and wrath, so I decided that we would stay and overwinter in Hyperborea and start out for home in the spring. But soon the natives with whom we traded, started to die from disease and the survivors became hostile, forcing us to leave our little island and head due south.

Marcus paused to take another sip of wine, as the faces around the table stared at him in complete, stunned silence.

'After that,' Marcus continued in a quiet voice, 'we followed the coast around what appeared to be a large island for a month until we reached a navigable river on the eastern shore. Sailing inland up this stream, we soon found a suitable spot along a heavily-wooded stretch of land and here we remained for the long winter. And what a winter we had. Snow so deep you could drown in it; cold like we had never experienced before and endless days of blizzards, raging storms and little sunlight. If it had not been for the friendly welcome from a native settlement, who supplied us with food, I think we would have frozen or starved to death, long before spring came. Calista was pregnant with Jodoc's child, and her father, Alexandros, had lost an eye. Cunomoltus and I would often go out hunting in the vast forests, together with the natives, and during this time I learned a few words in their language and I learned to love the herbs which they like to smoke. During this time, my brother fought with a bear and killed it and even had enough energy left, to fall in love with a native girl and get her pregnant. But when spring finally arrived, we were forced to leave her behind, for her family would not consent to see her go with us. Instead they gave us a man called Matunaagd, who had managed to learn a little of our language and who would come with us across the ocean, but he soon died from disease and we were forced to bury him at sea.'

Marcus paused and glanced across the table at Cunomoltus. His brother however was gazing down at the table, lost in sombre thought.

'So,' Marcus sighed, 'with the arrival of spring, all of us, having survived the winter, set out for home. Initially we sailed north, until we reached a wooded coast, which we followed eastwards as far as it would go. At its most easterly point we made contact with a small native settlement, whose inhabitants explained that there was no more land to the north or east of us. When we told them that we were nevertheless heading east, they advised us to follow the course of the huge, black sea-demons, which guard the ocean and which we had already encountered on our outbound journey. These sea beasts would show us the way to the rich, fishing-grounds and the river in the ocean, as the natives described it. If we caught it, the current, would propel us eastwards at great speed. So, not without a certain amount of anxiety, we set out eastwards into the endless and vast ocean. The winds and current favoured us and we made good progress, but the power of the ocean is beyond anything you can imagine and the sea gods were not about to let us go so easily. For thirty-two days, we were out there, alone on the wild ocean, and during that whole time, we did not sight land once. The sea gods threw storms, icebergs and huge waves at us. They tried to trick us by hiding the sun behind clouds; withdrawing the winds and striking us with lightning bolts. But we persevered and eventually with our drinking water running low, we finally sighted land, which turned out to be the western coast of Hibernia. Here we made land fall and replenished our supplies, but we told the Hibernians nothing about where we had been, for I do not wish the druids to know about our journey. From Hibernia it was an easy journey back to the port at Deva Victrix, although all of us were much worried by my brother's deteriorating condition.'

As Marcus's story came to an end, the room remained silent for a long time, as all tried to digest the momentous journey Marcus had just described.

Then at last Petrus stirred and shook his head in disbelief.

'That tale, Marcus, is about as good as Jason and the Greek poem Argonautica. But tell me, honestly, when you were in Hyperborea, did you see anyone who was a Christian? Did you see anyone wearing a cross?'

'Of course we didn't,' Cunomoltus interrupted looking annoyed. 'Why would anyone want to be part of a tiny, insignificant Jewish religious sect. The Hyperborean's had far more important things to do. They are good people.'

'Apart from the ones who tried to kill you,' Petrus retorted sarcastically.

Marcus raised his hand for silence and then, carefully undid the small canister, contained Corbulo's ashes from around his neck, and placed it on the empty plate. For a moment no one spoke as an anxious, tense mood settled on the people around the table.

'Emogene, the druid burned his body and kept his ashes inside that canister,' Marcus said quietly, his eyes finding Efa. 'The canister was a prison. She intended to keep Corbulo's spirit trapped inside, her eternal prisoner, never to join our ancestors, never too be free and never to find peace. It was a wicked act but I have freed him. I have honoured my father like I said I would, and our ancestors will approve. When I have sorted out our affairs here on the farm, we will all travel to the battlefield and bury him beside Quintus and his comrades. Then his spirit will finally rest in peace.'

Around the table no one spoke. Then slowly Efa rose to her feet with a little tear in her eye.

'A toast,' she muttered. 'A toast to Marcus and his brother, for the honour they have brought this family and for what they have done for us and my Corbulo.'

Quietly and respectfully all around the table rose to their feet and raised their cups, all except for Dylis, who remained seated, with a sudden flushed, annoyed expression on her face.

'Oh it's alright for you Marcus,' she hissed with sudden anger. 'You go away for years, you whore, you fight, you do what you like, then you come back and within a few weeks you are off again, leaving us to cope on our own. What have you contributed? What have you done to turn this farm into a prosperous place? Nothing!" Sharply Dylis rose to her feet, her anger growing, as she glared at Marcus. 'You were never here to help us. You didn't make the hard decisions about which crops to grow. You didn't buy the best slaves. You didn't manage our finances. You didn't negotiate with the merchants in the forum. You just left us with Elsa and Armin, two extra ungrateful mouths to feed. You were never here to solve our problems or do the hard work, or see my children grow up or even take care of your own wife.' Bitterness filled Dylis's voice as she stared at Marcus with a brutal look. 'But now you have returned, the great man is back and he presumes to tell us what we should do. He presumes to tell us how to run this farm. Who gave you that right?'

A shocked silence engulfed the dining room. Marcus's face remained unreadable as he glared at his half-sister.

'I have come home for good this time,' Marcus replied sternly fixing his eyes on Dylis, 'and I have plans for us. You may have done a good job in looking after my property but you are not the head of this family.'

'Dylis,' Efa snapped as Dylis opened her mouth to interrupt.

'That's enough.'

Across the table Dylis closed her mouth but her anger remained, streaming out of her like molten lava flowing from a volcano. Marcus too looked angry, but his anger was tempered and controlled.

'Marcus,' Efa said turning to him with a grave expression, "now that you and your brother have returned, you need to be aware that there are some pressing issues that need to be discussed. The first concerns your brother Cunomoltus. Whilst you were away a man came to visit us. I did not like the look of him, a big brute of a man. He wanted to know where Cunomoltus was. How he found us is a mystery, but Jowan and Petrus sent him on his way. But he may come back.'

Across the table Marcus sensed Cunomoltus looking at him.

'Did he give a name,' Marcus snapped. "Nectovelius perhaps?"

'He didn't give us a name,' Jowan replied hastily, with a firm shake of his head. 'But whatever business he has with Cunomoltus, it can't be good. He was a violent man; no good.'

Marcus grunted and looked down at the table.

'There is more,' Efa continued with a weary sigh. 'Petrus is in trouble with the priests of the temple of Neptune and Minerva in Noviomagus Reginorum. Apparently, he drank too much wine in one of the taverns with his Christian friends and ended up urinating all over the temple floor and over the statue of Minerva. The priests are livid and would have hanged him if I and Kyna had not intervened. Now the priests are trying to get the Town Council to ban Petrus and us from entering Reginorum."

'It was a joke,' Petrus muttered weakly as he raised his hand in the air. 'I was drunk. I needed a place to piss and their temple seemed convenient.'

'Well it won't be happening again,' Marcus growled angrily, turning to look at Petrus. 'It is your business what you do in the tavern but when it sullies the reputation of this family, it no longer becomes just your concern. Reginorum is where we bring the farm's produce to market. It would be a disaster if we had to go elsewhere. So, see to it that you keep out of further trouble with those priests.'

Embarrassed, Petrus waved his hand in the air avoiding Marcus's gaze.

'And there is something else,' Kyna interrupted, as she turned to Efa with a defiant look. Shocked, Efa shook her head in a vain attempt to silence Kyna, but Marcus's wife ignored her. 'Efa has been coughing up blood for the past month,' Kyna said as she turning to look down at the table. 'She has tried to hide it from me but I have seen it. She is ill and I cannot heal her. She needs expert help. She needs to travel to Londinium or Camulodunum to see the doctors there.'

'I am alright,' Efa murmured, reaching out to lay a hand on Kyna's arm. 'I am alright.'

'No,' Kyna said sharply. 'You are not alright; you are ill Efa and you know it.'

Marcus rubbed his forehead as he stared at Efa. 'Is it true.' he said in a concerned voice.

In her seat around the table, Efa sighed and nodded wearily. 'It is true. Every morning I cough up some blood but I do not want to be a burden on anyone.'

Marcus looked away, and for a long moment the table was silent. Then slowly Marcus turned to stare at Elsa who was sitting quietly in her seat, staring down at her hands in her lap. The thirteen-year-old girl and her younger brother had not uttered a word all evening.

'Elsa,' Marcus growled, "look at me girl.'

Obediently but with a sullen look, Elsa turned to look at Marcus. Marcus sighed and his face softened a fraction. 'I remember that you are good with herbs and healing potions,' he said nodding at the girl. 'You have a skill and you got rid of my brother's cold when we first met. Do you know what ails Efa? Do you know how we can help her?'

Elsa gave Efa a quick glance, then lowered her eyes and shook her head.

Marcus sighed and quickly turned to Kyna, 'Alright,' he muttered. 'I will take Efa to Londinium to see what we can do. We will leave as soon as we can and I will take Elsa with me.'

'But I am not the most pressing and serious of our concerns,' Efa exclaimed as her eyes came to rest on Dylis. 'Would you like to explain, or shall I?' Efa asked Dylis.

'You can do it,' Dylis muttered bitterly.

'What concern is bigger than Efa's health?' Marcus growled in alarm.

Around the table, no one seemed to want to meet Marcus's gaze. Then Efa shifted uncomfortably in her seat.

'About six months ago,' she said, 'we heard from our partners in Reginorum that one of the town's leading Roman citizens, a knight of the Equestrian order, a man named Priscinus, had started to make claims about our farm and land here on Vectis. This man wants our farm, Marcus. He is after our land. He is claiming that our farm was left to him by Agricola and he says that he has proof, although we have not seen anything since he first started making these claims. But these are no idle threats. Priscinus is a wealthy man, he is a citizen, a knight and he has powerful and influential friends. He is threatening to take the matter to court and evict us. If that happens we will lose everything.'

Efa fell silent and looked down at her finger-nails, as around the table all remained silent.

'No one is going to drive us from our land,' Marcus growled. 'This is our home.'

Chapter Nine – The Confrontation

The acres of golden wheat swayed gently in the breeze, stretching away to a line of willow trees and a ditch that marked the boundary of the farm. It was noon and in the clear blue sky, the hot July sun beat down on the land. Marcus stood in the shade of an old oak, sucking on his Hyperborean pipe and surveying his property. He was clad in sandals and a simple, white tunic with his focale, neck scarf tied around his throat. On his head, he was wearing a low, wide brimmed sun hat. He was sending small puffs of smoke rising into the air. At his side Dylis, Efa, Jowan and a slave boy were all silently gazing at the fields. Jowan was clutching a wooden ledger and a small, iron-tipped stylus pen. Behind them and half a mile away, the sunlight reflected on the red roof-tiles and neat, white-washed walls of the fine-looking farm and its collection of barns, outhouses, granaries and storage sheds. Nearby, two slaves were working in a dry drainage ditch, clearing it of debris with their hand-held sickles. Further away, three more slaves, watched by Petrus and his two, sleek, brown, hunting dogs, were repairing the wooden fence that enclosed the farm's herd of cattle, pigs and chickens. The slaves were singing to themselves as they worked. Marcus grunted in approval. A few days had passed since he'd returned home and now that he had fully recovered from his long journey, he was keen to see for himself the state that the family business was in. Turning to Efa he gestured at the golden wheat fields with his pipe.

'Once you told me,' he murmured, 'that I would make a very poor farmer and that I would soon grow bored of life on this farm. But now, when I look at this place I see a home, land worth fighting for.'

'We have worked hard to make this farm what it is today,' Dylis replied defiantly. 'Profits are up on last year and we have added more cattle. If market prices remain the same, we are looking at a record year.'

Glancing at her, Marcus nodded. Then he turned to Jowan who was clutching his ledger. 'So what is the full list of our assets and liabilities? What plans do we have for the future; what are our problems; what improvements can we make? I want to know everything.'

Jowan scratched his head and gave Marcus a wary, respectful glance.

'Well,' he said clearing his throat, 'our land is fertile. The harvest is looking good and there is growing demand for our produce. The Roman towns are booming; there are more people and they all need to eat. We have also heard that the harvest in parts of Gaul has failed. So, market prices are high, but these can change of course. Much of the produce is purchased by the army. The fact that you Marcus and Corbulo and Fergus were, and are soldiers, helps us in the negotiations with the buyers. We also have the barley field, which can be used to make beer. Our herd of cattle is growing, although it is not prudent to sell the beasts just yet; better to use them to increase our herd.' Jowan sighed as he glanced at his ledger. 'Taxes are stable and affordable but could rise. We have set aside money for this contingency. All in all, I would estimate that our assets including the farm, slaves and land, now total over a hundred thousand denarii, maybe even up to one hundred and fifty thousand denarii.'

Marcus frowned in surprise. 'That much,' he exclaimed.

Jowan nodded.

Marcus turned to stare at the wheat fields and took another draw from his pipe. Compared to a legionary's standard salary of three hundred denarii a year, a hundred and fifty thousand denarii was an unbelievably huge sum of money.

'And we have earned every single denarii,' Dylis hissed.

'What about liabilities,' Marcus said ignoring his half-sister. 'What about the slaves, any trouble, any runaways?'

'We have no debts if that is what you mean,' Jowan replied. 'Efa and Dylis forbade the borrowing of money. Like my wife said, Marcus, we have earned every denarii the hard way through blood, sweat, wise decisions and luck. What you see here is the result of many years work and hard graft.'

'And the slaves,' Marcus growled glancing at the silent, slave boy.

'The odd dispute amongst themselves,' Jowan shrugged, 'apart from that, nothing. We have had no runaways. We treat them well and there is enough food for all. There are many worse owners. Petrus keeps an eye on them.'

Marcus nodded in approval. 'Good,' he muttered sending another little cloud of smoke rising into the air. 'This is good news.'

'So now,' Efa said quietly turning to Marcus, 'you can see why a man like Priscinus wants to own our farm and land. We have been noticed, Marcus. What are we going to do about him and his claims?'

Marcus was silent for a moment as he gazed out across the fields.

'No one is going to drive us off this land,' he growled at last. 'This is our home and I don't care who we are up against, but we are going to have to prepare ourselves to fight for this land.'

'So do you have a plan?' Dylis asked with a hint of challenge in her voice.

Marcus nodded again and slowly tapped his pipe against his chin. 'Tomorrow you and I shall go into Reginorum to meet this

Priscinus,' he said turning to his half-sister. 'Afterwards I, you, Efa and Cunomoltus will head north to bury Corbulo on the battlefield, beside his comrades. We will take the girl, Elsa with us. I also need to visit Londinium. There is important business and people there, which can help our cause.' Marcus turned to look at Jowan. 'Whilst we are away, you will be in charge of the farm. I want you to start building defensive structures around the main villa, a ditch and a sturdy palisade at least six feet high. If everything you have told me about this Priscinus is true, then we will need to prepare ourselves for a long struggle which may become violent.' Marcus turned to glare at his companions. 'Agricola is dead now and we do not have any wealthy and powerful patron to protect us. So, we are going to have to look after ourselves.' Marcus turned to Jowan, sizing him up. 'I want the defences complete by the time I return. Do you think you can handle the work?'

Jowan eyes had widened in surprise, and for a moment he said nothing. Then he nodded, dipping his head respectfully. 'It will be done,' he said.

'What important business do you have in Londinium,' Dylis snapped, glaring at her brother suspiciously.

Calmly Marcus turned to look at her. 'Efa is ill and needs to see a specialist. Those kinds of doctors can only be found in the city, in Londinium,' he replied curtly. 'And there is something else,' he muttered, looking away. 'Our children need a future and I am going to give them a future. That is now my concern, to secure a future for all of them. The law states that if a man owns more than a hundred thousand denarii, he will become eligible to join the Equestrian Order, the Order of Knights. In Londinium I intend to lodge our application to join their ranks. Men of equestrian rank are important men, many of them hold senior positions in government; in commerce and the army. As Equites, our children and their children will have a chance of becoming governors of provinces, they could become tax collectors, bankers, senior army officers, miners and exporters.

They will be able to enter commerce and compete for government contracts to build roads, bridges or aqueducts. None of this is possible without being a knight. There are only a few thousand such men in the whole Empire but they run everything. It is the first step on the path to becoming a senator of Rome.'

'You want to become a knight,' Dylis blurted out. 'And how will that help us keep our farm?'

Marcus glared at his half-sister. 'For a start it would give us the same rank as Priscinus,' he growled, 'and for Romans, rank and status are everything. Beyond that it will mean that our name will be on the lists viewed by the Emperor himself, when he decides on his appointments for public office.' Marcus paused as his eyes blazed with sudden ambition. 'We are not only going to defend our farm and land,' he snapped. 'We are going to become an important family. Being a member of the equites will help advance our family in society. That is what I want for our children. A chance for them to make a name for themselves. We are going to become a family to be reckoned with throughout the whole province of Britannia and maybe,' Marcus looked away with sudden emotion, 'maybe one day,' he muttered, 'our descendants will be someone; someone who will be recorded in history like Caesar.'

***

Marcus and Dylis were silent as they trudged along the dusty, forest-path closely followed by a slave, a few paces behind. It was a hot day and the fierce, unrelenting, summer sun glared down on them from a clear blue sky. Marcus looked irritated. Annoyed, he slapped his hand against his neck trying to silence the flies and insects that buzzed through the air around his head, attracted by the sweat covering his neck and arms. The three of them had set out from the farm at dawn and, after having crossed the narrow sea straights, they'd headed inland on foot, to the town of Noviomagus Reginorum, Chichester.

Sullenly Marcus glanced down at his sandals. His irritation he knew, had nothing to do with the weather or his sister's disrespect. He was down to his last reserve of Hyperborean smoking herbs and when they were gone, his pipe would be useless. He would have to learn to live without the soothing Hyperborean smoke and he sensed that it was going to be hard. At his side Dylis strode along, her head held high, her eyes fixed determinedly on the road ahead, but there was no hiding her fidgety mood as he noticed her picking at her finger nails. She was still annoyed with him. He could sense that too. She didn't like the fact that he'd taken away her role. Contemptuously Marcus looked away. But that was her problem. The welfare of his family was his responsibility.

Up ahead the forest was coming to an end and beyond, set amongst the cleared fields, sat the small and prosperous-looking Roman town of Noviomagus Reginorum. An earthen bank topped by a timber palisade surrounded the town and smoke was drifting upwards into the blue sky. In the parched, green, yellow fields dotted with sheep and cattle, that surrounded the settlement, a few labourers were at work and except for the odd barking dog, everything was quiet and peaceful. Warily Marcus peered at the town as he remembered the last time he'd visited, when he'd stayed the night in a tavern on the final stretch of his long, journey home from the Dacian frontier. As an empty ox-drawn wagon with a single driver rumbled towards them across the dusty track, Marcus turned to Dylis.

'Who is our agent? Who is the man whom arranges buyers for us? I would like to speak to him before I see Priscinus,' Marcus growled.

'That would be Ninian,' Dylis muttered with a sour look, 'He has an office beside the Temple to Neptune and Minerva.'

'Is that the temple which Petrus defiled?'

Dylis nodded and Marcus looked away, shaking his head. As if he didn't have enough problems to worry about.

The gateway into the settlement was guarded by two elderly armed civilians who were deep in conversation with each other, as they leaned against the wooden gates. They made no effort to stop or question anyone and Marcus, Dylis and their slave slipped quietly into the town. The settlement street pattern still seemed to follow the lines of the old Legionary Winter Camp of the Second Augusta Legion, which had first arrived at this spot some sixty years earlier. The soldiers however had long since departed, leaving their winter camp to be taken over by civilians; Roman traders; retired veterans and the wealthier individuals of the local Regnenses tribe. Marcus strode down the dusty, unpaved, main street and the three of them were soon lost in the busy, market traffic. The town was filled with farmers, who'd come in from the surrounding countryside, to sell their produce, and the streets were noisy and packed. At a corner, scaffolding had been erected and workmen were toiling over the new, stone public-bath house. Further down the street, close to the cattle market, more scaffolding and more workers were labouring away on a new amphitheatre.

Without saying a word, Dylis steered them through the busy traffic towards an impressive looking, stone building. Marcus grunted as he recognised the Temple of Neptune and Minerva. As he drew closer, he caught sight of a marble dedication slab, which had been proudly erected in front of the temple doors. The inscription on the marble was easy to read.

'To Neptune and Minerva, for the welfare of the Divine House, by the authority of Tiberius Claudius Cogidubnus, great King of the Britons, the Guild of Smiths and those in it, gave this temple at their own expense. Valens, son of Pudentinus, erected this.'

Someone had scratched the sign of the Christian cross into the marble just below the inscription and Marcus's eyes narrowed suspiciously, as he caught sight of the graffiti. Had that too been Petrus's doing?

'Ninian, Ninian,' Dylis called out in a loud tense voice, as she approached the open, front door of the narrow, strip house that stood beside the temple.

A moment later a man with a fat, fleshy face poked his head out of the doorway. The man's forehead glistened with sweat. Catching sight of Dylis, an enormous smile appeared on his lips. Stepping out into the street Ninian affectionately grasped Dylis by her shoulders and quickly kissed her twice on her cheeks.

'Always a pleasure to see you Dylis,' the agent said smoothly.

'This is my brother, Marcus,' Dylis said sourly gesturing at Marcus. 'He has been away but now he is back.' Then she turned to Ninian. 'We need to talk with you; it's about Priscinus.'

'Of course,' the broker said lowering his eyes to look at the ground. 'You had better come inside. Things are starting to get ugly I'm afraid.'

***

Marcus leaned against the doorpost just inside the small front room of the building and folded his arms across his chest. Ninian had installed himself on a wooden bench beside a table and Dylis had sat down opposite him. Around them the small office was filled with dozens of small, wooden, writing-tablets, scrolls and files. The place stank of leather and glue.

'So what is the latest news?' Marcus growled.

Ninian glanced quickly at Dylis and turned to look up at Marcus with a respectful look. Then carefully he wiped the sweat from his forehead with the back of his hand and sighed.

'It's not good for you, I'm afraid,' Ninian replied in a quiet voice. 'Priscinus is an unpredictable man, a dangerous man, a clever man. When he decides to do something, he does not give up. He is like a dog that refuses to let go of a bone. He is tenacious. His family have deep roots in this district, ever since the days when Claudius was Emperor. Their business is to supply horses to the army and they have done very well for themselves.' Ninian paused and gave Dylis a sympathetic look. 'I have heard that he has hired a top lawyer from Londinium. This lawyer has been tasked with looking into legal ways in which he can take over your farm. Priscinus is preparing his case. He claims to have evidence that Agricola left your farm to him.'

'That's horse shit,' Marcus growled. 'What proof can he possibly have?'

'He says he has a document signed by Agricola, leaving the farm and land to him which supersedes your claim,' Ninian replied smoothly. 'I haven't seen it personally, no one has, but Priscinus is confident that he has the authority.'

'It must be a forgery,' Marcus snapped glaring at Ninian. 'I knew Agricola. The man employed my father to look after his estates here in Britannia. If anyone is speaking the truth it is us.'

'In court the truth doesn't really matter,' Ninian said with a sad sigh.

Marcus frowned. 'What chance of success does he have,' he snapped. 'The farm and its land belonged to Agricola and he left it all to my father Corbulo and myself. I still have the document in which Agricola confirms this. I have proof.'

Ninian shrugged. 'I don't doubt your claim or sincerity. If I was the court judge in this matter I would rule in your favour but I am not the judge, and that is the problem.'

'What problem?' Marcus growled angrily.

Ninian sighed again and peered up at Marcus with a weary, sympathetic look. "If the matter goes to court, who the judge will be, will be of critical importance. Priscinus is friends with nearly all of them. He's a knight after all. He and his family have the connections. They are part of the ruling class. The judges will rule in his favour; despite what evidence you can produce. The best way to protect yourself is to have a powerful patron, who can defend you, but alas you don't have one.'

'So what can we do?' Dylis interrupted.

'Well,' Ninian said looking down at the table. 'The next best thing would be to try and get the case heard by a senior figure from within the army. Your family are retired veterans. An army judge may look more sympathetically on your situation. Or you could try and make a deal with Priscinus, in which he drops his claims. Or you could try and bribe the judge, but that is a dangerous game and even if you are successful it will cost you a fortune.'

'So if the verdict is already all but certain,' Dylis cried out in sudden frustration, 'why go through all this charade of going to court? What's the point of going to court, wasting our time and paying lawyers, when it makes no difference?'

Quickly Ninian raised his hand in the air and glanced anxiously towards the doorway.

'The law,' he hissed, 'must be seen to be followed and obeyed. I agree that sometimes it's pointless. The rich and powerful are never going to lose a court case against the poorer and lower classes. That's just the way it is. But as long as the correct court rituals and procedures are followed, and justice is seen to have been administered, no one, apart from the losers, gives a shit.'

'What if my family were members of the equites,' Marcus grunted. 'Would it make any difference if I were of the same class and rank as Priscinus?'

For a moment, Ninian fixed Marcus with a curious look. Then he shook his head.

'It won't make any difference,' the broker replied. 'It is the person who has the most power and influence who decide these things. Priscinus may be a little bit politer to you in court, but the brute truth is that he has the resources and connections to win and he knows it.'

Marcus turned to look at Dylis. His half-sister was furiously biting her fingernails as she stared at the ground.

'And another thing,' Ninian exclaimed. 'I have heard that Priscinus is gathering together a band of armed fighting men. Court cases can mean bad publicity even for the victor. So, it is possible that in order to avoid going to court, Priscinus is planning to use violence to shift you from your land.' Ninian turned to look at Marcus and Dylis with a genuinely sad expression. 'I am sorry,' he murmured. 'You should be careful, both of you.'

For a long moment, the small room remained silent. Then at last Dylis rose to her feet and gracefully reached out and grasped Ninian's hand.

'Thank you Ninian,' she said quietly. 'You have been a good friend to me and my family. It will not be forgotten.'

***

Priscinus's farm lay a mile outside the town boundary. As Marcus, Dylis and the slave approached the front gate, six dogs came charging towards them, barking loudly. Ignoring the animals Marcus marched down the dusty, rutted-track towards the gate and low wooden fence that demarked the property. Beside the gate in an alcove, a stone bust of the head of Emperor Trajan silently glared at the newcomers.

'I will do the talking,' Marcus hissed giving Dylis a warning look. 'I will try and reason with the man. That seems to be our best option. Maybe he is willing to consider a deal.'

His sister did not reply. Her eyes were fixed on the sumptuous Roman villa that sat in the shade of a copse of trees, fifty paces away. In the enclosed fields beyond the farm, dozens of horses milled around a pond, their long necks stretched down towards the water. Calmly Marcus reached out to the small bronze bell that was attached to the gate and gave it a ring. On the other side of the fence the pack of dogs was still barking at them. The six, big powerful, drooling animals, their keen, alert eyes fixed on the strangers, had their mouths open, displaying rows of razor sharp and menacing teeth. Thick streams of saliva were hanging from their jaws and behind him, Marcus sensed his slave start to back away nervously. As Marcus stood waiting, a woman appeared, hastening towards them. As she came up to the gate Marcus saw that her left eye and cheek were covered by dark blue bruises. She gave Marcus and Dylis a nervous, embarrassed glance.

'We are here to see your master, Priscinus,' Marcus said, 'Is he at home?'

'He is,' the woman replied lowering her eyes respectfully. 'Who shall I say is here to visit him?'

'You can tell him,' Marcus said sharply, 'that my name is Marcus and that I own the farm and land on Vectis which he is trying to steal from me. I have come to discuss the matter with him.'

'Wait here,' the woman said in an emotionless voice. Abruptly she turned away and headed back towards the house.

'So now we know what kind of man we are dealing with,' Dylis hissed. 'A man who protects his property with a pack of aggressive dogs and who likes to beat up his slaves. Did you see her face?'

Marcus nodded. 'That's not all,' he muttered. 'Look over there.'

He gestured in the direction of some large stables. Outside the barn doors, a dozen or so men were facing each other, practising their fighting skills with wooden swords and old legionary shields. The clatter and clash of their weapons and the cries and curses of their trainer, mingled with that of the barking, dog-pack. As the dogs continued their barking, a few of the fighters turned to peer in Marcus's direction.

'Looks like they may be the armed men that Ninian spoke about,' Marcus growled. 'He was speaking the truth then.'

Dylis said nothing. Her face seemed to have become set in stone as she coldly stared at the main entrance to the house. The woman had re-appeared and behind her came four slaves, carrying a specially modified chair, upon which sat a young man in his early twenties, with a shock of blond nearly white hair. The slaves groaned and strained under the weight of the chair, but the occupant seemed completely oblivious to their situation. As they approached the gate Marcus grunted in surprise as he caught sight of the young man's wasted and deformed legs. Priscinus was a cripple. Beside him, Dylis went very still.

'Silence,' the young blond haired man cried, turning to glare at the dogs and obediently the animals lowered their heads and stopped barking. When the party was only a few paces away, the four slaves, their faces expressionless, halted, but instead of placing the chair on the ground, they kept it up in the air so that their master looked down on Marcus and Dylis. From up on his chair, the young man turned to study Marcus. Then his eyes flicked to Dylis and he smiled as he seemed to recognise her.

'I am Priscinus,' he said grandly. 'So, you have come to have a word with me about your farm have you?'

'Are you not going to invite us into your house,' Marcus growled.

'We have travelled a long way to speak with you. It is common courtesy.'

Slowly Priscinus turned to gaze at Marcus. 'No,' he replied sharply. 'I don't think I will. You are just fine where you are now. So, what do you wish to discuss?'

Marcus placed his hands on his hips as he glared at Priscinus. He'd not been expecting Priscinus to be such a young man, and he had not been expecting him to be a cripple either or for him to refuse them entry to his property.

'What happened to your legs?' Marcus said.

'Childhood disease, incurable, the Gods didn't want me to walk,' Priscinus replied. 'But really have you come all this way just to discuss my useless legs?'

Marcus's face darkened. 'My name is Marcus,' he said. '"I am the owner of the farm and land on Vectis, the farm which you are claiming as your own. I want to know on what legal basis you think my property belongs to you? I want to see the proof that you claim to have.'

Up on his chair Priscinus's eyes twinkled and a smirk appeared on his face.

'You know,' Priscinus said lightly, 'I was looking forward to contesting this issue with your lovely sister here, but now I suppose I will have to deal with you.' Then he leaned forwards in his chair and the smirk turned into a sneer. 'Your farm does not belong to you. It belongs to me. Agricola gave it to my family. I have the written proof and will produce this in court in due course. Until then you will just have to wait.'

'I knew Agricola,' Marcus retorted, "He never mentioned you or your family. It is easy to produce proof these days. Forgeries are common.'

On his chair Priscinus pointed a finger at him.

'Careful,' Priscinus whined. 'You had better start choosing your words carefully or else you will find yourself in court on a charge of slander.'

'Why now?' Marcus said angrily. 'Why press your claims on my farm now, after all these years.'

'I wanted to see if you would make a success of the place,' Priscinus retorted. 'And now that you have, I am going to take it all.' Once more the young man leaned forwards in his chair and sneered at Marcus. 'How does it feel to know that all that hard work, that back breaking hard work, planning and investment, has all been for nothing? All this time you were just slaving away to make me a wealthier man. You just didn't realise it.'

'You will not be taking my farm and home away from me,' Marcus growled as his hand dropped to the pommel of his sword. 'Just you try.'

At Marcus's side, Dylis was silently staring at the woman with the bruised face, who was standing quietly behind her master, her eyes facing the ground.

'It hurts doesn't it," Priscinus sneered. 'Oh, it must burn, the fact that you are going to lose your home. It's so unfair. A bit like the gods taking away my ability to walk. But I am not a completely heartless man.'

For a moment Priscinus studied Marcus with a speculative look.

'I will make you a deal,' he called out. 'Walk away from the farm and never come back and I will pay you twenty-five thousand denarii. That's a good sum. You and your family will be wealthy and will be able to live well.'

'That's barely a quarter of what the place is worth,' Marcus cried out, his face darkening with anger. With an effort, he managed to control himself. 'No, I have a better offer,' he said forcing himself to speak in a calmer voice. 'Your farm supplies horses to the army. I am willing to supply you with fodder for your horses, below the market price. We could be partners. There is no need to take this matter to court. There is no need for violence. What do you say?'

'Violence?' Priscinus's face cracked into a sudden sheepish smile. 'Who said anything about violence? I am not a violent man. I am a law-abiding citizen.'

Marcus muttered something to himself as he glared up at Priscinus. "Well," he growled, 'do we have a deal?'

On his chair Priscinus leaned forwards. 'Fuck off,' he spat, 'If you are not willing to accept my offer then I am just going to have to take your farm and land. I was being generous but you have made the wrong decision.'

'No, you have made the wrong decision,' Marcus retorted. 'You will come to regret crossing paths with me.'

'Whatever,' Priscinus sneered. 'Back to the house,' he barked turning to his slaves. 'We are done here.'

As Priscinus and his party moved away, Marcus, seething with rage, watched them go in impotent silence. Then he glanced quickly at Dylis. His sister too was watching the chair and its occupant being carried away. Then she turned and fixed her cold, emotionless eyes on Marcus.

'So that went well,' she hissed sarcastically. 'A good strategy brother. And you wanted to negotiate with that man.'

'That's our best hope. I had to offer him something,' Marcus said unhappily. 'You heard Ninian's advice. It was worth a try and now I have gained an insight into what we are up against. Priscinus is willing to negotiate.' Marcus paused. 'And he is also willing to kill to get what he wants.'

Dylis looked away.

'So now what?' she hissed.

Marcus took a deep breath and glared at the distant villa.

'This is just the start,' he murmured. 'The sensible thing to do is to prepare for trouble but to seek some sort of deal with Priscinus which will be to our mutual advantage. This situation will only be resolved by a compromise. It will only be solved by doing a deal with that monster. However hard and unpleasant that may be. We don't have a choice. Our options are limited.'

At his side Dylis turned to give her brother a contemptuous glance.

'The love of those Hyperborean smoking herbs has made you weak,' she hissed.

Chapter Ten – The End of Us

Marcus, Efa, Dylis and Cunomoltus stood in a semi-circle in the mud looking down in silence at the simple, altar stone that had been erected in the wet grassy field. A little way off, Elsa and one of the household slaves stood watching them. The shivering, and trembling girl clutched the reins of the horses, her cheeks rosy from the cold and her hair plastered to her skull by the heavy rain. Above her in the sky, dull grey rain clouds covered the heavens to the horizon. A week had passed since the encounter with Priscinus, but on this sombre and wet day all that was momentarily forgotten. Marcus, clad in a long, black, travelling cloak, with the hood pulled over his head, was the first to look up from the Roman army altar, that had been erected to commemorate the soldiers who had died here in this place, fighting against Boudicca, the Barbarian Queen. He sighed as he surveyed the grey rain swept fields trying to imagine the battle in which Corbulo had fought all those years ago. His father had spoken little about the battle, other than to say that it was the most important day of his life. Idly Marcus glanced around the non-descript landscape. The forests on either side of the battlefield were still there. The six thousand or so heavy infantry of the Twentieth and Fourteenth Legions, he knew, would have been concentrated in the centre, facing the vast horde of tribesmen and women which Boudicca had brought with her to this decisive spot. Governor Paulinus had placed his lightly armed auxiliaries and what little cavalry he still possessed, on the flanks, knowing they would be protected by the dense woods. But it had been the Roman legionaries who had won the day. Severely outnumbered, it had been they who had received the fierce, tribal charge and it had been they who, through sheer guts and brutal determination, had fought the Britons to a standstill and then slowly started to drive them back, massacring the tribesmen in their thousands.

Marcus turned, as silently Efa grasped him by the arm and gently started to lead him away from the altar stone and towards the middle of the field. As they picked their way through the wet grass, he spotted a solitary memorial stone. The stone looked out of place, all alone in the grass.

'That is the spot where we buried Quintus,' Efa said pointing at the stone. 'And beside it, is where we shall lay my Corbulo to rest.'

'Are you sure,' Marcus muttered.

'I am,' Efa nodded firmly. 'This is where he wants to be.'

For a moment Marcus said nothing as he stared at the patch of wet grass beside the stone. Then he turned and beckoned for the slave to join him. At his side Dylis and Cunomoltus were silent as they stared down at the grass.

'The end of us,' Efa said in a calm composed voice. 'This is how it will be. One day all of us will go back to the embrace of the earth mother and we shall be whole again. My Corbulo has waited long enough, but today his long wait is over and he will be at peace.'

As the slave approached, carrying the heavy looking memorial slab, Marcus grasped hold of it and carefully lowered it to the ground. Then he knelt and together with Cunomoltus and Dylis, the three of them, using their hands, quickly dug a deep and thin, rectangular hole in the ground and slid the stone into place. As the other two got back up onto their feet, Marcus remained on his knees scraping out some more earth in front of the stone to create a deep hole. Reaching up he took the leather bag proffered to him by Cunomoltus and, from within it, he carefully took Corbulo's skull and the small urn containing his father's ashes and placed them both at the bottom of the hole.

'The coin,' Marcus muttered, glancing at Cunomoltus, as he raised his hand.

'It should be a gold coin,' Dylis said in a hoarse voice. 'A gold coin will get him a better seat on the boat that crosses the river.'

Without saying a word, Cunomoltus dropped a large, gold coin into Marcus's outstretched hand and Marcus carefully placed it in the skull's open mouth. Then he sat back on his haunches, staring down at the gleaming, white skull that was looking back at him from the bottom of the muddy, waterlogged hole. For a moment, no one spoke and the only noise was the incessant patter of the rain. Then quickly Marcus filled in the hole with the displaced earth and finally replaced the tufts of grass, stamping them into place. As he got back to his feet and wiped his hands on his cloak, Marcus glanced at Dylis and his brother. The two of them, clad in their long travelling cloaks, looked sombre and pale. A solitary tear was making its way down Dylis's cheek as she gazed at the grave stone and Cunomoltus looked haggard, frail and cold. He had still not fully recovered from the illness that had beset him on board the Hermes, Marcus thought. Taking a step backwards, Marcus turned to look down at the abbreviated inscription that had been carefully chiselled into the stone. The words had only been agreed amongst the family, after a lengthy and emotional debate.

'To the spirits of the dead
And to Corbulo
A soldier of the Twentieth Legion
He served twenty-five years
Faithful to his vow and promise, he lies here in eternal rest, together with his comrades
His wife Efa, daughter Dylis and his sons Cunomoltus and Marcus made this
Do not walk here'

As Marcus finished reading the inscription, he felt Efa's cold wet fingers grasp his arm. The old lady, her head covered by her white sheep skin hood, was looking up at him with a gentle happy smile.

'He was a good man,' Efa said. 'I am confident he will go to the Elysian Fields. And you have been a good son, as good as any father can expect.'

Marcus did not reply as he turned to look out across the rain-swept field. He was not so sure that the spirits of the dead would send Corbulo to the Elysian Fields, the paradise that awaited a man who had led a good, heroic life, but wisely he kept those thoughts to himself.

'As his first-born son, I have a few words which I would like to say about my father,' Marcus growled turning to look at the grave.

'Life is about simple fulfilment,' Marcus began. 'It does not matter if we are rich or poor. At the start, we all have a choice. We must decide what is most important to us and follow that, throughout our lives. A man who stays loyal to his wife and family is a man who has led a full life. A man who stays loyal to his principles leads a full life. A man who loves his country and dies for his country has lived a full life. A man who never wavers from what he sets out to do, leads a full life.' Marcus paused and glanced around at the faces that were watching him. 'Now Corbulo, my father, was none of these men, even though later he tried to make amends. So, the only thing I can say about him is this. He was a soldier. He was loyal to the Eagle of the Twentieth Legion. In that loyalty, he never wavered, and for that we should honour him. For that reason, I ask the spirits of the dead, to allow him to spend his days in the Elysian Fields."

And as he fell silent, Marcus suddenly felt a great weight being lifted from his shoulders. At his side Dylis was choking back her tears and Cunomoltus face was ashen. Only Efa seemed happy and composed. Turning to the slave, Marcus took the small jug of wine from the slave's hand and slowly and carefully poured the libation onto the ground around the grave.

For a long moment, no one spoke. Then from amongst the trees of the forest, some fifty paces away, Marcus suddenly caught sight of movement. Frowning he peered towards the trees and then grunted in surprise. Sitting quietly watching them was a grey wolf. In shock, Marcus stared at the beast, hardly daring to breath. Then wrenching his gaze from the animal, Marcus turned to look at Elsa standing in the sodden field clutching the reins of the horses.

'Come,' he muttered, 'we head for Londinium. The living need looking after.'

Chapter Eleven – Hierarchy

Marcus paused on the pavement of the busy street and warily gazed up at the palace of the Governor of Britannia. The last time he'd been inside that building had been during his court martial some fifteen years ago. It had not been a pleasant experience but Agricola himself had been his patron then, and his influence had been enough to get Marcus pardoned by the military court and reinstated to the Second Batavian Auxiliary Cohort as a common soldier, never to hold a senior rank again. But times had changed. Agricola was dead and Marcus had no patron to protect him now. This time he would have to fight his corner on his own.

The imposing stone palace, stood on the northern bank of the Thames river and its fine, stone-walls was several storeys high. Its sloping roofs were covered in neat red-roof tiles and the entrance was dominated by a large, stone-statue of the Emperor Trajan. Two armed guards stood flanking the gateway into the building. As he approached, Marcus caught sight of the proud letters SPQR chiselled into the stonework above the entrance. A queue of petitioners hoping to gain an audience with the Governor or his staff, were waiting patiently to be allowed to enter. Quietly Marcus joined the queue and waited until it was his turn. It had taken them a few days on horseback to cover the distance from the battlefield where Corbulo now lay buried to Londinium, capital of the province of Britannia. Where Watling street had met the road leading south to Reginorum he'd said goodbye to Dylis and Cunomoltus, sending them back to the farm, whilst he had taken Efa and Elsa a bit further on to where they had found accommodation above the Cum Mula Peperit II tavern.

'State your business?' a harassed looking junior official snapped, as he made a note on his wooden tablet.

'Land Surveyor's Office,' Marcus muttered. I want to see an Agrimensore, a land surveyor.'

The official didn't look up from his tablet as he made a quick note on the wood with his iron tipped stylus, pen.

'Name, rank, place of residence?' the official asked.

Marcus gave him his details, and quickly and efficiently, the official pointed him down a corridor. The Land Surveyor's Office was a small, rectangular room with an open doorway into a second room, in which Marcus could see a huge, stack of ledgers and tablets, lining the walls. The land surveyor was sitting behind a desk with a pile of documents, lying opened on the desk. He glanced up at Marcus with a disinterested, weary look.

'How can I help you?' the surveyor muttered.

'I own a farm and land on the Isle of Vectis, Marcus replied. 'Business has been good and I need a surveyor to come down to the property to include it in the official census. I estimate that the place is worth more than a hundred thousand denarii but I need official recognition of this.'

'I see,' the surveyor grunted. 'You wish to be enrolled in the Equestrian Order. You wish to become a knight and you want my office to help you.'

'I will pay the survey fee,' Marcus said hastily.

'Of course you will,' the official said with a weary, bored expression as if he had heard it all before. 'But I must warn you that even if you have the right property qualifications, you will not get yourself onto the official lists of Equites. Only someone who is personally approved by the Emperor himself, gets to be enrolled as a knight with Equus Publicus. Your name will not appear on any of the official lists from which the Imperial Government make their appointments. Only a knight with Equus Publicus makes it onto those lists. Do you understand?'

Marcus frowned. He had not been expecting it to be so complicated.

'So what happens,' he said. 'What happens if my property qualifies me?'

A thin, cold smile appeared on the surveyor's lips.

'You will become a knight,' the official declared. 'You will simply enjoy equestrian status, but you will not be officially part of the order. You will be allowed to wear a toga with a thin, purple stripe; you will be able to wear the gold ring and you will gain reserved seating at the arena. And if, and only if, someone important, truly important, recommends you to the Imperial Government will you be enrolled as a knight with Equus Publicus.' The surveyor sighed and looked around sadly at the documents that surrounded him. 'And in this miserable provincial outpost the only person of true importance is the Governor himself so good luck with that.'

Marcus looked down at the floor. Then he nodded.

'I would like to arrange for a surveyor to include my farm and land in the census,' he said. 'How soon can you arrange it?'

'All in good time,' the official growled reaching for a clean wooden writing-tablet. 'You said you live on Vectis. There are seven Roman farms on the island. What was the name of your farm again?'

'It used to belong to Governor Agricola,' Marcus replied with a hint of pride. 'It lies close to the sea in the south-eastern part of the island...' Marcus's voice trailed off as he saw the surveyor looking up at him in sudden horror.

'You are the owner of *that* farm,' the official exclaimed, his face growing pale, 'You own the farm that used to belong to Agricola?'

'That's what I said,' Marcus growled irritably.

The surveyor looked down at his desk and then hastily rubbed his forehead.

'What's wrong,' Marcus snapped, his face darkening in alarm.

The official shook his head. 'I am sorry, I can't help you,' he muttered. 'In the current circumstances I cannot survey your property, it will only get me into trouble.'

'What,' Marcus cried out. 'But you just said you would. And what do you mean, the current circumstances?'

'Please, you should go; our business is finished,' the official stammered as he rose to his feet and gestured at the doorway.

'I am not leaving until I have an answer,' Marcus said stubbornly.

Furtively the surveyor glanced at the doorway, and suddenly Marcus noticed that the man was frightened. Fumbling in his pocket, Marcus slammed a single silver coin down onto the table.

'Tell me what you know,' he hissed.

For a long moment, the official remained silent as he stared down at the coin, torn by indecision. Then hastily he pocketed the coin.

'I can't survey your land,' the man whispered, avoiding Marcus's gaze. 'You have no idea how much trouble you are in. There is a man; his name is Priscinus. He is after your land. He has laid claim to your farm. He has powerful friends. Your farm is not going to be yours for much longer.'

'This I already know,' Marcus growled.

The official swallowed nervously and glanced at the doorway, as if he was expecting someone to be listening in to their conversation. Then quickly he looked up at Marcus.

'Priscinus's family used to be of senatorial rank,' the official whispered. 'His father used to be a senator in Rome for fuck's sake. They are a very important family but since Priscinus became their most prominent member, the family have run into financial difficulties. Their declining fortunes have been so great, that the Imperial Committees have kicked them out of the Senatorial Class and down to the Equites.' The surveyor nodded eagerly. 'So you see promotion can go both ways,' he hissed. 'But you seem a decent man so it is proper that you know what you are up against.'

Marcus gazed at the official.

'What am I up against,' he snapped.

The surveyor rubbed his forehead again. 'I can only tell you what I have heard,' the man muttered. 'Priscinus's family no longer qualify for admittance into the Senatorial Class, because they have lost a fortune. Now Priscinus wants to get it all back, and he thinks seizing your farm will help him to get back into the senate. That's why he will drive you out. He won't back down.'

'He is not going to drive me from my land,' Marcus said quietly.

On the opposite side of the desk the official shook his head.

'You still don't understand how much trouble you are in,' the surveyor whispered. 'Who do you think is backing Priscinus's claim to your farm?' The official stared at Marcus with wide incredulous eyes. 'The Governor of Britannia himself,' he whispered. 'Yes that's right. The Governor is backing Priscinus. He is that man's patron. You won't stand a chance when they make their move. What can you do against such powerful men? The Governor commands three fucking legions for Jupiter's sake. Priscinus is going to crush you. Get out now whilst you are still alive and by all the gods don't mention that I have told you this.'

Chapter Twelve – Leadership

It was a short walk from the Mule tavern, where they had been staying, to the doctor's house close to the Forum. It was just after dawn and the streets of Londinium were already crowded, noisy and smelly. Marcus strode along, supporting Efa with one arm around her waist. Elsa followed a few steps behind them, picking nervously at her fingernails, her face sullen, her eyes fixed on the stone pavement. Marcus glanced sideways at Efa with a concerned look. The old lady looked her usual formidable and confident self, but underneath she was not well. In the morning's it had become increasingly hard for her to hide her blood-soaked rags from everyone. And now she had started to rapidly lose weight.

'I can still walk by myself,' Efa snapped crossly as if she had read his thoughts. 'I am not in my grave just yet.'

Marcus said nothing as he looked away but he kept his arm around her waist. His family were frightened, depressed and worried. He'd seen it on their faces and heard it in their voices. Danger and disaster were circling the family and none of them knew wherever they would soon be homeless and destitute. They desperately needed some hope and reassurance. He needed to rally them. He needed to give them hope. As they approached the Forum the three of them paused to stare at the truly huge, stone Forum and Basilica that had arisen in the centre of the city. Some of the scaffolding was still in place and workmen were still swarming over the construction site, but the enormous, colonnaded, multi-storey office and market square was nearly complete. The structure, home to the banks, money lenders, lawyers and city merchants dwarfed, every single building around it and, presiding over the magnificent entrance gate, was a huge statue of the Emperor Trajan, crowned with the laurels of victory, his right hand raised in salute.

'He may be the Emperor but he can't stop the pigeons shitting on his statue,' Efa snapped bad temperedly as she gazed up at the statue.

Silently, Marcus steered her in the direction of the doctor's house. Efa had not wanted to go to see the doctor. She had said she did not wish to be a burden and that the doctor's time would be better spent looking after the poor and those who needed it more than her. But Marcus had brooked no opposition and, quietly but firmly he'd coaxed her into having herself examined. He needed her to get better, he had explained, for the family was counting on her, in this dark hour. They were all counting on her strength and wisdom. That had silenced her.

As the doctor ushered Efa into the back room of his narrow, strip-house he shut the door behind him, leaving Marcus alone with Elsa. Marcus glanced around at the simply, furnished front room. Elsa was sitting on a chair with her hands neatly folded in her lap, looking sullenly down at the floor. She had barely said a word to him since he and Cunomoltus had returned. Now Marcus sat down and studied her carefully. Their lack of interaction was not only her fault. There had been so much to do since he had returned and he'd had so little time to spend with her.

'Are you enjoying your new home?' Marcus muttered.

Across from him, Elsa nodded obediently but did not look up.

'The other children are treating you and your brother well?' Marcus inquired.

'I am not a child,' Elsa snapped sullenly.

'No, you are not,' Marcus replied sternly. 'And I am glad to hear it.' For a moment. he was silent as he studied the girl. 'You know,' he said at last, 'I was only a few years older than you are now when I ran away and joined the army. That is the bravest thing I ever did.'

Sullenly Elsa stared down at her hands, determined not to look up at him. Kyna had told him that the girl felt abandoned and it had made her sullen and resentful.

'Why,' she muttered at last. 'Why did you do that?'

Marcus shrugged. 'It was hard, because I had to leave my mother behind on her own. But I wanted to belong somewhere,' he muttered. 'My father had served in the legions and maybe I thought that, by joining the army, I could prove that I was a better man than he was.'

'And are you?'

Marcus said nothing and turned to look at the door behind which Efa was being examined.

'We have not had much time together since your father's death,' Marcus said at last, turning to look at Elsa. 'But I remember when we first met, that you told me that you wanted to become a healer with a practice in Londinium. Well here we are, in the house of one the finest physicians in the province.' Marcus paused and gazed at the girl. 'Do you want me to ask him if he needs an apprentice? He is just there, beyond that door. If you want to do this, now is the time.'

Startled, Elsa looked up at the door but she remained silent, fidgeting with her fingers, avoiding Marcus's gaze.

'Well, that's what you want isn't it?'

'If my brother can come with me,' Elsa muttered. 'I promised my father that I would look after him, that we would never be separated.'

'No Elsa,' Marcus firmly shook his head. 'You and your brother are part of my family now. You cannot look after him on your own. Your brother will stay with us on the farm on Vectis and you shall see him when you come to visit us or when he is old enough to visit you. We are family now, you, I, all of us and family look out for each other. There is nothing more important than family.'

'But you promised,' Elsa cried out, looking Marcus straight in the face, her eyes glowing with bitterness. 'You promised that I and my brother would never be separated.'

'You are not a child anymore,' Marcus replied sternly. 'You are a woman now and you must learn to trust me. Your brother will be safe on the farm. It is time you grew up and became what the gods want you to be. I need you to do this, all of us do. It would be a great shame to waste a talent like yours. And having a doctor in the family will help all of us. Think about it.'

Elsa looked away and suddenly there were tears rolling down her cheeks. For a moment, she was silent, and he could see she was struggling to make a decision.

'Why?' she said at last in a hoarse voice turning to glare at Marcus. 'Why do you care about me and my brother? Our father betrayed you. You owe us nothing. We are just two more useless, ungrateful mouths to feed.'

But Marcus shook his head.

'No, you are as much a part of my family as my own son,' he said sharply. 'And nothing will change that. I want to be your friend Elsa for I have a sense that you are going to make a great doctor one day.'

Marcus rose to his feet and looked down at the girl.

'So don't let me down,' he said.

***

When the door to the back room finally opened, Efa appeared and smiled brightly at Marcus. She was followed by the doctor who was not smiling. Marcus rose to his feet as Efa came and sat down beside Elsa. The doctor lingered in the doorway.

'Marcus, can I have a word,' the surgeon muttered beckoning for Marcus to join him in his surgery.

Frowning, Marcus joined the doctor in the back room and the surgeon quickly closed the door behind him.

'So,' Marcus exclaimed. 'How ill is she?'

The doctor scratched the back of his head and sighed. Then he looked up at Marcus and Marcus's spirits sank, as he caught sight of the man's expression.

'The cancer and infection is too widespread,' the doctor said wearily. 'There is nothing I or anyone else can do. Death is certain.'

Marcus took a deep breath and looked down at the ground. Then he nodded.

'How long has she got?'

'Six months, maybe a little longer, it is hard to say,' the doctor replied grimly. 'But before that she will weaken. It will happen quickly and suddenly. You should be prepared for this.'

'Does she know,' Marcus said.

'I think she does but I thought I should speak with you first,' the doctor replied. 'I haven't told her what I think and maybe its best if you don't either. She will be happier that way.'

'Shit,' Marcus said, taking a deep breath as he looked away.

Chapter Thirteen – The Ludi Magister

From the outside, the Ludus Maximus looked like any other wealthy Roman town house Marcus had seen. The stone villa with its sloping, red-tiled roof, stood in a smart and quiet district of Londinium. A freshly-painted sign with the school name hung above the entrance gate and beside the door, in a vestibule, a fine, stone bust of Emperor Trajan reminded visitors who the school's patron was. Marcus paused beside the gate and glanced back at Efa and Elsa, who were still a few steps behind him, coming down the quiet street. It was afternoon and barely a few hours had passed since the doctor had given him the grim news that Efa was dying. But if Efa knew, she was not showing it. Instead she seemed in a cheerful and talkative mood as she strode along, clutching Elsa's arm. And as they approached Elsa suddenly burst out laughing at one of Efa's comments. Marcus frowned. The girl had never done that before. As he waited for them to catch up, Marcus looked away down the street so that the women would not see the expression on his face. Since arriving in the capital, the news had been relentlessly bad. The refusal of the Land Surveyor's Office to conduct an official census on his farm had been bad enough, but it was positively catastrophic that Priscinus enjoyed the favour and protection of the Governor of Britannia. It had proved that he had been right to be cautious with Priscinus and try to negotiate with the man. And now Efa was dying and there was nothing he could do about it. But at least he'd been able to arrange something for Elsa. The doctor had been impressed by Elsa's knowledge and skill at healing and after some negotiation Marcus had managed to get her an apprenticeship, with the doctor, starting at the end of the summer. And now he thought wearily, they had come to the Ludus where Ahern, Jowan's bastard son, was studying because the school fees needed to be paid.

A slave opened the door and, on hearing the purpose of their visit, he gestured for the three of them to wait in the small hallway. Impatiently Marcus paced up and down over the fine, black and white mosaic floor showing a teacher instructing a class of students. He waited for Ahern to show himself. At last footsteps echoed on the stone floor and a tall, elegant-looking man with a white beard appeared, clad in a simple toga. A short, wooden-cane hung from his belt and for a moment it reminded Marcus of a Centurion's army vine-staff, which was used to beat their men for the slightest disobedience. The man clasped his hands behind his back.

'I understand that you have come to see one of my students,' the man said in an accent Marcus could not quite place. 'I am the Ludi Magister, the school master,' the man continued quietly. 'You have come to visit Ahern?'

'Yes, that's right,' Marcus replied. 'I have also come here to pay his school fees,' he added reaching for a bag coins from inside his pocket and tossing it at the school master.

Startled, the man hastily bent forwards and stretched out his hands to catch the bag. For a moment, he looked down at the money with distaste. Then he snapped his fingers and the slave came hurrying over.

'Take this to the master,' the teacher snapped. 'Tell her it is for Ahern's account and bring Ahern here from his room. His family have come to visit him.'

Smoothly and politely the school teacher turned and dipped his head in a gracious greeting to Efa and Elsa.

'Ahern will be here shortly,' he said.

'How many boys do you instruct in this place?' Marcus muttered as they stood waiting for Ahern to appear.

'We have thirty boys, aged between six and eleven; no girls,' the Ludi Magister sniffed. 'We do not take commoners. Lessons start at the sixth hour each morning and finish at noon every day. We teach them maths, reading, writing, poetry, geometry and rhetoric. We are the best school in Londinium, believe me. The boys here are destined for greatness. Your son is getting a fine education.'

'I don't doubt it by the amount it costs,' Marcus growled. 'But he is not my son. He belongs to my brother in law.'

'I see,' the teacher muttered.

Just then a little boy of around six came waddling down the corridor towards them. The boy was clutching his wax tablet and he was smartly dressed. He looked nervous and, as he caught sight of Marcus he stopped, and his face grew pale.

Marcus opened his mouth but it was Efa who was the first to speak.

'There you are Ahern,' she exclaimed with a broad smile as she strode towards the little boy and stretched out her hand. Gingerly he grasped it and she led him into the hall way. Marcus too tried to smile as he looked down at Ahern.

'How are you boy?' Marcus said.

Without saying a word Ahern nodded, not daring to look up at Marcus.

'He is still terrified that you are going to kill him,' Efa said scolding Marcus with a little wink. 'But you are not going to do that are you Marcus?'

Marcus did not reply as he squatted down on his haunches, and gently turned Ahern's head so that the boy was forced to look at him.

'Remember me?' Marcus growled.

Ahern nodded.

'Let's have a look at you,' Marcus said patiently. 'Let's see what kind of boy you are.'

For a long moment Marcus studied Ahern's face. Then he grunted.

'So who are your heroes' boy?'

Ahern bit his lip as he looked down at his wax tablet. 'Heron of Alexandria,' he said in a soft childish voice. 'He was the greatest scientist who has ever lived.'

'Who?' Marcus frowned.

'Heron of Alexandria, he was a Greek scientist,' Ahern replied. 'He lived three hundred years ago and he invented a machine that was driven by steam. One day I will carry on his work.'

Marcus leaned back and shook his head in puzzlement. The boy's answer had caught him by surprise. He had heard of Alexandria, although he would not be able to place it on a map, but he certainly had never heard of a scientist called Heron. He'd been hoping the boy would have said he wanted to be soldier.

"Well, we must all have our heroes,' he muttered rising to his feet. 'Even if they are Greeks by the name of Heron.'

'Ahern is one of our finest and brightest students,' a confident female voice said suddenly from the doorway leading into the villa. 'He is brilliant. His mind is one of the most gifted I have ever encountered.'

Marcus turned and saw an old and elegant woman, bedecked in fine rings and jewellery standing in the doorway. She was clad in white robes and her head was covered in a hood made of pure silk. She looked in her fifties. Marcus frowned. The woman looked strangely familiar. Then abruptly some colour shot into his cheeks as he recognised her. It was Claudia, the Legate's wife, with whom he'd had an affair at the Fort in Luguvalium, all those years ago, when for a brief summer, Marcus had been the Prefect of the Second Batavian Auxiliary Cohort. For a moment, no one spoke. Then a little smile appeared on Claudia's lips as she recognised Marcus.

'It's been a long time Marcus, since you rescued me and my daughter from the rebels,' Claudia said smoothly, inclining her head in gracious gratitude. 'I always wondered what had become of you and now you are here in my school. What a happy coincidence.'

'Your school,' Marcus muttered, trying to look as normal as possible.

'Yes, Claudia said confidently with a mischievous twinkle in her eye. 'I own the school. Its creation was my idea and Ahern is one of my star pupils, aren't you Ahern?'

In response, the little boy nodded and clasped Claudia's outstretched hand.

'Then that makes me feel even more confident about his future,' Marcus said looking down at the ground.

'You know each other,' Efa interrupted glancing from Claudia to Marcus.

Claudia nodded. 'Marcus was the Camp Prefect at Luguvalium during the great northern rebellion,' she said, smiling at Efa. 'It was years ago now but he saved me and my daughter from being captured by the rebels. We are alive because of him and his Batavians.'

'I am glad to see that you are doing well,' Marcus said, trying to change the subject.

'Oh I don't know,' Claudia sighed. 'My husband is a Senator now in Rome. I am waiting for him to call me to Rome, to be at his side, but so far he has declined to do so. But I have the school and that is something I suppose.'

Marcus nodded and looked down at Ahern.

'I am pleased that he is doing well,' Marcus exclaimed. 'And when I am next in Londinium I shall come to visit him again. But we must go now. There is urgent business that cannot wait.'

As Efa and Elsa turned to say goodbye to Ahern, Claudia came up to Marcus and took hold of his arm running her fingers lightly across his skin. She smiled as she looked up at him, her eyes twinkling in delight and for a moment Marcus was back in his quarters at the Fort in Luguvalium watching her lithe, naked body lying on his bed.

'If you ever need anything from me,' she said quietly, 'then all you have to do is ask. I reward those who have helped me and you have done more than most. I want you to know that you have an ally here in Londinium.'

***

Looking troubled and somewhat embarrassed, Marcus led Efa and Elsa back to the Cum Mula Peperit II tavern, where they were staying. As they walked down the street Marcus remained silent as Efa chatted to Elsa in a cheerful voice. The chance meeting with Claudia had thrown him. What was she trying to do? Was the woman trying to become his patron? It would certainly be useful to have such a wealthy and influential woman as his ally, but for any favours granted to him she would surely demand favours in return and that made him nervous. He wasn't yet sure whether he wanted to become her client, indebted to her kindness and support.

'There is history between you and that woman isn't there,' Efa said suddenly, turning to give him a wise, thoughtful look.

'There is,' Marcus growled. 'But this is the last time that we are going to talk about her.'

The Cum Mula Peperit II tavern stood close to the busy Forum and as they entered the building Marcus gestured for Elsa to take Efa upstairs to their room.

'We leave for home at dawn tomorrow,' he snapped. 'So get packing. I want to get back to the farm as soon as possible.'

Without looking again at the two women, he ambled over towards the bar where the bar owner, a hulk of a man, was cleaning cups with a wet rag. On the opposite side of the tavern, hanging from the wall, were numerous Batavian military artefacts, old swords, helmets, knives, shields, a captured Brigantian battle-axe, a human skull and an old, boar-headed, Celtic war trumpet. For the Mule was not only a commercial tavern, it had also become, under its new management, the social meeting place for the province's Batavian military veteran community.

In front of the bar, Marcus paused as thoughtfully he looked down at the two remaining fingers on his left hand.

'Any news from the boys?' Marcus muttered. 'We leave for Vectis tomorrow at dawn.'

The tavern owner glanced at him, as he replaced the cup on a shelf. 'I spread the word like you asked me too,' the retired Batavian veteran replied. 'If anyone is interested, they will be here before nightfall. They know the deadline. That's all I can do. You will just have to wait and see who shows up.'

Marcus nodded and grunted something to himself.

'You look like you have had a shit day,' the tavern owner said with a faint smile.

'It could have been better,' Marcus replied. 'Civilian life is so complicated. Sometimes I miss the simplicity of the army.'

The tavern owner reached out and picked up the next dirty cup. 'Well the news from the Dacian frontier is encouraging,' the veteran said. 'We've heard from all our cohorts on that front. They are being prepared for action. Lucky bastards. The loot and spoils that they will win will turn them into rich men. The Brigantes and Caledonians never did have many riches. That was our luck, to have to face those poor miserable fuckers. But Dacia is a different story. They have goldmines.'

Marcus sighed wearily as he suddenly thought of Fergus on his way to the front thousands of miles away to face an uncertain, dangerous future. And there was nothing he could do to help protect his son.

It was dark outside when Marcus realised that no one else would be coming. Grimly he rose to his feet and turned to look at the eight Batavian veterans lounging about around the tavern. He'd been hoping to get at least twelve men to come back with him to help protect his farm on Vectis but instead of twelve he had eight. The men, all of them retired soldiers stared back at him silence. All of them were sturdy, seasoned and battle hardened veterans with many years of military service. They were clad in simple grey travelling cloaks with hoods and they had brought their own weapons. Their travelling packs lay dumped on the floor in a heap.

'Alright, listen up,' Marcus said in a loud voice. 'Thank you all for coming. I do appreciate it. The conditions will be as promised. I shall pay for your expenses and a small daily salary. My farm is well stocked with food and it is a pleasant place. You won't go hungry. You are free to leave at any moment. The man who is trying to take over my land is called Priscinus. He is not going to succeed but he has been training men to fight and I think he may try and drive me and my family from my farm by force. If this happens I intend to fight.'

Marcus paused and looked around at the faces watching him. For a moment, the tavern remained silent. Then one of the veterans cleared his throat.

'We are all with you Marcus,' the retired soldier growled. 'And if it comes to violence then we will protect your farm. Don't worry about us. That's why we are all here. But there is one other matter that we wanted to discuss with you.'

'What's that?' Marcus frowned.

The veteran who'd spoken glanced round at his comrades who nodded at him.

'In addition to what you have promised,' the veteran said in a serious voice, 'we want you to make a donation to the Batavian Veteran's Fund which we have recently created to help our poorer and less well-off members and veterans. Do this and no fucker called Priscinus is going to take your farm from you.'

Marcus glanced around the tavern and then across the bar at the tavern owner. The owner nodded that he was in agreement with the men.

'Alright, it's done,' Marcus snapped. 'Now get some rest, we leave for Vectis at dawn.'

Chapter Fourteen – Hope in the Face of Despair

The eleven riders rode along the country track in single file, raising clumps of dirt and dust as they went. The flanks of the horses were heaving and streaked with sweat and around them, Vectis's peaceful countryside looked a parched yellow and green. It was afternoon and in the clear, blue sky the sun was a glorious ball of intense light and heat. The thud of the horses' hooves reverberated along the path and among the dry bushes and thirsty trees, the fresh grassy scents of summer filled the air together with a multitude of buzzing insects. Grimly, Marcus peered ahead along the track as he led the small, mounted-party towards his farm. Had he left it too late? Had Priscinus already made his move? Would he find a smoking, blackened ruin and his family's scattered, decaying corpses? But on the horizon, he could see no towering column of black smoke nor had the boatman, who had ferried them across the water, mentioned anything about seeing a party of armed men crossing to the island. Riding closely behind him came Efa and Elsa, both looking tired after their long journey from Londinium, their faces stained with dust and sweat, as were those of the eight silent, stoic Batavian veterans who brought up the rear.

Tensely Marcus bit his lip, as at last, he caught sight of his farm in the distance. The golden wheat fields that surrounded his property looked magnificent and undisturbed. A new palisade of sturdy-looking, if rather amateurishly constructed, wooden tree-trunks and branches surrounded the main house and agricultural buildings, partially shielding them from view. A party of slaves were busy digging a V shaped trench around the outside of the new defences. Marcus grunted in satisfaction as he eyed the fortifications. At least Jowan had done what he'd asked him to do. The palisade would not be able to hold off a determined, experienced military force for long, but it should be sufficient deterrence for the men he'd seen at Priscinus's farm. However, as he and his companions approached the main gate, a dog started to bark and Marcus's eyes narrowed suspiciously as he saw two figures hurrying towards him. From a distance, he recognised Jowan and Kyna. There was something about the way they moved that didn't feel right. Reining in his horse at the gate he quickly slid to the ground just as Jowan reached him and as he saw his brother-in-law's face, Marcus suspicion exploded into alarm. Jowan was not his usual placid, stoic, unshakeable self. Instead he looked ashen-faced, unsettled and in one hand he was clutching a spiked, war-club.

'What has happened?' Marcus cried out.

'Marcus,' Jowan called out in a strained voice. 'Thank the gods you are back. Dylis has gone missing. We haven't seen her for days.'

'What?'

Shocked, Marcus stared at Jowan and then turned to look at Kyna, as she came hurrying up to the gate.

'Dylis is missing,' Kyna gasped. 'We have searched everywhere for her. We have made inquiries with the neighbouring farms but no one has seen her. She went missing the day after she and Cunomoltus returned to the farm. She has been missing for days.' Kyna paused to catch her breath, her cheeks flushed, her face creased with worry. 'And there is more bad news. A messenger arrived from Reginorum with a summons. Priscinus is taking us to court. You are going to have to appear at court to defend yourself. The date has been set for ten days' time. The judge is the town's magistrate. He's one of Priscinus's friends, we are sure of it. And that is not all. Ninian came to us a few days ago. He told us that the priests of the Temple of Neptune and Minerva in Reginorum, the ones who Petrus insulted, have managed to persuade the local merchants to stop buying our produce. They have placed an embargo on us.'

The scowl on Marcus's face deepened.

'What about the army supply agents?' Marcus snapped. 'We sell most of our produce to the army. Have they too joined this embargo?'

Jowan shook his head. 'We don't know,' he said in a weary, dispirited voice. 'We don't know what the army buyers think. None of us have been to Reginorum since Dylis went missing. Finding her has been our priority. She is my wife, Marcus. The children are badly affected by her absence.'

Marcus nodded and looked down at the ground. 'I know,' he muttered, 'and we will find her, don't you worry.'

'What are we going to do about the summons?' Kyna blurted out, her lower lip quivering as she spoke.

Silently Marcus glanced at Efa and Elsa. Then he turned to look at the eight Batavians who were still mounted upon their horses. 'If we have been summoned then we will go,' Marcus replied turning back to Kyna, 'We have nothing to be ashamed of, nor do we have anything to hide. We have done nothing wrong. You all know what this is, a simple land-grab by a powerful man. It happens all the time, but make no mistake.' Marcus's face grew grim. 'This is our land and we are not the kind of people who are easily frightened or driven away. No one is going to take this farm from us. In the end, you will see, all will be well.'

Turning to Jowan, Marcus placed his hand on his brother-in-law's shoulder and gave him a little encouraging smile.

'I have brought these men back with me,' Marcus muttered gesturing at the horsemen. 'They are all old comrades, Batavian veterans; men who know how to fight. They are going to help us defend our home. See to it that they are given some hot food and that their horses are looked after. Have the slaves prepare quarters for them in the large barn. After that, I want the whole family gathered in the dining room. We are going to find Dylis, your children are going to get their mother back.'

'My daughter is still alive,' Efa exclaimed suddenly in a calm, confident voice. 'I can feel it. She is alive.'

Jowan was staring at the eight, silent Batavians sitting on their horses. Then he turned to Marcus and nodded grimly before hurrying away accompanied by the farm's hunting dogs. Marcus gave Efa a little appreciative glance. Then Kyna was at his side and as she embraced him. He felt the nervous tension in his wife's body.

***

They were all there except for Dylis, his sister of course. Marcus stood at the head of the long dining table, grimly clutching the edge of the wood with both his good hand and his injured one. His family looked worried and nervous as they silently crowded around him and for a moment, Marcus wished that Fergus was with him, standing at his side, supporting him. But Fergus was far away and his son had no idea what was happening to his family. With a weary sigh, Marcus raised his head and gazed at the faces peering back at him. They needed a bit of hope. They were waiting for him to explain his plan, to show them a way out, but what little of a plan he'd been able to put together had been hastily done in the last hour, and he had his own doubts about wherever it would work.

'So this is what we are going to do,' Marcus growled, trying to sound as confident as he could, 'The Batavians are here to protect our home. They will sleep in the barn and during the day they are going to train the male slaves how to fight. We need everyone who can hold a weapon.' Marcus paused as he drummed his fingers on the table. 'If Priscinus is so foolish as to come here in person with his men, we are going to meet him at the palisade. That will be our perimeter. There are not enough of us to defend the whole farm, so we shall concentrate on protecting the house. Everyone except the children are to be armed with whatever you can find, and I want two slaves on a permanent picket a mile down the track plus another on top of the roof with a bell which they are to use to sound the alarm. That way we should have some advance warning.' Marcus paused again. 'And in the unlikely event,' he muttered, 'that we are overrun, Kyna will lead all the children, including the children of the slaves, towards the beach and along the coast to safety with the neighbouring farm.'

'It sounds like we are going to war,' Efa muttered with a sigh.

'I have collected a dozen or so hunting bows from my friends,' Petrus interrupted helpfully. 'They are in my room. I will give them to the Batavian's.'

'That's good,' Marcus said glaring at him. 'But that doesn't release you from the debt you owe to all of us. Your stupidity in insulting those priests has now turned the whole town against us. You are going to have to do better than that to make things right.'

Embarrassed Petrus looked down at the table.

'What about Dylis?' Jowan said sharply as two of his children clung to each side of him. The children looked scared.

'Cunomoltus and I will go into Reginorum,' Marcus replied looking at the children. 'It is the one place where you say you have not searched for her. Maybe Ninian has news. Maybe someone in town knows something, maybe someone can give us a clue to what has happened to her. I am also going to have word with these merchants who are refusing to buy our produce.'

'Shouldn't you take some of the Batavians with you,' Kyna said anxiously.

'No, they will stay here to protect the farm. Cunomoltus and I can handle ourselves,' Marcus said resolutely.

'Priscinus has summoned us to court,' Kyna said shaking her head. 'What will happen if we go and the judge rules that our farm no longer belongs to us? What are we going to do then? We can't fight against Roman law. We can't disobey the law.'

The room fell silent and for a long moment no one spoke. Then Marcus stirred and suddenly his deep mellow voice was filled with confidence and strength.

'I know that you are all anxious and worried,' he said quietly. 'But we are going to have to be strong. These are testing days but they will pass. Fortuna favours those who dare stand up and fight for themselves. And I want you to remember something. My father never lost faith in us. And we are not going to lose faith in each other now. Corbulo is watching us. This was his farm once. So, don't let him down.'

***

Reginorum was not as large and grand as Londinium but it was undeniably Roman. As Marcus and Cunomoltus strode down the straight, main street of the small town, the tightly-packed rows of long strip houses, with their narrow frontages, workshops and stores, spilling out into the street, seemed to loom over him, trapping the pedestrians in a whirl of noise, smells and activity. Ox-drawn wagons rumbled down the street kicking up dust and the metallic hammering of a blacksmith dominated the chatter of the people in the street, and the advertising calls of the street-merchants. Wood-smoke rose into the air and down a side, narrow, street, a pack of feral dogs was barking and fighting amongst themselves. Marcus, clad in his wide-brimmed sunhat and carefully avoiding the piles of horse-manure in the street, cautiously glanced around him, as he and his brother made their way towards the Temple of Neptune and Minerva. None of the people in the street seemed to take any notice of them. As they approached the fine, stone-temple, a priest clad in his ceremonial robes appeared in the doorway and handed out some loaves of bread and a jug of wine to the ragged, miserable-looking beggars who sat clustered on the stone steps leading into the building. Ignoring the priest, Marcus headed straight for Ninian's small office that butted up against the Temple.

Ninian was sifting through a pile of documents as Marcus and Cunomoltus stepped into his office. He gave Marcus a concerned look, as he quickly rose to his feet and silently extended his hand towards Marcus.

'Dylis has gone missing,' Marcus said gravely as he grasped Ninian's hand. 'She has been missing for several days. I was wondering whether you had seen her or heard from her?'

The broker nodded and looked down at his desk. 'I heard about this,' he muttered. 'It's worrying. But I have not seen her. If I do hear anything I will let you know at once.'

Marcus grunted his appreciation.

'It's not like her to go missing like this,' Marcus said quietly. 'It's perplexing. My family have searched for her everywhere.' Marcus paused. 'You have heard about the court summons. I hope Dylis's disappearance is not linked to this but if you hear anything, anything at all, do let us know.'

Ninian nodded again. Then he straightened up.

'You have another problem,' he said lightly. 'The priest's next door, they have persuaded your buyers to stop doing business with you Marcus. I tried to argue your case but the merchants do not dare go against the will of the priests. It's troubling and its bad business for everyone but unless you can change the mind of the priests there is very little that I can do about it I'm afraid.'

'I will deal with the priests,' Marcus growled. 'But what about the army buyers? Have they joined the embargo too?'

Ninian sighed in relief. 'The influence of the priests does not extend to the army,' he said with a little encouraging nod. 'The soldiers must eat after all or else there will be a riot. But the priests are nevertheless going to put a big dent in your profits and they have also been whipping up sentiment against you amongst the town's people. They are calling you a Christian. They are spreading the rumour that you don't recognise the authority of the old gods and that of the Emperor.' Ninian sighed again. 'I think it may be wise if you and your family did not show themselves in Reginorum for a while, at least until matters have calmed down.'

'A Christian?' Marcus scoffed glancing at his brother. 'The people are stupid and ignorant if they believe that I am a Christian.'

'If the priests say it, they will believe it,' Ninian replied.

'We want to speak to the merchants, our buyers,' Cunomoltus interrupted. 'Where can we find them?'

Ninian turned to look at Cunomoltus. Then he shook his head.

'They won't listen to you. They are terrified of the priests but if you insist you will be able to find them all in the cattle market on the outskirts of town.'

Marcus glanced at his brother and then turned to Ninian.

'Matters are coming to a head on the farm,' Marcus said quietly. 'Priscinus may make a move against us before the court date so if you hear of anything do warn us. It may still come to bloodshed.'

'I will Marcus,' Ninian said with a little respectful nod.

***

As he emerged from Ninian's office and into the street, Marcus paused to look around him hoping perhaps to catch a glimpse of

Dylis, but there was no sign of her. The main street was busy and on the steps of the Temple the beggars were devouring the free bread they'd been given.

'Come on, let's try and see if we can talk some sense into these buyers,' Marcus muttered, as he turned and started to walk away down the street. He was closely followed by Cunomoltus. His brother too, was looking around, cautiously hoping to catch a glimpse of Dylis.

'What are we going to say to them?' Cunomoltus said as the two of them pushed on down the street towards the cattle market.

'We are going to remind them that the benefits of business go both ways,' Marcus snapped. 'And that if they aren't prepared to buy our stuff, we will find someone else who will.'

'But we don't want to do that.' Cunomoltus said with a frown.

'Yes, but they don't know that for sure,' Marcus growled. 'It's worth a try.'

The street ahead still followed the contours of the old Roman fort and as the two of them passed a tavern that had been built into the original defensive embankment, a man suddenly screamed out Cunomoltus's name.

'Cunomoltus,' the man roared again, and this time his shout silenced the pedestrians in the street and people stopped, and turned to stare. Slowly Marcus and Cunomoltus turned to look at the man who had challenged them and, as they did Marcus's heart sank as he recognised the huge, towering hulk of the man standing in the street a few paces away. It was Nectovelius, the man who had come looking for Cunomoltus at the farm earlier in the year and whose wife Cunomoltus had shagged in Londinium. Nectovelius was staring at Cunomoltus with blazing, furious eyes, his red cheeks glowing and even from a few yards away, Marcus could smell the wine on the man's breath.

'You fucking bastard,' Nectovelius roared slurring his words as he glared menacingly at Cunomoltus. 'So I have finally caught up with you. I knew that if I waited long enough you would show up like a bad smell. And now you bastard I am going to kill you,' he said drawing a knife from his belt.

'What.' Cunomoltus cried out as he staggered backwards in alarm. 'I thought we had gotten past all of this. The debts that I owed have been repaid. There was an agreement with the 'Blues.' You were there. And I never want to see you or your wife again. Can't we just move on?'

'No!' Nectovelius roared, as Marcus and Cunomoltus hastily stumbled backwards as he lunged at them with his knife. The aim was poor and it was clear that Nectovelius was drunk as a skunk.

In the street, the crowd gasped and someone cried out in warning as they stared at the developing fight in the middle of the street.

'Why not,' Cunomoltus shouted as he yanked his own knife from his belt. 'My debts with your brothers have been settled. I owe you nothing.'

'Because she has left me,' Nectovelius roared. 'She ran off and it's all your fault. So, I am going to kill you for that. Now stand still lecherous pig and take what is coming to you.'

But, as Nectovelius lunged again he stumbled too far to his left and into Marcus's path and, with a quick decisive movement Marcus thrust his short army pugio knife straight into the man's head. The blade slid straight into Nectovelius's eye with a sickening crunch sending blood gushing down his face. Nectovelius dropped his knife and with a vicious kick Marcus sent the big, howling-man tumbling to the ground, covered in blood and clutching his forehead. In the street, Marcus, his chest heaving with exertion, stood staring down at the writhing figure, lying in the dust. But before he could make another move, Cunomoltus pounced with a shrill, vindictive yell and grasping hold of Nectovelius's hair, he sliced open the man's throat sending another torrent of blood flooding onto the street.

'Bastard deserved it,' Cunomoltus cried out as he staggered back from the corpse, 'You heard him. He is better off dead.'

Marcus said nothing, as he stared down at the body and the rapidly growing pool of blood.

Amongst the crowd that was staring at the gory bloody scene in the middle of the street, a sudden angry muttering arose. Then as Marcus turned to look at them, some from within the crowd started to hiss.

'Christian! Murderer!' A man suddenly yelled raising a fist in the air.

'That's the man who insulted the priests and the gods,' another cried out.

In alarm, Marcus took a step backwards. What was this? The crowd was turning against them. Then a priest, clad in his ceremonial robes suddenly appeared amongst the onlookers and as he caught sight of Marcus, his face darkened and he raised and pointed a finger straight at him.

'Christians,' the priest roared furiously. 'Christians have no place in this town. Get them! Let's string them up from the nearest tree.'

'Run,' Marcus cried, turning to Cunomoltus. His brother needed no further urging. As the two of them fled down the street, with a great enthusiastic roar, the angry lynch mob set off in pursuit. As he ran, a man tried to grasp hold of Marcus, but Marcus violently shoved him out of the way. Ahead of him a woman and two small children hastily scampered to safety down an alley, as he and Cunomoltus raced down the street with the loud, baying mob close behind. From an alley, a dog came bounding into the street, barking madly as it ran alongside them. Just as they were nearing the edge of the town a stone struck Marcus on his back and another went flying just over his head. Marcus groaned as he suddenly caught sight of the two elderly town guards standing beside the gateway, that was the only way out through the town's palisade and earthen embankment. The guards were armed with spears but, as they turned to see the large town mob bearing down on them, with Marcus and Cunomoltus out in front, the men flung down their weapons and fled through the gates.

As Marcus and Cunomoltus shot out through the gates and into the fields beyond, most of the baying mob came to a ragged, panting halt and a final stone hit Marcus on his elbow. Risking a quick glance behind him, Marcus saw that the last of their pursuers had given up and were furiously shaking their fists in the air instead.

'Damn you and damn you Petrus,' Marcus panted as he gave Cunomoltus an angry scowl. 'Damn you both for getting us into such unnecessary trouble.'

Chapter Fifteen – Resolution

Marcus was inspecting the V shaped trench, dug by the slaves around the main complex of farm buildings, when the warning bell rang out. Startled, he looked up in the direction of the lookout post on top of the roof of the main villa. The slave had risen to his feet and was standing, staring at something along the track to the north and shaking his small, iron bell for all it was worth.

'Get to your positions,' Marcus roared, as he started to run towards the house. In the trench the slaves, clutching their entrenching tools, were already scrambling out of the ditch. As Marcus reached the front door, one of the Batavian's joined him, holding a bow with a quiver of arrows slung over his shoulder.

'Has the prick come?' the Batavian growled.

'I don't know,' Marcus snapped. Inside he nearly collided with Kyna, who was hurriedly ushering the children into one of the rooms. She looked pale, but Marcus was glad to see that, although they looked scared, none of the children was crying. As he emerged into the courtyard at the front of the house he turned sharply and looked up at the lookout, standing on the roof.

'What can you see?' Marcus shouted as one of the hunting dogs started to bark.

'Single horseman coming down the track Sir,' the slave cried out. 'He is moving at a fast pace. Will be here very soon.'

Marcus grunted and turned to stare across the courtyard towards the newly constructed, palisade and the gap left at the front gate. A single horseman was not what he had been expecting. For a moment, he bit his lip as he considered telling the lookout off for raising the alarm unnecessarily, but then decided against it. A moment later both Cunomoltus, clutching a bow and a spear, and Petrus armed with his hunting bow and quiver, came rushing up to him, looking flushed and excited. Without saying a word Marcus started out towards the front gate with them trailing behind. As he reached the gate, he heard the thud of hooves coming towards him. Quickly he glanced up at the morning sky. It was still dry and warm but to the west, a line of dark, grey-clouds was moving towards them, bringing rain. Turning to glare at the solitary rider thundering towards him, Marcus frowned as he recognised the owner of the neighbouring farm.

As he reached the front gate, the rider reined in his horse and the beast snorted and came to a halt. The horseman's face was streaked with dust and he gave Marcus a quick anxious, respectful nod which Marcus returned.

'Trouble coming Marcus,' the farmer called out in a tense voice as he sat on his horse and wiped his brow. 'My son says he saw Priscinus and maybe thirty to forty armed-men landing on the island this morning. They are accompanied by a few priests and townsfolk from Reginorum. It looks like they have come for a fight. My son came straight over to warn me. He says that the last he saw of them, Priscinus and his men were heading inland in your direction. I thought I should warn you.'

Grimly Marcus turned to stare down the deserted track leading northwards. Then he turned to look at his neighbour and nodded. 'Thank you,' he replied. 'We appreciate it.'

The farmer sighed and cast a quick glance down the track.

'You know I would help you if I could, Marcus,' the man exclaimed. 'But Priscinus is coming in force and I have my own farm and family to consider. You understand, don't you?'

'Yes,' Marcus replied. 'I understand. You are a good neighbour. But we will still be here tomorrow.'

'I hope so,' the farmer said with an anxious nod as he wheeled his horse around and started back down the track.

Marcus remained silent as he, Cunomoltus and Petrus watched the man ride away. Then sharply Marcus turned to his brother.

'Take up your positions,' he growled. 'We will wait for them to appear. Tell the others we have an hour or so.'

***

Marcus patted the Batavian on his shoulder as he slowly made the rounds along the rough, but sturdy-looking palisade that surrounded the farm house and out buildings. At intervals along the wooden wall Jowan, and the slaves had constructed raised platforms from which the defenders had an unobstructed view of the golden and glorious looking wheat-fields. The Batavians, armed with bows, proper swords, shields, helmets and thick, leather-armour had divided into pairs, each pair manning one of the platforms, which were spread out around the oval-shaped perimeter. The slaves were strung out in between them, forming a ragged-looking band of men and women, equipped with spades, sickles, knifes, stones and axes but nothing else. As he strode along the wall, Marcus called out to them with reassuring words but the slaves, tight lipped and tense said nothing in reply. As he came around to the front gate, he saw Cunomoltus, Jowan and Petrus anxiously staring up the track to the north. The gate had been barred and a barricade of old planks, sharpened stakes, barrels and prickly thorn-bushes had been piled up against it. The men glanced around, as they saw him coming, their faces betraying their emotions. Marcus glanced up the track. Still nothing. More than two hours had passed since their neighbour had ridden up to warn them. Idly he glanced at the farm house. Efa and Kyna were inside, looking after the children. They knew what to do if matters went badly. Marcus sighed. Ideally that was where he would have placed his reserve too but this was not the army he had to remind himself. Apart from the Batavians, the people who were going to fight were not trained to do this. They were his family and his farm's slaves. Marcus took a deep breath as he came and stood beside his brother at the front gate. Around him the farm was strangely quiet, except for the barking of a dog and the mooing of the cattle in their pen.

'There,' Petrus said quietly pointing at something in the distance.

Marcus peered down the track in the direction that Petrus was pointing. Then he too saw it. A solitary wagon was coming down the path towards the farm kicking up a cloud of dust. The cart was being pulled along by two horses and on both sides of the vehicle, columns of armed-men in single file and on foot were plodding towards the farm. For a moment Marcus did not move. Then his face darkened and he opened his mouth and quietly growled like a wolf.

'When I give the order I want you to skewer the first bastard who comes within range,' he said harshly turning to Petrus. 'They need to know that we are serious. But don't go for Priscinus. He's not to be targeted. I need him alive. The prick can't walk anyway.'

'I can't promise you that,' Petrus said tensely. 'Arrows have a habit of going astray and my aim is sometimes poor.'

Marcus said nothing, as he stood staring at the approaching column. Then slowly his hand came to rest on the pommel of his sword and both Petrus and Cunomoltus notched an arrow to their bows and carefully raised their weapons into a shooting position. On the nearest raised platform to him, beside the palisade, Marcus saw the two Batavians do the same, stretching their bows and taking aim.

Down the track the wagon came trundling towards them and as it drew closer Marcus caught sight of Priscinus, sitting in a large, comfortable-looking chair that had been raised and lashed to the cart. Two slaves stood behind him, one of whom was holding up the personal banner of Priscinus's house. Priscinus was clad in a fine, white toga with a broad, purple-stripe running down one side. Marcus's mouth curled in contempt. Priscinus was clad as if he was still a Roman senator, even though he had lost that privilege. The driver of the wagon, astride one of the horses, seemed to have an uncanny instinct for self-preservation for he brought the wagon to a halt just out of arrow range. And, as the columns of armed men halted, and started to cluster around the wagon, Cunomoltus groaned in dismay.

'There are more than thirty or forty of them, Marcus,' Cunomoltus sighed. 'Looks more like sixty and some of them have bows.'

Marcus said nothing, as he stared at the mob that was gathering around the wagon. His brother was right, the numbers were larger than he had expected and amongst their ranks he caught sight of a few priests, clad in their ceremonial robes. Priscinus's men seemed relaxed, confident in their superior numbers, and some of them started to raise their voices, taunting the defenders and shaking their fists in the air. But as Marcus's keen experienced eye studied the enemy ranks, he grunted in relief. The men facing him might be numerous but they were not trained or experienced soldiers. Nor did Priscinus seem to know what he was doing. The mob was sticking together in a single clump of men and silently Marcus prayed, that they would remain like this. For, if Priscinus ordered his men to spread out around the whole perimeter, he would be able to overwhelm the thin defences in a mass attack from all sides.

'I don't see Dylis amongst them,' Jowan exclaimed grimly as he ground the butt of his spear into the earth. 'They don't seem to have her. Unless they are keeping her as a hostage somewhere else.'

'Well, we are going to find out soon enough,' Marcus growled gesturing at the solitary priest who was coming towards the barricade with both his arms held up in the air. 'Looks like they are sending someone to talk to us. Let him pass. I want to hear what he has to say.'

When the priest was five or six yards from the barricade, he halted and slowly lowered his arms. For a long moment, the holy man was silent, as his small, eagle-eyes took in the barricade, the ditch and the wooden palisade and the men training their arrows on him. Then he turned and looked straight at Marcus.

'Priscinus offers you terms,' the priest called out in a loud, arrogant voice, 'This farm and this land no longer belong to you. They are Priscinus's property now. You and your family should leave right away. If you do this Priscinus will let you all go with whatever you can carry and he will spare your lives. But you must go now and never come back and the Christian will remain behind. Those are the terms. What is your answer?'

'You are a brave man,' Marcus replied. 'To come out here, all alone, to give us this message.' Marcus took a step forwards, his face suddenly harsh and cold. 'Now go back to your master and tell him this. Tell him that we do not need to do this. No blood needs to be shed today. I am prepared to negotiate with him. But if thinks he is going to have my farm, then he is going to have to come here and take it from me.'

'Is that really the answer you want me to give to him,' the priest sneered.

'Fuck off prick,' Petrus yelled as he provocatively brandished the large cross that dangled from around his neck. 'You heard our answer. Now be a good dog and run back to your master. Go on, he is over there.'

The priest gave Petrus a disgusted glance and then, without another word he turned and started back towards the mob that clustered around the wagon.

'What's the plan, Marcus?' Cunomoltus muttered in a tight voice as the four of them watched the priest walk away. 'With their numbers they can overwhelm us, trained men or not.'

'We wait,' Marcus snapped. 'We wait to see how far they want to take this.'

'They don't have her,' Jowan hissed. 'They don't have Dylis.'

Beyond the barricade the priest had re-joined the mob and seemed to be talking with Priscinus in an animated fashion. As Marcus peered at them Priscinus suddenly turned and gestured at someone standing behind the wagon and out of view. A moment later, six men detached themselves from the main group and keeping a respectful distance between them and the wooden palisade they started out into the golden, ripe wheat fields and as they did Marcus spat out a curse. The men were carrying burning torches.

'Bastards,' Jowan hissed as he realised their intention.

One by one the men started to set fire to the crops in the field and as the flames began to spread, smoke started to rise into the noon sky. Marcus turned and took a step towards the barricade as he stared in alarm at the growing destruction. Across the space that separated the two sides, the priest was once again coming towards him, his hands raised above his head as the smoke and flames tore across the glorious, golden fields devouring everything in their path.

'Petrus,' Marcus hissed. 'Shoot the bastard.'

'But he's coming under a sign of truce," Cunomoltus cried out in protest as he turned to stare at Marcus. 'If you kill a priest of Neptune and Minerva, we will never be welcome in Reginorum again, Marcus.'

'I don't care,' Marcus snapped. 'Petrus, shoot him.'

Petrus said nothing as he carefully took aim and then with a soft whirring noise he released. The arrow hurtled through the air and with deadly pinpoint accuracy, the projectile slammed straight into the priest's face, knocking the man backwards onto his back. For a stunned moment, no one made a sound. On the ground the priest, with Petrus's arrow sticking out of his head, lay motionless.

As the smoke came wafting across the ground towards them, the mob stared in disbelief at the lifeless corpse of their negotiator. Then as one, outraged, the men raised their weapons in the air, screamed and charged straight towards the barricaded gate. Marcus felt the hair's rise on his neck as he felt the familiar terror that an enemy charge elicited.

'Kill them,' he roared in a savage voice. 'Kill them all. They must not break through the barricade.'

As the first arrows went flying towards the charging mob, Marcus heard a familiar cry. 'Thunder and lashing rain so Wodan cometh,' and as he heard it the shout was taken up by others.

But there was no escaping the terror of the furious, yelling, charging mob. At Marcus's side Petrus whimpered in fear, as the screaming attackers came charging towards them and beside him Cunomoltus's face had drained of all colour.

'Stand your ground, they won't get through,' Marcus roared. His voice savage and brutal as he reached out and gripped Petrus firmly by the shoulder. But even Marcus felt the fear shaking his legs. Barricade or not there were just four of them defending the front gate. They were outnumbered over twelve to one.

The first of the mob were only a few paces away, when Marcus drew his sword. At the barricade Jowan, his eyes blazing was roaring as if he had gone completely mad and, as one of the attackers tried to rip aside the obstacles, Jowan savagely thrust his spear into the man's exposed chest. Marcus ducked as a spear flashed past his head and landed harmlessly in the courtyard behind him. The mob had reached the barricade and was furiously trying to tear it apart, hacking at it with their weapons and grasping the barrier with their bare hands. Crying out Marcus thrust his sword at the men in front of him, forcing a few of them backwards. Then he cried out as a sharp pain cut across his left arm, as one of the attacker's spears grazed him. Furiously he hacked and stabbed at the men trying to clamber over the gate. At his side Jowan, Petrus and Cunomoltus were all doing the same, desperately trying to hold back the mass of squealing, yelling bodies that was trying to break through. From their raised platform, the Batavian's kept up a relentless, constant and deadly barrage of arrows and amongst the tightly, packed group of attackers it was impossible to miss their targets. Marcus snatched a glance at Cunomoltus as he heard his brother suddenly cry out in pain. Cunomoltus was bleeding heavily from a gash to his head, but he was still on his feet and the bodies of two his assailants lay slumped over the barricade in front of him adding to the obstacles. Beside him Petrus was screaming in rage and terror, as he dodged the enemy spear thrusts, furiously jabbing at the attackers with his spear. But there were too many attackers and, as Marcus stabbed a man in the neck three more of the mob finally managed to clamber over the barricade and land on their feet close to him. Swiftly Marcus turned to face the three men. They were armed with swords and knives. With an outraged cry, Marcus took a step towards one of them and dodging the man's wild thrust he kicked him in the balls, sending the attacker groaning and stumbling backwards against the palisade. But as he turned to face the other two they were upon him and Marcus was flung to the ground in a confused, vicious, snarling tangle of arms, legs and bodies. The sharp point of a knife drove through his leather armour and into his leg and Marcus roared in sudden pain. Desperately he tried to push the men off him and stagger to his feet, but they were too strong and too heavy. He could hear their heavy laboured breathing and curses as the two attackers tried to finish him off. Then suddenly, one of the men's heads exploded into a ball of blood, broken bone fragments, brains and clumps of hair as an iron spiked club embedded itself into the attacker's skull. Instantly the pressure on Marcus slackened and he grasped hold of the remaining attackers throat and started to squeeze. Jowan suddenly loomed over him, forcibly yanking his club from the dead man's skull and, as he did Marcus, with a sudden surge of energy forced the third attacker onto his back. The man was wheezing and his face was turning blue as he ineffectively tried to stop Marcus from throttling him.

Wildly Marcus risked a glance at the barricade. Petrus and Cunomoltus were still on their feet and they had been joined by six Batavians who were cutting the remaining attackers to pieces with their long cavalry swords. The Batavian's must have seen the danger and had arrived just in time. The bodies of Priscinus's men were piling up against the barricade. To his right, two Batavians were finishing off a small band of men who'd managed to break through the palisade. One of the mob stood with his back pressed up against the wooden wall, impaled to it by a spear which had been driven straight through his chest. And on the ground, one of his colleagues was screaming in pain and terror as he tried to crawl away from the fight, dragging his bloodied, useless legs through the dust. As Marcus stared at the man, one of the Batavian's stepped over him and finished him off, with a swift thrust of his knife into the man's neck. Underneath Marcus, his attacker had stopped moving and his head had lolled to one side. Grimly Marcus reached out and grabbed hold of a discarded knife from where it lay on the ground and swiftly slashed the man's throat, sending a stream of blood gushing out into the earth. Then painfully and with a grimace he staggered to his feet. His tunic was stained with blood, gore and someone's brains and he was bleeding from a wound to his arm and leg. At the barricade the Batavians, Jowan, Petrus and Cunomoltus were crying out in relief and triumph and raising their bloody weapons in the air, as the remaining attackers fled back towards the wagon where, upon his raised chair, Priscunus had been following the fight. Grimly Marcus surveyed the desolate and bloody scene. More than half of Priscinus's men lay dead, wounded and dying in front of the gate, their bodies slumped over the barricade, scattered across the track and fields and littering his courtyard; felled by arrows and hacked, stabbed, decapitated and throttled to death. As he stared at the grim scene, black smoke came wafting towards him on a gust of wind and he tasted the acrid smell on his lips. A few of the badly-wounded attackers were groaning, where they had fallen and others were trying to crawl back to their own lines. His plan had worked Marcus thought with savage satisfaction. Killing the priest had lured Priscinus's men into a rash attack, upon the gate and without knowing it they had run straight into his killing field. Then Marcus grimaced, as a searing hot pain shot down his leg. As he staggered towards the barricade Cunomoltus, his face turned red by his own blood, rushed to his side and steadied Marcus with his arm.

'Take Priscinus,' Marcus roared ignoring the shuddering pain in his leg and arm. 'I want him taken alive. Get him!'

'No good Marcus,' one of the Batavian's panted as he paused to gaze across the smoke-filled space between the gate and Priscinus's wagon. 'He's still got his archers. They will shoot us down before we can even get close to him. There is no cover out there. We must stay within the protection of the palisade. The man has lost, Marcus. He is done for today. He knows it.'

And as the Batavian spoke, Marcus suddenly saw Priscinus's wagon slowly start to turn around and begin to move away. Priscinus had seen enough. He was retreating. The cart was followed by a gaggle of subdued, nervous survivors from the attack, some of them limping and casting fearful glances at the farm. Their numbers had been severely depleted.

Furiously Marcus forced his way up to the barricade, hobbling as he went and brushing aside Cunomoltus's steadying arm.

'It did not have to be like this,' Marcus roared in fury as he stared at the retreating wagon and band of attackers. 'I gave you a choice Priscinus. You arrogant prick. The dead are dead because of you. I would have talked to you about a compromise. The only way this dispute is going to be resolved is through a negotiated settlement and now you are running away. You coward. You fucking weasel! You don't deserve to wash the feet of the lowest criminal.'

Then a great curtain of black smoke intervened blotting out the view and Marcus turned and started to cough.

'We stopped them Marcus,' Jowan said his eyes bulging in sudden shock as if he had only just realised what he'd being doing. 'We stopped them and slaughtered them. They are all dead.' His voice trailed off. Petrus, clutching his large cross that hung on a cord from around his neck, was picking his way through the dead and broken bodies muttering to himself in a low urgent voice.

Marcus finished coughing and ignoring Jowan, he turned to stare at the ruined, blackened and burning wheat fields. His family and the Batavian's seemed to have suffered no dead but the victory had come at a cost for the farm's harvest had been completely destroyed.

'What now Marcus?' Cunomoltus muttered as his brother gave him an anxious glance.

Marcus sighed as he gazed at the fire and the towering column of smoke. There was nothing he could do about his crops.

'Collect the bodies of the dead in a heap,' he growled grimacing in pain. 'We will burn them before nightfall, beyond the perimeter, over there alongside the track. And we will tend to our wounds.' Turning to Cunomoltus he grasped hold of his brother's shoulder. 'I am too fucking angry and exhausted to think about what to do with Priscinus right now. We will discuss him tomorrow.'

***

Marcus was sitting up in his bed, his heavily bandaged leg stretched out in front of him, studying the inventory and list of accounts for his farm when loud, excited shouting erupted. The noise was coming from the courtyard. Alarmed he snatched up his gladius sword that was lying on his bed and reached for the wooden crutches. Had Priscinus and his men returned? A whole day and night had passed since the assault and the destruction of his crops and during that time the only people who'd shown themselves had been one or two of his neighbours, who'd come to see the damage done to the fields. As he hobbled down the corridor, grimacing in pain Kyna came rushing towards him but instead of looking alarmed, her eyes bulged in excitement. Her cheeks were flush and she had difficulty in speaking.

'What's happened woman?' Marcus bellowed irritably as he grasped hold of his wife's arm.

'It's Dylis,' Kyna blurted out. 'She is back. She is in the courtyard now. She is alright. She just walked through the main gate as if nothing had happened.'

'What,' Marcus exclaimed.

Kyna broke free from his grip and raced away down the corridor, followed swiftly by Marcus hobbling along on his crutches, as fast as he could. Outside it was nearly dark and as he came stumbling and swaying into the courtyard, Marcus cried out in sudden emotion as he caught sight of his sister. Burning torches had been placed at intervals along the palisade and beside the gate and in their flickering, reddish light Marcus saw Jowan embracing Dylis, together with Petrus and two of Dylis's children. They were swiftly joined by Efa and Kyna. Out of sight a dog was barking and the smell of smoke still hung thickly over the farm. As Marcus approached, Jowan let go of his wife and the small gathering fell silent as they respectfully turned to look at Marcus.

'Where have you been?' Marcus exclaimed shaking his head as he came to a halt a few paces from his sister. 'What happened to you? Do you know how worried we all were?'

Dylis was clad in a dirty, stained and torn tunic, partially covered by a dusty cloak and hood that was pulled down around her neck. A knife dangled from her belt and she looked completely normal. She regarded Marcus coolly and there was a faint hint of contempt in her voice as she spoke.

'Hello Marcus,' Dylis said. 'I thought you would like to know. Priscinus is dead. I saw his corpse this morning. So, our problems are over. The man who burned our fields is no more.'

Around Dylis the gasps were audible. Marcus cocked his head to one side as he stared at his sister in stunned silence.

'What do you mean, dead?' Marcus muttered at last.

Dylis's face grew scornful as she gazed back at him. 'You didn't understand what needed to be done,' Dylis snapped rounding on Marcus with sudden anger. 'You didn't have the guts. But when such a dangerous man as Priscinus is threatening our farm, our family, our future, then there is only one thing that you can do. I poisoned him. I sent him to spend eternity with the furies of hell. I wasn't going to let that arsehole take away everything that I and this family had built up over the years. Over my dead body. That's why I disappeared. That's where I have been all this time, preparing to kill Priscinus, because that is how you stop people like him.'

Marcus opened his mouth and gazed at his sister in utter shock. 'You poisoned Priscinus,' he muttered in confusion. 'How?'

Dylis wrenched her gaze from him and turned to look at the ground.

'It took me a while,' she replied sullenly. 'That's why I have been gone for so long. Do you remember that woman, the slave, with the bruises to her face? The one who met us at the gate when we went to speak with Priscinus.'

'I remember,' Marcus growled.

'Well I used her to get the poison into his house,' Dylis snapped.' 'Turns out that Priscinus was abusing her on a regular basis. She was happy to help me. Priscinus died choking to death. He's gone. We no longer have to fear him.'

Suddenly Marcus groaned and closed his eyes in despair. Ofcourse Dylis had not been there with him in Londinium when he'd gone to meet the land surveyor. She did not know that Priscinus's patron and ally was the Governor himself. And now Priscinus was dead, murdered in his own home. The Governor would never let that go. The Governor of Britannia would never allow his clients and friends to be murdered, especially the head of a family of former Roman senators. There would be an investigation, resources would be thrown at the case and there were going to be consequences, massive consequences. And if the trail led back to his family it would be all over for them.

Marcus groaned again as the full realisation of what Dylis had done sank in. Then he stepped forwards and embraced his sister in a tight hug.

'You don't know what you have done,' Marcus muttered.

Chapter Sixteen – Castra Bonnensis

(Province of Lower Germania, early August AD 105)

The harsh cries of the weapon instructors rang out across the large, sandy, training-area of the legionary fortress where several hundred legionaries of the Twentieth Legion were practising their weapons drill. It was a clear, fine day and in the brilliant, blue, sky the merciless sun bathed Castra Bonnensis, the legionary fortress on the Rhine in heat and light. Fergus, clad in a short-sleeved white, tunic and clutching a large, wicker-shield and a heavy, wooden, training-sword grimaced as he aimed cuts and thrusts at the six-foot-high, wooden post before him. The wooden training-shield and sword had been intentionally made much heavier than his normal equipment. The instructors had said that this was meant to build up the strength in his arms. Fergus's face glistened with sweat and his back and neck were drenched as he concentrated on attacking the wooden post. A few paces away, his mess mates were doing the same. Behind them, the instructors slowly, strode along the lines intervening if they were not happy, whilst the senior company officers looked on. Fergus grunted in satisfaction as he struck the wooden place in exactly the place he'd been aiming for. Titus, the company Centurion was driving his men hard, and for the past few days, ever since they had arrived at their new, temporary home on the Rhine, he'd been keeping them busy with one training exercise after the other. As he stepped back to once more attack the wooden post Fergus snatched a glance in the Centurion's direction. Titus was easily distinguishable by his magnificent, red plumed helmet. The men were convinced the continuous training was because Titus wanted to show off to the legionaries and officers of the 1st Minervia Legion, in whose camp they had been billeted.

A few paces away, Aledus suddenly swore as he missed his target and instead, in frustration, lashed out at the wooden post with his foot. Fergus grinned as, moments later, one of the weapon instructors blew his whistle and came stamping towards

Aledus shaking his head. Aledus shot Fergus a little, cheeky smile as he saw him watching. The men's morale was high, Fergus thought, as he turned and concentrated on attacking the wooden post. And so was the mutual respect and team spirit within his squad. When he had finally re-joined the company in the port of Rutupiae, he had found out that his squad had been brought up to full strength of eight men. The two newcomers were young, inexperienced and brand-new recruits, straight out of basic training, but on the short sea voyage to Gaul and the subsequent march to the Rhine, he'd made a concerted effort to turn his whole squad into an efficient, effective team, and now at last, his efforts seemed to be paying off.

A sudden shout made Fergus hesitate. Turning he caught sight of Titus, Furius and the company standard bearer, striding into the middle of the training area.

'Squad against squad, form up, form up,' an instructor yelled.

Along the line, the legionaries, in their white, sweat-stained, tunics, hastily started to cluster around their leaders. Fergus lowered his sword and shield, as Aledus, Catinius Vittius and the others quickly assembled around him.

'First squad versus second, third versus fourth, fifth versus seventh,' the weapon's instructor yelled as he strode across the sand, 'sixth versus eighth, ninth versus tenth, form up, single line of eight.'

Fergus frowned and quickly glanced in the Centurion's direction. His squad had been pitted against Fronto and his men. If the traditional training order had been followed that should not have happened. What was Titus up to?

'You heard,' Fergus snapped turning to his men, 'form a line of eight and boys, I am not going to lose this one, not against Fronto, not with Titus watching, so put your backs into it.'

Hastily his squad arranged themselves into a line, as opposite them, their opponents did the same. Across the six paces that separated the two squads, Fergus caught Fronto glaring at him with a calculating, contemptuous look. Fergus hissed as he glared back at his rival. Since the incident on the march to the Rhine, it had been commonly agreed amongst the men of the company that Fergus and Fronto had emerged as the front runners to claim the position of Tesserarius, third in command of the company. The company seemed to be split in their loyalties on this issue and Titus, the company Centurion had remained tight-lipped about who would get promoted.

'Drop your training swords,' an instructor yelled. 'The engagement will be fought with standard issue equipment.'

Obediently Fergus and the others threw their heavy, wooden, training-swords down onto the sand and stood waiting for the instructor to come up to them and hand them the legionary's short stabbing sword, the Gladius. As he took his sword, Fergus stared at the leather disc that covered the sharp point and which was meant to prevent any serious injuries during the mock battle.

'We're going to beat the shit out of you,' Fronto cried out glaring at Fergus with a contemptuous look.

Fergus did not reply as he crouched and brought his wicker shield up in front of him. Then he glanced at his comrades. The men seemed ready.

'Attack,' the instructor shouted.

With a wild yell Fronto's squad surged forwards. Fergus braced himself as the man opposite him came crashing into his shield, the weight of his charge pushing Fergus backwards. The legionary was thrusting with his sword, trying to find an opening around Fergus's shield. Grimly Fergus parried the man's thrusts and blows and then seeing his chance he swiftly struck a low blow, slicing at the man's exposed leg. His opponent screamed in pain and staggered backwards as a red line of blood instantly welled up across his leg. Fergus cried out to Tiber, the new recruit beside him and quickly stepped into the gap that had opened up in Fronto's squad line. Along the line, the legionaries of each squad were pushing and jabbing at each other in a furious, snarling fight. Fergus had barely made it into Fronto's line when a figure launched himself at him with terrifying strength and speed. The impact knocked Fergus's shield from his hand and as he crashed onto his back in the sand he lost his sword as well. In horror Fergus saw Fronto lying on top of him. His rival too had lost his shield and sword but his hands were groping for Fergus's throat. Fronto was snarling and whining like a starving, wild animal. With a startled cry, Fergus rammed his elbow into Fronto's face, eliciting a howl of pain. But the man did not loosen his grip. A moment later Fergus groaned as Fronto punched him in the face. His rival was terrifyingly strong and for an instant Fergus was back in the Lucky Legionary Tavern at Deva on the night that Fronto, in a drunken fit, had tried to murder him. With a howl Fergus shifted his weight and rolled over, flinging Fronto onto his back and, as he felt the blood streaming from his nose, he launched a flurry of punches at his rival. But Fronto seemed to be made of stone and for every blow that Fergus landed, he received one in return. Then with blood pouring from a multiple of cuts to his face and impeding his eyesight, strong hands were suddenly dragging the two of them apart.

'Enough, enough,' Titus roared in a furious voice. 'This is supposed to be a training exercise. Not an excuse to settle personal rivalries. You are a disgrace, both of you! This is not what I expect from my NCO's.'

Bleary eyed and with a heaving chest, Fergus sat in the sand and glared bitterly at Fronto as he wiped the blood from his nose. His rival's face was as bruised and bloodied as his own but the raw, vicious, hatred on Fronto's face was unmistakable. Around them, the two squads had stopped fighting and were silently and sheepishly staring at their battered leaders sitting in the sand.

'Fergus,' the Centurion shouted. 'Get yourself cleaned up and report to my quarters. The rest of you get back to attacking those posts. And if this happens again, I will have all of you on half pay. Move, move, move!'

***

Fergus stood waiting in the hall to Titus's quarters. He'd washed himself and stopped the bleeding but his face was still a mess of cuts and angry bruises. One of the Centurion's slaves stood motionless by the door staring into space. It wasn't really Titus's quarters Fergus thought sullenly. The Centurion, like the rest of them had been billeted in the barracks that was normally the home to the auxiliary cohorts attached to the First Legion Minervia. They were just here temporarily. The rumour going around the camp was that a battlegroup consisting of the bulk of the First Legion and the thousand man vexillatio of the Twentieth would soon be marching south towards the seat of the Dacian war on the Danube. Wearily Fergus looked down at his army boots as he waited. Crossing the sea from Britannia to Gaul had been an experience that not all had enjoyed, with most of the men being terrified of the open sea and sea sick to boot. The sailors had laughed at them. And as he and his comrades had finally come ashore, Fergus had realised that he'd never before been outside of the province of Britannia. In northern Gaul he'd been able to understand the local Gaul's who had come to the side of the Roman road to sell their goods to the marching column. But here, in lower Germania, right up against the Rhine, the locals were different; fiercer, taller and more primitive and he and his comrades hadn't understood a word of their harsh guttural Germanic language. But inside the army camp he and his men had instantly felt at home, for the layout and routine of the stone fortress was the same as their home base at Deva Victrix.

The slave beside the door was still staring into space. Fergus cleared his throat. Kyna, his mother and the rest of his family on Vectis had been overjoyed to see him but he'd not been able to do anything for them in the short leave allotted to him. And now he worried about them for his family were in trouble. Their ownership of the farm was in doubt, but stuck here on the Rhine there was nothing he could do about that now except pray to the gods for help, which he'd done every night since he'd left the farm. And there had still been no news from his father. It was likely that Marcus was not going to return from his ocean voyage. It was likely, he, Fergus had become the head of his family without realising it. Tensely and nervously, Fergus fiddled with the small circular Celtic amulet around his neck, that Galena, his wife had given him. Maybe he should be at home with his wife preparing for the birth of his child. Maybe he should be on the farm on Vectis defending his property. Maybe he shouldn't be here on this distant frontier. Irritably Fergus muttered something under his breath. Stop being such a woman he told himself. This was the life he'd chosen to lead. This was Corbulo's life and this was what he had dreamed about doing when he was still a boy. His whole family, four generations, had been soldiers and he would be no different. It was an honest, honourable way of life, even though sometimes he wished he was somewhere else.

Behind him the door to the barrack's block opened and Furius, acting Optio and second in command of the company, strode into the hall. The young officer was clad in a short-sleeved, white tunic similar to that worn by Fergus. He raised his eyebrows and sighed as he caught sight of Fergus.

'Ah it's you,' Furius said lightly with a hint of a smile. 'In trouble again? As I recall you and your squad are always getting into trouble.' Furius paused to stare at Fergus and for a moment it seemed as if he was trying not to burst out laughing. 'Now let's see,' Furius continued, 'when I was still your Decanus there was that incident with the Brigantian prisoner who you killed. Then in Deva last year you were chased down the street by Fronto, which resulted in Aledus having the shit kicked out of him and spending weeks in hospital recovering and then there was that brawl in the Lucky Legionary Tavern. Titus must be getting sick of you.'

'You know full well *why* Aledus and I were chased across Deva that day,' Fergus said quietly, as he kept his eyes on the floor.

'I do,' Furius replied cheerfully. 'It was one of the best days of my life. And when Lucullus our Optio was wounded, that was another.'

'What about the incident between me and Fronto on the march across Gaul,' Fergus said raising his chin with a hint of defiance. 'You forgot to mention that fight. But it was not my fault, just like today was not my fault. He struck me. He was the first to take a swing at me. I didn't provoke him.'

'Fronto is a prick,' Furius said with a nod. 'Everyone knows that. But your problem Fergus is that you allow him to bait you. He is doing it on purpose and you always bite and every time you do so, you piss Titus off. My advice,' Furius said slapping Fergus cheerfully on his shoulder, 'is to ignore him even if he shits on your food.'

'That's easy for you to say,' Fergus muttered under his breath as Furius disappeared down the narrow corridor.

Then the door to the Centurion's quarters suddenly opened and Titus was bellowing for Fergus to enter. Quickly Fergus strode into the middle of the room, saluted smartly and stood stiffly to attention as the Centurion's second slave, swiftly and silently exited the room closing the door behind him. Titus was sitting in a chair behind a desk, frowning as he read something written down on a wooden tablet. He didn't look up as Fergus entered. Standing in a corner Fergus suddenly became aware of a second man, clad in a fine, white toga. The man was tall, elegant and in his thirties and he had his hands clasped behind his back. He was studying Fergus with a curious, interested look on his handsome face. Whoever the stranger was, Fergus thought, he was a senior ranking officer, of that he was sure. No one else could look that cool and confident in Titus's presence. 'Sir,' Fergus said clearing his throat. 'You wished to see me.'

'Yes,' Titus growled laying the wooden tablet on the desk and fixing Fergus with a resigned, weary look. 'We have only just arrived here on the Rhine and already it seems that you are causing quite a stir, Fergus.'

'Yes Sir,' Fergus said staring straight ahead into space.

Awkwardly Titus placed the tips of his fingers together and then glanced quickly at the stranger and, for the minutest moment, Fergus thought he saw resentment in the Centurion's gaze.

'This is not about your disgraceful conduct on the training field today,' Titus said sharply turning to Fergus. 'This is something else. Something that I have only just been made aware of this morning and I must admit it comes as a bit of a surprise.'

Fergus said nothing as he stared straight ahead.

Titus sighed and rubbed his forehead as he looked down at the desk.

'An allegation has been made against you Fergus,' he said at last. 'An allegation from an anonymous source within the company. The allegation is that you are not actually a Roman citizen, that you had someone pretend to be your father and write a letter of recommendation to us upon your enlistment and that you are therefore not legally entitled to be a member of the Twentieth Legion.'

Fergus cheeks flushed but he did not move an inch.

'This man over there,' Titus said gesturing at the tall handsome stranger, 'is a lawyer attached to the First Legion, our hosts. He is here to investigate the allegation and see if it contains any merit.' Titus sighed. 'You understand Fergus, these sorts of allegations are extremely serious and I have a duty to report them to my superiors. The army must conduct a full investigation. It's the law. And I must warn you, that if you are found guilty, you could be kicked out of the Legion and given a dishonourable discharge. Do you understand how serious this is?'

'It is not true Sir,' Fergus said in a tight voice. 'I am a citizen.'

'That's not what your accuser claims,' the lawyer suddenly interrupted as he took a step towards Fergus. 'He says that your father was an auxiliary cavalryman in one of the Batavian cohorts and, that when you enlisted your father was not a Roman citizen, meaning that you aren't either. He says you got one of your grandfather's comrades, a veteran named Quintus to claim that he was your father and write your letter of recommendation.'

Fergus shook his head. 'I am a citizen,' he muttered and as he spoke he was suddenly aware of Titus watching him closely. This was Fronto's work, Fergus thought angrily. These allegations had his name written all over it, but how had his rival managed to come by this information? Only a few men had seen Quintus's letter of recommendation and even fewer knew the truth and those men, his three closest friends and Galena would not have said a word to anyone, of that he was sure. So how had Fronto stumbled upon the truth?

For a moment, the room fell silent. Then the Centurion stirred and glanced at the lawyer. 'Fergus is one of my best NCO's,' he exclaimed. 'I understand that you must investigate these allegations but as you can see we are a vexillatio of the Twentieth Legion and all our administrative records are at our home base at Deva, several hundred miles away. It will be impossible to check the records especially as we are to march south to Dacia within the coming days. I need this man in my company, I need him with me when we go. It would be absurd to leave him behind pending the investigation into these allegations.'

'And yet I must investigate,' the lawyer said with a shrug. 'As you said, it is the law.'

Titus growled in frustration.

'So what do you recommend we do,' he snapped glaring at the lawyer. 'My man here has denied the charges.'

The lawyer glanced at Fergus and thought for a moment.

'Well the allegations cannot be ignored,' the lawyer said smoothly. 'But if your man can produce witnesses, independent and unaffiliated to him, who are happy to testify that he is indeed a citizen, then this will help his cause. And there is something else,' the lawyer said carefully. 'But for me to explain that to your man, I do need to be alone with him.'

Titus grunted and looked down at his desk. Then with a weary sigh, he rose to his feet and strode towards the door, closing it behind him. Slowly Fergus turned to look at the tall lawyer as the man approached. There was something not quite right about the way the man was looking at him. The lawyer came to a halt close to Fergus, too close for Fergus's comfort.

'Do you want to know the name of your accuser?' the lawyer said in a smooth silky voice.

'Maybe,' Fergus muttered coolly standing his ground but inside his thoughts were in turmoil. What was going on? Had the lawyer just offered to name his anonymous source? And why was he standing so close.

'If you do, I will want a favour in return,' the lawyer replied.

Fergus suddenly felt uncomfortable. The conversation was getting weird.

'Some men like women, but I don't,' the lawyer suddenly hissed. 'So here is the deal, I give you a name and I drop the charges against you in return for favours, sexual favours, I think you know what I mean.'

Fergus stared stonily ahead, trying to control himself. Striking a superior officer was a major offence and would land him in very serious trouble. But at that very moment he wanted to do nothing more than smack this pervert straight in the face.

'I think I will pass,' Fergus growled instead. Then in a louder voice. 'Will that be all Sir?'

'Suit yourself,' the lawyer hissed turning away abruptly. 'But this matter is not closed. And good luck in finding those independent witnesses,' the officer snapped. 'Your accuser is confident that no one in your company is going to come forwards to support you. The allegations will stay on your record until the matter is closed.'

***

It was getting dark when Fergus approached the sober stone barracks block in which he and his squad were billeted. As he was about to enter the small, two room quarters he was met at the doorway by Aledus and Vittius. His mess mates were looking worried and agitated and their expressions instantly alarmed Fergus.

'What's going on? What's happened?' Fergus blurted out.

'Trouble,' Aledus said in a tense voice. 'One of the new recruits, Tiber. He has vanished. He should have been here for his evening meal but we haven't seen him. He has been gone for hours.'

'What," Fergus growled.

'We think he may have deserted,' Vittius muttered. 'He's taken all his personal belongings and he left us note.'

'A note,' Fergus exclaimed in disbelief.

'He says he is sorry, that's all,' Aledus said shaking his head.

Fergus was staring at his two friends in horror. Then he turned to look away into the gathering darkness.

'Shit,' Fergus muttered.

Chapter Seventeen – The Deserter

'So what are we going to do?' Aledus muttered looking at Fergus.

Fergus and the rest of his squad stood around the doorway to their barrack's block. It was growing dark and in the sky, the first twinkling stars had already appeared. Upon the walls of the legionary fortress the guard was being changed and the cries of the watch commanders rang out across the vast camp. Slowly Fergus tore up Tiber's note, written on a scrap of papyrus, and let the fragments drift to the ground. Then he shook his head in dismay.

'Why would Tiber desert?' he snapped. 'He knows the penalty for that. He didn't seem unhappy. It doesn't make sense.'

'None of us saw this coming Fergus,' Catinius replied. 'And who knows what his reasons are, but he's gone and that's all that matters.'

'He hasn't been gone for long," Vittius growled, grinding his boot into the sand. A few hours at the most I reckon, and he can't have much money. Our salaries are held by the standard bearer and I know for a fact that Tiber, because he is a brand new recruit, has never been paid. He didn't have any savings either. He's not a wealthy man. So, if Tiber is planning on heading home to Britannia, he won't get very far, not without much money. He will have to beg for food and transport. The stupid fool. What was he thinking?'

Fergus nodded and glanced thoughtfully at Vittius.

'Titus will have him executed if he's found,' Fergus said quietly. 'You know the punishment and you know the Centurion's attitude. Titus will show no clemency for deserters. He will have no pity. Tiber's fate is sealed, if he's not present at tomorrow morning's roll call.' Fergus's face darkened. 'And boys, Titus may well decide to punish all of us if he suspects that we knew something and did not report it, or try to stop it from happening. We're all going to get shit for this.' Grimly Fergus turned to look around at the anxious faces of his men. 'So there is just one thing for it, we need to find Tiber and bring him back before anyone notices that he is missing.'

'Decimation?' Catinius exclaimed in horror. 'Titus wouldn't do that, surely? How could we have stopped Tiber from deserting if we didn't know about his plans?'

'He won't care,' Fergus said harshly. 'His main concern is maintaining discipline, especially as we are about to march off to war. He may punish us all just as an example to the others.'

'Fergus is right,' Aledus interrupted. 'We have no choice. Tiber may be acting like a fool but he is still part of the squad, one of us, and so we need to find him before the dawn roll call.'

Around Fergus the others nodded in silent agreement.

'But how?' Catinius blurted out glaring at the men around him. 'Have you forgotten. There is a curfew in place. None of us are allowed to leave the camp. You all heard the announcement. The Germans are celebrating a religious festival in the civilian town tonight. No Roman soldier is to leave the fortress. Those are the orders. How can we look for him if we are not allowed out?'

Fergus turned to glance at the stone walls of the legionary fortress.

'We have no choice,' he muttered. 'We'll have to risk it and we don't have much time.' Fergus turned to his men in a conspiratorial manner. 'Aledus and I will go over the wall and search for Tiber in the town,' he said quietly. 'Maybe he is holed up in one of the taverns or whorehouses or maybe he is down in the river harbour, trying to sneak aboard one of the ships.

Catinius and Vittius, you will search the camp. Check the baths, the stables, the gambling and drinking den's and anywhere else you can think of. The rest of you will remain here in case Tiber returns on his own accord.'

'How will you get over the wall without being seen?' Catinius said unhappily.

'There is a section of the wall, facing the river,' Aledus replied quickly, his eyes shining with sudden excitement. 'The guards on this part of the wall are not very attentive. They are lazy and don't always walk the full length of the wall. If we had a sturdy rope, with the darkness to protect us, we could be up and over the wall without anyone seeing us.'

'And how will you get back inside,' Catinius snapped. 'And what happens if you are spotted in town or if Tiber has already left Bonna?'

'Oh you do always have to bring up all the negatives, don't you,' Aledus snapped in irritation as he rounded on Catinius.

Catinius was about to retort when Fergus grasped him by the shoulder.

'We'll climb back up over the wall and we won't be spotted,' Fergus said sharply. 'And if Tiber has already left Bonna, well then there is nothing more we can do. It will be too late and he'll be gone and that will be that. But we need to make sure. There is a possibility he hasn't gone far.'

'I have a rope,' Vittius exclaimed helpfully.

***

In the darkness, the patter of the rain was loud and constant and for once Fergus was grateful for the weather. He crouched on the stone rampart peering into the gloom. The guards on this section of the wall seemed to have taken shelter near the watch tower and all seemed peaceful and quiet apart from the occasional drunken, cry coming from the civilian settlement to the south, the rain and the blast of a hunting horn. Wiping away the rainwater that plastered his face, Fergus turned to stare at the silver-coloured Rhine which was just visible in the pale moonlight, two hundred yards away. It was the first time he'd had a proper look at the Rhine. The mighty river was placid and wide and he could not see the eastern bank. So, this was where the Empire ended he thought, this was the frontier. Beyond lived the unconquered free German tribes in their endless forests and marshes that were said to stretch to the very edge of the world. The few men from the First Legion with whom he'd spoken, had described the eastern bank as an unfriendly place full of stinking Germans who refused to wash and who one could never fully trust. They were best left alone to sulk in their hovels in the ground the legionaries of the First had added.

'Ready,' Aledus whispered, as he gave the rope, which he'd tied to the battlements, a sharp tug. Then before Fergus could say anything Aledus clambered over the side of the wall and quickly vanished into the darkness. Fergus turned to look in the direction of the watchtower as he waited. But there was no alarm. The sentries had not seen them. With a grunt, he grasped hold of the rope, slithered over the side and began to lower himself to the ground. The rope creaked and groaned under his weight but it held. As he reached the bottom, he slipped and slid awkwardly down into the deep muddy V shaped ditch, ending up on his back in a puddle of dirty water. Cursing softly Fergus picked himself up and on all fours clambered out of the ditch. Nearby Aledus was crouching in the gloom, staring out across the marshy, reed-infested ground that separated the legionary fortress from the river.

'So what now?' Aledus whispered.

'We'll start with the taverns and whorehouses,' Fergus said softly. 'And if he isn't there we will check the harbour. Come on, let's go.'

As Fergus and Aledus approached the outskirts of Bonna, the settlement which lay just to the south of Castra Bonnensis, the dark German long-houses made of oak and roofed with straw, hove into view in the pale moonlight, clustered around the main Roman road in an unplanned, chaotic fashion. Revellers were everywhere, staggering about in drunken stupor, pissing beside the road, singing, vomiting, wrestling with each other or lying comatose in the mud. From the barbarian huts Fergus could hear the noise of feasting, screams, laughter, barking dogs and excited cries. The Germans were loud, brash and pissed and Fergus suddenly understood why the authorities had imposed a curfew on the Roman soldiers.

'They sure like a party,' Aledus muttered quietly, as the two of them moved on down the road and passed the drunken and rowdy town's folk.

'The local farmers must have come into town from the countryside to celebrate the festival of their gods. Be on your guard,' Fergus replied warily.

The centre of Bonna was built up around the main Roman road that followed the Rhine southwards to the legionary fortress at Castra Mogontiacum, Mainz, a hundred miles away. As he caught sight of the familiar looking Roman terraced, stone, houses, with their smart, red-roof tiles, Fergus heaved a sigh of relief. The narrow, but long Roman strip-houses flanked the main street, their shops and workshops shut and locked up for the night, but even here the Germans swarmed across the street, leaning out of doorways, shouting, drinking and singing whilst others, clutching flasks of beer and wine, appeared out of the side streets that petered off into the darkness. The language of the locals was harsh and guttural. Marcus would have been familiar with the language from serving in his Batavian Cohort,

Fergus thought, but he himself couldn't understand a word of what was being said.

'What did Titus want with you today?' Aledus hissed as the two of them headed on deeper into the town.

'There have been allegations made against me,' Fergus muttered as he strode along keeping a wary eye on the people around them. 'Someone in the company is saying that I am not a Roman citizen and that I faked by letter of recommendation. It's Fronto,' Fergus growled sourly. 'I am sure that he is behind this. Titus has been forced to report the matter up the chain of command and now this lawyer has got involved.'

'No, shit,' Aledus murmured in horror. 'How did Fronto find out? How is it possible he could know about that?'

'Yes, that's a good question,' Fergus snapped, turning sharply to look at Aledus, 'Only you, Catinius, Vittius and Galena know the truth.'

'I have not said a word to anyone,' Aledus protested as his cheeks turned red. 'I swear it Fergus, on my cock and my honour.'

'Alright, I believe you," Fergus said. Then slowly he shook his head. "Do you believe that this lawyer tried to get me to perform sexual favours in return for dropping the investigation?'

'That's illegal,' Aledus growled in disgust. 'You could report him for that. The army doesn't tolerate that kind of behaviour.'

'He's a senior officer,' Fergus replied wearily. 'If I accuse an officer like him of such behaviour, it is going to bring a whole shed load of shit on top of me. You know what I am talking about. No, maybe it's better to just let it go unreported. I have enough problems to deal with right now.'

'Alright, let's start with that tavern over there,' Aledus said turning to point at a two storey stone building with a gaily painted sign hanging above the doorway. "I always wanted to go there. The boys from the First Legion say that they only employ virgins.'

***

It was already deep into the night, when Fergus and Aledus emerged from the tavern and turned to stare forlornly down the street. The drinking place had been the fifth one they'd searched and once again they had come up empty handed. No one had seen Tiber and no one knew where he could be hiding. Several hours of searching had produced absolutely nothing and Fergus was tired, irritated and hungry. The Germans too had not been particularly happy to see them and they had found few people who had been able, sober and willing to speak to them in Latin.

'Where next?' Aledus growled in a dejection voice.

'I think there is another place down near the river, which we could try,' Fergus said as he started to cross the road and head down a side street.

Wearily and silently the two of them trudged on down the street and into the darkness towards the Rhine, trying to avoid the vomit, piss and rowdy, celebrating Germans. The tavern, when they finally spotted it, was nestling alone, close to the edge of the river, away from the other buildings and the four, silent and dark Roman galleys that lay at anchor along the river bank. The reddish glow from a fire was just about visible through the cracks in the doorway and walls. The wooden and thatched German style long-house had been raised up onto a large, wooden platform by a series of thick, sturdy wooden-posts and a short, timber ladder led from the ground up onto the platform. And out beyond the building, the placid and silver waters of the Rhine flowed silently onwards on their long journey to the sea.

'Why did they do that?' Aledus said with a yawn as he gazed at the house.

'Probably to protect themselves from flooding,' Fergus muttered. 'Isn't it obvious?'

Aledus did not reply and tactfully let the remark go. Bad temperedly, Fergus clambered up the ladder and onto the platform and taking a quick, last look around, he opened the door and stepped into the long house. He was greeted by a blast of heat. In the middle of the long rectangular room, over the hearth, a piglet was roasting upon beautifully forged iron, fire-dogs. Drips of fat hissed and exploding in the flames and the rich, juicy smell of pork filled the room. A small group of men had turned to stare silently at Fergus, and against the far wall two stark-naked women were reclining on wooden chairs. Coolly the women stared at Fergus and Aledus, but made no effort to cover themselves up. Without a word Fergus turned and made his way towards a fat man, standing behind a makeshift bar. In the dim, reddish light, the barman's forehead glistened with sweat.

'I am looking for one of my men, a Roman soldier,' Fergus said slowly in Latin. 'His name is Tiber. He has a white scar on his right forearm. He's eighteen, black haired and about my height. Have you seen him?'

The fat man quickly glanced past Fergus at the group of men beside the doorway. Then he frowned and shrugged and rattled off a reply in his guttural Germanic language. Fergus sighed wearily and idly turned to glance at the naked women.

'Does no one in this shit hole speak Latin,' Fergus muttered. At his side, Aledus was staring at the naked girls.

'It's been a while,' Aledus replied in a distracted voice. 'Maybe we should ask those two beauties over there if they have seen Tiber?'

In reply one of the women raised her eyebrows, slowly rose to her feet and came towards Aledus. Running her fingers lightly across his chest she said something in her Germanic language which drew a laugh from her companion. Aledus grinned stupidly as he touched her bright, blond hair and then carefully reached out to cup one of her breasts with his hand.

'Maybe the search for Tiber can wait for a while,' Aledus muttered.

'We're not here for that,' Fergus snapped irritably. 'We don't have any time. Come on, what's the German word for deserter?' 'I haven't got a clue,' Aledus replied as he smiled at the girl. 'The only words that I know are fuck, pussy and how much,' and as he said the words, the girl burst out laughing and stepped away.

Suddenly Fergus sensed movement behind him, and heard the wooden floor creak. Turning around he saw that the four men who'd been sitting beside the door were all on their feet and barring the way out. Fergus's face darkened. The Germans blocking the way had folded their arms across their chests and were staring at him with sullen, unfriendly eyes. They were pale-faced, big brawny-looking men, at least a head taller than Fergus and Aledus and their long, wild, blond-hair fell to their shoulders. And to Fergus's surprise they all appeared to be stone cold sober.

'Now look what have you done,' Fergus hissed at Aledus.

One of the men took a step towards Fergus and snapped something in his harsh sounding language. Fergus frowned and shook his head, indicating that he had not understood and the man repeated himself, louder this time.

'What?' Fergus growled. 'I don't speak your language. I am here to find one of my men, a boy called Tiber.'

Again the German spat something in his own language and this time he gestured at the naked women, who'd retreated to their chairs and were watching the confrontation with amused, excited looks.

'Look,' Aledus snapped taking a step towards the German. 'We don't speak your language, don't you get it you Barbarian arsehole, so stop jabbering away and speak some proper Roman Latin.'

'He says that you fuck girl, so now you must pay for her service,' a voice behind them said suddenly in thickly accented Latin.

Both Fergus and Aledus whirled around and gazed in surprise at the man who'd spoken. Fergus swore under his breath. Tiredness was playing with his judgment for he had not noticed the man sitting quietly on his own in the shadows.

'What do you mean?' Fergus blurted out.

'He says you fuck girl, now you must pay,' the man shrugged. 'They will not let you leave until you have paid.'

Fergus's eyes narrowed and his hand dropped to rest on the pommel of his sword strapped to his belt. The man who'd spoken in Latin looked around forty. He was clad in an expensive-looking, black, sheepskin tunic, Roman army sandals and his fingers were adorned with beautiful and colourful amber rings that glinted and gleamed in the firelight. There was a crafty, intelligent gleam in his eyes as he studied Fergus with a faint, amused smile.

'What are you talking about,' Aledus hissed. 'I never fucked her. I just touched her, that's all. You saw what I did. We only just walked in.'

And as he spoke Aledus grew increasingly angry. 'Is this how you treat the men who protect your homes? What is this bullshit? You are not getting a single, copper coin. Not a single coin.'

Behind Fergus the Germans blocking the way broke into bad tempered muttering.

'Still they say you must pay,' the man with the amber rings on his fingers replied.

Aledus opened his mouth to reply but Fergus silenced him by quickly raising his hand.

'How come you speak Latin?' Fergus growled staring at the German.

'It's a long story and I don't think your friends over there have the patience,' the man replied. 'I would advise you to pay.'

'Or else what?' Aledus snapped jutting out his chin.

'Or else they will drown you in the river and let the fish feast on your corpses,' the man replied sharply. 'Like I said, I advise you to pay.'

Fergus paused for a moment as beside him Aledus growled in frustration.

'How much?' Fergus said suddenly.

The man with the amber rings turned to the Germans at the door and said something quickly in their rough harsh language and in return one of the tall giants spat out a word.

'Two denarii,' the man said turning to Fergus.

'We will give you one Denarii,' Fergus said quietly staring at the older man. 'In exchange you and your friends will tell us if you have seen one of my men, a Roman soldier by the name of

Tiber. He has gone missing. I have come to take him back to his barracks before his absence is noticed. And that is the best deal that you and you your friends are going to get.'

For a moment, the room remained silent except for the hissing and spitting meat that was roasting over the fire. Across the floor, the older man was staring at Fergus. Then slowly his lips curled into a broad grin.

'They are not my friends,' the man said in a changed voice. 'My name is Adalwolf and I am an amber merchant and you shouldn't be here.'

Adalwolf's eyes gleamed with sudden interest. "Do you know that Lord Hadrian, Legate of the First Legion has ordered that all Roman soldiers be confined to their barracks until our religious feast is over. There is a curfew and you have broken it by coming here. I could report you for that. I am good friends with the Legate.'

'You,' Aledus sneered, 'you know Hadrian, the Legate of the First Legion? I don't think so.'

'Shut your man up,' Adalwolf said calmly looking at Fergus. 'He and his big arrogant mouth are getting on my nerves. But I do know Hadrian and he is a good friend. I serve him as a guide, advisor and translator. No one knows Germania Magna and its people better than I.'

'Do we have a deal or not?' Fergus snapped.

Adalwolf gazed at Fergus in silence for a moment. Then he rapped out a sharp word to the men clustered around the door and stretched out his hand towards Fergus with the palm open.

'It's done,' Adalwolf replied. 'They have agreed. Now show me your money.'

'What have you got?' Fergus muttered turning quickly to Aledus. Irritably Aledus fished around in his pockets and then sullenly handed Fergus a couple of coins. Fergus grunted, looked up at Adalwolf, showed him the money but instead of handing it over he closed his hand.

'So one of your men has deserted,' Adalwolf said with a patient smile, 'and you have come here, broken the curfew, to find him and take him back. That is quite a risk you have taken. I know the punishment for desertion. This soldier must mean a lot to you. I am impressed. You have courage.'

'I don't leave my men behind,' Fergus growled. 'We are a unit. We look out for each other. We trust each other. Now do you know anything about Tiber or am I wasting my time here?"

Adalwolf sighed and glanced at the two naked women.

'Your man is hiding out near the Roman ships, down by the water front,' he said turning to look at the floor. 'He is hoping to get aboard one of the galleys. He has been there for a few hours now.'

Fergus stared at Adalwolf, trying to read his mind, but the German merchant looked like he was telling the truth.

'Thank you,' Fergus replied at last as he flipped the coins at Adalwolf. 'We will be going now.'

Smoothly catching the coins in his hand, Adalwolf turned and nodded at the men standing beside the door.

'One more thing,' the amber merchant called out in his accented Latin, 'tell me your name and unit, Roman?'

Fergus hesitated.

'What do you what to know that for,' Aledus hissed. 'Do you think we are going to give you our names so that you can report us to Hadrian?'

'I am just curious,' Adalwolf replied with a twinkle in his eye. 'Let's say that your loyalty to your comrade has impressed me.'

'You can tell the Legate Hadrian that my name is Fergus,' Fergus snapped as he pushed his way towards the door. 'And that you have had the pleasure of doing business with the Second Company of the Second Cohort of the Twentieth Legion. The same company that will come back here and burn this place to the ground if I find that you have been lying to me.'

***

'Now why did you have to tell that prick our names,' Aledus growled as he and Fergus stomped off into the darkness towards where the Roman galleys lay drawn up along the river-bank.

'Don't be daft. He's not going to report us,' Fergus snapped in reply. 'Did you not hear what he said? Did you not see how easily he convinced those Germans to let us pass? That man has some power and influence. I bet he was telling us the truth. He's a merchant, he's interested in profit. Why would he report us, what possible advantage would that give him? If he is indeed a friend of the Legate, then he won't be interested in wasting his time on common soldiers like us. And anyway we will just deny everything.'

'But you still didn't have to take the risk. It was still foolish to give him your name,' Aledus hissed in an annoyed voice. 'And you owe me one Denarius.'

'I wanted to show him that I was not afraid of him,' Fergus said sharply, "I don't like to be threatened. Alright, so there it is, now shut up and keep your eyes open. Dawn is not far away. We don't have much time.'

Aledus muttered something under his breath and turned to glare into the darkness. Close by the river, water was gently lapping up against the low, muddy bank and in the distance a hunting horn blasted away.

'The boys from the First are none too happy with Hadrian,' Aledus muttered sulkily as the two of them approached the small, river harbour. 'They told me that Hadrian has only recently been appointed as their Legate and that he is a second rate commander. Before he was made Legate he was part of the Emperor's retinue. Apparently he was an up and coming man, until he fell out favour with the Emperor. The boys from the First think he has been posted to Bonna as punishment by Trajan but no one knows why. That's the rumour anyway.'

'That's fascinating,' Fergus growled tiredly. 'Now keep your eyes open for Tiber. I am sick of tramping around all night looking for that miserable fuck.'

Before them the outlines of the Roman galleys suddenly loomed up out of the darkness. The four galleys with single masts and small deck houses, gently rose and sank in the swell of the river current and the thick, mooring ropes creaked and groaned. On board, the sails had been furled and the oar holes in the sides of the vessels were empty. Fergus paused and turned to look around him. In the pale moon light, the Rhine stretched away into the gloom. It was easily the largest and widest river he'd ever seen. The shore of the river around him looked deserted and apart from the creaking ships and the lapping water he could hear nothing.

'Tiber,' he hissed loudly. 'Tiber, where are you. It's us, Fergus and Aledus.'

From the darkness, there was no answer.

'Tiber, you prick,' Aledus called out softly. 'We have been looking for you all night. Now come out and show yourself. We're your mates.'

Again the night remained silent. Fergus sighed and cast about in the darkness.

'Tiber,' he called out. 'We're here to take you back to the barracks. Whatever issues you have, deserting is not going to solve them. Titus is going to punish all of us if you are not present at roll call at dawn. Come on back with us. No one has noticed your absence yet. All of this can still be forgotten. We're your mates. We wouldn't be out here if we weren't worried about you.'

Suddenly Fergus heard movement from near the water's edge. Then in the moonlight a figure appeared.

'I am here, Fergus,' a sour and sullen voice muttered.

And a moment later Tiber appeared from out of the gloom looking dishevelled and glum.

Fergus sighed in relief as he caught sight of him. Then with an annoyed grunt he reached out with his hand and firmly grasped hold of the young man's chin and vigorously shook Tiber's head. 'Don't you ever fucking do this again,' Fergus hissed angrily. 'You have no idea of how much shit the rest of us have had to endure because of you. I am not going to report this, but do it again and I won't be so lenient, got that?'

In the gloom Tiber nodded glumly.

'What's the matter with you,' Aledus said in a concerned voice as he grasped hold of Tiber's shoulder. 'What got into to your head to make you do something stupid like this?'

'I was homesick,' Tiber muttered.

***

The company stood in perfect formation in front of their barracks. The ten rows of eight legionaries were clad in their short-sleeved, white tunics and were staring straight ahead into space, their straight arms held stiffly against their sides. It was early morning and Titus, clad in full armour and wearing his red-plumed helmet and backed up by the signifer holding up the company standard, stood in front of his company glaring at his men as Furius silently and efficiently went down the ranks checking that all were present and correct. As the Optio came down the ranks he paused in front of Aledus and frowned.

'Looking a bit tired today,' Furius exclaimed suspiciously, as he inspected Aledus from top to toe. 'What was it this time? Drinking or gambling?"

Fergus turned his head ever so slightly and glanced down the squad line. They were all there, including Tiber who was staring stoically into space. Their mess mate's absence seemed to have gone unnoticed and the whole squad had been mightily relieved when, just before dawn, Fergus had finally slipped him back into their barracks. Aledus however looked exhausted and was struggling to keep his eyes open.

'Couldn't sleep Sir,' Aledus replied with an effort. 'Afraid of the dark Sir.'

'Afraid of the dark," Furius repeated as his face darkened. He shook his head in disgust. 'You should be afraid of me boy if I catch you sleeping whilst on parade.' And with that Furius continued on down the line. When he had finally completed the inspection the Optio strode up to Titus and saluted smartly.

'Company all present and correct Sir,' Furius cried out in a loud voice.

The Centurion acknowledged his Optio and raised his vine staff in the air.

'Today we shall practice what we have been practising all week,' Titus bellowed. 'We will start with a run of two laps around the fortress walls. This will be followed by physical exercises and a talk from a doctor on how best to treat wounds and infections. Pay attention to what this surgeon has to say. We are marching to war and his advice may save your life. In the afternoon, there will be weapons drill and training, individual, pairs, squad versus squad and at the end of the day we shall engage with the First company, in a company versus company mock battle which I do not want to lose.'

Titus paused and looked around at his men. "Now I am sure that you will all be glad to hear that tomorrow at dawn we and our colleagues from the First Legion will be leaving this fortress and will be starting on our march southwards to the Dacian frontier. It's going to be a long journey, several weeks at least, so make sure that all your kit is in good working order by dawn tomorrow. So, because this is our last night at Castra Bonnensis, our battlegroup commander and Legate of the First Legion, Hadrian, has decided to give you all the evening to yourselves. The curfew has been lifted until the second hour after dark and you are free to spend your money in town and say goodbye to your favourite whores.' Titus paused and glared at his men and Fergus tried desperately to stifle a yawn. 'Rome conquers all,' the Centurion cried out.

As the company fell out and the men began to trudge towards the southern gate of the vast legionary base in preparation for their morning run, Furius however caught Fergus by the arm and pulled him aside. The Optio and second in command looked serious.

'Titus wanted me to have a word with you,' Furius said quietly.

'It's about that matter yesterday with the lawyer and the allegations against you.' Furius sighed and then affectionately patted Fergus on his shoulder. 'Seems that some of the men from the other squads are willing to speak up for you in your defence. I don't know what has changed from yesterday; then no one wanted to come forward. But it means that for the moment you are off the hook. Titus has already spoken with the lawyer and his superior officers and he has managed to get the whole thing buried.' Conspiratorially Furius leaned in closer to Fergus. 'Just between you and me, but I think that lawyer annoyed the hell out of Titus. The old man doesn't want some pen pusher interfering with the running of his company and treating one of his NCO's like shit. But when we return to Deva there may still be some questions to answer. Alright, understood, Fergus?'

'Understood Sir,' Fergus said quickly.

Furius took a step backwards and examined Fergus. Then he frowned.

'You look exhausted,' the Optio growled. 'Just like Aledus. What's the matter with your squad today? No,' Furius said with a sudden shake of his head. 'Actually I really don't want to know what you get up to. Just stay out of trouble.'

Fergus swayed lightly on his feet as he watched Furius walk away. Then two of his fellow squad leaders were coming towards him. Fergus acknowledged them with a little nod.

'We heard about Tiber,' one of the Decanus said quietly. 'And we heard about what you and Aledus did about it. That was a decent thing to do Fergus. Risky but decent. The men like it. We'll put in a good word for you about these allegations, whatever Fronto says.'

Chapter Eighteen – The German Frontier

(Late September AD 105)

The rhythmic tramp of the legionaries' iron studded boots on the stone road was so familiar that Fergus no longer noticed it. The noise drowned out everything else and the annoying dust, kicked up by the marching column had gotten everywhere, in his mouth, hair, throat, eyes, ears and under his tunic. The battlegroup of around 8,000 men was strung out along the road, the men's boots kicking up the dust as eight abreast, they took up the whole width of the paved road. It was noon and Fergus, clutching his large legionary shield encased in its protective leather cover, strode along on the extreme right-hand position of the eight-man squad.

His white focale soldier's scarf, was tightly wound around his neck to stop his armour from chafing and Galena's iron amulet dangled from around his neck. On his head he was wearing a standard infantry-man's helmet with wide, curved, cheek-guards. Suspended over Fergus's shoulder on a wooden pole, swaying as he strode along were; his pack; entrenching tools; grain ration; cup; spoon and bronze cooking pot. The sixty pounds of equipment jangled and clanged against each other. The pole had been tied to the shaft of his two, throwing spears, their long and narrow iron spear-heads, pointing upwards. Wearily Fergus reached up and wiped his forehead with his arm. His face, arms and lower legs were a deep brown and slightly sunburnt and his armour was dirty and stained and, despite the cool temperature, he was covered in beads of sweat that ran down his dust-covered cheeks.

They had been marching on the road for more than six weeks now, without a single day's rest. The long journey had taken a toll on the company, with six men forced to continue on with the baggage train due to sprained ankles, exhaustion and other injuries. But at least none of the dropouts had been from his squad, Fergus thought with grim satisfaction. His boys were holding their own. And there had been more good news, for that morning, as they had prepared to set out from their marching camp on the outskirts of Vindobona, Vienna, Titus had gathered the company together and had told them that their journey was finally coming to an end. They would be reaching their new temporary home by nightfall, the Centurion had assured them.

Stoically Fergus stared at the equipment packs of the men from the next squad who were marching just in front of him. Some of the legionaries seemed to have modified their uniforms to keep out bitter northern winds and others were wearing white woollen socks on their feet. And there was not a man whose uniform was not torn or worn out in some manner. Up ahead, the company was led by Titus, easily distinguishable by his red-plumed helmet and the signifer holding up the proud company standard. And just in front of the two officers were the rear ranks of the First Company of the Second Cohort.

A few civilians and ox drawn wagons, driven off the road by the marching column, stood in the fields beside the road, staring patiently at the soldiers as they waited for them to pass so that they could resume their journey. As the company reached higher ground, Fergus turned to peer down the slope at the broad river whose swampy, low-lying bank, lay half a mile away. The Danube had been their companion for the past few weeks now and the road had broadly followed its course in an easterly direction, sometimes veering inland, but they had never spent a day without glimpsing its placid waters. Fergus shook his head in silent amazement. He had thought the Rhine had been big but the Danube was even bigger. The long list of unfamiliar sounding Roman towns and forts through which the battlegroup had marched, Augusta Vindelicorum, Castra Regina, Batavis, Ovilava, Cetium and Vindobona had all been on or near the Danube, and the further east they'd gone the wider the river had become. And there had been another surprise, for only yesterday, as they had marched past an auxiliary fort on the river at Asturis, KlosterNeuburg, Fergus had learnt from a civilian selling water beside the road, that the auxiliary cohort stationed at the fort were none other than the Second Batavian Cohort, his father's old unit. But there had been no time or opportunity to see if any of the Batavians remembered Marcus.

From the front of the column, a sudden trumpet-blast rang out and a moment later Titus's loud bellowing voice was crying out.

'We rest alongside the road. Fifteen minutes,' the Centurion shouted. Silently the formation of heavily-laden troops came to a halt, broke up and started to drift to the edge of the stone road. As the legionaries wearily lowered their shields and marching packs onto the ground and reached for their water pouches, Fergus dumped his equipment beside his mess-mates, stretched and rubbed his shoulder. Along the side of the road as far as the eye could see, the fields were filled with soldiers sitting, standing and lying down in the grass. Fergus turned and gazed down the hill towards the Danube. The river was indeed getting wider the further east they went. To the east, across the open, deserted meadows he could make out a large dark, conifer-forest, which seemed to stretch away to the horizon. Along the river bank he suddenly noticed two watch towers, spaced around a mile apart. The squat, square-shaped timber towers, three floors high and protected by a square, wooden palisade, had a balustrade on the third floor that went right around the tower. The viewing platform, which afforded the sentries a 360-degree view, was covered by the distinctive overhanging roof. Slowly Fergus studied the river bank. There were more watch towers in the distance. It had been the same all along the river Rhine too. The frontier zone, the Limes, was the most heavily fortified area Fergus had ever seen and he and his comrades had marvelled at the vast network of military fortifications, roads, forts, watchtowers, signal-towers, frontier towns, fort-lets and supply depots. All manned and patrolled by thousands upon thousands of legionaries and auxiliaries from across the whole Empire. The Roman static defences, which sealed off the two river frontiers in depth, were like nothing he had ever seen before and, as their journey along the frontier zone had continued, Fergus had started to appreciate the sheer scale, interconnectedness and decades of planning and building that must have gone into these impressive-looking fortifications. The experience had left Fergus in little doubt that no part of the river frontier was not being watched by Roman eyes. Nor was all the activity limited to one bank of the river, for on their march they'd seen Roman forts and patrols on the other barbarian side too.

'What would I give to have a swim in that river,' Aledus muttered as he came and stood beside Fergus. 'It's going to feel good to wash this stink away. Gods, I hope they have a bath house where we are going.'

'Not far to go now,' Fergus muttered absentmindedly as he reached up to his neck and fiddled with the iron amulet that Galena had given him.

The two of them turned, as they heard the angry bellow of an ox. Coming towards them along the road, was a slow plodding convoy of oxen and horse-drawn wagons. The drivers of the baggage train, seated high up on the front of their carts, ignored the thousands of legionaries lining the side of the road. Behind them, piled up high in the wagons were the battle group's supplies, disassembled artillery and heavy equipment and sitting, sprawled across the sacks, barrels, amphorae and equipment of all kinds, were a motley assortment of stragglers and sick soldiers who had been forced to drop out from the march. Fergus and Aledus stared at the plodding convoy in silence. Filtering alongside the convoy towards them was a large troop of German Numerii, mounted irregulars, riding along the road in single file. As the Germanic horsemen drew level, Fergus peered at them keenly. They were some of the most exotic warriors he'd seen. The battle-group had picked up the detachment of Numerii at Mogontiacum and the savage-looking German tribesmen, with their beards and horned helmets were armed per their own individual preference and only the presence of the Roman liaison-officer, riding at their head, indicated that the unit was part of the Roman army. As the mounted irregulars trotted away down the road, Fergus turned back to gaze at the Danube and grunted as he caught sight of a Roman galley, rowing downstream. The warship's long bank of oars moved in perfect silent unison as the ship sped through the water like some strange wooden insect that was out hunting for food.

'That's a nice cushy life isn't it,' Aledus exclaimed as he too caught sight of the patrol vessel, 'Up and down on the river. Never having to put one leg before the other. Those marines from the fleet have got it good.'

'Yes, but boring as hell,' Fergus retorted. 'And less pay, plus you would be sea sick all the time, just like you were on the crossing from Gaul!'

'I wouldn't mind being bored as long as I never have to march again,' Aledus replied with a sheepish grin. 'My feet are killing me and I think my boots are about to fall apart for good this time.'

Fergus was about to reply, when a cry rose from along the road. Turning to stare in the direction of the noise, Fergus suddenly caught sight of a solitary rider galloping down the road towards him, his cloak flying behind him and a leather, despatch case slung over his back. The man was screaming at the soldiers and wagons to get out of his way. As he thundered past Aledus sniggered.

'He's in a hurry, isn't he?'

Fergus did not reply. On the horizon to the east he suddenly noticed a column of black-smoke rising into the air. Carefully Fergus turned to look towards the west, down the road from which they had come, and there too on the horizon, a column of smoke was rising into the sky.

'Shit,' Aledus muttered as he too noticed the smoke. 'What do you think that is? Barbarians?'

'Could be,' Fergus replied stoically. 'Remember that Centurion in Castra Regina. Remember what he told Titus?'

Aledus nodded. Titus had informed the whole company soon after. The Centurion had warned them that the Barbarian tribes across the Danube were restless and had been sending raiding parties across the river all summer. The Barbarians, the Centurion had explained, seemed to be testing the Roman defences, but for what purpose no one knew. And within a day of leaving Batavis the battle-group had come upon the first evidence of this guerrilla warfare. They had stumbled on the grizzly smoking ruin of a destroyed watchtower, overlooking the Danube. The eight-man squad, who'd been manning the post, had all been decapitated and their bodies hung from a nearby tree. The sight had had a sobering effect on the company.

'Gather round, gather round,' Titus was suddenly shouting beckoning for the company to come near to him. Obediently Fergus joined the rest of the eighty men as they silently clustered around their Centurion. Titus glared at his men as he waited for the stragglers to join him. And as Fergus stood waiting for him to speak, he suddenly caught sight of Fronto standing opposite him in the crowd. As Fronto noticed him, he grinned revealing a row of rotting teeth and then slowly and deliberately Fronto ran his finger across his throat in warning.

'What a fucking wanker,' Vittius hissed as he noticed the movement. 'Does he want to have his face kicked in?'

'Just ignore him,' Fergus said firmly. 'He is just doing it to annoy me. The prick will get what is coming to him but only when I say so.'

'Right,' Titus bellowed, turning to look at his men. 'Listen up. I have just been given some news. Due to the end of the campaigning season, we are not going to be taking part in any fighting against the Dacian's. Not this year anyway. Instead, the Legate Hadrian, our acting commander, has ordered us to go into winter quarters and await the new fighting season in the spring. The Second Cohort is to be billeted at the auxiliary camp Aquinoctium, which lies on the river, fourteen miles west of Carnuntum. Our temporary task will be to help defend and patrol the frontier until the spring. After that we will be heading east to kick Dacian butt. So, the good news is that we will be reaching our new home tonight. This is good news for the winters around here are long and bitterly cold and the first snows are less than six weeks away.' Titus paused as Furius leaned towards him and muttered something in the Centurion's ear.

'And I will say it again. The tribes beyond the river,' Titus cried out, 'the Marcomanni and the Quadi are restless and have been raiding our territory all summer, so the local auxiliaries are going to be glad to have us in support. But be on your guard. The Germans like to strike in small mobile groups, attacking our outposts and watchtowers, often at night, and then fleeing back to their own territory before our relief forces can appear. It is a cowardly way of fighting, but I never did have much hope that the Germans would be capable of much more. So, the lesson is, stay alert. Forget that and the chance is high that you may die like a fool, and boys, we have not just fucking marched half way across the Empire to die like fools. We are the best company in the cohort, so I expect you to act like the best.'

For a moment, the company gathered around their Centurion remained silent.

'What's the bad news Sir?' a brave anonymous voice suddenly cried out from the crowd of legionaries gathered around Titus.

'The bad news,' Titus bellowed, 'Is that our new quarters do not yet exist. We are going to have to build the barracks from scratch and they need to be finished before the first snows.' Titus paused. 'Rome conquers all,' he bellowed.

Chapter Nineteen – A Proper Punch-up

'It's not fair,' Aledus grumbled as he heaved one end of the felled, tree log onto his shoulder and waited for Fergus to do the same with his end. 'Apparently the Sixth Cohort have been billeted on the eastern edge of Carnuntum,' Aledus growled unhappily. 'And here we are living in the middle of a dank forest, with half a cohort of miserable and moody auxiliaries for company, and fourteen miles from a town of fifty thousand people. Fifty thousand people!' Fergus did not reply as he heaved the log onto his shoulder and the two of them started off through the trees towards the building site, where the legionaries were busy constructing their winter quarters. 'That's fourteen miles there and fourteen miles back,' Aledus grumbled as he continued talking. 'That's just too far for a night out. Oh, it's alright for the boys from the Sixth, who can sneak into Carnuntum whenever they like, but not for us. It's just not fair. I mean the dickhead who decided to place us out here, sure did not want us to be able to go into town and sample its delights. What did we ever do to deserve this? Carnuntum has a bath house and an arena.'

'Shut up Aledus,' Fergus growled, as the two of them approached the construction site and dropped their log onto a pile of wood.

Aquinoctium nestled on the higher ground in the middle of a man-made clearing in the dense conifer forest, less than a mile from the banks of the Danube. A muddy timber palisade and V shaped ditch surrounded the brown and dreary-looking barracks and extensive stables that housed the horses of the Hispanic Auxiliary Cavalry Cohort who's home this was. Half the auxiliary cohort's riders had already been transferred to the fighting, further east on the Dacian frontier, but the freed-up accommodation was still not large enough to house the five hundred men of the Second Cohort. The gate into the small auxiliary fort, was guarded by a tall solitary watchtower that rose above the gatehouse and around the fort, the muddy cleared-ground was littered with freshly-cut tree stumps. Wood smoke was drifting upwards from the cook-house and the two men on sentry duty high up, on their platform above the gate, were leaning over the balustrade watching the legionaries toiling over the new wooden barrack-blocks that were being built outside the walls of the original fort. A dog was barking and as Fergus paused to stare at the construction site, a tree slowly toppled over in the forest behind him and hit the ground with a great splintering crash. The legionaries clad in their short-sleeved white army-tunics, were labouring away and the noise of sawing, hammering and shouts, filled the forest and the cleared space around the fort. The men were making good progress and the foundations and walls of most of the barracks were nearly all complete. And it was just as well Fergus thought, for as he glanced up at the sky, he could see dark-grey rain clouds. Summer was over and in the past week the temperature had suddenly dropped.

Fergus turned back towards the forest where his company were busy chopping down trees. He had just reached the edge of the tree line, when from inside the fort a bell started clanging. Startled, Fergus and Aledus turned to look in the direction of the fort. The two sentries high up on their viewing platform were no longer staring at the construction workers. Looking animated, they were pointing in the direction of the river and shouting down to their comrades inside the fort. A moment later the gates to the auxiliary camp were thrown open and a squadron of thirty, heavily-armed cavalrymen came thundering out, and without, explanation galloped away down towards the river. The auxiliaries soon vanished into the forest.

'What's going on?' Vittius called out, as he came running up to Fergus. Along the edge of the forest, the men from the Second Company had downed their tools and had come to see what all the fuss was about.

Fergus shrugged. 'I don't know,' he replied. 'But those horsemen looked like the fast response squadron. I think there may be trouble down by the river.'

Inside the fort, the furious noise from the clanging bell abruptly ceased. Uneasily, Fergus turned to stare in the direction of the Danube. The forest beyond the gateway had been cleared to form a long, straight and narrow-looking fire-break, that went on for a mile, sloping down through the forest towards the edge of the river. Fergus had at first thought the cleared forest had been a road or path of some sort, but now suddenly he realised its purpose. The cleared break-line provided the sentries on the watchtower with a direct line of sight to the outpost, which stood on the banks of the Danube. And as he squinted and peered down the line, Fergus suddenly caught sight of large, coloured flags being whirled around by the men manning the watchtower on the river. The auxiliaries were signalling to each other.

'What are they saying?' a legionary cried out, as he too caught sight of the raised flags.

'Blue flag - R, red flag - A,' another legionary cried out, 'Green means - I or B I think and black can means V, O or D.'

'Raid,' Fergus hissed. 'They are signalling that the Germans have crossed the river.'

Stunned the legionaries around Fergus stared in the direction of the river. Then Fergus noticed the Senior Cohort Centurion hurrying towards him accompanied by the Cohort signifer and a Cornicen, a trumpeter clutching his cylindrical trumpet. Spotting Titus, the officer veered straight towards him.

'Titus, tell your men to get their armour on and grab their weapons,' the senior Centurion yelled. 'Hurry. There is trouble down by the river. Multiple raiding parties. You are to get your company down there right away and sort it out.'

***

The company had already crossed the main Roman road that ran between Vindobona and Carnuntum and were half-running and half-walking down along the heavily forested slope towards the signal tower on the river, when they heard the unfamiliar blast of a horn in the distance. Warily Fergus paused and peered into the dark wild forest around him, but amongst the trees, nothing moved, and as the seconds ticked by the noise did not come again. Silence returned. Up ahead Titus had started out again, and was setting a brisk pace through the trees accompanied by the signifer with his wolf's-skin draped over his head and clutching the precious company banner. As he followed Titus down the slope, Fergus could hear the metallic jangle of the legionaries' equipment and the men's laboured breathing and muffled curses. Clutching his rectangular shield, which covered him from ankle to shoulder, in one hand and his two throwing spears in the other, he glanced around at his squad. They were right behind him, staring tensely and apprehensively into the dark impenetrable forest, as if expecting the enemy to be hiding behind every tree.

The men in the squat watchtower with its square palisade, had stopped signalling and were nowhere to be seen, but the outpost itself seemed undamaged and there was no sign that the place had been attacked. As the company emerged from the forest and out onto the open floodplain, Titus raised his hand silently in the air and behind him his men came to an abrupt halt, and crouched down on one knee, their shields leaning against their bodies and their spears pointing outwards and resting on the shield rims. Beyond the watch tower, forty paces away, Fergus could see the Danube. The banks of the mighty river were covered by tall reed-beds and the ground looked treacherous, marshy and sodden. A good hiding-place, he thought. Downstream from the Roman watchtower, a white sandy beach was lined with a row of sharpened wooden stakes driven and slanted into the sand, so that they were pointing outwards at the river. Further along the river-bank, someone had built a series of earthen dykes and had flooded the land in between, creating a natural watery barrier. Cautiously, Fergus turned to gaze at the forest, which came nearly all the way to the water's edge. Wicked looking sharpened spikes had been driven into the ground and seemed to block every gap and path that led off inland. The anti-cavalry spikes seemed to extend deep into the forest. Fergus grunted in surprise. It was as if the whole landscape had been fortified and every possible defensive feature of the landscape moulded and turned into a gigantic physical barrier. He had never seen anything like it.

Crouching in the wet soggy ground Fergus waited for Titus to make up his mind. Then, just as the tension and silence was becoming intolerable, a man appeared on the balustrade that ran around the top of the watch tower. The soldier was holding a bow.

'Where is the enemy?' Titus called out impatiently.

Hastily the auxiliary soldier turned and pointed downstream.

'A big group of them came out of the forest a mile or so that way,' he called out in a thick Hispanic accent. 'Two of my men saw them. That was an hour ago. The Germans came from the south. They are laden with loot and they are preparing to cross back over the river. They are building rafts. They have women and children with them. Some of them could be prisoners taken as slaves.'

'How many of them are there?' Titus snapped looking up at the auxiliary.

'About two hundred,' the soldier called out. "But they are preparing to cross back to their side of the river. Maybe it would be wiser to just let them go.'

'Like hell,' Titus bellowed. 'That's not fucking likely. Those thieving bastards are going to get what they deserve which is my cold steel blade in their guts.'

For a moment, Titus paused and glared in the direction in which the auxiliary was pointing. 'I need one of your men to show us the way,' he called out at last. 'I don't want to step into one of your traps and skewer myself. Take us to this war band and we will do the rest.'

"I will show you myself,' the auxiliary replied glumly as he turned and vanished through a doorway into the tower.

***

'This is going to be a proper punch-up,' Fergus muttered as he stared at the German war band who had made their camp at the river's edge, fifty paces away across the flat grassy floodplain. Alongside Fergus, the legionaries, drawn up in a single straight line, were staring at the raiders in grim and tense silence. Fergus tried to slow his breathing. This was the first time he had seen the enemy up close, and this was going to be his first fight where the odds were not heavily stacked in the Roman's favour. A dozen half-completed rafts lay, drawn up on the soft muddy bank and the Germans were milling about, shouting and raising their weapons in the air as they defiantly gathered around their leaders. They were big, tall and fierce-looking men and were armed with a bewildering assortment of weapons, knives, axes, pikes, spears, bows, spiked clubs and swords, but few seemed to have shields and none was wearing any metal armour. Their clothes were made of wool and animal hides and some of the warrior's faces were covered in tattoos, whilst others were bedecked with looted rings, glittering jewellery and arm bracelets. And standing behind the warriors were groups of hard faced women, nearly as tall as their menfolk, their long blond hair, fluttering freely in the breeze. With a shock, Fergus noticed that the women too, were armed. They were going to fight.

'This is going to be a proper punch up,' he repeated quietly, as tensely he tightened his grip on his shield.

'Flying wedge! Form up into a flying wedge,' Titus bellowed as alone he calmly strode out towards the enemy. 'No mercy, no quarter boys. Remember what these people did to the auxiliaries in that watchtower.'

From the edge of the river the Germans replied with loud defiant roaring. They were joined moments later by the shrill high-pitched screeching from the women and as the women's screaming grew in volume, Fergus saw the faces of his legionaries grow pale. None of them had ever experienced this. The screeching women were truly unnerving and unexpected.

'Company will form up on me,' Titus's voice rose above the din. 'Form up, form up. Flying wedge!'

Hastily, Fergus and the company moved into the position, which they had practised a hundred times on the exercise field. When they were ready, the company had formed a tight V shaped formation with Titus at its very tip.

'Follow me,' the Centurion bellowed. 'No mercy.'

Silently and grimly the legionaries packed together in their tight V shaped formation and sheltering behind their large shields, began to advance towards the German raiders like an armoured crab. In response, the Germans rushed to form a crescent line, raising their weapons in the air. The screaming, yelling and shouting increased, as Titus headed straight towards the enemy.

'Raise spears, prepare,' Titus roared above the din as a few arrows hammered and thwacked into the legionary's shields. Fergus bit his lip, as around him the legionaries, crouching behind their shields, silently raised their Pila into a throwing position. Then when Titus was just ten yards from the baying and bristling German line the Centurion raised his sword in the air.

'Release!' Titus bellowed. 'Charge!'

With a howl, Fergus flung his spear at the Germans, wrenched his sword from its scabbard and charged. At such close, range the volley of spears was devastating. The Germans in front of Fergus went down by the dozens, impaled and skewered, screaming, groaning and collapsing to the ground. Their lack of shields and armour a catastrophic blunder. With a roar Titus and the legionaries behind him punched straight through the Barbarian line, scattering the enemy in all directions. A screaming German with a horned helmet on his head, came at Fergus, wielding an axe, which he swung straight into Fergus's shield with terrifying force, sending splinters of wood flying into the air. With a yell, Fergus pushed the man backwards with his shield, jabbing at him with his sword and with a groan the German sank to the ground. There was no time to finish the man off. The surviving Germans on the flanks, having recovered from the terrifying Roman charge, had begun to press and harry the Romans on both flanks and the battle began to descend into a furious, snarling and vicious hand to hand brawl.

'On me,' Fergus roared, 'form a wedge.'

There was no time to see if his squad had heard him or were obeying the order. A stone struck Fergus painfully on his shoulder and bounced off his armour and, at the same time a German lunged at him with his spear. Fergus grimaced and blocked the blow with his shield, just as two Roman's hastily took up position on either side of him, their shields covering his flanks.

'Form a wedge,' Fergus screamed. Then without waiting, he began to cut his way into the enemy ranks, pushing the Germans back with his shield and jabbing and stabbing at them with his nimble and deadly, short sword. At his side his two comrades kept pace, protecting his flank and stabbing at the enemy from behind the cover of their shields. The Germans howled and screamed in rage, but they were unable to halt Fergus's slow methodical advance and their blows and lunges slid off the legionaries shields and armour. Two more Romans had joined the wedge and behind him Fergus could hear laboured breathing and panting, as the tight little scrum of Romans pushed forwards. Around them the dead, dying and broken bodies of their enemy littered the ground.

'Kill them all, kill them all,' a Roman voice screamed, just to Fergus's right. Snatching a quick glance, Fergus caught sight of Fronto. Fronto too, had formed his squad into a wedge and they were busy cutting the Germans to pieces and driving them back towards the water's edge. Seeing Fergus a few paces away, Fronto gave him a crazy-looking grin. Then abruptly he disappeared from view.

As Fergus carefully stepped over a dead body, a warrior launched themselves at him and slammed into his shield, slashing at him with a knife. The knife raked the cheek-guard of his helmet knocking his head sideways. Recovering swiftly, Fergus punched his metal shield-boss into the woman's face, sending her staggering backwards. Then with a cry he was upon her driving his sword deep into her neck. As he straightened, up the woman coughed up some blood and stared up at him. Then slowly the light faded from her eyes. From close by someone howled in pain. It was followed moments later by a string of foul Roman curses. Fergus blinked as his two comrades on either side of him quickly closed the gap in the scrum. Ahead, Fergus could suddenly see the Danube. He had cut his way right through the enemy line. The realisation had only just sunk in when the Germans broke. One moment they were screaming and hacking at the Romans and the next the survivors were fleeing in a wild disorganised mob towards the river bank.

'After them, don't let them escape,' a Roman voice yelled.

The legionaries needed no further encouragement. With a loud victorious cry, they set off in pursuit. The Germans were running for their lives now. Their defiant blood-curdling yells had turned into terrified-screams and cries. But there was nowhere for them to go. They were trapped between the legionaries and the river. As he rushed after the fleeing mob, Fergus could see that some of the Germans in desperation and terror, had jumped into the water and were desperately trying to swim across the water. But the river was wide and the current strong, and most of the people in the water did not seem to know how to swim. They were going to drown. A small knot of warriors, seeing the chaos on the bank bravely turned to face the Romans, brandishing their weapons and screaming their defiance. But they were swiftly cut down, knifed and killed. As he reached the water's edge Fergus could see that the fight was over. Lifeless bodies were floating, face down in the river, and a group of survivors, mainly women and children, were huddled together on their knees, stretching out their arms to the Romans, their faces pale with terror as they pleaded and begged for mercy. Wide-eyed, his chest heaving, Fergus lowered his bloodied sword and turned to stare at the carnage of the battle field. The grassy field was littered with smashed, battered corpses, discarded weapons and broken shields and the groans and cries of dying men and the wounded were hideous. Here and there wounded men were trying to drag themselves to the river side or rise to their feet. Some of the Roman legionaries however were moving across the bloody-field finishing off the wounded with their swords. Others were stooping over the dead robbing them of their belongings and possessions.

Close by a harsh Roman voice suddenly cried out. 'Kill the prisoners. No mercy. You heard Titus. That will teach them not to cross the river again.'

Fronto's cry was followed by cold unfriendly laughter.

On the river bank Fronto and his men, with drawn swords, were advancing on the hapless survivors huddled together beside the water's edge and who were trying to surrender. Fergus hissed and before anyone could stop him, he strode over and barged straight into Fronto flinging him to the ground.

'It's over,' Fergus roared. 'The fight is over!'

Furiously Fronto scrambled back onto his feet and aggressively thrust his face right up against Fergus's face, his eyes blazing.

'You are a dead man walking,' Fronto snarled his face contorted in rage and hatred. 'Touch me again. Go on, do it, I dare you.'

'The fight is over,' Fergus retorted, raising his voice as he stood his ground. 'We will take this lot prisoner. They may have useful information. There is no need to kill them. They will be sold as slaves.'

'Titus ordered us to show no mercy,' Fronto roared splattering Fergus with spittle.

'The fight is over,' Fergus roared back.

'Fergus, Fronto, shut the fuck up,' a voice suddenly bellowed.

Fergus turned to see Titus coming towards them accompanied by Furius. The Centurion's face was smeared with blood and he looked furious.

'Fronto,' Titus roared. 'Get your squad to pile the dead onto a heap and see to it that you burn their bodies.' Furiously Titus turned to glare at Fergus as behind him Furius studied Fergus with a stern disapproving expression. 'And you,' Titus snapped, 'get these prisoners bound and chained. We will take them back to the fort. They should fetch the Cohort a good price in the market. All proceeds to be shared the usual way.'

Titus paused and for a moment glared at Fronto and then Fergus.

'And if I see either of you speaking to each other again today, I will have both of you whipped in front of the entire cohort.'

***

The silent prisoners, their heads drooping, sat in the mud just inside the auxiliary fort. It was evening and the grey, overcast October sky was growing dark and the temperature was dropping steadily. Towards the river, a thick column of smoke was still rising into the sky from where Fronto had burned the bodies of the slain barbarians. The prisoners, men, women and children looked miserable, frightened and dejected. Their hands had been tied behind their backs and their ankles bound together with rope. Fergus standing guard over the Germans, lightly ran his finger over the cheek guard of his helmet tracing the damage that the woman's knife had wrought in the metal. The helmet had saved his life but the realisation had only come long after the fight had ended. Standing guard around the prisoners, the rest of his squad looked bored and tired. They had all made it without any serious injury. The company however, had suffered one fatality and seven wounded of which one man was in a serious condition. Fergus could hear his screams, coming from inside one of the barracks blocks where the camp doctor was fighting to save the soldier's life. Wearily Fergus looked down at the Germans. The glum prisoners had not all been barbarians for amongst them, Fergus had soon discovered, were a few women and children who had been taken from local farms as slaves during the war-band's raid across the frontier. The freed women had wept and kissed Fergus and his companion's feet in pure joy at being liberated and it had comforted Fergus to know that he'd done the right thing by sparing their lives. And as the fear of immediate execution had receded, the Germans had started to talk amongst themselves. With nothing else to do Fergus had listened to the barbarians, even though he couldn't understand a word of what was being said. The Germans looked very like the ones he'd seen at Bonna on the Rhine and they had sounded the same too. He thought he could distinguish an accent. The officers may talk about different tribal groups inhabiting different parts of the frontier Fergus thought sourly, but to him and his squad the Germans all looked and spoke alike.

Catching sight of Furius, Fergus called out to him.

'How long are we to stand here Sir? It will be dark soon. It's getting cold. The others have already eaten. They have been resting in their tents for hours now.'

Furius glanced in Fergus's direction but did not pause as he strode along.

'They have sent a messenger to Carnuntum,' Furius replied evenly. 'Someone is coming to interrogate the prisoners before they are sold to the merchants. Standard procedure around here apparently. They should be here shortly. Your men will be able to get some rest after that.'

Muttering darkly under his breath, Fergus turned away. Standard procedure, he thought derisively. Titus was making him stand out here as punishment. He'd not seen Fronto since they had returned to the camp and that was just as well, because once again they had nearly come to blows. If Titus allowed the situation to continue, matters would soon get out of hand. The Centurion had to make up his mind soon about whom to promote to Tesserarius or else blood was going to be spilt. Surely Titus could see that?

The auxiliary camp was a hive of activity. In the stables the horses whinnied and the smell of fresh bread and a meaty soup came wafting over towards Fergus and his men. A couple of open, charcoal-fed fires were burning near the walls of the square camp and the Hispanic auxiliaries were clustered around them, cooking their evening meal and warming their hands. Beyond the ramparts of the forest fort, Fergus could hear the shouts of his comrades as they beavered away constructing their new winter quarters. A sudden warning cry from one of the sentries up on the watchtower made Fergus turn and glance towards the gates. A few moments later the big wooden doors creaked and swung open and two horsemen trotted into the fort, their horse's hooves scattering mud in their wake. Catching sight of the prisoners the two riders turned and trotted straight towards where Fergus was standing. And as the newcomers came to a halt and dismounted Fergus swore softly in surprise as he recognised one of the men.

'So we meet again,' Adalwolf said with a little smile as he stretched out his hand to Fergus in greeting.

Chapter Twenty – The Amber Merchant

'What are you doing here?' Fergus exclaimed in surprise as he grasped Adalwolf's proffered hand.

From the corner of his eye, Fergus suddenly noticed the Senior Cohort Centurion accompanied by a few men from his staff, coming towards the prisoners.

'They sent for me. I have come to interrogate your prisoners. With your permission,' Adalwolf replied in his thickly accented Latin as he took a little good natured theatrical bow. 'You forget that I serve the Lord Hadrian and go where he goes.'

Fergus glanced at Tiber, standing guard over the prisoners. Then quickly he took a step towards the amber merchant. 'If you say one word about the incident with my man in Bonna, you will regret it,' Fergus hissed. 'Not a word, understood.'

Adalwolf smiled and then to Fergus's surprise patted him on the shoulder. 'Don't worry I won't say anything,' he replied. Then he looked past Fergus at the Centurion who was approaching. 'But I would like you to do one thing for me in return. A favour done requires a favour in return.'

Fergus's face darkened. He didn't like where this was going. What did Adalwolf want? The Centurion and his men were nearly upon him.

'What?' Fergus hissed hastily.

'I don't know yet,' Adalwolf replied. 'I shall let you know when I do.'

Then abruptly Adalwolf turned away to face the Centurion and Fergus saluted smartly and took a few steps back.

'You the man who is going to interrogate my prisoners?' the Centurion growled as he looked at Adalwolf.

'Yes, Adalwolf nodded. 'That's my job.'

'Good,' the Centurion said turning to glance at the hapless Germans sitting in the mud. 'Let me know if they tell you anything important. And,' the Centurion paused as he turned to look at the civilian whom was accompanying Adalwolf, 'we will take the usual price for the slaves. I shall send a party of my men to collect payment from you in Carnuntum. Agreed?'

In response Adalwolf turned to look at his companion who nodded and, as he did so Fergus realised that the man was a slaver.

'Agreed,' Adalwolf replied. 'My companion will send his men to collect the slaves once I am done here. This is a large group, Centurion, larger than usual. It's a good haul.'

'Yes, well you should thank those men over there,' the Centurion nodded with a satisfied look as he gestured at Fergus and his squad. 'It was their company who brought them in.'

Relieved, Fergus watched the Centurion walk away and as he did, Adalwolf turned and strode purposefully towards the prisoners. The German merchant was silent as he slowly walked around the group, inspecting the hapless barbarians. Then without warning the merchant lashed out at one of the men toppling him onto his side. Planting his boot firmly on the prisoner's back, Adalwolf pushed the man's face into the mud and screamed at him in his harsh Germanic language. Moving on Adalwolf stooped and randomly grasped hold of a woman by her chin, forcing her to look up at him as he yelled a torrent of what sounded like abuse at her. Fergus remained silent as he watched Adalwolf work his way through the group. And when one of the prisoners raised his voice in protest, the merchant floored him with one brutal kick of his boot and went on kicking him until the man no longer moved. At last, Adalwolf however seemed to get what he wanted, as for a while he stood listening to a terrified and crying woman who kept on talking, her panic-stricken eyes darting everywhere. Looking satisfied, Adalwolf silenced the woman with a sharp word. Then he came towards Fergus and his expression softened.

'I told you that I do many things,' Adalwolf growled, as he turned to gaze at the miserable, terrified prisoners. 'Not all of them are pleasant but my Lord Hadrian demands results and I deliver.' With a sudden proud movement, Adalwolf raised his chin. 'My people are the Vandals. They live far to the north of this river, beyond the mountains. They are a great people. Rome knows them as the Lugii and when I was a young man, similar in age as you are now, I too raided Roman land. It is a rite of passage for any young warrior, for a man must prove his bravery, for warriors will only follow a man who is brave and fearless. My people will not accept a coward as a leader, not even a high-born coward and maybe this is where we differ from Rome.' Adalwolf sighed. 'But now I am old. I have travelled up and down the amber road from sea to river more times that I care to remember. I know the lands beyond the frontier better than any man and I also know my own people better than any Roman does. That's why I am useful to Hadrian and he rewards me well for my service.'

'What did the woman tell you?' Fergus muttered.

Adalwolf sighed again. 'The Marcomanni and Quadi are restless,' he muttered. 'All summer they have been raiding beyond the river. We don't know why the free tribes are so unsettled. There is enough land beyond the river to satisfy everyone. But it is easy for small war bands to cross the river at night and slip through the Roman defences. This lot here went even further. The woman told me they went as far the Roman town of Aquileia on the middle sea. That is more than two hundred miles into Roman territory.' Adalwolf frowned. 'But what should worry Rome is not the distance these people travelled, but the reason. They were not only here to raid. Their leaders told them that there was good land to be occupied, good farming land to be taken. They were told that the Romans were weak. That they could take what they liked. This is a new development, one that we have not seen before. Lord Hadrian will want to know about this.' Adalwolf turned to Fergus. 'Your company did well to bring this lot in. I shall make sure that Lord Hadrian is made aware of the role your unit played.'

Fergus turned to stare at the prisoners.

'I am not some dog that you can call when you wish,' he snapped.

'All men are in debt to someone, even the Emperor in Rome,' Adalwolf said sharply. 'It is the way of the world. Get used to it.' The older man paused to study Fergus with a little bemused smile. Then he raised his finger and pointed at him.

'You possess guts and you are loyal to your friends. I like that. Those are the qualities that will make a good warrior and leader. I was like you once. Yes, I think you are going to prove useful.'

***

It was nearly dark when Fergus and his squad were finally released from guard duty. Wearily the eight of them, clad in their white tunics and with woollen towels draped over their shoulders, silently strode through the forest towards the stream that ran down the slope towards the Danube. Behind them the noise from the forest camp slowly faded. The forest was silent, cool and damp and the air felt heavy and still. Beside a wide pool Fergus paused, stripped, laid his sheathed sword and leather belt carefully on the ground and without testing the water plunged naked into the stream, going completely under. He surfaced with a shocked cry at the icy coldness of the water. On the bank his mess mates laughed and in response Fergus splashed them.

'Who needs a bath house when we have this fine, natural, ice-cold water to wash in,' Fergus cried grinning as he wiped his face and sank back into the stream. 'Come on in, you cowards, this stream is going to make your cocks shrivel to an even smaller size than they already are.'

'Speak for yourself,' Aledus replied as he took a running leap and landed in the middle of the stream with a tremendous splash. A moment later he too was crying out in shock at the ice-cold water. Above the tree tops, the first stars had started to appear but it was still light enough for Fergus to see some way into the forest. As the others started to leap into the pool he went under again, surfaced, applied the sponge to his face and body and then, streaming with water clambered out onto the rocky ground. In the pool the men were calling out and fooling around with their sponges, and as he dried himself with his large woollen towel, Fergus grinned at their antics. Then he bent to pick up his tunic and as he did, an arrow struck the tree in front of which he'd been standing - just a split second before. Instinctively Fergus threw himself onto the ground and rolled behind a large rock as one of the men in the pool gave a startled cry. Fergus's eyes widened in horror. Someone had just taken a pot shot at him. Shocked he stared at his sword, lying just out of reach beyond the protection of the rock. Then he turned to stare at the forest. Someone had just tried to murder him.

In the pool the men were shouting and frantically scrambling out of the water. Fergus could feel his heart beating in his chest, as horrified, he stared into the trees waiting for the next arrow, but as the seconds ticked by none came. Then Vittius came scrambling into cover beside him kicking, Fergus's sword towards him as he did.

'Did someone just take a shot at you?' Vittius gasped in horror.

Fergus grabbed his sheathed sword and pulled the blade free, turned and slowly raised his head above the stone. In the gloomy forest on the other side of the stream nothing moved.

'Someone just tried to murder me,' Fergus blurted out in shock. 'Some fucker just took a shot at me. If I hadn't bent down to pick up my tunic he would have hit me.'

'Shit,' Vittius hissed as he turned to stare into the forest, clutching his sword. 'Who would do such a thing? Who even knows we are out here?'

'Fronto,' Fergus snapped, his eyes bulging in sudden rage. 'It has to be Fronto. This time that arsehole has gone too far. I am going to cut his throat. I am going to kill the mother fucker!'

Chapter Twenty-One – Roman Soldiers

Clutching his spear, Fergus leaned against the watchtower's balustrade and peered glumly into the darkness. It was late and cold but the night was quiet. In the darkness below him nothing moved. Fifty paces away, the pale moonlight revealed the smooth placid waters of the Danube and from somewhere in the vast forests beyond the river, a wolf was howling, but its mournful voice went unanswered. Tensely Fergus fiddled with the iron amulet that Galena had given him. Ten days had passed since the attempt on his life and for nine of those, he and his squad had been cooped up alone in this solitary, watchtower beside the river. Officially they were here on sentry duty. To keep an eye on the river. But in reality he had been banished, Fergus thought bitterly. That was why he was here. Titus had posted him to this watchtower to keep him away from Fronto. Titus did not want trouble within his company. That was why he was now freezing his balls off in this shit hole, whilst Fronto was spending his evenings in the warm, safe and newly completed winter quarters. But if Titus didn't want trouble within his company then why did he not decide on who to promote to Tesserarius? That would surely settle matters. Fergus tightened his grip on the amulet, squeezing the iron in anger. After the attack beside the stream he'd stormed back into the Cohort's camp intent on confronting Fronto but, as he had gone in search for him, he had run straight into the Centurion and Furius. Somehow the two officers seemed to have already known what had happened and had anticipated him and despite his furious protests, Titus had told him that without a reliable witness there was nothing he could do. No one had seen Fronto in the forest. It would just be his word against Fronto's. There was no proof that Fronto was involved. Titus had then ordered him to surrender his sword, Corbulo's old sword and after that, Furius had escorted him into the auxiliary camp, where he'd spent the night separated from his comrades. At dawn the next day they had given him his sword back, and he and his squad had been posted to the watchtower on the Danube, ten miles west of the Cohort's base. They had not even been allowed to say goodbye to the rest of the company. I hope this guard duty will knock some sense into you, had been Titus's parting words.

'Fronto you coward,' Fergus hissed to himself, as he thought about the attack and the fact that Fronto had not shown himself afterwards. 'You are nothing but a fucking coward. But you are not going to kill me.'

'What's that?' a sleepy voice yawned behind him.

Fergus turned and saw that it was Aledus. His mess mate was wearing his helmet and was clad in armour and he was armed with a spear.

'Nothing,' Fergus muttered, waving his hand in a dismissive gesture, 'just talking to myself. What are you doing up here?' he added quickly changing the subject.

'It's my turn on sentry duty,' Aledus yawned again. 'Have you forgotten? So, go on get some rest. Vittius has agreed that he will prepare breakfast.'

Wearily Fergus ran his hand across his face and sighed. Then he stretched. 'The night's been quiet,' he said. 'That wolf has been howling for a while but I have seen nothing move out there. Nothing on the river either.'

Aledus nodded and came to stand at Fergus's side and peered into the night. For a while the two of them did not speak. Then Aledus gave Fergus a mischievous grin.

'Do you know what they say about this watchtower,' he blurted out. 'They say it is the single most-attacked Roman outpost along the entire Danube frontier. I didn't want to alarm the others but that's what I heard.' Aledus nodded his eyes shining in excitement as he looked around at the wooden watch tower. 'And here we are. They say that the Germans beyond the river, use this place to test and train their youths, to harden them for battle and war. Apparently, they cross the river and attack at night, then melt away when our boys summon reinforcements. It's an easy target, what with us right up against the river and reinforcements several miles away. And have you ever wondered why we got this assignment? The last men to defend this tower were all slaughtered in a raid, just a few weeks ago. But better not tell that to the others.'

'How do you know that?' Fergus frowned shaking his head.

'Some of the Hispanic auxiliaries told me before we left,' Aledus replied. 'They told me to make my peace with my gods. Then they just laughed, bastards.'

'You are right,' Fergus grumbled as he turned and reached for the door handle that led into the tower. 'Keep that fancy tale to yourself. It won't do morale any good.'

'It can't be any worse than Vittius's cooking,' Aledus called out cheerfully, as Fergus vanished into the tower.

Inside the dark, square, top-floor room where the squad's supply of wheat and barley was kept, Fergus quietly descended through the hole in the floor down into the second floor, where the rest of his men were asleep on their rough straw mattresses. This room was warmer than the others and in the centre of the room, in a small stone hearth, a fire was burning low, its flames spitting and crackling. A pile of dry fire wood lay next to the hearth and the legionaries shields and spears lay stacked against the far wall. Carefully Fergus manoeuvred over the sleeping bodies, picked up a small, oil lamp shaped like a human foot and lit it from the fire. Then quietly he lifted the leather hatch that covered the hole in the floor that led down to the ground. Keeping the lamp steady, Fergus slowly descended the ladder to the ground. As he emerged from the doorway into the small, outside space between the tower and the square outer palisade he shivered. Quickly glancing up at the cold sky he saw a multitude of stars in the darkness. Clutching the tiny, flickering light, he strode purposefully towards the outer gate and hastily checked that the wooden bolts were in place. They were and Fergus silently shook his head. The gate was securely locked as he knew it had been, but he'd just had to double check. Aledus's talk had made him worry. He was just about to turn back towards the tower entrance when, in the distance, he heard the bark of a dog followed, by a sudden shout that rent the quiet night.

'Roman soldiers, Roman soldiers!' a desperate sounding voice cried out from close by in good Latin. Fergus stood very still. The voice had come from beyond the outer palisade.

'Let us in,' a voice cried as something heavy, suddenly slammed into the wooden gate, making Fergus jump backwards. 'For fuck's sake open the gate. They are nearly on us.'

"Who are you?" Fergus shouted as he held up the lamp and drew his sword. Then before any reply could come, up on his viewing platform, Aledus was suddenly crying out in warning. His shouts were followed a split second by the clanging of the tower's alarm bell.

'Who are you?' Fergus roared as above the din he heard another barking dog.

'Roman soldiers,' the voice roared from very close by. 'I have a wounded man. If you don't open up this gate we are going to die out here.'

'What's the password?' Fergus cried out as he hesitated.

'Oh for fuck's sake,' the voice on the other side hissed. 'You prick. I haven't gotten a clue. We have urgent news for Lord Hadrian. Open up for god's sake.'

'What can you see Aledus?' Fergus shouted as he looked up at the top of the tower.

'Nothing,' Aledus yelled. 'But there is definitely something out there. I can hear barking dogs and I can see a line of burning torches. They are coming towards us.'

Fergus bit his lip and turned to stare at the gate, torn by indecision. Was this all a German trick to get him to open the fort and get them all killed? But if the men out there were indeed Romans then he was condemning them to death if he did nothing. Acting on instinct Fergus made a reluctant growling noise, placed his lamp onto the muddy ground and carefully slid the bolts aside and flung open the gate, stepping backwards as he did, his sword raised and poised to stab anything that came at him from out of the darkness.

For a moment, nothing moved in the darkness beyond. Then a figure loomed up out of the gloom. The man was big and in the pale moonlight Fergus could see he had a beard and was wearing a rough Germanic cloak, fastened at the neck by an iron clasp. In his hand the stranger was clutching a gleaming German battle-axe. Ignoring Fergus, the man turned and whistled into the night and a few moments later, two men appeared half-dragging, half-supporting a fourth man in between them. The wounded man was groaning, his head drooping and he seemed unable to walk on his own.

'Shut the gate and barricade it,' the stranger with the beard hissed turning to Fergus. 'And prepare to fight. The barbarians have crossed the river. They will be here very soon. They have come to kill us.'

'Who are you? What unit do you belong to?' Fergus exclaimed eying the four strangers suspiciously whilst keeping his sword raised and ready to strike. The men were all clad in the same Germanic clothes and all their weapons looked foreign.

'Special forces,' one of the men snapped. 'You will just have to trust us. We were on a mission across the river. We have important news for the Legate Hadrian. Important news that must reach the Legate. You understand? But the fucking Germans intercepted us. They wounded Milo.'

'Bastards shot me,' the wounded man groaned and, as he looked down at the man Fergus suddenly noticed the stump of an arrow embedded in the man's leg and the dark blood stains.

'Fergus, what's going on? Who the fuck are they?' a voice cried suddenly from the entrance to the tower. In the dim light Fergus turned to see Vittius and Tiber, fully clad in their armour, clutching their swords and warily watching the strangers. But before Fergus could reply Aledus, up on his sentry platform, screamed in warning and an arrow thwacked into the tower close to where he stood.

'How many?' Fergus cried out turning to stare at one of the men.

'Maybe fifty, maybe more,' the man shrugged grimly. 'I don't know for sure but they have dogs and they want us dead.'

'Tiber, Vittius, barricade the front gate,' Fergus roared at the two men beside the entrance to the tower. 'Use whatever you can find. Catinius get up on the platform and light the warning beacon. Do it now and take the bow. Shoot anyone who approaches our perimeter. And you,' Fergus snapped, turning to the four men standing in the small muddy courtyard, 'get your wounded man into the tower, then join me down here. We must stop them from getting over the palisade. Move, move.'

The barking of several dogs was now horribly close. As the men in the courtyard exploded into activity, Fergus leapt up onto the elevated walkway that ran along the inside of the wooden palisade and cautiously raised his head above the parapet. And as he did he swore. Not more than twenty yards away in the darkness, a line of flaming torches was advancing towards the watchtower and in their devilish glow he could see dozens of armed men. The Germans were shouting out to each other in their harsh, unintelligible language as they came on. Some of the men were being led by great, wolf-like war dogs, which were barking and straining to break free from their master's leashes.

As Fergus stared at the approaching enemy in horror, high up on the sentry platform the warning beacon suddenly burst into flames.

'The signal won't save us,' one of the strangers hissed as he crashed down against the wall at Fergus's side. 'The other watch towers may see your signal but any patrol that they send out will not dare approach us until dawn. They will be too fearful of an ambush. It has happened before. They won't come.'

'Then we hold out until dawn,' Fergus snapped.

Another arrow embedded itself in the wooden wall, a couple of yards away and Fergus flinched. Down by the gate he could hear Vittius swearing, but he could not see what he was doing. Then, from high up on the sentry platform an arrow shot away into the night and a split second later the defenders were rewarded by a shriek. The shriek was followed by Catinius's triumphant yell. Fergus turned to snatch a look at the walkway around the square palisade and in the gloom he could just about make out seven figures crouching, and spaced out along the wooden wall. The defenders had drawn their swords and were clutching their spears, as they peered into the darkness. At least his squad were going to be able to defend themselves. They were not going to be slaughtered in their sleep.

'They are all around us Fergus,' Aledus screamed from high up on his viewing platform. 'We are surrounded by torches. Must be a hundred of them.'

'Don't let them get over the wall,' Fergus roared as the barking dogs threatened to drown out his words. 'We hold these walls or we die.'

'But if they do,' the stranger beside him hissed, 'we shall have to retreat into the tower.'

'No,' Fergus said sharply. 'If they get over the wall all is lost. If they trap us in the tower they can simply burn us alive. We hold them here. Not one step back.'

Beyond the ramparts the baying of the war dogs sounded horribly close. Then before Fergus had a chance to raise his head to take another look, something heavy thudded into the wall close by. Two yards away, fingers suddenly appeared grasping the top of the wall. They were followed by the head of a man. The German was straining and panting as he tried to climb over the top of the palisade. Silently and swiftly the stranger beside Fergus rose and swung his axe straight down onto the man's head nearly decapitating him. The blow sent the attackers body crashing down onto the ground. Moments later the night erupted in screams of dismay and fury. The noise seemed to swirl and grow like a storm around the small watchtower and suddenly all Fergus could hear was savage cries and screams and the thud of running feet. Fergus's eyes widened in terror as he realised what was happening. The raiders were storming his outpost.

The wooden wall trembled as it was struck by what seemed a herd of wild roaring beasts and, at the front gate, Fergus heard Vittius's defiant screams. Close by an iron grappling hook on a rope suddenly came flying over the wall and landed with a crash on the walkway, before rapidly slithering up against the palisade. The enemy was attempting to pull down the wall. Without hesitating, Fergus scrambled towards the hook and released it just in time, before it went taught. He'd only just managed to turn around with his back against the wall, when a volley of spears lobbed from over the opposite side of the tiny fort-let came hammering into the ground and palisade around him. In the gloom one of the projectiles seemed to catch his companion in the arm, forcing him to drop his axe and scream in agony. As Fergus stared in terror at his companion clutching his wounded arm, he sensed movement to his right. Whirling around he was just in time to see a barbarian rise above the palisade, his hands grasping the top of the wall. The man was just about to roll over into the fort. With a yell Fergus rose to his feet, grasped hold of the man's neck and stabbed him in the chest with his sword before shoving him backwards. The attacker disappeared into the darkness with a groan.

'Hold them, don't let them get over the wall,' Fergus screamed as a surge of adrenaline coursed through his veins. A few paces away, two more barbarians were just about to clamber over the top of the wall. One of them was clutching a burning torch and in its glow Fergus caught sight of a bearded face. With a defiant roar Fergus charged forwards and pushed the first man from the wall and drove his sword straight into the second attacker's face. Corbulo's old sword went deep with a sickening, crunching noise. Grasping hold of the dying man's hair, Fergus tore the burning torch from the man's grip and setting him ablaze, he shoved the German backwards over the wall into the mass of his comrades below. Then with a roar Fergus hurled the torch at one of the barking war-dogs. There was no time to see how his comrades were doing. It was every man for himself now. If they were dead or if the enemy had gotten over the wall, it would all be over very quickly. The whole perimeter of the watchtower had been transformed into a vicious, snarling fight for survival and the shrieks, yells and screams of men and the wild barking of dogs seemed to envelop everything. A few paces away, the wounded stranger was roaring in a savage furious voice. Despite his wounded arm, he had managed to retrieve his axe and was swinging it at every man who dared try and clamber over the wall. Transfixed, Fergus stared at the man as if watching him in slow motion and as he stared at the warrior, the stranger was suddenly struck in the chest by an arrow that knocked him clean off the walkway and into the muddy courtyard. Reality came back to Fergus in a sharp rush of noise, terror and violence. Three more barbarians were threatening to clamber over the top of the wall. Savagely, Fergus hacked at the fingers of one of them slicing them clean off and sending the attacker crashing back to the ground with a howl of pain. But before he could reach the other two they made it over the wall with triumphant yells. Fergus was suddenly aware that he lacked a shield. One of the Germans jumped down into the courtyard, clutching a spear but the second man came at Fergus wielding two knives, one in each hand.

Fergus dodged a vicious slicing blow and then another as he sprang backwards. Then, as his opponent seemed to stumble and reach out to steady himself against the wall Fergus struck, driving his sword into the man's exposed neck. The attacker gurgled, staggered and dropped one knife and desperately clutched his throat. Vainly the German slashed at him with his other knife but the blow lacked strength and Fergus caught the man's arm and kicked him backwards onto his back. But before he could finish the man off, close by Fergus heard a scream, and from the corner of his eye he saw Vittius come charging out of the gloom clutching a spear which he drove straight into a barbarian's stomach sending him stumbling backwards. The force of the charge impaled the German up against the palisade. Wild-eyed Fergus turned to look around him. In the distance a Roman trumpet was blaring. Something had changed. The noise around him was receding. Where were the attackers? But, as he turned to look around him he could see no more hands or bodies reaching up to clamber over the wall. Startled, he crouched down and turned to peer over the side of the palisade. The flaming torches were moving away and so was the noise of barking dogs. The barbarians seemed to have had enough. Or were they just regrouping for another assault? In the distance a Roman trumpet rang out again in the darkness.

'Fergus, they are moving away,' a triumphant voice yelled from high up on the viewing platform. 'We drove them off. The bastards are fleeing towards the river.'

There was no time to reply to Aledus's cry.

In the muddy courtyard Vittius suddenly emerged from the gloom. The young man's face was streaked with either blood or mud and he looked exhausted.

'Tiber is dead,' Vittius said in a voice shaking with emotion. 'He got hit by an arrow in the neck.'

Chapter Twenty-Two – Winners and Losers

Fergus sat slumped against the palisade staring into space. His pale face was unshaven and he looked utterly exhausted. It was morning and around the wooden wall, his comrades huddled under their blankets, staring at the ground. They too looked exhausted and no one seemed to want to say anything. The warrior who Vittius had impaled and pinned to the wall with his spear, was still there, hanging limply and silently over the weapon, his clothes stained with dark red blood. In the small space between the outer walls and the watch tower, Tiber's corpse had been laid out in the mud and covered by a simple army blanket. Slowly Fergus turned to stare at him, forcing himself to maintain his gaze. What a strange world this was. In Bonna he had thought he had been doing the right thing, when he'd set out to find and bring Tiber back to the company. But if he had let Tiber go, probably he would still be alive today. By bringing Tiber back, he had led him to his death in this miserable muddy outpost. Tiber was dead because of him. Fergus closed his eyes and blushed, as another wave of guilt swept through him. No, he couldn't think like that. He must not dwell on such things. The enemy had killed Tiber. It was not his fault. It was just his time. Wearily Fergus ran his fingers down his face. But however many times he told himself that, it did not make the guilt go away.

Tiredly Fergus lifted his head as he saw the commander of the Hispanic Auxiliary Cavalry Squadron coming towards him. The squadron of thirty riders had appeared at first light, approaching the watchtower cautiously and they were still here, milling around outside and shouting to each other. Soon after their arrival two of the special forces soldiers had left for Carnuntum with their precious message. The news was urgent and they must go at once, they had explained. Of the other two, one was wounded, unable to walk and the other dead. There had been no time to find out what the content of their message was. It had better be worth it Fergus thought bitterly.

Slowly Fergus got to his feet as the decurion approached.

'We found eighteen bodies beyond the wall,' the decurion said in his accented Latin, 'You boys must have put a terrific fight. Well done.'

'Thank you Sir,' Fergus replied quietly.

The officer nodded, glanced up at the watch tower and then reached out and gripped Fergus's shoulder in a sympathetic gesture.

'My men and I must go now,' the officer said. 'We have heaped the enemy dead in a pile. Burn the bodies. We will take the wounded scout with us. When I get back to camp, I will make a full report to your commanding officer. I have also sent one of my men to the naval base at Carnuntum, with the request that one of their ships should anchor in the river directly in front of your position. With a bit of luck that should dissuade the Germans from attacking again. The artillery and archers that they have on board those galleys are awesome. They will cover you, if the barbarians try anything. Expect them by night-fall and good luck.'

'We will be alright Sir,' Fergus said with a grateful nod. 'Thank you.'

The officer saluted and Fergus saluted in return. Then the decurion was striding away crying out to his men to saddle up.

When the auxiliary cavalry unit had finally vanished from view and they were alone once more, Fergus turned to his mess mates. The men were sitting or leaning against the wooden palisade, huddled under their woollen army blankets.

'Alright, listen up,' Fergus called out. 'Catinius, you will take first watch. We will change every two hours. Vittius I believe that you had promised us breakfast, see to it. The rest of you get some rest. I am going to inspect our defences and burn the enemy bodies. The auxiliaries have promised us some naval support tonight so we will not be alone out here.'

'Fergus,' Aledus said in a muted voice. 'What about Tiber? What shall we do with his body? We can't just leave him there.'

Fergus hesitated as he turned to look at the corpse. Then he nodded.

'Alright,' he muttered. 'We will bury him just outside the watch tower. This place I suppose is as fitting as any. I will do it myself.'

'No,' Aledus said firmly as he shook his head. 'We will all help. Any of us could have taken that arrow.'

'I think he had a girl back home in Lindum,' one of the men called out. 'She deserves to know what happened to him.'

Fergus hesitated again, as he gazed at Tiber. The man was right. He should have thought about that himself. Another wave of guilt came crashing over him. Then with a sigh he looked up at the men.

'Does anyone know if Tiber was part of a funeral club? Did he put any money aside for his funeral, for his family?'

The men were silent as they glanced at each other.

'We don't know,' Aledus muttered at last. 'He never mentioned it.'

Fergus nodded. 'That's alright,' he said gently. 'Well now is the time to dig deep boys. His woman and his family deserve something for Tiber's service. I say we all give twenty Denarii each. That's a hundred and forty in all. Less than a half a year's pay but at least they will be able to get a proper memorial stone made up. Tiber deserves that at least.'

Around him his men remained silent as they glanced at each other again. Then slowly they all nodded in agreement.

***

Fergus gazed at his neat hand writing scratched into the small, wooden tablet. The letter to Tiber's family had been the hardest letter he'd ever had to write, and it had taken him the whole day to do so. But now it was finished and, as he looked down at the words, Fergus suddenly gasped in relief. He had told them everything. How Tiber had been a good friend; how he had tried to desert and how and where he had died, fighting bravely to protect his mates. There was nothing more to add. The letter and the money would be given to the next available soldier or messenger, who was heading back to Deva Victrix. Wearily Fergus rose to his feet and slipped the wooden tablet into his tunic pocket. Then, extinguishing the candle with his fingers, he turned and started up the ladder towards the third floor of the watchtower. He desperately needed some fresh air.

Two days had passed since the attack, and although the days and nights had remained quiet, the men's morale had steadily sunk to new lows. As Fergus appeared in the doorway and placed one foot on the viewing platform, he caught sight of the flaming torches aboard the Roman naval galley, that lay anchored in the middle of the Danube, a couple of hundred yards away. The warship had not moved from its position for two days. Casting a quick glance into the darkness, Fergus turned and nodded at Vittius, who was on sentry duty. Vittius acknowledged him with a little flick of his head.

'Seen anything out there?' Fergus muttered as he leaned on the balustrade and peered out into the night.

'Nope, nothing,' Vittius replied. 'The marines seem to have scared the enemy off.'

Fergus said nothing as he peered at the galley in the middle of the river. Then sharply he turned to Vittius.

'Fuck the marines,' Fergus growled. 'It was we who scared the shit out of the Germans! It was we who stood up to them - you, me, Tiber and the others. After the fight we put up, they will think twice about attacking us again. We killed eighteen of them - eighteen!"

Vittius nodded in silent agreement.

'And when we get back to the company,' Fergus said quietly, 'I am not going to have anyone say otherwise. The men are going to know what we did here. No one is going to take the piss out of us. I am done taking shit from the likes of Fronto. We are not raw recruits anymore. We are the equal of any man.'

'So say we all,' Vittius snapped. 'But what are you going to do about that piece of shit? He has twice now tried to murder you, Fergus.'

'Sliding a knife between his ribs would be the easy part,' Fergus said quietly as he peered into the night. 'It is what comes after that which is the hard part. The army would have me executed.'

Fergus sighed and slowly shook his head.

'And here was I, thinking that I only had to worry about the enemy. They never told me when I signed up that I was more likely to get knifed by a fellow soldier,' Fergus paused. 'There has to be another way to get that arsehole off my back,' he muttered sourly. But how? I haven't got a clue.'

***

Fergus was woken by an excited yell. Instantly he was on his feet and reaching for his spear and shield. The shout had come from the sentry platform at the top of the watchtower.

'What's going on?' one of the men cried out as he poked his head up through the hole in the floor.

'I don't know,' Fergus snapped as he hastily clambered up the ladder. 'Get to your position.'

As he emerged onto the platform, Aledus, who was on sentry duty, cried out again and pointed with his finger at a small troop of horsemen who were galloping towards the watchtower. Hastily Fergus joined him at the edge of the platform, grasped hold of the wooden balustrade and peered at the riders. As the newcomers drew closer Fergus suddenly frowned.

'That's Furius,' Fergus exclaimed in a surprised voice. 'What is he doing here?'

Without waiting for an answer, Fergus disappeared back into the tower. Vittius, clutching his spear and shield, was guarding the outer gate as Fergus came hastening towards him. Around the small fort the others had taken up their positions, crouching along the raised walkway. Vittius looked anxious.

'It's Furius,' Fergus gasped laying a reassuring hand on the soldier's shoulder. Then turning swiftly to the other's he cried out. 'Stand down men. The Optio has decided to pay us a visit.'

Outside the fort, horses were snorting and whinnying. As he stepped through the gate Fergus saw Furius. The Optio looked uncomfortable and clumsy riding a horse and Fergus struggled to suppress a smile, as the officer finally managed to dismount, nearly falling over in the mud.

'This is a surprise Sir,' Fergus said saluting smartly.

Furius gave the horse he'd been riding, a look of disgust and then turned to glare at Fergus. Around him the silent Hispanic auxiliaries who had escorted Furius remained in their saddles.
'So are you still alive then?' Furius snapped as he came towards Fergus.

'Yes Sir,' Fergus replied.

'I have brought you new orders,' Furius said glancing up at Aledus, who was watching them from his position at the top of the watchtower. Then, quickly the Optio turned to Fergus and for a split-second Fergus thought he saw a new wariness and respect in Furius's eyes.

'There have been some developments on the other side of the river since, you left us,' the Optio growled. 'The Cohort has received new orders. Apparently, our scouts have discovered that a large Marcomanni raiding force is being assembled with the intention of crossing the river and raiding our territory. This is not some small-scale attack. This is a major raid. The enemy group is several thousand strong and they have a camp a few miles north of the river. The Cohort is going to be part of a force that is being sent against the Germans. We are going to smash them up, before they can move against us. So, you and your men are to return to the company at once. The auxiliaries with me will take over the watchtower. We are to leave at once. Get your men ready.'

'We are going to cross the river and attack the enemy,' Fergus exclaimed.

'That's right,' Furius snapped as he turned back towards his horse. 'Did you think we just sit here on our side of the river waiting for the Germans to attack us? Two can play that game, Fergus.'

***

As the Cohort's winter quarters hove into view through the trees, Fergus tensely tightened his grip on his spear. If he ran into Fronto he was not sure how he would react. The bastard had twice tried to murder him. But any action or revenge on his part would not be tolerated by the army. There would be consequences. Titus had made that very clear, before sending him to guard the watchtower. It was late in the afternoon and, as the small detachment led by Furius strode towards the newly built barracks, Fergus could see the men were still working on the defensive palisade and V shaped ditch. The forest was alive with shouts, hammering and sawing.

'Fergus,' Furius said turning sharply. 'Titus said that he wants to see you right away. The rest of you find a spare barrack room and get your shit together. The Cohort is moving out to Carnuntum tomorrow at dawn. The cooks are preparing a hearty battle meal, so make sure that you are fed. This will be your last, hot meal for a while. The next few days are going to be tough.'

Fergus nodded at Aledus as Furius led him away towards one of the long grey wooden barrack blocks that lined the ground just outside the auxiliary fort. One of the Centurion's slaves was languishing at the door to the Centurion's quarters. He gave Fergus a curious, respectful look. Furius strode straight past him and into the newly-constructed building, with Fergus following close behind. Titus was sitting in a chair whilst Lydia, his young wife, was busy cutting his hair. Seeing Furius and Fergus, Titus grunted and quickly waved his wife away. Obediently Lydia packed away her scissors and other hair cutting kit and, giving Fergus a little friendly wink, she strode off into another room, drawing the heavy curtain behind her.

'Sir,' Furius snapped, straightening up and saluting. At his side Fergus did the same.

Irritably Titus rubbed his forehead. Then he turned to look at his two subordinates and for a moment his eyes lingered on Fergus.

'So it seems that you are a bit of a hero,' Titus growled in a quiet voice. 'According to the scouts who you rescued, you defended that watchtower with skill, courage and determination. They say that you saved their lives.'

'I did what any man would have done,' Fergus replied. 'It was fight or die Sir.'

'Good,' Titus exclaimed giving Furius a quick glance. 'And I hear that you lost a man?'

'Yes Sir, his name was Tiber. We buried him beside the watchtower. He was a good man Sir.'

Titus nodded in agreement and turned to look away. Then he tapped his fingers on the back of his chair.

'You are probably wondering why you have been called in to see me,' Titus said in a grave sounding voice. 'Well I have some good news for you Fergus. As of this moment I am promoting you to company Tesserarius. You are now third in command after myself and Furius. You are now Furius's second in command. Congratulations.'

Fergus's cheeks exploded into a furious blush and as he stood staring at Titus in disbelief, he seemed unable to speak for some seconds.

'Thank you Sir,' Fergus stammered at last. 'I will not let you down. But what about Fronto?'

'Don't worry about Fronto,' Furius interrupted. 'There have been some changes within the company since you were last here. One of the other companies had a sudden vacancy for a

Tesserarius, so Fronto has also been promoted and transferred. He is now with the fourth.'

'I am not sure I understand,' Fergus muttered.

"The Tesserarius of the fourth is gravely ill. He's in a hospital in Carnuntum. The company needed a replacement, so we have given them Fronto,' Furius snapped. 'And you two have been forbidden from speaking to one another. We do not want any further trouble, is that clear?'

'Yes Sir,' Fergus replied.

'Do you have a good man who can take over as Decanus of your old squad,' Titus said as he came up to Fergus.

Fergus blinked, still not fully recovered from his surprise. Then hastily he nodded.

'Aledus is a good man, he would make the best choice. He has the respect of the others.'

'Good then that is settled,' Titus growled. 'I will have the signifer make the changes to your personnel files and salary. The company will be informed at the dawn roll call tomorrow.'

For a moment, the room was silent, as Fergus took a deep breath.

'You are probably thinking about why did I chose you and not Fronto,' Titus said patting Fergus on his shoulder before slowly retracing his steps to his chair. 'Well the truth is that Fronto is a better soldier than you. He is stronger and more experienced and he will make a fine company watch-commander,' Titus paused to look at the ground. Then he looked up at Fergus. 'But I like you. You may be young but you are a natural leader of men. Maybe one day you will make it to become a Centurion. I have observed how your squad treat you and you are not so full of yourself as some of the others. That is refreshing. And there is something else.' Titus gave Furius a quick sideways glance. 'Those scouts, special-forces who you helped save. They were carrying important news for the Legate Hadrian. It is because they survived, that we now know about the large Marcomanni raiding force that is assembling on the other side of the river. By saving their lives, you have provided Hadrian with some vital information and saved gods know how many lives.'

'Thank you Sir, I didn't know,' Fergus said quickly.

'Well you do now,' Titus said as a rare smile appeared on his lips. "Now the role of Tesserarius is not just to keep the company watchword. No, the watch commander is the Optio's deputy. It is an important role. I hope that you will take the responsibility seriously, Fergus.'

'I will Sir.'

"That will be all, Watch-Commander,' Titus said gesturing for Fergus to leave.

Outside and alone once more, Fergus took a deep breath and then clenched his fist in an outburst of fierce joy and satisfaction. He'd made it. He'd been promoted to Tesserarius, the highest rank that his grandfather, Corbulo, had ever reached, and he was only a shade over twenty years old. Galena and his family would be proud and so would Corbulo. Pulling his grandfather's sword from its scabbard, he gazed at the cold steel and then stifled an excited laugh.

'Are you watching old man,' Fergus whispered glancing up at the dull grey sky.

Then replacing the sword, he suddenly looked troubled. The gods had a cruel and strange way of managing the fates of men. Tiber had lost his life but he, Fergus, had been promoted.

The gods were cruel and they played terrible games. Winners and losers, Fergus thought, as he set off to find his mess-mates. Winners and losers; that was what it all came down to in the end.

Chapter Twenty-Three – Across the Danube

The river harbour of Carnuntum was packed with over a thousand soldiers. It was growing dark and the temperature was dropping sharply. The men were languishing all over the harbour, taking up every available piece of space, their shields, spears and armour glinting in the torch-light. Some of the legionaries were asleep, curled up in their thick woollen army-blankets whilst others, wrapped up in their winter cloaks, sat around in small groups, playing dice games, resting and talking to their mates in quiet, subdued voices. Fergus carefully picked his way through the dense throng of bodies and equipment, as he headed towards the waterside where the galleys of the Pannonian fleet lay moored against the stone embankment. Carnuntum served not only as a legionary base but it was also the HQ of the Pannonian fleet whose vessels patrolled the river. Behind him, away from the Danube, the huge walled city of Carnuntum stretched away into the gloom. The city was quiet and sentries had been posted to bar the roads leading to the harbour and keep away prying civilian eyes. The legionaries were waiting for the order to board the ships that would ferry them across the river. But that order would not come for another few hours yet, Fergus thought as he glanced up at the sky, clutching the small tessera tile tightly in his fist. The realisation that he had been promoted to Tesserarius, Watch Commander and third in command of the company had barely sunk in before he'd been thrown into his new role. Upon their arrival in the harbour after the short march from their winter quarters, Titus had called an 'O group meeting', where he issued his subordinate officers with their orders. The Centurion had gathered Furius, the signifer and Fergus together and had explained what was going to happen. The battle-group, consisting of the entire vexillation of the Twentieth Legion plus eight squadrons of Batavian cavalry and a Cohort from the First Legion, would embark onto the galleys at midnight. The navy would ferry them across the river under the cover of darkness. Once on the barbarian shore the battle-group, consisting of some eighteen hundred men, would advance northwards and inland. Special forces scouts already on the northern bank would guide them to their enemy. The Marcomanni were said to have their camp in the middle of a forest some five miles from the river. The Roman force would wait until first light and then launch their assault on the enemy encampment, hopefully catching the tribesmen completely by surprise. That at any rate was the plan.

Clutching the small tessera tile tightly in his fist, Fergus picked his way through the crowd. Titus had written the day's watch word onto the tile and it was Fergus's responsibility that every man in the company was made aware of what the password was. In the darkness and confusion of the pending night march, not knowing the correct password could mean the difference between life and death. As he reached the stone embankment, Fergus paused and turned to stare at the ships lying neatly anchored in rows, along the river-side. The galley oars had been withdrawn and the ships sails were furled and the spars of the masts were pointing up at a crazy angle. A few sailors and rowers were lounging about on deck but no one seemed in any hurry. And as Fergus gazed silently at the timber vessels with their fearsome colourful painted eyes adorning their bows, he suddenly thought of his father. What had happened to Marcus? Had he finally returned home or had he been lost at sea, his spirit condemned to drift on the waves for all eternity? Had he managed to retrieve Corbulo's mortal remains and given him the burial he had wanted? Fergus sighed. No, he should not do this. He should not think about his father, or the trouble his family were in on Vectis, or Galena and the perils of childbirth which she would soon endure. If he thought too much about them, he would go crazy. There was no way of knowing how they were doing and there was nothing he could do to help. All he could do was hope for the best and pray to the family guardian spirits to protect and watch over his loved ones. But, as he stood on the stone embankment staring at the naval galleys, Fergus struggled to contain the homesickness from welling up behind his eyes. The chances that he would see all his family again were slim at best.

'You again,' a voice exclaimed in a thick Germanic accent. 'Everywhere I go, you seem to pop up, Fergus. This cannot be a coincidence.'

Fergus turned and glared in the direction of the man who had spoken. Adalwolf was coming towards him with a friendly grin. The German was dressed in a long leather winter cloak, which he'd fastened with an iron clasp and a short axe was stuffed into his belt.

'If not coincidence, what then?' Fergus snapped embarrassed that the amber merchant had caught him in a moment of weakness.

'It must be the work of the gods,' Adalwolf replied with a humorous twinkle in his eye. 'I take it that your company will be accompanying me across the river tonight?'

'You are going too?' Fergus sniffed.

'That's right,' Adalwolf nodded turning to glance at the galleys. 'I wouldn't miss this for the world. The coming battle is going to be very lucrative.'

Fergus frowned. 'What do you mean, lucrative?' he said sharply. But Adalwolf nonchalantly waved his question away. 'You will see,' the older man replied. For a moment, he paused and Fergus frowned again. Adalwolf seemed to be considering whether to tell him something.

'One of the ways in which I serve Lord Hadrian,' Adalwolf said at last, turning to Fergus with a grave look, 'is through my knowledge of our enemy. I help train our special-forces scouts. I teach them the ways of my people. I help recruit the best men for the job. The two scouts who brought us the news that the Marcomanni were planning a major raid across the river, those two men were working for me. You,' Adalwolf said pointing his finger at Fergus, 'you could work for me. I have the connections to make it happen. The pay is better than what you get now. You have potential, Fergus. Why don't you think about it?'

For a moment, Fergus stood staring at Adalwolf in stunned silence. The merchant however, looked deadly serious.

'Thank you,' Fergus muttered turning to look away. 'But I belong to the Twentieth. It was my grandfather's unit and it is mine too.'

***

Fergus drew his cloak tighter around his shoulders. The night was cold and in the darkness he could see nothing. He stood on the crowded deck of the galley as the rowers, sitting at their benches, quietly propelled the vessel across the river. The only noise came from the gentle splash of the oars in the water. Around him, the legionaries stood packed together, clutching their shields and spears, unable to move. The men were all staring into the darkness trying to spot the barbarian bank. They seemed eager to get ashore. Warily, Fergus turned to look at the water. One slip or accident and a soldier, with all the armour he was wearing, would go straight to the bottom. No wonder the men became jittery when they were forced onto a boat. A dozen paces away, across the placid river, he could just make out another galley, packed with legionaries, its oars moving in perfect synchronised harmony. A soft cry from the front of the galley made him turn. In the darkness ahead three torches had appeared. The light flickered and then began to wave about.

'Those are our scouts,' Titus growled. 'That's the signal boys,' the Centurion called out in a louder voice. 'Prepare to go ashore.'

With a soft grinding bump, the galley ran onto the muddy river-bank and the signifer, clad in his wolf skin cloak and clutching the company standard, jumped boldly down into the water. Seeing that the water only came up to his knees, the legionaries quickly began to scramble over the side of the ship. Onshore

Fergus could hear muffled shouts and not far away another ship, came sliding up onto the mud flats. Fergus landed in the mud with the ice-cold water swirling around his knees. Hastily he made it up onto higher and drier ground. The night was filled with laboured breathing, curses, the rattle and jingle of the men's armour and the muffled shouts of the officer's as they tried to get their men organised.

'Second Company, Second Company, form up on me,' Fergus heard the standard bearer calling out in the darkness.

In the flickering light of a flaming torch, he caught a glimpse of the signifer holding up the company banner and hastened towards it. The standard bearer had chosen a large stone as the rallying point, and over his shoulder, he was carrying a large coil of rope. Some of the men from the company were already there, kneeling on one knee in a calm, disciplined fashion; their large shields resting against their bodies; their spears pointing at the sky and their helmets glinting in the torchlight. In the darkness along the river bank there seemed to be chaos and confusion as hundreds of troops continued to pour ashore from the ships. Quickly Fergus took up his position beside Titus and Furius as more men from the company came hastening towards them. In the distance he suddenly heard the whinny and snorting of horses.

'Fergus,' Furius said softly in the darkness, 'count the men and report back to me. We should have 79 legionaries and NCO's, not including officers.'

'Yes Sir,' Fergus muttered as he turned and silently began to count the men kneeling around the company standard. It was a hard to do with just the flickering torch light to guide him, but at last he seemed to have the number.

'Company are all accounted for Sir,' Fergus said smartly as he reported back to Furius, '79 men and NCO's, not including officers.'

'Good,' Titus growled from the darkness, sounding satisfied. "Now we wait until the Cohort commander gives the signal to advance. The other companies are slow, slower than us at any rate.' In the darkness the Centurion paused. 'Fergus,' he snapped at last, 'once we move out, make sure that the men know that they are to keep hold of the guide-rope. In this darkness it will be easy to lose one's way in the forest. I will be damned if that happens to this company. Any man who let's go of that rope will get five lashes from my vine stick. There is no excuse. Make them understand.'

'Sir,' Fergus muttered turning away. As he picked his way through the kneeling ranks, muttering Titus's instructions to the men, Fergus's thoughts suddenly turned to Corbulo. He was now doing the job that his grandfather had done for most of his army career. Company Tesserarius, Watch Commander. Would Corbulo be proud of him? The rank was not very senior and it paid only one and half times the salary of a normal legionary. His grandfather had served for twenty-five years and old Quintus had always maintained that he could have made it to become a Centurion if it hadn't been for his poor disciplinary record and consistent lack of respect for his commanding officers. In the darkness, a little smile appeared on Fergus's lips. And yet, and yet, Corbulo was a hero. He had sacrificed his life to save his children. He was a legend in the Twentieth, for it had been he who had saved a whole battle-group from annihilation in Hibernia. How had he managed to do that? That achievement alone had made up for all the lost and wasted opportunities. That deed had set the family on the path to prosperity. Yes, Fergus thought, with growing certainty, one day, he Fergus, was going to make his grandfather proud. Warily he glanced up at the dark sky. The old man was watching him, judging him. He was certain of that. He could practically feel the presence of his spirit. He would not let him down.

The forest was quiet and amongst the trees and undergrowth nothing moved. The legionaries, formed up into two ranks, were down on one knee their shields leaning against their bodies and their spears pointing in the direction of the enemy encampment, which lay less than a mile away through the forest. The two lines of legionaries stretched away through the forest until they vanished from view. It was dawn and to the east the sun was a red-ball rising majestically into the clear, crisp sky. Fergus stood close to Titus and Furius, as they all waited for the order to advance. Fergus looked tired but he didn't feel tired. Adrenaline was pumping through his veins. Tensely he reached up to touch the amulet Galena had given him. The amulet would protect him she had said. It had powerful magic. This was not his first fight but it was certainly the largest fight he had ever been involved in. Titus seemed to have been deliberately vague, when asked how many German warriors they would be facing, and Fergus suspected that he was deliberately withholding that information. 'It's dawn Sir,' Furius muttered.

'I know. We wait until the signal is given.' Titus growled staring moodily into the wilderness beyond the Roman lines.

For a while the officers were silent. No one seemed interested in talking. Impatiently Titus began to tap his vine staff against his leg.

Then suddenly, from somewhere out of sight, a Roman trumpet rang out, shattering the silence and peacefulness of the forest and sending birds soaring up into the air.

'That's the order to advance,' Titus bellowed, as the trumpet blast was repeated all the way down the line.

'Second Company will advance!'

Along the Roman line the men rose to their feet in a disciplined manner, hefted their shields off the ground and began to slowly advance through the trees; their spears pointing straight ahead. Fergus, keeping close to Titus, followed. Ahead of him the soldiers' armour and helmets glinted in the early-morning light -

an alien looking sight in the natural world of wood, fallen leaves, mud, stones and grass.

'Was that wise to use the trumpet like that,' Fergus muttered turning to glance at Furius. 'Surely the enemy would have heard that too?'

'Who knows about such things,' Furius shrugged. 'The senior officers must have considered that. Focus on what is to come, Fergus.'

Tensely Fergus turned to stare into the forest up ahead. He could see nothing amongst the trees. But surely he thought, the use of the trumpets to signal the start of the attack must mean that the battle-group had lost the element of surprise. In front of him, the lines of heavily-armoured legionaries continued to pick their way through the forest, maintaining an unbroken line.

'Upon contact we will attack in wedge formations,' Titus said in a calm voice. 'Kill everything that crosses your path. No mercy. But we must maintain a single line with the companies on our flanks. The enemy must not be allowed to get through the gaps and into our rear. Furius, you will lead our right flank, Fergus you will take the squads on the left and I will lead the centre. And remember to keep contact with the companies on your flanks. Do not be lured into a full-scale pursuit of a fleeing enemy. They could be trying to lure us out of formation. If all is lost, you will fall back on your standard and defend it to the last. Do you understand your orders?'

'Yes Sir,' Furius and Fergus said at the same time.

'Good,' Titus muttered grimly as he turned to gaze into the forest.

'How large is the enemy force Sir?' Fergus said quietly.

Titus gave Fergus an annoyed look.

'Thousands,' he growled.

Chapter Twenty-Four – War beyond the Imperial Frontier

Up ahead the forest was starting to thin out, and through the branches and trees Fergus could make out wide-open fields. The smell of wood-smoke filled his nostrils and a strange silence seemed to have descended upon the land. As he stepped out from the tree cover, he took a deep breath. Covering the fields in front of him was the barbarian camp. Hundreds of small cooking fires dotted the grassy plain. Smoke was rising into the sky in little twisting wisps. Drawn up facing the forest, fifty paces away from Fergus, was a solid looking shield wall bristling with thousands of armed Germans. And as the Roman companies emerged from the forest, a great defiant and thundering roar rose from the packed barbarian ranks. Fergus took another deep breath as he forced himself to keep walking towards the enemy. He'd been right. They were not going to be taking the Germans by surprise. The enemy had chosen to fight instead of melting away into the forest. But at least the barbarian camp did not seem to have any fixed defences. The space between the forest and the German shield wall was unobstructed.

A Roman trumpet blared out and abruptly the Roman legionaries came to a halt. Across the open-space between the two sides the Germans raised their weapons in the air and screamed and roared. Then, as the legionaries stared at their enemy in passive silence, the Germans began to chant, a deep-throated chant taken up by thousands of voices.

'Out, out, out!' 'Out, out, out!'

'Fergus, Furius, take your positions on the flank in the first line,' Titus roared above the chanting. 'Company will advance when you hear the signal. Kill everything that crosses your path.'

Tensely Fergus hastened to his allotted position on the extreme left of the company's section of the battle-line. Hefting his shield protectively in front of him, he glanced quickly down the Roman line. The legionaries were staring at the barbarian lines as they awaited the order to attack. Turning to look at his own men, Fergus suddenly saw Aledus standing in the front line. And beside him, Catinius, Vittius and the others and suddenly Fergus felt very exposed. He should have been with his comrades. What was he doing here all alone in the line? But there was no time to dwell on that. Above the chanting Germans, he could hear the Roman officers screaming orders to their men.

'Wedge formation,' Fergus yelled at the men closest to him. 'Once we attack you will form wedges just like we have trained for. Form up on your Decanus. Stay within formation, cover your neighbour and kill everything that crosses your path. No mercy. Those bastards over there may be loud but they are no match for us.'

There was no more time to say anything else. Across the fields a Roman trumpet rang out and, to his right Fergus heard Titus's ferocious bellowing voice.

'Second Company will advance!'

Silently the Roman line began to advance towards the German shield wall. Then one by one the legionaries began to bang their spears against their shield's until the whole Roman line was clashing their weapons against their shields. The rhythmic noise began to compete with the German chanting. Grimly, Fergus stared at the enemy as he strode towards them. The barbarians, clad in their drab, grey and black clothing, looked formidable and terrifying and, amongst their numbers he caught sight of women and children armed in the same fashion as their menfolk.

When the Roman front line had closed to within fifteen yards of the enemy, a great roar rose from the Roman ranks and drawing back their spears, they flung them at the German shield-wall, drew their short swords, and charged. The volley of spears hammered into the enemy ranks, cutting down countless warriors. Shrieks and cries rose from the German line and the survivors stumbled backwards, but the shield wall held and the Germans stood their ground. Fergus, released from an unbearable tension, screamed as he came charging straight into the German line. His shield slammed into a warrior, sending the man tumbling backwards into his comrades. Wildly Fergus thrust his sword at the Germans but his thrust was parried. The next moment he was staggering backwards under a flurry of furious hammer-blows that landed on his shield, as an enraged barbarian attacked him with a huge spiked-club. The warrior was a full head taller than Fergus and his face was contorted in rage. There was no time to issue orders. In the vicious hand-to-hand combat, it was every man for himself now. Another German joined the attack on Fergus, trying to skewer him with his spear but, just as he thrust his weapon at Fergus, a Roman gladius sliced into his stomach, tearing a gaping and bloody hole in his guts, which promptly spilled out. Fergus thrust his shield into a barbarian trying to push him backwards, but the man would not budge and for an insane moment, the two of them stood screaming at each other as they struggled and jostled trying to push one another back. Then with a furious cry Fergus raised his sword and managed to drive it into his opponent's neck.

On both sides of him the whole Roman front line had become embroiled in a vicious, snarling and brutal fight with the German shield-wall. In the bloody chaos men were furiously pushing, hacking and stabbing at each other and around them the dead, dying and wounded were piling up. Shrieks, screams and yells shattered the plain and there was no way of knowing who was winning. To his right, a Decanus had managed to form a small V shaped wedge with himself at the tip, and the small tight Roman scrum was beginning to fight its way deeper into the German line. Leaping sideways, Fergus joined the rear of the formation, his right flank protected by the shield of the next man.

'Forwards,' the Decanus roared as he took a step forwards, crouching behind his shield that was protecting him from the furious enemy battering and thrusts. And as he stepped forwards, the men on either side of him did the same presenting a continuous shield wall from behind which, they jabbed and stabbed at the Germans with their short swords. The tactics had been practised so often on the training field that every legionary knew them instinctively. They had a devastating impact on the barbarians.

'Forwards,' the Decanus roared again and once again crouching behind his shield he took another step forwards. Around the little V shaped Roman scrum, the barbarian line began to buckle as the Germans seemed incapable of breaking the tight armoured formation and the legionary swords jabbing and stabbing at them from behind the protection of their shields began to exact a terrible toll. Fergus cried out as his sword went straight into a man's chest. Violently he twisted the blade free and pushed the warrior to the ground with his shield.

'Forwards,' the Decanus yelled in a hoarse voice. Quickly Fergus stepped forwards keeping contact with the Roman V shaped scrum. Then to his right, above the din he suddenly recognised Titus's ferocious bellowing voice. The Centurion seemed to crying out in warning, but his words were lost in the din of battle. Wildly Fergus turned to look to his left and as he did, he immediately understood Titus's warning. A gap was opening in the Roman line between his company and their neighbours. The Germans had not yet spotted it, but they would soon.

'Hold the fucking line,' Fergus screamed. 'We are losing contact with our left flank.'

The Decanus leading the advance showed no indication that he was listening. All along the battle line, the Romans had got stuck into the barbarians, trying to push them back with their shields and stabbing at them with their deadly effective short swords. The horrific screams of the fighting men on both sides had become indistinguishable. But as he staggered and strained under the weight of a furious attack by a German wielding an axe, Fergus saw that the front of the tight Roman V shaped scrum, was no longer moving forwards.

'Move to the left,' Fergus roared as he flung the barbarian backwards, trying to smash the metal boss of his shield into the man's face. 'Move to the left. Don't let them get through the gap.'

And slowly the Roman soldiers around him, began to edge towards the left. From the barbarian lines a furious howl rose as a few barbarians tried to rush into the gap, but they were swiftly cut down by the legionaries that came at them from both sides. Within seconds the Roman line had closed the gap, once more forming a continuous line of formidable armour, shields and jabbing swords. A blow struck Fergus's shield sending the shock vibrating through his entire body. Grimly he slammed his iron shield boss into the barbarian who was trying to cut him down, and followed it up with a vicious thrust of his bloodied sword. His blow sliced through an arm and he was rewarded with a howl as his opponent dropped his axe. Furiously Fergus knocked the German to the ground and killed him with another sword-thrust to the man's exposed neck. A stream of blood erupted like a fountain splattering Fergus's shield and face.

'Forwards,' a Roman voice roared.

And once more the Roman scrum began to advance into the German line. Crouching behind his shield Fergus grimly stepped forwards, bracing himself as another barbarian came at him. The Germans were putting up a stubborn fight. His opponents were huge, wild-looking men, at least a head taller than him, but what they had in courage and strength, they lacked in weapons, armour and training. Dimly Fergus became aware of a trumpet blaring out across the battlefield. Straining to hold back the German battering and pushing against his shield, he suddenly became aware of the thud of horses' hooves. The next moment the pressure pushing against him slackened, then broke completely. Astonished, Fergus saw the barbarians in front of him start to fall back in confusion. Then with incredible speed the confusion turned into a full-scale rout. Snatching a glance to his right, Fergus saw a group of Batavian horsemen galloping through the running figures, slashing at the enemy with their long cavalry swords. The defiant screams and yells of the barbarians had abruptly changed to shouts of terror. There was no time to wonder about what had happened. Raising his sword in the air, Fergus turned to the men around him.

'After them, after them,' he roared.

And with a ferocious blood-curdling yell the Roman legionaries began to pursue the fleeing enemy. As Fergus stormed forwards through the remains of the barbarian camp, he was overwhelmed with a furious, heady sense of triumph and rage. It was time to finish the Germans. It was time to slaughter them all, to take revenge on the men who had tried to kill him. The fields around him were littered with corpses and dying men. Up ahead more Batavian cavalry had appeared and were mowing down the fleeing barbarians as they attempted to reach the relative safety of the forest. The shrieks and high-pitched screams of the fleeing men grew louder and louder. The rout was turning into a massacre. As he leapt over a corpse, Fergus suddenly heard a woman scream. A few yards away beside a smoking camp fire, he caught sight of a Roman legionary wrestling with a young barbarian woman on the ground. The soldier had dropped his shield and sword and seemed to be trying to throttle the girl. Without thinking Fergus leapt towards the fight and with a ferocious kick sent the Roman soldier tumbling away into the grass. The girl screamed, as she saw Fergus's bloody sword and blood spattered face. Terrified she tried to scramble to her feet but harshly Fergus knocked her to the ground and pointed his sword at her neck.

'Stay down, stay down,' he screamed.

The next moment the Roman soldier whom he had kicked into the grass was coming at Fergus with a wild, crazed look in his eyes. But as the man tried to grasp hold of Fergus's throat, Fergus struck him with a vicious blow to his head and swiftly sent the soldier tumbling back to the ground with his shield. Wildly Fergus turned to stare at the girl. He didn't know why he was doing this. Some instinct and reflex had kicked-in but as he stared at the girl cowering on the ground the raw violent blood lust inside him started to subside.

Around him all was confusion as the Roman legionaries swept through the enemy camp, killing, looting and finishing off the remnants of the barbarian force. Horrific screams and pleas for mercy rang out everywhere. Fergus stood over the girl, pointing his sword at her neck, suddenly unsure of what he was supposed to do. The fight was over. The surviving Germans were fleeing for their lives and from somewhere to the rear a trumpet rang out. The Roman soldier who he had knocked to the ground was gingerly picking himself up. The man gave Fergus a murderous look as he reached for a sword and stomped off. On the ground close to the German camp-fire lay the bodies of two women. Fergus, his chest heaving from exertion stared at the girl as she whimpered and crawled over to one of the corpses, cradling its head in her arms. Fergus growled as he stood over her unsure whether he should kill her or let her live. Around him the legionaries had begun to plunder the dead of anything of value. A few of the men cast envious glances at the girl but as they saw Fergus standing over her they seemed to change their minds and move off to find easier pickings.

At his feet, the German girl was whimpering as she cradled the dead woman's head in her arms. The girl looked around sixteen and had long coal-black hair and strange Germanic runes tattooed onto her forehead. From the corner of his eye Fergus caught sight of Titus's plumed helmet. The Centurion was moving across the battlefield, crying out orders to his men. With a grunt Fergus made up his mind.

'You are mine now,' Fergus cried kicking the girl's legs. 'You belong to me. You are my slave. Mine, do you understand.'

Chapter Twenty-Five – The Slave Markets of Carnuntum

The Forum, the central market place of Carnuntum, was packed with shoppers, merchants, pedestrians and off duty soldiers. In the large, open square, lined with dozens and dozens of market stalls and shops, the noise of hundreds upon hundreds of voices, bellowing oxen, barking dogs, mingled with the advertising cries of the merchants and a multitude of street entertainers, prostitutes, religious-nuts, all trying to lure the town's citizens and soldiers to spend their money with them. It was noon. Fergus and a large group of men from the Second Company, slowly pushed their way through the crowds, past the large stone statue to Emperor Trajan and on towards the section of the Forum reserved for the slave trade. The men were clad in their white tunics over, which they were wearing their long, winter cloaks. Their sheathed swords hung from their belts, and as they pushed through the crowd, the civilians hastily and respectfully moved aside. A full day had passed since the battle on the other side of the Danube and Hadrian, in recognition of the resounding Roman victory, had ordered that the soldiers who had taken part, would be granted two days leave. And that had meant two days of freedom to visit the brothels, the amphitheatre and other attractions that Carnuntum had to offer.

As they made their way towards the slave pens, Fergus glanced around at his legionaries. The company had suffered three dead and six wounded, two of which were in a serious condition. But from his old squad none had been killed or seriously wounded and for that he was glad. The battle had been a sobering experience and afterwards, none of them had wanted to talk about it. But now as they strode through the crowded Forum the soldiers with him looked relaxed and happy and so they should Fergus thought. In addition to the two days leave, the Legate Hadrian had also decreed that the soldiers would be allowed to keep all the loot and booty that they had taken from the defeated enemy. And for some of the men, including him, that had meant that they could keep the prisoners who they had captured. The soldiers were about to become rich by selling their prisoners as slaves to the slave traders in the Forum.

Through the noisy crowds the slave pens hove into view and eagerly Fergus peered at the large, iron cages, hoping to spot the girl who he had captured. The German prisoners and slaves, languishing inside the large cages, looked utterly miserable and dejected. They sat around on the ground, their ankles and hands bound together in iron, slavers-chains. Others stood on their feet, clasping the side of their cages and staring vacantly into the crowds of onlookers. Most of the slaves were silent, still clad in their blood-smeared and torn clothing. But here and there a defiant spirit was shouting and cursing the onlookers. The crowds however, seemed to be taking no notice, as if they had seen it all before. Eagerly Fergus searched the cages. Men and women seemed to have been separated, but in the female cages he saw no sign of his girl with the long, black hair and tattooed forehead. The slavers who had come to round up the prisoners after the battle, had branded each one on the shoulder with a number and had given their owners a token, with the corresponding number as a receipt. And now the time had come to cash in his bounty. Fergus sighed. And now too, he understood what Adalwolf had meant, when he'd said that the battle was going to be lucrative. The girl could be worth over a thousand Denarii; his mates had suggested. That was over three year's salary. A huge sum. It all depended on the skill of the auctioneer who would sell the slaves on the soldier's behalf, his comrades had said.

As the soldiers reached the slave pens and began to eagerly and excitedly gather around the auctioneers, Fergus left them and came towards the iron cages containing the female slaves. Slowly, searching for his girl, he strode along the iron bars, gazing at the miserable looking humanity. Inside the cages, the female slaves were silent and avoided his gaze. The girl had not said a word to him. She had refused to speak when the slavers had talked to her in her own language. The only noise she had made, after he had pulled her away from the corpses beside the fire, was to scream when the slavers had branded her with her number; twenty-one. But she had understood him, when he'd said she was his slave, Fergus thought. He was sure that she had understood that, for when the slavers had come to take her away she had turned to stare at him, as she was being led away.

Then suddenly he saw her. The girl was sitting in the far corner of one of the cages, furthest from the crowds and she was staring sullenly at the ground. She had not seen him. Fergus paused, and for a long moment, he gazed at her through the bars of the cage. She looked around sixteen. Her long, black hair was stained with mud and dried blood and she was still wearing the same clothes, in which she had been captured. She wasn't too bad-looking either if he overlooked the strange runes tattooed onto her forehead. With a sigh, Fergus turned to look away. On the raised, wooden platform in front of the slave pens, the first of the prisoners had been dragged up onto the stage and was being sold to the crowd of slave merchants who had gathered around the platform. The soldiers from the Second Company looked on eagerly, as the auctioneers skilfully began to raise the bidding price, selling their humans as if they were in a cattle market. Suddenly Fergus turned to look the other way, filled with disgust. Efa and Dylis, his grandmother and aunt had once been slaves in Caledonia and, as a boy, they had told him about the degrading things that they had been forced to do. Turning to look around him, Fergus sighed. He didn't like this place. What was he doing here? This was no place for him to spend his day off. But as he was about to walk away, he paused as his fingers closed around the small, stone-token in his hands. The girl belonged to him. She was worth a lot of money. Money, which might help his family back on Vectis. If he left her here without, claiming her then she would still be sold and someone else would just get her premium. No, he would still have to do this. But, as he turned to stare at the miserable looking girl through the iron bars, Fergus was suddenly torn by indecision. Efa and Dylis would never forgive him if he sold her. Wearily he cast a quick-glance up at the heavens. What would Corbulo have done in this situation? But there was no answer from the grey clouds.

'Number 21,' an auctioneer cried out in a loud voice, as the girl was dragged from her cage and led up onto the wooden platform. Expertly the auctioneer turned to address his audience. 'As you can see she is a young female, around sixteen, good teeth, strong and in excellent health,' he cried. 'Would make a great kitchen-maid, field-worker or house-hold slave. Limited grasp of Latin, but nothing a whip cannot teach. We will start the bidding at eight hundred Denarii.'

Around the platform the slave merchants and citizens gazed up at the girl. Then one of them raised his hand. Then another. Fergus took a deep breath as he looked on. Upon the stage, the girl looked terrified as she struggled with the slavers who held her fast. Then a stream of urine came running down her leg. But as one of the punters stepped forwards and reached up to touch her, she turned and spat at the man. The action resulted in a smattering of laughter amongst the crowd.

'Nine hundred denarii, do I have any bids for Nine fifty?' the auctioneer cried out glancing around at the crowd.

'No, I am sorry,' Fergus suddenly called out, raising his hand and showing the auctioneer his stone token. 'I have changed my mind. The girl is no longer for sale. I am going to take her with me now. Undo do those chains.'

Startled, the auctioneer turned to stare at Fergus. Around the stage the surprised crowd fell silent, as they too turned to look at Fergus. Up on the platform the girl was gazing at him with wild, frightened eyes.

'Undo those chains,' Fergus cried out again, as he pushed his way to the front of the stage and clambered up onto it and handed the auctioneer his token. 'She is no longer for sale.'

The auctioneer stared down at the token in his hand. Then slowly he shook his head.

'You are mad,' the man hissed quietly. 'What are you, a soldier, going to do with a slave? She will run away at the first possible chance. You would do much better if you let me sell her and pocket the money. Think about it.'

'I have,' Fergus growled. 'And she is not for sale.'

'Alright, suit yourself,' the auctioneer snapped angrily, as he gestured for his men to unchain the girl. 'But you will still pay the auctioneer's fees.'

'What are you doing Fergus,' one of his soldiers called out from the crowd. Ignoring the man, Fergus fished into his pocket, slapped a single, silver coin into the auctioneer's hand, then roughly grasping the girl by her arm, he led her off the podium.

The girl was silent as Fergus led her away through the crowd. Then, when they were out of sight of the slave pens, he forced her to stop. Tensely Fergus turned to look at the girl but she refused to meet his gaze.

'Shit,' Fergus muttered as he looked away. He'd acted on impulse and now that he had done so, he had no idea of what to do with his new slave.

'Alright, listen,' he said in Latin. 'My name is Fergus. You remember me, don't you? I took you prisoner on the battlefield. You belong to me. You are forbidden from running away, do you understand?'

The girl did not reply. Clasping hold of her chin, Fergus forced her to look up at him.

'What is your name?' he growled.

But the girl remained silent, staring at him with stubborn, defiant eyes.

'Can you understand what I am saying?' Fergus said speaking slowly.

Again the girl made no sound, nor did she move her head. She just stared back at Fergus with her large, pale-blue eyes.

'Oh this is fucking great,' Fergus hissed. 'What are you, a mute? Someone cut out your tongue?'

On impulse, he tried to force the girl to open her mouth, to show him that she did indeed have a tongue, but she squealed and refused to open her mouth, and after she had bitten his hand twice, he gave up.

'Suit yourself then,' he snapped angrily. Then roughly he undid the belt from around her waist and used it to bind her hands together.

'Don't you dare run away,' he cried pointing a finger at her. 'Now for the last time, what is your name?'

But the girl refused to answer and sullenly, lowered her eyes to the ground.

Bewildered Fergus shook his head. Maybe this had been a mistake? Maybe the slave auctioneer was right and he should just take the money. How was he ever going to look after a slave, like this girl? What use did he have for her? What was she going to do? How was he going to feed her? Where was he going to put her? He hadn't thought about any of that, when he'd made his decision to take her away from the slave merchants. All he knew was what he didn't want to sell her to those fat, lecherous men in the Forum.

For a moment, he stared at the ugly scar and the number 21, branded into her shoulder with a white-hot poker. The girl would carry that mark with her for the rest of her life. It would be an eternal reminder to everyone that she was a slave.

'Alright,' Fergus said in a calmer voice. 'If you don't want to speak, then I will give you a name. You can't be known forever as number twenty-one. So, from now on you will be called Titula. Got that. Titula, that's your name. When I say Titula, you listen.'

The girl raised her head and stared at Fergus.

'Titula,' Fergus muttered with a little encouraging nod. 'My name is Fergus. I am a soldier. I am the man who captured you on the battlefield. You remember me, don't you?'

The girl was staring at him blankly and with a sigh Fergus looked away. He had been a fool. Ofcourse the girl would not understand Latin. She was from beyond the Imperial borders, a barbarian and she would know as much Latin as he knew about her language, which was nothing.

'Oh fuck me,' Fergus muttered rubbing his forehead wearily. What had he done? What was he going to do with this girl?

'Fergus, what are you doing?' a voice called out from close by.

Deflated, Fergus turned to see Aledus and some of the other men coming towards him through the crowds. Some of the legionaries were clutching small leather bags in their hands, their faces beaming with happiness and excitement. Aledus was peering at Fergus curiously. Then he turned to examine the girl. 'What are you doing man?' Aledus repeated as he came to a halt beside Fergus, his eyes still on the girl. 'Are you insane? Don't you realise how lucky you are to have caught her? If you sold her, she would fetch over three year's salary. Don't you want the money? All the others have made a huge profit.'

'I can't do it,' Fergus muttered. 'I just can't do it.'

'You are mad,' Aledus replied, shaking his head. 'What are you going to do with her? We are soldiers Fergus. We have no time to look after slaves. If you are looking for a quick shag, then have it done with and then return her to the slavers. You are a fool if you do anything else.'

'That's enough,' Fergus growled. 'I have made up my mind. She is not for sale. That's the end of it.'

'Fine,' Aledus said raising his eyebrows. Then he gave him a playful slap on his back. 'Most of the company are off drinking followed by the whorehouses and the amphitheatre but I was wondering, now that you are such a rich man, whether you would like to come and join me for some proper gambling? I know a few veterans who organise a game close by. They seem to have deep pockets. Come on, I am feeling lucky today.'

Chapter Twenty-Six – Number Twenty-One

The five-army veterans, older men clad in civilian attire, sat on the stone steps of the temple staring unhappily at the dice.

'See I told you that it was my lucky day,' Aledus cried out with a wide grin, as he scooped up the coins lying beside the dice. 'Better luck next time boys. You should pray to Jupiter harder. Maybe he will throw you a bone.'

'Cocky bastard,' one of the older men growled with an annoyed shake of his head. 'I bet you won't be lucky like that twice in a row. Well, what do you say punk. Fancy another wager?'

'I am in,' Fergus snapped as he looked down at the three dice and placed his last silver coin into the growing pile. He shouldn't be doing this he knew but he was going to do it anyway. The excitement of the game, the lure of the stakes was too much. He could do this. He could win again. He'd had moderate success in the early stages of the gambling, but for the last six straight throws he'd lost. But on the seventh go his luck would turn. It had to, Fergus thought. The eight of them were sitting on the temple steps in the middle of the Forum. It was afternoon and the dull, grey clouds covered the whole sky. Around the gamblers the Forum was crowded with people coming and going, but no one seemed to pay them the slightest interest. Titula, her hand bounds tightly together with her belt, sat behind Fergus staring at the dice in sullen silence. She had still not said a word but in the excitement of the game, that was just as well Fergus thought.

'Sorry boys but I think I am done for the day. The whores are getting impatient. They are lusting after my presence,' Aledus said with a cocky grin as he glanced at the veterans. 'You will just have to play this hand without me.'

'Suit yourself,' one of the veterans growled. Then smoothly the man turned to carefully size Fergus up. 'This round we are tripling the odds, so that's three silver from you,' the man said gesturing at the pile of coins.

Fergus froze. He didn't have any more money. From the corner of his eye he noticed Aledus turn to look at him. His friend gave him a little shake of his head. Slowly Fergus turned back to stare at the coins. The money glinted in the light beckoning to him. He shouldn't be doing this. He shouldn't.

'I don't have any more coins on me,' he grunted.

One of the veterans, a hard-looking man of around fifty with an angry white scar across his cheeks sneered.

'You look like a wealthy man. What with a slave in tow? It's three silver coins or you can fuck off.'

Fergus sighed and stared at the coins. If he won this round, he would win back all his losses and then some. He could do this. His luck was bound to change.

'Alright, I shall have to owe you,' he growled. 'Like I said I don't have the coins.'

'Like hell you will,' one of the gamblers growled. 'We don't do credit. You pay up now or you fuck off.'

But the man was sharply cut off by another of the veterans.

'No,' the man said with sudden authority. 'He has that slave girl. He is not going to default on his debts if he loses. She will cover his debts, no matter what.'

'The girl is not for sale,' Fergus snapped.

The man with the angry scar grinned and around him his comrades broke out into unfriendly laughter.

'We don't want to buy her,' one of the veterans said. 'If you lose we will just use her for an evening. That should cover your debts. We will return her to you in one piece.'

Fergus took a deep breath and looked down at the money. Then without warning from behind him Titula suddenly leaned forwards and clasped hold of Fergus's wrist and as she did, the veterans burst out laughing.

'See, she does understand Latin,' one of the men cried out with an amused look. 'The girl knows exactly what is going on.'

Irritably, Fergus wrenched himself free from Titula's grip and turned to look at her. The girl was staring at him with a frightened look.

'Alright, I am in,' Fergus growled turning back to the gamblers, 'but you are not touching my slave. If I lose I will pay you the debts within three days. I make that promise on the honour of the Second Company of the Second Cohort of the Twentieth Legion.'

Around the pile of coins, the veterans sucked in their breath. For a moment, they were silent as they glanced at the man with the scar.

'If you don't pay,' the man said at last staring at Fergus with a calm but menacing look, 'we will find you and cut your balls off and feed them to the fish in the river. Do you understand what I am saying? We don't take kindly to pricks who don't pay their debts?'

'Shut up,' Fergus retorted glaring at the man. 'I have given you my word. That is enough. Anyway, I am not going to lose.'

The man with the scar turned to his comrades and gestured at the dice.

'Let them speak,' the man growled.

Tensely Fergus stared at the dice lying in the bottom of the leather cup. His luck had held and four of the five veterans had been knocked out of the game. The only ones' left was himself and the man with the angry scar. Across from him the veteran glared and leaned forwards.

"I will raise you," the man sneered, "Triple again, nine silver coins. You think you have the balls to follow that?"

Fergus hesitated and then slowly exhaled. Nine silver coins was a lot of money, which he didn't have. Wearily he looked down at the dice in the cup. There was only one man left to beat, a fifty-fifty chance.

"Bring it on," he snapped defiantly, jutting his chin at the veteran.

With a grin the man picked up the cup, gave it a shake and rolled the dice. Then the veteran hissed in delight. A six, a five and a four.

Fergus reached out, grasped hold of the dice and dropped them into the cup and gave them a good shake. Then silently he muttered a prayer to the gods and rolled the dice out onto the stones. A one, another one and a two. Fergus groaned and closed his eyes in dismay as his opponent whooped in delight.

'Come on mate, we should go,' Aledus said quietly.

Fergus nodded as he stiffly rose to his feet and, as he did the veterans did the same. 'You owe me eight silver coins,' the veteran with the scar snapped, jabbing a finger at Fergus. 'I will expect payment in three days' time. Come and find me here on these temple steps. And don't think about not showing up. If you don't, we will come and find you and don't think that the army will protect you. We know everything there is to know about the legions, so you had better have the money by then, punk.'

And with a final sneer at Titula, the five veterans scooped up the coins and dice from the temple steps and stomped off into the crowd.

'Stupid, stupid, stupid,' Fergus hissed hitting his forehead with his fist. 'What was I thinking? Why do I always do this?'

'I don't have that kind of money,' Aledus said looking away. 'None of the boys have. You shouldn't ask them Fergus; it's too great a sum.'

'I know, I know,' Fergus muttered glumly. Then he took a deep breath and turned to look at Titula. The slave girl lowered her eyes and stared down at her feet.

'Alright, I will figure something out,' Fergus said with a sigh. 'Maybe Furius will lend me the money. I shall have to ask him.'

'Don't mess with this those men,' Aledus said turning warily to look in the direction in which the veterans had disappeared. 'They are not men you should cross. They are locals. They will know what goes on around here. We are going to be here all winter so you are not going to be able to avoid them.'

'I said I would figure something out,' Fergus said in an irritated voice as he rounded on his friend.

'Good,' Aledus retorted turning to look away.

A sullen silence followed. Then Aledus shook his head in disbelief and chuckled.

'Damn Fergus, you are shit at gambling. Did you know that. You always lose. You never know when to stop do you.' Aledus chuckled again. 'So I am thinking about joining the lads in the tavern and drinking until I pass out. What are you going to do? What are you going to do with the girl?'

Fergus glanced at Titula.

'I told you, I am not going to sell her,' he growled. 'And about tonight, I am sorry, I won't be joining you.'

'That's probably for the best, none of the boys would want to buy you drinks all night anyway,' Aledus said with a cheeky grin. 'I will take her back to our camp,' Fergus said ignoring the jibe. 'I am going to ask Titus if he will allow her to stay in the same quarters as his slaves. The girl will be able to help cook, clean, repair stuff and whatever other chores that need to be done. She will have a roof over her head and she won't starve. That's the best I can think of right now.'

Aledus glanced at the slave girl and then slowly shook his head. 'I still think you are mad,' he muttered. 'She is going to run away at the first chance she gets. I would if I was her.'

***

It was morning when Fergus, accompanied by Furius set off into the forest. Both were clad in their winter cloaks with hoods and both were carrying hunting bows. Quivers, filled with arrows, were slung over their shoulders and both were carrying their short swords strapped to their belts. It had been Furius's idea that they go hunting on their second day of leave and Fergus had not objected. Above them the sky was overcast and it was a dry October day. The morning air felt crisp and cold, a perfect day to go out hunting. Behind them, amongst the newly-completed barracks of the Cohort's winter quarters, smoke from the legionary cooking fires curled lazily into the sky. The silence was broken by a single, barking dog. The men who had decided to remain in the camp would be taking it easy today Fergus thought, and most would no doubt be wanting to sleep off their hangovers. Most of the company however had elected to stay the night in town, sampling its delights. They were expected back before nightfall.

As they slipped away into the forest, Fergus silently notched an arrow to his hunting bow. Titula had not spoken a word to him on the fourteen-mile walk, back from the city to their base in the forest. After trying to engage her, Fergus had given up, and the two of them had completed the walk in sullen, annoyed silence. On the walk back he'd come to the conclusion that the sheer horror of the events the girl had been through in recent days, must have made her mute. But despite her condition, the girl had made no attempt to escape. At the auxiliary camp, it had been Titus's young wife, Lydia who had come to his rescue, when he'd shown up at her door with Titula in tow. It had been Lydia who had told Titus that she would be happy to accept another slave, into her quarters. After a brief inspection of the girl, Lydia had announced that she would do and Titula had been immediately set to work cleaning and helping the cooks. That had been yesterday.

'So Fergus, it seems that the gods want us to work together," Furius said, with a faint smile as the two of them made their way deeper into the forest. 'Can't say I am unhappy with that. After all we both seem to have done rather well out of our last cooperation, back in Deva.'

'My thoughts exactly,' Fergus replied as he followed Furius through the forest. 'That jug of wine was a well-timed gift. Titus made the right decision, even if it meant poor Aledus ended up in hospital with his face kicked in.'

'Shit happens,' Furius shrugged.

'And I am glad that Fronto was transferred,' Fergus growled. 'Titus made another good decision there. If he hadn't done that I would have killed Fronto, that bastard.'

"Yeah right," Furius said pausing and turning to look at Fergus in disbelief. 'That's tough talk but I doubt you would really have done it. You are a pussy Fergus. You may think you are tough but you are still a pussy.'

'Think what you like,' Fergus growled as Furius resumed walking. 'But that bastard deserved a knife in his ribs.'

'That he did,' Furius said quietly. 'Arsehole once tried to stab me as well. It was before you joined us. Did you know that?'

'No,' Fergus replied in a surprised voice.

'Yes, well, best forgotten now,' Furius said sullenly. 'But Fronto is my enemy as much as he is yours Fergus and one day he is going to get what he deserves.'

'Does that make you a pussy as well,' Fergus said as a little smile appeared on his lips.

'Shut up,' Furius snapped.

***

The small fire, enclosed by a ring of stones and piled high with dry twigs and branches, crackled and spat and the wood-smoke rose through the trees. Fergus and Furius sat on opposite sides of the fire, staring at the roasting carcass of a young deer, which they had managed to stalk and kill in the woods. The animal had been skewered onto a long, metal-spike, which Furius had placed over the fire, held up by two metal supports that he'd driven into the ground. Fat was dripping down into the flames, causing the fire to hiss and explode. As Fergus sat staring at the meat, Furius slowly rose to his feet and reached out to turn the roast over.

'Here, have some of this,' Furius said tossing across a drinking pouch. Fergus caught it, undid the pouch and sniffed. Then, with a grunt he held the pouch to his mouth and emptied some of the wine into his mouth. Tossing the pouch back to Furius, the Optio did the same, burped and wiped his mouth with the back of his hand.

'You know,' Furius said with a sigh as he stared into the flames. 'I am only the acting Optio. When Lucullus returns to health he will get his old job back.'

Fergus frowned. He hadn't thought about that. Warily he picked at the hole and tear in the cloth of his cloak.

'But I am the Tesserarius now,' Fergus muttered at last. 'So what will they do with you when Lucullus returns to claim his old position?'

'Transfer within the Legion most likely,' Furius said gloomily. 'They will post me to another company, just like we did with Fronto.'

"Maybe they will promote you to Centurion?"

'Nah,' Furius said with a little amused smile, 'promotion up to the rank of Optio can be rapid but there is a huge gap between an Optio and a Centurion. Most men must wait ten or fifteen years before they are promoted to Centurion. As you can imagine it is a sought-after position and not too many come free each year. And you need to be in with the senior officers if you know what I mean. No, they will probably make me an Optio in some other fucking company.'

Fergus nodded and looked down at the ground. Now was the right time to ask Furius if he would lend him, eight silver coins. But asking Furius would be a humiliating experience and as, he struggled to ask the question, the moment passed and Fergus remained silent.

Furius was about to say something else, when Fergus heard a twig crack in the forest. Jumping to his feet he drew his sword and turned to peer into the forest in the direction from which the sound had come.

'Who goes there?' Furius cried. He too had leapt to his feet and had drawn his sword. The cold steel glinted in the firelight.

A few moments later a face appeared from behind the trees. It was Lydia, Titus's young wife. She smiled as she came towards the camp-fire, clutching a wicker basket under her arm. And to Fergus's surprise she was followed by Titula, clutching a similar-shaped basket. The girl gave Fergus a stoic look.

'We were gathering mushrooms in the forest when I saw the smoke from your fire,' Lydia said as she gave both Furius and Fergus a broad smile. 'Looks like your hunt was successful.'

'It was,' Furius said, sheathing his sword, "You are welcome to join us. There is plenty of meat. Enough to feed the whole company.'

But Lydia shook her head as she glanced at the roast. 'No I should be getting back,' she said quickly. 'And I think so should you Furius. Just before we left a messenger on horseback arrived. My husband has received new orders and he doesn't seem to be very happy about them. I think you had better come back with me. Titus will want to speak with you right away. Sorry to break up your day like this but I know my husband. He is properly pissed off.'

Then, before either Furius or Fergus could reply, Lydia turned to look at Fergus and gave him a friendly wink.

'Your slave doesn't say much,' Lydia exclaimed. 'But she does what she is told and she is a hard worker. I will leave her with you. Maybe you will loosen her tongue.'

'Thank you,' Fergus muttered inclining his head respectfully.

'Alright,' Furius said turning to glance at Fergus. 'I will leave it to you two to bring that roast back to the camp. I am not going to miss out on eating it. You have your orders, Fergus. See to it.'

***

When Lydia and Furius had disappeared into the forest, Fergus turned to look at his slave girl. Titula was standing at the edge of the fire, staring at the fat dripping down into the flames. She seemed to be waiting for him to speak. Her long, black hair had been tied up and fixed with a small bone fibula and she looked a little awkward wearing her new, Roman style clothes. Lydia must have given her those, Fergus thought. The girl was only a few years younger than himself. Slowly he sat down and gestured for her to do the same and, after a moment's hesitation, she did.

'Are you hungry?' Fergus said glancing at her. 'If you want to eat then take some of the meat,' he added gesturing at the roast.

But the slave girl did not move, nor did she say anything.

Wearily Fergus looked away. It was the same old story all over again. The girl would not or could not speak. It was pointless trying to communicate with her. And yet this time, part of him was not ready to give up.

'I hope that Lydia and the other slaves are treating you well,' Fergus exclaimed. 'I hear some masters abuse their slaves, but I want you to know that I am not like that. You will find me an honest, honourable man.' Fergus paused and glanced at Titula. 'All I require from you is that you serve me well, and don't run away. In return I shall feed you, cloth you and treat you well and see to it that no harm comes to you, and then,' Fergus sighed, 'in time you shall earn your freedom and I shall let you go home, but not yet, you understand, not yet.'

Across from him, where she was crouching on the ground, the girl picked at her finger-nails and said nothing.

Fergus sighed again and then laughed. This was ridiculous. Was the girl trying to make him look like a fool?

"What am I going to do with you,' he said wearily. 'Gods tell me what I am going to do with this slave girl?'

Suddenly the girl rose to her feet, fumbled for something in her pocket and silently came and sat down beside Fergus. Startled he did not move. Carefully Titula reached out and poked her finger through the hole and tear in his cloak and, as Fergus looked on she held up a fine, bone needle and a patch of cloth and began to repair the hole. When she was finished, she patted the patch and looked up at him.

'Thank you Titula,' Fergus muttered looking away in sudden embarrassment.

For a moment, she stared at him with her pale, blue eyes, as if she was examining him for the first time. Then slowly she rose to her feet and gestured at his hunting knife that was stuffed into his belt. Frowning Fergus pulled the knife from his belt and held it up in the air.

'What are you going to do with this?' Fergus said guardedly.

Titula said nothing as she patiently undid his fingers around the knife before slipping it out of his grip completely. Turning towards the roast, she expertly sliced off a couple of pieces of meat and skin and handed them over to Fergus, together with the knife. Fergus looked down at the meat in silence. Then with a grunt he handed one piece to Titula whilst, he stuffed the other into his mouth. At his side, the slave girl did the same, devouring the meat as if she had been starving.

'Thank you,' Fergus muttered again, when he had swallowed the last of the meat. 'Now at least I know that you like meat.'

The girl was crouching on the ground watching him carefully. Then slowly and silently she lay back, hitched up her tunica and spread her legs, exposing herself to Fergus. Beside the fire Fergus quickly rose to his feet.
'No, no, no,' he exclaimed hastily. 'I already have a woman. Her name is Galena. She is my wife. There is no need to do that. I do not require you to do that.'

Hurriedly he gestured for her to cover herself up. For a moment Titula looked confused. Then slowly she pulled down her tunica and sat up looking at the ground, in sudden embarrassment.

Fergus turned to look away and exhaled sharply. Corbulo, his grandfather would not have hesitated. Quintus had made that clear. Fergus turned to look at Titula. The girl was a pretty and fairly-attractive woman and he wouldn't normally have hesitated either, before having a go. But he'd made a solemn vow to Galena. He could not betray her. No, he had promised to stay true to her, and however hard that had proved so far, he had managed.

Sitting down beside Titula, he held out the iron amulet Galena had given him.

'My wife gave me this,' Fergus exclaimed. 'Her name is Galena. She is carrying my child. So, I already have a woman. Do you understand? One day I will go back to Britannia and see them both.'

Titula remained silent but as he showed her the amulet she reached out to touch it, examining the fine metal work curiously. Then abruptly she got up and moved away around the fire and, as she did, Fergus thought he saw a sudden look of sadness appear in her eyes.

Fergus rubbed his forehead and turned to look at the roasting meat.

'We should head back,' he said rising to his feet. 'I will need your help carrying this carcass back to the camp.'

***

As Fergus and Titula, with the young deer slung on the metal pole in between them, came striding up towards the Centurion's quarters, Titus accompanied by Furius suddenly appeared in the doorway to their barracks. Titus looked unhappy.

'Fergus,' he barked, 'get your butt over here. I want to have a word with you.'

Obediently Fergus gestured for Titula to lower the roast to the ground. Then hastily he came towards the Centurion and saluted smartly.

'You may not believe this,' Titus growled fixing his eyes on Fergus, 'but this morning I received a messenger from the Legate Hadrian himself. Yes, that's right. Hadrian has sent me a message. He has ordered our company to report for special duties at his HQ in Carnuntum in seven days' time. It has already been approved by the Cohort commander. Apparently, we have been chosen for some special mission beyond the Danube.'

'I understand Sir,' Fergus said frowning, 'but what has this got to do with me, Sir?'

'Only this,' Titus snapped glaring at him. 'The messenger who came to me this morning was a German officer on the Legate's staff. He gave his name as Adalwolf. He said that he knew you personally and that based on his acquaintance with you, he had personally recommended to Hadrian that the Legate choose our company for this mission. He said we were the best and that he had complete confidence in us. He had nothing but praise, for you in particular.'

A little colour shot into Fergus's cheeks as he stared at Titus.

'That doesn't sound too bad Sir,' Fergus stammered.

Grimly Titus took a step towards Fergus, so that the Centurion's face was right up against Fergus's. The Centurion looked furious. 'He also said that our expedition was likely to take us hundreds of miles beyond the Imperial frontiers and that we would be gone for at least two months,' Titus bellowed.

Chapter Twenty-Seven – Roman Diplomacy

The company stood drawn up in its square parade-ground formation facing Titus. At the Centurion's side, the signifer, clad in his wolf's-head skin cloak, was clutching the company banner. Six days had passed since they had been ordered to report to the naval harbour at Carnuntum and Titus was still in a foul mood. Now, wearing his splendid uniform, armour, plumed helmet and red cloak, he stood glaring at his men, tapping his vine-staff moodily against his thigh, as if he was a volcano that was about to explode in rage. Not a man moved and not a man made a sound. Fergus, staring into space, stood in front of the foremost ranks, facing Titus, whilst Furius stood behind the rearmost ranks, clutching his long, wooden staff. Titus had kept the company standing like this for nearly an hour. What was he waiting for? What was he trying to prove? Behind the high walls of the harbour of Carnuntum there was no one to see them. Sourly, Fergus continued to stare into space. Titus had barely said a word to him since he'd told him about the company's new orders. He still blames me, Fergus thought. Well it wasn't fair. How could he have known that Adalwolf would choose his unit for this special mission? In the dull November morning sky, dark thunder-clouds were gathering in the east and it was cold.

From the corner of his eye, Fergus suddenly noticed movement. Four men were coming towards the company. They looked like senior officers.

'Company,' Titus's voice boomed out across the small parade ground, 'Company will stand to attention.'

In front of their Centurion, the seventy-five legionaries stiffened and straightened up in a smooth collective movement. Clutching their shields and spears, each man stared straight ahead with an expressionless look. As the four officers came up to Titus, the Centurion turned to the newcomers and saluted. A few yards away, Fergus silently swore to himself. Leading the small group was the Legate Hadrian and, at his side was Adalwolf.

Hadrian had a beard. Their twenty-nine-year-old commander was of average height and he was a handsome man. Dressed in the uniform of a legionary legate, with muscle cuirass armour covering his chest and a fine red cloak draped over his shoulders, Hadrian looked every inch the dashing young aristocratic general. Fergus stared at him with growing curiosity. The Legate had been with the whole battle-group, all the way from Bonna on the Rhine to their new winter quarters, but this was the first time that Fergus had actually seen him close up. The men had discussed their commander on the long march. Some had called him a clown, an Imperial appointee lacking any military experience but others had said that he was a tough and accomplished soldier with a strong respect for the men under his command. Quickly Fergus averted his gaze as Hadrian idly turned to glance at the company. Then with a little nod to Titus, the Legate turned to address the men.

'Legionaries,' Hadrian cried out in a voice that seemed used to command. 'For those of you who do not know me, my name is Hadrian, Legate in command of the First Legion.' Hadrian paused to peer around at the soldiers. 'Now, I am sure that you will be asking yourself, what am I doing here on this cold day? No doubt you would prefer to be warming your hands over an open fire and filling your bellies with piping hot stew or perhaps hunting in the forest. But Adalwolf here,' Hadrian said gesturing at the German amber merchant, 'he has told me that you are the best company in one of Rome's finest Legion's. And if that is so, then I am going to need you. Tonight, under the cover of darkness we will be crossing the river and heading north. Our destination lies hundreds of miles beyond the Imperial frontier, a sacred grove in the land of the Vandals. Now the reason why we are going there is to conduct diplomacy on behalf of the Emperor and the People of Rome. The Vandals are Rome's allies and we need them to remain our friends. We are going to need their friendship when spring comes again and the war in Dacia resumes.' Hadrian grinned as he gazed at the company. 'But leave the diplomacy to me. Your job is to get me to this sacred grove alive and in one piece and then back again. Now because of the secrecy, which we need to maintain, none of you today will be allowed to go beyond these walls. None of you will be allowed to tell anyone about where we are going. So, I hope all of you have already said goodbye to your loved ones. Our mission will last at least two months,' Hadrian cried. 'You will be issued with winter clothing and whilst you are away your pay will be doubled. Now get some rest. We have a long and difficult journey ahead of us. Long live Emperor Trajan and the People of Rome.'

'Long live Emperor Trajan,' the company roared.

Hadrian looked pleased as he gazed at the men. Then he turned and accompanied by his companions, he strode away.

'Company,' Titus boomed. 'Company will fall out. Dismissed.'

With a relieved murmur the men broke ranks and began to drift away across the open space. Here and there a few little groups started to form, as the men laid down their shields and spears and sat down on the ground. Fergus exhaled and reached up to scratch his forehead. Then he glanced quickly at Titus. That morning Titus had said farewell to his wife Lydia, and for such a tough man like the Centurion, their farewell had been surprisingly touching in its affection. Fergus ran his fingers over his forehead. Titula had still not said a word to him. She didn't seem to have understood when he had told her, he was going away. He'd left her in the company of Lydia and, as a last gesture, he had given her his hunting knife. He wasn't sure why he'd done that, but it had made him feel better. At least that way the girl would have a chance to protect herself whilst he was away. Afterwards Furius had laughed at him telling him that he was getting far too close to his slave girl and that he should start to treat Titula as a slave, property, an asset, to do with however he saw fit. You are a fool, Fergus. She is going to run away whilst you are gone, Furius had warned him.

From the corner of his eye, Fergus suddenly noticed movement beside the gates leading from the naval harbour into the city. A column of auxiliary horsemen, clad in their distinctive chainmail armour, came clattering into the open space between the walls and the harbour front. Grunting in surprise, Fergus recognised the proud banner, which one of the horsemen was holding up. The riders were Batavians and not just any Batavians. These men were from the Second Batavian Cohort, his father's old regiment. A little smile appeared on his face, as he stared at the cavalrymen. Would some of the riders still remember Marcus, his father? There were thirty or so of them, led by a young Decurion; a full squadron. The horsemen were followed by a column of shaggy, tough looking mules, heavily laden with sacks and wooden boxes that were strapped to their backs. Each mule seemed to be attended to by a single slave holding a whip or stick. There were fifteen of them, led by a fat slave-master with a limp.

'So, looks like you are not going to repay your debts to those veterans after all,' Aledus said quietly as he suddenly appeared at Fergus's side. 'Weren't you supposed to meet them on the temple steps today with the money?'

Fergus turned to glance at his friend and shrugged.

'Yes, I won't be there,' he muttered. 'I don't have the money anyway. They will just have to wait until we get back. Double pay, Aledus, double pay, that should help.'

'It's a dangerous game you are playing Fergus,' Aledus said with a troubled look in his eyes. 'I know those kinds of men. They will not forget. They will want their money with interest. You need to watch your back.'

Fergus was about to reply when he noticed Titus, Furius, the signifer and the young Batavian Decurion coming towards him.

'Fergus, with me. Now,' the Centurion growled.

Giving Aledus a quick goodbye, Fergus hastily strode away to catch up with Titus.

'What's going on?' he muttered casting a glance at the Centurion as the five of them strode across the parade ground.

'The Legate has requested our presence,' Titus snapped.

***

The small harbour-master's office had been built up against the harbour walls and inside it seemed to have been completely taken over by Hadrian and his staff. Bowls of half-eaten food and drinking cups lay scattered across a large wooden table, upon which lay a papyrus map and, along the walls sacks of grain, amphorae and boxes lay stacked up against each other. Oil lamps burned from their holsters along the walls, bathing the room in a flickering light and, in a corner a small fire crackled in a hearth. Hadrian and his three companions were standing around the table examining the map, as Titus and his officers entered the room. Seeing them, the Legate beckoned for them to join him around the table. As he approached, Fergus gave Adalwolf a quick, annoyed glance but the German ignored him.

Once they were all standing around the table, Hadrian cleared his throat.

'Gentlemen,' Hadrian said in a grave voice, turning to Titus, "it is of vital importance that all my officers are fully aware of the importance of this expedition. I need you all to understand what is at stake here. So, I am now going to give you a brief overview of the strategic situation along the frontier and how our mission fits into this. After that Adalwolf will talk you through our planned route and what we can expect to encounter on our journey.'

Titus slowly turned to look down at the map on the table. Across the papyrus, small iron-counters denoting infantry, cavalry and naval forces, lined the entire frontier from the German sea in the north-west to the Black Sea in the south-east. The counters were supplemented by hundreds-upon-hundreds of map markings lining the entire frontier in depth and denoting forts, watch towers, roads, supply-depots, fixed defences, naval harbours, walls and towns, villages and cities.

Fergus stood up straight with his hands respectfully clasped behind his back, as he studied Hadrian. The Legate did not look like or sound like a clown. There was a quiet competence about how he spoke and moved and yet, Fergus struggled not to laugh. The rumour amongst the legionaries was that the Legate had only been posted to Carnuntum and the command of the First Legion because he'd fallen out of favour with Trajan the Emperor. This command was a demotion. Was the great man now trying to make up for it, by pulling off a diplomatic coup that would impress the Emperor? If so, Fergus thought with sudden weariness, he and the company were mere pawns on a board he did not fully understand. The other rumour about Hadrian doing the rounds amongst the ranks however, was worse. Some had sworn that Hadrian was not a real man at all, and that he preferred the company of men to that of women.

'So,' Hadrian said in a clear voice, glancing around the room. 'Our expedition will consist of myself, Adalwolf, my German adviser, translator and two of my freedmen who are familiar with the strategic situation. The Second Company, Second Cohort of the Twentieth Legion; your men, Titus, will act as our main escort. In addition, we shall be joined by a squadron of auxiliary Batavian cavalry, who will act as scouts. Finally, we will have fifteen mules to carry our supplies. Each mule will be tended to by a slave and will carry our food and tents. That makes a total of six officers, one hundred and five soldiers and fifteen slaves plus four civilians.'

Slowly Hadrian reached forwards and picked up a small counter of a legionary infantryman.

'Now this is the Legionary base at Carnuntum,' he said looking up at the men around the table. 'Normally the fifteenth Legion is based here but the bulk of that Legion has already been transferred south and east to the Dacian frontier. The same applies for my own unit at Bonna, and many of the other legions guarding the Rhine and Danube have likewise sent vexillatio to the Dacian front. The Emperor Trajan is gathering a force of over a hundred thousand men to conquer Dacia in the spring of next year. It is a formidable force, but it also means that many of our forts and fortresses are severely weakened and undermanned.' Hadrian paused to study the map for a moment. 'Now the Emperor has instructed me to keep the frontier to the north quiet and peaceful, during his Dacian campaign,' he continued. 'That means that the German tribes must not be allowed to take advantage of the situation,' he growled. 'They must not feel tempted to invade Roman land whilst most of our best men are away fighting in Dacia. And gods forbid, they must not be tempted to form an alliance with the Dacian's against us. On our stretch of the frontier, that means the Marcomanni and Quadi must be kept in check. That is why we need the Lugii and Vandal confederation to remain our allies.' Hadrian tapped the map with his finger. 'The Vandals are a powerful group of tribes. They live here in the mountains and plains to the north beyond the Marcomanni and Quadi. If we can keep the Vandals as allies of Rome the Marcomanni and Quadi will think twice about attacking us. They will not want to expose themselves to attack from their northern neighbours.' Hadrian looked up sharply. 'Remember, the German tribes hate each other far more than they hate us. Our expedition to the Vandals will be to ensure that our alliance with them continues. It is of vital strategic importance that it does.'

'Very good Sir,' Titus interrupted with a sour looking expression as he looked down at the map. 'I am just a soldier so I know nothing about diplomacy. But if there is something that I have learned in twenty-two years' service it is that men seldom do anything that is not in their self-interest. How then are we going to ensure that our alliance with the Vandals continues?'

'A good question Centurion,' Hadrian nodded. 'And I was coming to that. Our diplomacy is based on two methods of persuasion, the stick and the carrot. Now because the Vandals live hundreds of miles to the north they cannot be threatened with military force so we must resort to the carrot.' Hadrian straightened up and looked at Titus. 'Your men will not only be escorting me, and my staff to the Vandal sacred grove. We will also be carrying with us six strong boxes filled with gold and silver. Our cargo will be worth over a million denarii. The Emperor has authorised me to give this Roman subsidy to the Vandal leaders; one box for each chieftain of the individual tribes that make up the Lugii and Vandal confederation. We are going to pay the Vandals to remain our allies. That is why this mission must remain a secret. There will be many men out there, who would love to get their hands on that gold and silver if they knew about it.'

At Titus's side, Fergus suddenly saw Furious break out into a flush. A million denarii he thought. That was incredible wealth; wealth beyond imagination.

'A million denarii!' Titus muttered slowly shaking his head. 'Shit, for such an amount every man within a thousand miles will be willing to risk his life. If anyone finds out about this, we are going to become dead men walking.'

'Precisely,' Hadrian snapped. 'Which is why the knowledge of the gold and silver subsidy will not go beyond the walls of this room. It is the reason why tonight we will be leaving under the cover of darkness. It is the reason why the men are not allowed to leave the harbour. The soldiers should not know what we are carrying. It is for the best. Is that clear?'

Around the table, the officers nodded in silent agreement.

'How do you intend to keep such a large cargo a secret from the men?' Titus asked. 'Gold and silver is heavy. It takes up space. It makes noise.'

Hadrian glanced at one of his officer's. Then he looked down at the map. 'The gold and silver will be carried by the mules,' he muttered. 'We have arranged for it to be hidden in boxes which are also filled with grain and barley. Everyone will think they are just part of our food supplies. No one will know any different by taking just a casual glance.'

The room fell silent.

'How will we find our way to this sacred Vandal grove?' Fergus said.

Slowly Hadrian turned to look at Fergus.

'A good question, Tesserarius,' the Legate muttered. 'On our expedition we will be accompanied by a Vandal prince, a man named Gaiseric. He has agreed to take us to the sacred grove of his people. It is the place where they worship their gods. The other Vandal chieftains will meet us there.' Grimly Hadrian turned to look at the men assembled around the table. 'Gaiseric has promised to give us free passage through the lands to the north. He claims to have authority to do this. He is an important man amongst the Vandals. He will be our principle go-between; between us and the Germans.'

'Does he know about the gold and silver?' Titus growled unhappily.

Hadrian shook his head in slight exasperation. 'He knows about the subsidy,' the Legate snapped. 'He helped set the price. I know what you are thinking Centurion but you are just going to have to trust the man. He has proved himself a loyal and useful ally in the past.'

'If you say so Sir,' Titus growled.

'What about you?' Fergus suddenly piped up turning to Adalwolf with a challenging look. 'I thought you said that you were a guide. I thought you said you knew the land beyond the frontier better than any living man. Why are you not taking us to this Vandal temple?'

Across the table Adalwolf surveyed Fergus coolly, with a hint of irritation. But before Adalwolf could reply, Hadrian interrupted him.

'Prince Gaiseric is our guide,' the Legate snapped. 'It has already been settled. There will be no more discussion. I am going to need him during our discussions with the Vandal leaders. He is an important man amongst our allies.' Exasperated Hadrian glanced around the table. 'Now Adalwolf here will give you a briefing on what you and your men are likely to expect beyond the frontier. You will do well to listen to this.'

Giving Fergus a disapproving look, Adalwolf ran his hand across his chin as all eyes turned to the German amber merchant.

'If you look at the map,' the merchant said quietly in his thickly accented Latin as he placed his finger on Carnuntum. 'Once we cross the river we will head north following the amber road until we reach the Moravian gates. For those of you unfamiliar with the amber road. It is the main route from the amber producing regions far to the north, to their markets within the Roman Empire. Carnuntum is the point where the road enters the Empire. There is no road of course, not like any Roman road that you are used to, but there is a well-trodden trail and we should be able to barter for supplies along the way with the local villages. The Germans along our route are used to seeing traders and Roman merchants. Our food stores will not last us for the two months in which we will be gone. So, we must supplement them with barter and hunting.'

Adalwolf paused as he stared down at the papyrus. Then slowly his finger moved northwards and into an area of blankness on the map.

'The Moravian gates are a pass through the mountains,' Adalwolf muttered, "To the east the Carpathian mountains and to the west the Sudeten mountains. Once we are through the pass we will swing north-west, leaving the amber road as we strike out for the Vandal holy grove that lies on top of Mount Sleza, here.'

Adalwolf tapped the map with his finger. Then he looked up and his eyes found Fergus.

'Our best defence is to keep a low profile and to keep moving,' Adalwolf said sharply. "The Marcomanni and Quadi are certainly no friends of Rome but then they are not as well organised as Rome. Hopefully we will have passed through their territory before their leaders can mount an effective response. Beyond the frontier, in the barbarian lands, there are no roads, no towns, no cities, no baths, no forts, no Roman civilisation. The land is covered in vast, dense forests with scattered villages. The German tribes do not live like Romans. It is possible for a small group like us, to slip through their territory without meeting any serious opposition. If we are challenged, we are a party of merchants heading north on the amber road. Prince Gaiseric and his men should also help.'

Adalwolf turned to Titus.

'Now the other problem that we are going to encounter is winter. The winter in the mountains and forests is truly horrendous and something none of you have ever experienced. Freezing temperatures, a lack of food, no wild-game and snow-storms so thick you will hardly be able to see the next man in front of you. In such conditions, you are going to find it hard to move and our pace will slow dramatically. So, Lord Hadrian has arranged for all your men to be issued with special winter cloaks, socks, gloves and other cold weather equipment after my own design. Your men will also be given specially-designed covers for their shields and oil to keep their swords from freezing in their scabbards.' Adalwolf paused and raised his hand to stroke his chin. "But if any of your men become ill and incapable of keeping up with us, they must be left behind. We cannot be slowed down by stragglers. Make sure that your men are aware of this.'

'I will not leave any of my men behind,' Titus said calmly turning to Adalwolf.

Adalwolf sighed and turned to look at Fergus.

'I wouldn't worry about that Centurion,' the German amber merchant muttered. 'As your company is the finest in the whole Legion I don't expect this to happen anyway.'

'Alright, any questions?' Hadrian said.

But around the table the assembled officers remained silent.

'Good,' the Legate exclaimed turning to look at the officers around the table. 'Then have your men collect their equipment from the harbour master and tell them to get some rest. We leave tonight as soon as it is dark. That will be all.'

***

It was dark and in the heaven's, there was no sign of the stars or the moon. The two naval transports that had brought the expedition to the other side of the Danube had already silently vanished back into the night. In the darkness, the men from Fergus's company were down on one knee, their shields protecting their bodies and their spears facing outwards into the night. Fergus picked his way carefully along the small crescent shaped, perimeter that the company had thrown up around the beach upon which they had landed. Behind him, down by the water's edge the mule drivers and Batavian cavalrymen were still getting themselves organised and their curses and the soft, protesting-whinny of horses and the braying of the mules was the only sound. Beyond the perimeter, in the darkness of the night, all seemed quiet and peaceful.

'What are they doing back there, Sir?" one of the men whispered in the darkness, as Fergus came past, counting and tapping each man on the shoulder.

'Fuck knows,' Fergus muttered.

He moved on down the line and in the darkness, he could feel his new thick-woollen socks on his feet. His heavy white winter cloak, which he'd pulled over his body armour was certainly warm but it made him feel a lot heavier. The men had at first complained about the weight of their new white-woollen winter coats but the muttering and protests had subsided when Fergus had explained how cold it was going to get in the mountains, and how the new cloaks would probably save their lives. On the spur of the moment, he had told the men that it would be a court martial offense if they lost or discarded their winter equipment.

'Think I saw something move in the darkness, Sir,' a legionary said quietly as Fergus tapped him on the shoulder.

Fergus paused and silently turned to stare into the darkness.

'What do you think you saw?' he murmured.

'Not sure,' the soldier replied. 'It was fleeting but something definitely did move. Could be an animal I suppose.'

'Keep looking,' Fergus said as he continued along the perimeter.

Strange, he thought as he reached the river-bank. Ever since the company had boarded the transports, he'd had this feeling that they were being watched. But by who? Wearily Fergus shook his head. He must be just imagining things like the soldier he'd passed on his rounds. No one knew that the company was out here. In the darkness, no one would have seen them cross the river. But the unease would not go away and, as he stomped off to report to Titus that all men were present and accounted for, the moon suddenly appeared from behind the clouds and in its pale light, Fergus caught sight of the glimmering waters of the Danube. For a moment, he paused to stare at the calm, peaceful, gently rippling river. Would this be the last time he saw the Danube? Were any of his men going to come back from this expedition?

'All men present and accounted for, Sir,' Fergus murmured as he found Titus. The Centurion grunted and turned to look back at the river. The Batavians cavalry and the mule drivers had finally managed to sort themselves out and stood around in small groups looking lost.

'If your men are all ready,' Hadrian whispered from the darkness. 'Then let's go. We have a lot of ground to cover before me make camp. Give the order, Centurion.'

'Yes Sir,' Titus muttered as he started off into the darkness.

A few moments later Fergus heard Titus's softly-called orders ringing out. In the darkness, the legionaries rose to their feet, reached for their marching packs, slung them over their shoulders, lifted their shields up and began to file into the night after their Centurion. Fergus exhaled and was just about to follow the column that had begun to wind its way inland, when he felt something soft touch his cheek. Startled he looked up at the sky. In the heaven's the moon had vanished again, casting them all back into blackness. But something was moving on the air currents and suddenly Fergus realised what was happening. It was snowing.

Chapter Twenty-Eight – The Amber Road

Fergus strode along the forest path with one hand holding the wooden-pole that was slung over his shoulder together with his two spears and from which, all his personal equipment hung. He was clutching his shield in the other hand. The weight of his heavy white winter-cloak and all his equipment, felt like a ton pressing him down into the earth and despite the fresh layer of snow on the ground, his forehead was covered in sweat. The white linen-cloth that covered his shield had already gotten stained with mud. Wearily he peered up the path. It was nearly noon and the column was moving slowly but steadily through the forest in single file. Men, horses and mules were spread out along the forest path, and he could not see the advance guard. The trees closed in on both sides of the sandy track, dense, dark and their stark, rigid-branches covered in snow. Slowly, Fergus reached up to wipe his forehead with the back of his hand. It had been four days since they had left the Danube and for the past three days they had not emerged from this endless, cursed forest. Nor had they encountered a single-living soul apart from a hunting party who had swiftly melted away into the forest. Bored, Fergus lifted his head and stared at the slaves and their fat limping-master, who was leading their mules down the path ahead of him. The mules too were heavily laden with sacks and boxes, weighing over two hundred pounds, strapped to their tough, rugged backs and carefully balanced on either side of them and in some of those boxes, hidden under the grain and wheat, was an enormous amount of gold and silver. Enough to fund your own private little army, Fergus thought. He licked his lips, at he stared at the slow-moving beasts of labour as they trudged along the path. Titus had placed him here, in the centre of the column, so that he could keep a careful eye on the precious cargo which the mules were carrying. That was his job. To keep an eye on the Emperor's gold and silver.

It was an hour or so later and the column had still not emerged from the forest, when Fergus suddenly noticed Adalwolf coming down the path towards him. The German merchant nodded a greeting as he caught sight of Fergus.

'It's your fucking fault that I am here,' Fergus hissed, as Adalwolf began to walk alongside him. 'If you hadn't chosen my company I would be now be snug and safe inside my winter quarters. But now guess what? I am out here in the barbarian wilderness, protecting an Emperor's ransom. And it's all your fault.'

'Double pay, that's what the Lord Hadrian has promised you,' Adalwolf retorted. 'Is that not something?'

'Shut up,' Fergus growled looking away into the trees.

'Come, let's not fall out over this,' Adalwolf said soothingly. 'I thought you may like some company. Can't imagine these slaves and their mules are much fun.'

'I think I prefer the mules,' Fergus snapped.

Ignoring the jibe Adalwolf sighed. 'You made a good first impression on the Lord Hadrian,' the merchant murmured. 'He likes you. He told me.'

Next to Adalwolf, Fergus shook his head.

'I think you have the wrong man,' Fergus hissed. 'I do not have sex with men. If the Legate thinks I do, then he is very much mistaken and if he dares touch me, I will report him. Homosexuality is forbidden by the army.'

'Oh that,' Adalwolf chuckled. 'No that is not what I mean. He doesn't like you in that way. He was impressed by you as an officer. You showed no fear or hesitation when you spoke up in our meeting before we left. Lesser men might have been too intimidated to speak out, but not you.' Adalwolf paused and looked down at the ground. 'He is a special man, Lord Hadrian,' he said at last in a fond, respectful voice. 'He understands his soldiers. He knows what they feel and he cares for their wellbeing. He likes being around his men. He is a good leader and he is a good soldier, just like you. You know that he is going to be Emperor one day, don't you?'

Fergus shook his head.

"The rumour going around is that Emperor Trajan had him demoted and sent to lead us as punishment. Is that true?"

Adalwolf turned to look around to see who was within earshot. Then slowly he nodded.

'There seems to be some hostile politics at the imperial court but it will pass. Lord Hadrian will not be out of favour forever. One day, Trajan will recall him and forgive him and when he does I will go with him to Rome, Fergus.'

'Well good luck with that,' Fergus said in a tight voice. Then quickly he glanced at the German. The amber merchant had not just found him to engage in idle chat. Something seemed to be weighing on Adalwolf's mind. Something he seemed to be having difficulty in saying.

Adalwolf turned to gaze into the forest with a sudden nostalgic look. 'Ah,' he muttered half to himself, 'The days of my youth seem so long ago now. When I was a young man like you are now, I used to love these wild places, the endless forest, the high snow-capped mountain peaks. I thought this was the whole world. But then one day I crossed the Danube with a raiding party and I saw the greatness that is Rome. I saw what true civilisation was and I became an admirer of Rome. We Germans, we spend all our time and energy fighting one another. We destroy; we hack each other to pieces; our blood feuds cross generations but, in the end, we leave nothing of any worth or note behind, unlike Rome.' Adalwolf paused, as a distant look appeared in his eyes. 'I have seen the great libraries of Rome, Fergus. I have seen the palaces, aqueducts, inventions and machines of the Romans. I have laid eyes upon a great civilisation. I have seen what Rome has achieved and I long to be part of that. The only way my people, the Vandals, will ever be remembered will be in the histories that you Romans write down in your books. But every time I start to believe that I am a Roman, I am reminded of my people, my proud and primitive, blood-thirsty Vandal kinsmen and family out there in their wild forests.' Adalwolf sighed. 'I cannot let go of them, Fergus. A man must remain loyal to his ancestors. He cannot be something he is not. So, I became a German in service of Rome.'

Slowly Adalwolf turned to look at Fergus with a sad little smile.

'When I was a young man,' Adalwolf said, 'I too was a Prince of the Vandals just like Gaiseric. My father was leader of his tribe and I was his eldest son, destined to take over when he died.'

'So what happened,' Fergus said with a frown as he plodded on along the sandy forest track.

'I murdered a man,' Adalwolf said calmly. 'I killed my brother and because of that I was banished, forbidden from returning to my people. My bones will never be allowed to lie beside those of my ancestors.' Adalwolf sighed again. 'That was twenty years ago and I have not seen my family since. But now, Fergus, now at last I am going home.'

Slowly Fergus shook his head in confusion. Was this why Adalwolf had come to talk to him?

'Your brother,' he muttered. 'You killed your own brother. Why?'

'Because Rome has forced all the German tribes to make the same choice,' Adalwolf snapped in a sudden harsh voice. 'My bastard brother wished for the Vandals to be enemies of Rome and I wanted peace and an alliance with Rome. We quarrelled and he lost and as punishment they banished me.' Adalwolf turned to stare at Fergus, his face transformed, aggressive and cold. 'But now I am going home, Fergus, not to beg them for mercy and forgiveness but to prove to them that I was right all along. To show them that I was right to seek an alliance with Rome.'

Fergus blew the air from his mouth and gave Adalwolf a crazy look.

'So why does Hadrian not seem to trust you enough to let you lead us over the mountains to this holy German temple?' Fergus retorted.

At Fergus's side, the older man shrugged and turned to look away.

'That's just politics,' Adalwolf snapped. 'Prince Gaiseric is an important Vandal nobleman even though he is also an arrogant prick. He will become the leader of his tribe when his father dies so, Lord Hadrian must show him respect. My people are proud, Fergus. Insults are remembered for life, blood feuds fester across generations and every warrior is easily insulted and quick to reach for his battle-axe. Death is never far away in our politics. They are a touchy-lot my kinsmen. Remember that.' Adalwolf took a deep breath. 'But they are also the greatest of all the German tribes, for my kinsmen are the bravest under the stars and as numerous. Hadrian is wise to seek an alliance with them. He is doing the right thing.'

'Does Gaiseric know who you are?' Fergus asked looking puzzled.

'Gaiseric is a prick,' Adalwolf sneered turning to look out into the forest as the two of them continued down the path. 'His mouth says one thing but his heart says another,' he added bitterly. 'Gaiseric may pretend to be Lord Hadrian's friend for now because it suits him, but in his heart, he is just like my bastard brother. He is no friend of Rome. I don't trust him and neither should you, Fergus.'

'But Hadrian seems to trust him,' Fergus replied.

'Hadrian is smarter than you think,' Adalwolf retorted, 'For the moment he needs Gaiseric. That is why it is he who is acting as our guide and not me. But his usefulness will not last forever.'

'I agree,' Fergus murmured as he wearily adjusted the pack over his shoulder. 'Sometimes it feels as if our guide is leading us in circles through this endless forest.'

Carefully Adalwolf turned to gaze at Fergus.

'That is why I have come to talk to you,' Adalwolf said in a quiet, deadly serious voice. 'When the time comes, Fergus, Lord Hadrian is going to need you to kill Gaiseric.'

Startled Fergus turned to stare at the German merchant.

'What,' Fergus exclaimed. "What are you talking about? Why would the Legate want to do that?'

'Because,' Adalwolf snapped as he started to stride away up the path, 'Gaiseric is going to lead us all to our deaths.'

Chapter Twenty-Nine – The Watcher in the Forest

A sharp cry along the forest trail brought the plodding column to an abrupt halt. Hastily Fergus left his post and strode past the mules and their attendant slaves until he reached the fat slave master, who'd been placed in charge of the slaves and animals. Up ahead, along the path, the legionaries and Batavian horsemen had come to a halt, stretched out in a long, single file amongst the trees. What was going on? As he peered down the track, Fergus suddenly saw Furius hastening towards him.

'What is going on? Why have we stopped,' Fergus called out as the Optio came up to him.

'The scouts say there is a barbarian village up ahead,' Furius replied glancing at the heavily laden mules. 'Titus wants you to take a squad and accompany Gaiseric and his men into the village. The rest of us are going to hang back in the forest. You are to purchase hay from the villagers. The horses and mules need to eat. Get as much of the stuff as you can.'

'Can't Gaiseric handle that?' Fergus grumbled.

'No,' Furius said shaking his head. 'Titus wants a Roman to be present. Don't ask me why, just do it, Fergus.'

With a resigned sigh, Fergus patted Furius on the shoulder and started off down the path towards the front of the Roman column. As he strode past the men from his old squad, he beckoned to Aledus, their Decanus.

'Aledus, I need your squad, follow me,' Fergus snapped.

Obediently his old comrades began to file after him, casting wary glances into the dark, snow covered forest. Up ahead at the front of the column, a small group of men stood amongst the trees, clustered around Hadrian and Titus. As he approached, Fergus caught sight of the tall, lanky figure of Gaiseric, standing

294

beside Hadrian. The Vandal prince was clad in a black tunic, over which he was wearing a thick bearskin cloak. He looked around twenty. His head was covered in a fine, brown fur hat and an axe hung from his belt. In one hand, he was holding a spear and he was laughing. As he came towards the men, Fergus took the opportunity to carefully examine Gaiseric. So, this was the man who Adalwolf had told him he should kill. Was this the man who was going to lead them to their deaths? Scepticism crept across Fergus's face. It was more likely that Adalwolf's dislike of Gaiseric was nothing more than personal rivalry between two Vandals, - a contest to see who would become Hadrian's most favoured and trusted advisor. That had to be the reason why Adalwolf disliked the man. Well, Fergus thought, he would be damned if he was going to carry out Adalwolf's dirty work for him.

***

In the forest, Gaiseric suddenly paused and peered at the trees ahead. Tensely Fergus raised his fist in the air and, behind him, the six legionaries came to a halt and crouched, ready to hurl their spears at anything that came at them. But in the forest around them, all was silent and nothing moved.

'Over there, see,' Gaiseric said quietly in his thickly accented Latin, turning his head slightly towards Fergus, as he pointed at something amongst the trees.

Softly Fergus swore to himself. He had not spotted what Gaiseric had seen. There, thirty paces away through the trees, he suddenly noticed a small hut with a rough, low-hanging conical roof made of turf, straw and tree branches and covered in fresh snow. The primitive house seemed to be half subterranean with only the roof showing above ground, but it was definitely man-made. Fergus frowned as he stared at the hovel. Then as his eyes moved, on he noticed another and then another hovel. The constructions seemed to form a small circle in the dense forest. Then softly but clearly he heard the whinny of a horse, and a moment later the warning bark of a dog.

Without uttering a word Gaiseric, began to stride towards the small German settlement. Silently Fergus pumped his fist in the air, the signal for his men to follow him. Then he started after Gaiseric and his three German companions. The Vandals showed no sign of hesitation as they headed straight towards the village. Fergus and his men, trailing, emerged cautiously from the trees into a forest clearing to see that Gaiseric had already found the villagers. The Germans had gathered around him as he rapidly spoke to them in their harsh sounding language. They were tall, bearded men, stern faced and serious looking, clad in thick animal hides, and all of them were armed, some with what looked like Roman knives. Close by, a dog stood barking at the strangers. As Fergus drew nearer, he saw that the dwellings all had dark openings that sloped downwards into the ground. There were five of them. And just as he was staring at the doorways, a blond-haired woman clutching a baby in her arms emerged from one of the hovels. She stopped in alarm as she caught sight of Fergus and his men. The woman was nearly a head taller than the Romans and her cloak was fastened by a fine Roman fibula, brooch, made of bone. Ignoring her, Fergus slowly moved over to where Gaiseric and his three companions were in conversation with the villagers.

'Ask them if they have any hay,' Fergus said turning to Gaiseric, 'Tell them that we are a party of amber merchants and that we need hay for our horses and pack animals. Tell them we will pay them for it.'

Gaiseric did not acknowledge Fergus. Instead he kept up his furious barrage of words, speaking so fast, Fergus wondered what he could be possibly be talking about and how the villagers could take it all in. As he patiently waited for Gaiseric to reply to him, he turned to gaze at the villagers. Some of the men too, seemed to have lost interest in Gaiseric and were giving Fergus curious glances. Then abruptly one of the villagers, an older man raised his hand and pointed straight at Fergus and spat something out in his intelligible language. Gaiseric hesitated and turned to give Fergus a quick glance.

'They say they are happy to trade with you Roman,' Gaiseric growled in his thick Germanic accent. 'But they say that they need all their hay for their own animals. They say that the winter is going to be long. But if you like you and your men are welcome to drink some beer with them whilst they discuss what else they can sell to you. They are used to seeing Roman merchants.'

Once again the older man pointed at Fergus and spat out something in his own language. Then he opened his mouth in a wide, welcoming grin, revealing a few yellow rotting teeth.

Gaiseric turned to look away.

'They say they are surprised to see Romans on the amber road so late in the year,' the Vandal prince growled. 'They are asking if you have brought any wine with you or Roman cups, bowls or amphorae? They will trade with you for these. They have honey, beeswax, furs and blond women's hair. They say it can be made into wigs.'

Fergus sighed in disappointment and shook his head. 'No, we came here for hay. If he won't sell, then we are done here. We should get back.'

Raising his hand at the German villagers in greeting, Fergus turned and started to walk away.

Behind him however the villager suddenly called out, speaking rapidly in his own language and slowly Fergus turned around to stare at him. Gaiseric was studying the villager intently. Then sharply he turned to Fergus.

'Wait,' Gaiseric snapped. 'He says that ten miles or so to the north, a large band of warriors has made their winter camp beside the route used by the amber merchants. He says that if we are heading north we will run straight into them. He says these men are forcing all merchants to pay a fee for safe passage up the road.'

'What,' Fergus exclaimed in alarm. 'How many men are we talking about?'

Gaiseric turned to the village elder and after a short exchange he turned back to Fergus.

'He thinks there may be a few hundred,' Gaiseric growled. 'He says they are a strong group. They will not let us pass without payment.'

For a moment Fergus said nothing. Then slowly he turned to look at the village elder.

'Titus needs to hear about this,' Fergus said quickly. 'Come on, let's get back.'

Fergus was half way to the edge of the forest when he heard a strangled cry. It was followed by a thud, as something hit the ground and then a shout. Startled, Fergus turned around to see what was going on. Two of the villagers lay in the snow that was rapidly darkening in a growing pool of blood. Their throats had been cut. A third man had been stabbed in the chest and was down on his knees, his head tilted to the ground and the knife still stuck into his body. And another of the villagers was fleeing towards the forest. Stunned, Fergus stared at the scene as the man with the knife in his chest slowly toppled sideways. Gaiseric was speaking rapidly to his three companions, clutching a bloodied knife in one hand and gesturing at the huts. Fergus's eyes widened in shock. The Vandal prince was murdering the villagers in cold blood.

'What the hell are you doing?' Fergus roared, as he recovered from his shock.

But Gaiseric did not reply and as Fergus stared at the bloody and gory mess, an axe went whirling through the air embedding itself in the back of the fleeing villager, bringing him crashing down into the snow. Across the clearing, Gaiseric's three companions were already racing towards the dark entrances to the huts with drawn weapons.

'Gaiseric!' Fergus roared furiously.

But the young Vandal prince was not listening. He stood alone in the middle of the clearing staring down at the three corpses and the spreading pool of blood. A sudden hysterical scream erupted from one of the subterranean huts and, as Fergus turned towards the noise, his eyes widened in horror. A screaming woman brandishing an axe came rushing straight towards Aledus. Startled, Aledus had just enough time to turn and face her and raise his shield, when with a vicious blow she hammered her axe into the wood. Aledus cried out in shock, staggered backwards and instinctively stabbed the woman with his spear, knocking her to the ground. Horrified Fergus turned to stare at the huts. Hysterical screams were coming from the German dwellings into which Gaiseric's companions had vanished, and at the edge of the trees, Fergus suddenly saw a few women and children fleeing into the forest.

'What have you done,' Fergus roared as he strode towards Gaiseric. 'These villagers were no threat. They were willing to trade. We came here to gather supplies. Instead you have massacred them for no reason. This was unprovoked. You, murderous bastard.'

Slowly Gaiseric turned to stare at Fergus. There was a cold, harsh look on his face.

'They were nothing,' he said contemptuously. 'These people were nothing. They were weak. They deserved death.'

'What the fuck are you talking about?' Fergus roared.

'We came for the hay, for the animals,' Gaiseric retorted his eyes narrowing as he glared at Fergus. 'Now you can take all the hay you want. The animals can eat and we can move on. These people had to die so that we may live. It's simple. What is there to discuss?'

Abruptly Fergus looked away. His hands trembled in fury but there was nothing more he could do now. Across the clearing Gaiseric's three companions had emerged from the huts and one of them was dragging a young, screaming girl through the snow by her hair. As the men came up to their leader, the man dragging the girl along laughed and with a vicious stamp from his boot, he broke the child's neck. Stunned Fergus looked down at the child's broken body lying in the snow.

'What do you care Roman,' Gaiseric hissed from close by. 'Why should you care about these people? You didn't know them. They are not your family. And besides as soon as we would have left, they would have gone to warn that group of warriors camped up the trail. They would have sold us out for a few common trinkets. They had to die.'

Titus sighed as Fergus finished recounting what had happened in the German village. For a moment, the Centurion said nothing. Then he nodded and reached out to grip Fergus by the shoulder.

'Swine, the lot of them. I never liked the Germans,' Titus muttered. 'But what is done is done. I will send some men to collect the hay. They are not going to be needing it anymore.'

Fergus took a deep breath. 'What about this group of warriors blocking the path to the north? The villagers said they were several hundred strong. We will never get past them without a fight, Sir.'

'I will leave that decision to the Legate,' Titus replied. 'I had better go and speak to him now. And you,' Titus said pointing at Fergus, '"you stay away from Gaiseric, understood. I don't want any trouble. That German enjoys Hadrian's favour, remember that.'

Fergus nodded and watched the Centurion stride away down the column of men, horses and mules that were strung out along the forest path. Suddenly amongst the trees, Fergus caught sight of Adalwolf. The German merchant was watching him. Then slowly and deliberately Adalwolf raised his finger and ran it across his throat, before silently turning away into the forest.

***

It was late in the day and the expedition was once more strung out on a forest path. Sullenly Fergus strode along at his post beside the mules and the slaves. The tough, heavily-laden animals plodded on, silent and uncomplaining and Fergus had begun to appreciate their qualities of endurance. No wonder the legionaries had once been called Marius's mules he thought. A day and a night had passed since the massacre in the village, and after some discussion, Hadrian had decided to veer off course and go around the war-band blocking the more direct route. The diversion would add a couple of days to their journey. Slowly Fergus wrenched his gaze away from the mules and turned to gaze into the forest. The tall pines were covered in fresh snow and the brown, green and white landscape was eerily quiet. But last night, as the men had made camp and huddled around their fires and tents, they had all heard the mournful howling of wolves in the distance. The noise had unsettled the horses and mules and the slaves had spent a lot of time trying to calm the beasts down. With a grunt, Fergus drew his heavy, white winter-cloak tighter around his shoulders. Winter was steadily closing in and the weather was getting colder. And there was something else that he couldn't shake off. The strange sense that the expedition was being watched had returned. He had felt it again last night as he had made his rounds, checking on the sentries. Something or someone was watching them, from the cover of the forest.

As the column plodded on through the forest, Fergus caught sight of one of the Batavian horsemen standing at the side of the track. The auxiliary cavalryman was wearing a similar, white winter-cloak as Fergus and he was examining his horse's hoof. As Fergus drew level the man shook his head and started up the path on foot, leading his horse by hand.

'Thunder and lashing rain, so Wodan commeth,' Fergus said suddenly turning to the Batavian as his mouth split into a wide grin.

Startled, the rider turned to look at him. The Batavian looked a few years older than Fergus. Then the man frowned.

'Thunder and lashing rain, so Wodan commeth,' the rider repeated quietly in a thick Germanic accent. 'How do you know about this?'

'My father served in the Second Batavian Cohort,' Fergus said. 'He was stationed at Luguvalium and after that on the Dacian frontier during the first war. When he was my age he fought in the battle of Mons Graupius in Caledonia.'

The Batavian stared at Fergus with sudden interest.

'What was his name?' the rider said.

'Marcus. My father's name is Marcus. For a short while he was Prefect of the whole Cohort,' Fergus replied.

'That Marcus? You are his son,' the Batavian blurted out, his eyes widening in shock. 'Marcus, the man who saved the whole

Cohort during the Brigantian uprising. The man who led the cavalry in Hibernia. The man who they demoted after the rebellion had been crushed?'

'That's right,' Fergus replied.
For a long moment, the Batavian stared at him as if struck dumb. Then hastily he looked away.

'I was too young to serve with him,' the Batavian said at last, 'but there are some older men within my squadron who remember him. Your father is a legend. A hero. Wait till I tell them who you are.'

With a flush on his cheeks, the Batavian turned to look at Fergus again.

'Tonight when we make camp, promise me that you will come and find me and the boys. They will want to meet you.' The Batavian's face broke into a spontaneous grin. 'Who would have thought of it. Marcus's son and us, out here. Of all the co-incidences, the gods choose this one.'

***

It was getting dark when Hadrian finally called a halt and the men set about erecting their tents and getting their cooking fires going. As the soldiers busied themselves around the forest camp, Fergus began to post his sentries. He had just completed his task when in the gloom he suddenly heard a shriek, followed by shouting. The noise had come from out of the forest. Hastily he jogged through the crisp snow and through the dark forest towards the noise. As he drew closer, another shriek rent the evening. It was followed by harsh Roman voices. Amongst the trees, up ahead he could see a couple of men holding burning torches and, in their flickering light, he caught sight of two legionaries crouching in the snow holding down a writhing figure. The figure was hissing and whining as he struggled violently to free himself.

303

'What is going on here?' Fergus cried out as he approached.

'We were out collecting fire wood when we caught this bitch, Sir,' one of the legionaries exclaimed, gesturing at the writhing, whining figure who was being pinned down in the snow.

'She?' Fergus said frowning.

'That's right Sir,' a legionary called out, "she was watching the camp. Spying on us. But now we have got her she doesn't want to calm down. She has already bitten Julius twice and she had a knife on her.'

'Get her up on her feet,' Fergus snapped.

Obediently the two legionaries in the snow grasped hold of the woman's arms and yanked her roughly up onto her feet. The girl's long black hair was dishevelled, but as he caught sight of her face, Fergus staggered backwards and gasped in shock. The defiant looking girl standing before him was Titula. Speechless, Fergus stared at her. It was Titula alright. There was no mistaking the tattooed Germanic runes across her forehead.

'What,' Fergus stammered in confusion. 'What are you doing here?'

Titula stared back at him in silent defiance, but upon seeing Fergus she had ceased to struggle. Then, with a speed that took everyone by surprise, she wrenched herself free, stepped forwards and flung her arms around Fergus's, waist burying her head against his chest.

'You know this woman Sir?' one of the legionaries asked in a puzzled voice.

'I do,' Fergus said hesitantly, as he looked down at the girl clinging on to him in a tight embrace. 'She is my property.'

Then as he noticed she was shivering with cold, he reached out and gently placed his arm across her back.

'It's alright boys,' Fergus said in an embarrassed voice. 'I will take her back to the camp. She is with me.'

***

The campfire crackled and the flames and sparks leapt up to die in the black night. Sitting in the snow around the fire Fergus, Furius, Adalwolf, Vittius and Catinius were all staring in fascination at Titula, as the slave girl hungrily and silently devoured a leg of mutton. The girl looked like she was starving and her cheeks were hollow and bony. Fergus could only guess how long ago it had been since she had eaten. He'd found a winter cloak and even though it was too big for her, she seemed grateful. Now she sat stuffing her face with food, with the woollen cloak wrapped around her shoulders. She had remained silent since Fergus had brought her into the camp, but she had caused no more trouble and she had gone where he had told her to go. Her arrival had however, caused a bit of a stir amongst the camp but after a quiet word with Titus, the Centurion had agreed to let her stay on the condition that she didn't cause trouble.

'What in the Gods name possessed her to follow you out here, Fergus?' Furius said with a little bewildered shake of his head. 'I mean, this is not some town down the road from our winter quarters. We are way beyond the Imperial frontiers.'

'Our young friend must have made an impression on the girl,' Vittius said with a little smile. 'Best not tell Galena about this though when you next send a letter home. She will cut your balls off when you return home.'

Fergus did not reply as he stared at the girl. He was truly lost for something to say. The shock of Titula's appearance had been so unexpected, so weird, that he still didn't know how to handle it.

'She must have been following us since we crossed the Danube,' Catinius muttered. 'Question is why? She is a German slave. Why didn't she just go home? Unless of course she has nowhere to go, no family. But I agree with Vittius. Our friend Fergus has made one hell of an impression. What did she do again when you first saw her? She gave you a hug.'

Fergus silently nodded.

'So much for the secrecy surrounding our mission,' Furius growled, flicking another stick into the fire. 'Rome's finest, tracked and followed by a sixteen-year-old girl. Makes you wonder who else knows about our expedition.'

At Fergus's side, Adalwolf suddenly rose to his feet and silently came around the fire, kneeling beside Titula. The slave girl paused in her eating, to glance warily at the German merchant. Then she bared her teeth at him and hissed.

'She has spirit, that's for sure,' Vittius chuckled.

Adalwolf suddenly reached out and grasped Titula's head with both hands, carefully pushing away her long, black hair. She squealed and dropped her hunk of meat, but Adalwolf held her in a tight grip as he stared at the runes, tattooed onto her forehead. Then abruptly he let go of her and sat back down in the snow, with a sudden troubled look on his face.

'What?' Furius growled suspiciously peering at Adalwolf. 'What is the matter?'

For a moment Adalwolf stared at Titula. Then slowly he turned to look at his companions sitting around the crackling campfire.

'The runes,' he muttered in a troubled voice. 'Most men cannot read but I can.' He paused to stare into the flames. 'The girl,' he exclaimed suddenly looking up at Fergus, 'the runes say she has been marked by the Gods. They say she is a Valkyrie. That she is one of the six ladies of the war Lord, Odin, destined to ride with him across the sky.'

'What?' Furius exclaimed with a puzzled frown.

'The girl is a Valkyrie,' Adalwolf snapped with sudden tension in his voice. 'She rides through the sky with Odin, Lord of War. Don't you fools understand? She has the power to choose who lives and dies in battle.' Adalwolf turned to stare at Fergus and to Fergus's surprise he saw that Adalwolf suddenly looked afraid.

'Fergus, what is she doing here with us?' Adalwolf murmured.

Chapter Thirty – The Moravian Gates

Hadrian stood looking down at the crude map that Gaiseric had drawn in the snow and dirt. Adalwolf, Titus, Furius, Gaiseric and Hadrian's two freedmen had gathered around the Legate and were doing the same. At the edge of the 'O group meeting,' Fergus stood watching the senior officers, as he waited for them to issue their orders. A few days had passed since Titula had come out of the forest. The expedition had been making steady progress northwards through the endless forests and frozen swamps, but the further they had gone, the shorter the days and the colder the weather was becoming. And now the flat plains had started to give way to rolling hills, covered in dense dark, pine-trees.

Gaiseric knelt beside the map and pointed at two small pebbles. 'Now this is our position and here is the war band that my scouts spotted,' he said glancing up at Hadrian. 'They are maybe five or six miles away. Most of the warriors are on foot and they seem to be moving parallel with us. Apart from hunting and squabbling amongst themselves, they seem to be moving around without any aim or purpose.'

'Have they spotted us?' Hadrian replied, looking serious.

Gaiseric sighed and shook his head. 'No, my men think they don't know about us just yet, but that could easily change. My scouts say we haven't been seen but the size of our group; the tracks we are leaving and the villagers who we come across; any of these will eventually give away our presence. We should assume that it will be only a matter of time before this war band discovers us and comes to investigate.' Gaiseric paused as he looked up at Hadrian. 'They are a threat. I recommend that we change our course before they discover us. We will never be able to outrun them, not with the mules and the cargo that we are carrying.'

Hadrian sighed as he peered down at the map.

'That would mean heading up into the mountains,' the Legate muttered. 'Deeper snow drifts, more difficult terrain, less food. Our progress will slow.'

Gaiseric nodded. 'But better than having to fight our way into the Moravian Gates,' he replied. 'Look,' the Vandal Prince added, gesturing at the ground. 'Once we are into the pass that separates the two mountain ranges we should be able to find the head-waters of the Oder river. When we find the river,' Gaiseric said looking up at Hadrian, 'you should get your men to build rafts. We then load the mules and the men onto the rafts. On the water, we will make quicker progress and it will be safer too. The Oder will take us north and west; the direction in which we want to go. The river journey is around a hundred miles. But when we reach the point where we come ashore, it will be only one or two days walk to Mount Sleza.'

Hadrian nodded as he stared at the ground.

'What about our horsemen?' Hadrian growled. 'The mules may be able to be persuaded to board the rafts but the horses won't.' 'The cavalry will follow us along the banks of the river,' Gaiseric said quickly. 'There are settlements along its course. We will be able to barter for food and fodder.'

Gaiseric was looking up at Hadrian, and slowly the others, clustered around the Legate, did the same, waiting for him to speak. Hadrian remained silent as he considered the options. Then he seemed to make up his mind.

'Alright, we will go up into the mountains,' he said nodding at Gaiseric. 'We have not come here for a fight. Take us into the Moravian Gates.'

***

It was late in the afternoon and it was snowing again, as Fergus struggled up the path, his boots disappearing completely into the snow with each step. The expedition was winding its way up the slope of a forested hill, and the slaves were cursing and using their whips to keep their mules on the path, as the heavily-laden animals stoically plodded on. The slave master had bound the beasts together with a sturdy rope, to stop them floundering and slipping down the steep slopes of the hill. Wearily, Fergus paused and turned to gaze down the path at the rest of the mules and their slave attendants. It was his job to keep an eye on the beasts and the precious cargo they were carrying. Beyond the mules, bringing up the rear of the column, he could see a line of legionaries, pushing on through the snow in a single file. The men were huddled under their white, hooded, winter cloaks and were clutching their spears. Their large rectangular shields were covered in white, protective dust-covers. Fergus grunted. The soldiers were indeed hard to spot in the white, winter weather. He hadn't expected the winter camouflage to work, but it did.

A hand was tugging at the sleeve of his winter cloak. Fergus turned to see Titula standing beside him, holding up a piece of stale, old bread. Gratefully he took the bread from her and stuffed it into his mouth. Then he started plodding up the path again and, at his side Titula did the same, the bottom of her long, oversized, white winter-cloak trailing through the snow. To Fergus's relief, the slave girl had started to make herself useful around the camp, by mending and fixing the soldier's clothing and boots - a skill which she seemed to be particularly adept at. And, as she had become a familiar face, the only woman in the expedition, word had crept out that she was a Valkyrie, with the power to choose who would live or die on the battlefield. Some of the men had greeted the news with scepticism, but most of the soldiers chose to avert their eyes and not look at her, when she was close by or fixing their clothing.

As they struggled up the slope of the hill, Fergus gave Titula a cautious glance. He and Adalwolf had both tried to talk to the girl. They had tried every manner of persuasion but Titula had remained silent, and at last Fergus had concluded that the girl could not speak. Some deformity must be prevented her from speaking. But despite this, he'd been able to communicate using signs and hand signals.

'Heh,' Fergus muttered reaching out and running his finger slowly across his own forehead. 'Why do you have these? Who gave you these runes?'

Titula was watching him carefully. Then she seemed to understand, shrugged and looked away into the trees.

Fergus muttered something to himself.

'Why are you here?' he said glancing at her again. 'Why did you follow me? Why did you not return to your own family?'

The girl was watching him carefully but it was clear she had not understood. With a frustrated grunt, Fergus pointed at her and then at himself, then at the landscape around them, before throwing up his hand in a questioning gesture.

For a moment Titula did not respond. Then she looked down at her feet and a sudden flush appeared in her cheeks, as she seemed to understand. Silently she reached out and placed her hand against Fergus's chest and then, swiftly she sank to her knees, facing him in the snow and with infinite grace she slowly bowed her head. Fergus frowned as he looked down at her, and along the path some of the slaves turned to stare. With sudden insight Fergus understood. Ofcourse. He had saved her life on the battlefield and then probably again, by not letting the slave merchants sell her in the markets of Carnuntum. And as the realisation dawned, Fergus gasped. The girl could easily have run away and gone back to her own people, but she must feel duty bound to stay at his side. It had to be either that or she had nowhere else to go.

'Shit,' he muttered as his cheeks turned red. The girl's simple devotion was touching, but he could hardly return home to

Galena with a young slave girl in tow, who believed it her solemn duty to be at his side and look after him. That could get rather awkward.

A startled cry from one of the slaves suddenly shattered the tranquillity of the late afternoon. Fergus turned to stare in the direction from which the sound had come. Then, before he could react, a spear came hurtling out of the trees, slamming into one of the heavily-laden mules and sending the beast crashing sideways into the snow. The spear was followed by loud screams and shouts and to Fergus's horror, armed men came pouring out of the forest, running towards the slow-moving column. At his side, Titula flung herself onto the ground beside one of the mules.

Instinctively Fergus dropped his equipment and drew his sword. They were under attack. The column was being ambushed.

'Defend the mules, they are going for the mules,' a voice shouted and to his surprise, Fergus realised it was his own.

There was no more time. A screaming warrior, naked from the waist upwards, came racing towards Fergus, his face contorted in rage, his arm raised to plunge his spear into Fergus's body. At the last moment Fergus raised his shield and the man's weapon slid off harmlessly, but the force of his impact sent them both tumbling backwards into the snow in a wild, confused flurry of arms and legs. Fergus lost his shield in the melee, but as the German tried to rise to his feet, Fergus lunged upwards with his sword and caught the man in his exposed chest. With a groan the warrior collapsed onto Fergus, splattering him with blood. Savagely Fergus pushed the dying man off him, rolled away and swiftly rose to his feet. Around him all was chaos. The mules were braying in terror and trying to flee up the path, but they had got hopelessly entangled and were being prevented from escaping by the two dead animals, lying in the snow. Half the slaves had fled, but to Fergus's surprise the others were putting up a fight using their sticks and whips to defend themselves and their charges from the German warriors. But it was an unequal fight, and already two of the slaves were lying motionless on the ground, with blood seeping out into the virgin snow. And as Fergus stared at the fight unable to move, he saw a German decapitate the fat, slave-merchant with an axe. Then as if released from a spell, Fergus could move again. A warrior came at him, clumsily slashing at him with a spear, which Fergus easily evaded. Wildly Fergus lunged at the man, but the German backed away. Then with a roar the warrior raised his spear, took a step forwards and flung it straight at Fergus. Fergus's eyes widened in horror, as instinctively he dodged sideways and the projectile went hurtling through the air, inches from his face. But as the moment of terror passed, bloodlust welded up within Fergus, and with a furious cry, he leapt at the now weapon-less warrior. The man realising the stupidity of his mistake, just had enough time to scream in panic, as Fergus buried his sword into his chest. With a savage kick, Fergus freed his bloodied sword and sent the man tumbling back into the snow. Behind him he heard the terrified braying of the mules. But as he turned to face the next attacker, all he saw were the white cloaks of the legionaries as they came rushing up the path, scattering the few remaining Germans before them. Wildly Fergus turned to look around him, but there was no one left to fight. The attackers had been fewer in number, than he had realised and those who weren't already dead or dying were fleeing back into the forest. Gasping for breath Fergus stared at the bloody carnage along the path. The cries and screams of the men merged with the braying mules and the pristine snow was stained with corpses and fresh blood. Dimly Fergus became aware of Furius and Titus hastening towards him down the path. Then suddenly he felt a cold hand slip into his own, and as he turned to look around, he saw that it was Titula. Her face was ashen and her lower lip was trembling, as she stared at the carnage around them. For a split crazy moment Fergus had a vision of her riding through the skies in the company of the German war god and pointing her finger at the men who were destined to die on the battlefield.

313

'What happened here? Report.' Titus's harsh voice boomed out as the Centurion strode towards Fergus.

Fergus blinked and focussed on Titus.

'They came out of nowhere Sir,' he snapped. 'Fuckers just ambushed us. I think they were after the mules. They got two of them. I did what I could Sir as did some of the slaves.'

'It's alright Fergus,' Titus said in a softer voice as he turned to stare at the dead and broken bodies littering the path. 'You did what you could. That was your job. Are you alright?'

Fergus blinked again. Titus had never ever asked him if he was alright. Silently he nodded and shakily exhaled as he tried to steady his nerves.

'Shit,' Titus muttered suddenly.

Fergus turned to look in the direction in which the Centurion was staring, and then he too grunted in dismay. On the path one of the dead mules lay on its side, with a spear sticking out of its body. The supplies, sacks and wooden boxes that the animal had been carrying lay strewn and scattered across the path, and amongst one of the smashed boxes, glinting and gleaming in the sunlight for all to see, were hundreds upon hundreds of fine Roman gold and silver coins.

Chapter Thirty-One – A Man's Choices

In the forest, Fergus could hear the axe-men at work felling trees. For a moment, he paused on his way to inspect the sentries, and turned to gaze at the small Roman camp beside the river. The white tents, barely distinguishable from the rocky, snow-covered ground, stood in two neat rows, and beside the rushing, gurgling stream a party of legionaries were busy lashing newly-felled long logs into a crude raft. Their spears and shields lay stacked within easy reach. Smoke was rising from a couple of camp fires and a little way off, under the watchful eye of some Batavian riders, some of the horses and mules had lowered their heads to the water to drink. It was the second morning since they had reached the headwaters of the Oder and had entered the Moravian Gates - the pass that would lead them through the mountains. Lifting his gaze away from the camp, Fergus turned to stare at the distant Carpathian Mountains to the east. It was a crisp, cold morning and in the clear light he could make out the rolling foothills, covered in an endless carpet of pine trees, stretching away to the horizon. Slowly, he turned to look towards the west and there too, in the distance he could see a mountain range, lower and less imposing than the Carpathians, but mountains nevertheless.

With a grunt, Fergus set off to check up on the sentries. There had been no more encounters with tribesmen, but the attack had brought home how vulnerable they were out here in this foreign, trackless land. Since the ambush, Titus had ordered that the sentries be doubled and although it meant less men to help build the rafts, the Centurion had considered that was a price worth paying. The expedition had lost two of the mules during the ambush and a third had been too badly wounded to continue and Furius had been forced to cut the beast's throat and leave it behind. And only nine of the slaves remained, badly shaken by their encounter with the German tribesmen. And now the whole company was aware of the precious cargo that they were carrying. None of the men had mentioned it, but it must be on their minds and the fact that the soldiers were now aware of the fortune they were guarding had made the officers nervous. If the soldiers decided to take the money, they would all instantly become very wealthy men.

As he pushed on into the forest where the woodcutters were at work Fergus sighed as he realised he, Titus, Furius and the signifer would be vastly outnumbered if the men mutinied. But they wouldn't do that he thought. He knew more than half of the men by name. They were loyal. They wouldn't mutiny over a bit of gold and silver. They were the finest company of men in the whole of the Twentieth Legion. Was that not why Adalwolf had recommended them to Hadrian? Startled Fergus came to an abrupt halt. Had that been the reason why the German merchant had chosen them? Had he been thinking about just such a situation?

As he was weighing up the matter a hand suddenly touched his arm. Startled he turned around to see Titula playfully dancing away from him through the trees. She seemed to be in a good mood. Fergus grinned as he watched her raise her arms in the air, as she silently twisted and danced around the trees, her long, winter cloak whirling through the air. A quick glance around him confirmed that they were alone. The slave girl smiled sweetly as she danced back towards him. Then without warning she reached up with her hand and pulled Fergus's face towards her, trying to kiss him. Startled Fergus backed off, staring at her in confusion. What was this? Unperturbed Titula reached up and tried to pull the iron amulet, that Galena had given him, from around his neck.

'No,' Fergus protested as he caught hold of her hand. 'I have a wife. She is going to bear my child. I made a vow to her. I will not break it.'

At his side Titula did not seem to be listening. Wantonly she pressed herself up against him, running her hands over his body. Then slowly she looked up at him with her coy, sweet smile. Fergus groaned. This was too much. In his wildest dreams, he had never expected to be chased and pursued like this by a woman, a slave! Was it not supposed to be the other way around? His grandfather Corbulo would not have given it a second thought but he couldn't. He wasn't like Corbulo, not in that way. Something held him back. He could not break his vow to Galena. She was waiting for him back at Deva, and when he returned he would meet his son or daughter. They would be waiting for him. Carefully but firmly, he pushed Titula away from him.

'No, this cannot happen,' he said shaking his head.

Titula took a step backwards and suddenly her mood changed. Anger blazed from her eyes and she opened her mouth, bearing her teeth. Then abruptly with a glare that bordered on contempt, she turned on her heels and stomped off into the forest. Slowly Fergus shook his head in bewilderment as he watched her go. He had made a vow, did the slave girl not understand or did she not care? Then a little colour shot into his cheeks. Had it been wise to refuse the advances of a Valkyrie? Nervously Fergus gulped and picked at his fingernails. Adalwolf had been adamant that she was marked out to be Valkyrie. And now he, Fergus had just pissed off the woman who had the power to decide who lived and died on the battlefield. With a weary resigned sigh, Fergus closed his eyes as he inclined his head upwards towards the sky. It was as if he could already hear Corbulo's laughter coming down from the heavens.

***

The Oder river was narrow and fast-flowing and, strung out in a line, the twelve rafts bobbed up and down on the current. The precarious looking rafts were crammed and packed with soldiers, supplies and mules. It was morning and the river was silent except for the occasional splash of a steering oar and the nervous braying of the mules. Fergus crouched on the sodden, slippery and freezing tree-trunks and steadied himself against the side of the square raft, as the current swept them onwards downstream. The raft was nothing more than two or three layers of tree trunks, lashed together with rope and iron nails and there was precious little to stop the ice-cold water from swamping them. Around him, his eight companions were silent as they stoically crouched on the raft, trying not to move and holding onto whatever they could get a grip on. In between them, lay piles of supplies, sacks and wooden boxes. Titus had thought it best to unload the mules in case one of the beast's panicked and was lost in the river. At the back of the raft, one of the handpicked legionaries was the only man standing upright, holding onto a crude wooden steering-oar, with which he was trying to keep them in the middle of the stream.

It was cold and overnight the temperatures seemed to have plunged. As he exhaled, Fergus could see his breath steaming in the air. Wearily he brought his fingers to his mouth and tried to warm them by breathing on them. At his side one of the legionary's teeth was chattering uncontrollably, despite the thick winter-cloak the man was wearing.

'Tonight boys, we will make a fire,' Fergus said in a loud voice, trying to sound encouraging as he turned to look at the men. 'You will be warm and we will have a chance to dry our clothing.' No one replied. The glum, freezing men around him huddled under their sodden, white winter-cloaks and gazed morosely at the river. Theirs was the last raft in the fleet. Wearily Fergus rubbed his fingers across the red beard that was developing across his chin and cheeks. Titus had given him the responsibility of guarding the rear of the expedition and making sure that no one was left behind. Ahead of him he could see the other rafts bobbing up and down in the water, joined together with lengths of rope so that the whole fleet was connected to each other. The crowded rafts were packed with every inch of space being used, and the only men standing up were the helmsmen, pretending to be in control of where they were going. It had not been smooth sailing. Already they had lost another mule which had fallen into the river and several men had started to come down with bad head colds and fevers, including Furius.

Fergus groaned. And since their encounter in the forest, Titula was shunning him. His slave girl was avoiding him. It had started with her refusing to sleep around the same fire as himself. And now she had chosen to go with one of the other rafts. Fergus raised his fingers to his mouth and blew on them once more. It was an absurd situation. She was his slave after all. She should do what he told her to do. But she just did her own thing and try as he might, he just didn't know what to do about it. Furius had advised him to beat some sense into the girl.

On both banks of the river the land had started to flatten out, as they had come down from the mountain pass. Now the dull, flat land and featureless pine forest closed in on all sides. There had been little sign of the locals, apart from a primitive dugout canoe and occupant on the river and brown smoke rising into the sky from a settlement in the forest. The bleak, snow bound and featureless land seemed uninviting and harsh and somewhere out there, the thirty or so Batavian riders would be following the rafts along the river-bank.

'A hundred miles of this,' Fergus said grimly turning to Adalwolf who crouched at his side, staring down river. 'Maybe it would have been better to keep to land? At least that way we would be moving and keeping warm. On these raft's all we can do is get cold and wet.'

'No,' we shall make much faster progress like this,' Adalwolf replied. 'Gaiseric is right. The river will take us nearly all the way towards our destination. She forms part of the Amber Road. You Romans call the river, the Suevus.'

'If you say so,' Fergus grumbled.

At Fergus's side, Adalwolf sighed and shifted his weight so that he was sitting more comfortably. Then carefully he reached for something in the folds of his cloak and withdrawing his hand he held up a small, red rock like object.

'This is amber,' Adalwolf muttered staring at the beautiful transparent object. 'This is what all Romans crave. Have you ever seen amber before, Fergus? Do you know why it is such a valuable commodity?'

Fergus frowned as he peered at the small red stone like object.

'My father and grandfather once possessed some amber,' he muttered at last. 'They took it from a sea cave in the far north of Caledonia. My grandfather used it to start a stone haulage business in Londinium but that was twenty or so years ago now.'

Adalwolf nodded. 'Interesting,' he replied. 'Amber in Caledonia, I never knew that.' Then he turned to look at the piece of amber he was holding up. 'Roman women like to use it as jewellery,' the merchant said slowly. 'Amber is only found along the shores of the sea to the north of Germania. It is a rare commodity so it is precious. But it's real value is not as jewellery or bullion.' Adalwolf paused and a glint appeared in his eyes as he gazed at Fergus. 'No, it's real value lies in it's magic. Yes, Amber has magic,' he grunted. 'Amber has magical properties, oh yes.'

Fergus turned to look at Adalwolf, as a little disbelieving smile appeared on his lips.

Unperturbed Adalwolf turned to look at the red resin stone in his hand. 'Look,' he muttered, 'If I rub this piece of amber against a needle and I float that needle in a bowl of water the needle will always turn to point to the north.'

Adalwolf fixed his eyes on Fergus, looking deadly serious. 'So you see, the amber always points the way back home, to the place where it came from in the north,' he hissed.

***

The camp fires flickered and crackled in amongst the trees and along the river bank. It was night and along the frosty, low-lying river bank, the rafts lay pulled up onto the land. The men had raised their tents in the snow, close to the water's edge and were now sitting huddled around their fires or settling down to sleep under their thin, army blankets. In the dark sky, high above the camp, a countless multitude of stars glinted and twinkled in the darkness. The Batavian cavalry horses, stood close together tied to trees by their riders. The beasts seemed to be clustering together for warmth and many of the animals looked malnourished and exhausted.

Moodily, Fergus sat around one of the camp fires, huddled under his blanket, chewing on a piece of stale cheese and trying to keep himself warm. Titula had once again chosen to defy him and had joined another camp fire. Sullenly Fergus lowered his eyes to the ground. Maybe Furius was right and he should give her a beating to show who was in charge, but deep down he knew he would never be able to do that. The women in his family would be furious with him and, even if they never knew about it, he would still know what he'd done. Beating up a girl, even a slave girl, to show one's authority, was a coward's way of trying to exercise control. No, he would have to find another way.

A heavy hand suddenly landed on his shoulder, and startled Fergus looked up to see three Batavian cavalrymen standing over him. Two of the men were older, in their late thirties, and their hard, tough Germanic faces looked serious. The third man was younger and Fergus suddenly recognised the trooper he'd spoken to, on the forest path so many days ago. Without a word the three Batavians sat down around the fire, forcing the other occupants to make space.

'You claim to be Marcus's son,' one of the older Batavian's growled in his accented Latin as he stared at Fergus with a deadly serious look. 'You had better not be taking us for fools. I knew Marcus. I served with him at Luguvalium and in Dacia.'

'Marcus is my father. He was the Prefect of the Second Batavian Auxiliary Cohort, I am telling you the truth,' Fergus replied firmly meeting the man's gaze. 'I was born inside the fort at Luguvalium. I was three years old when my father became Prefect. I was there when the Brigantes tried to take the fort. If you were there like you say you were, you will remember me. My father made me a little wooden sword which apparently, I liked to wave around when I was about in the fort.'

'He looks a bit like him,' the other Batavian muttered, 'same facial features, same red hair.'

The first Batavian grunted something to himself as he studied Fergus intently. Then he looked away and his features softened. 'Alright Fergus, son of Marcus,' the man growled, 'let's say I remember you. I remember that three-year-old called Fergus with his little wooden sword. Your father is a great man, a living legend amongst us. If you are his son, there is not a man amongst us who would not ride into the gates of hell for you.'

Fergus blushed as he looked down into the crackling fire. Then he nodded and smiled.

'Let's hope that won't be necessary,' he exclaimed. 'But as my father always said, the Batavians are amongst the finest soldiers in the Empire.'

Across the fire the second Batavian leaned towards Fergus, his mouth twisting into a crooked grin.

'And another thing Fergus,' the Batavian hissed. 'Sort out that woman problem of yours. The whole expedition knows what is going on. If you won't put us all out of our misery and fuck her then one of us will do the job for you.'

The three Batavians rose to their feet in unison and, as a furious blush appeared on Fergus's cheeks, they vanished into the darkness. Fergus however barely had time to consider their words, when from a neighbouring camp fire a loud, abusive argument shattered the tranquillity of the night. Startled, the men around Fergus's camp fire turned to stare at the altercation. Fergus rubbed his forehead in dismay. Across from them, Adalwolf and Gaiseric had risen to their feet and were facing each other, shouting and spitting at each other in a furious argument.

***

The Oder had widened and slowed, as the river had taken them north west into the flat plains beyond the mountains. It was after noon and it was snowing. On the river, the twelve Roman rafts crammed with men, supplies and beasts and bound together, were slowly floating down stream. Beyond the river, the flat featureless plains were covered in vast snow-bound pine forests. From his raft, bobbing up and down on the water, Fergus pulled the hood of his white winter-cloak over his forehead and peered into the bleak, dim light. Several days had passed since the expedition had embarked on their river journey and by now all the men were thoroughly sick of the dull, slow moving waters of the Oder. There had been several encounters with local tribesmen and they had come across several native settlements, built along the river. Most of the Germans had come out to trade with them, and sometimes Fergus had caught groups of small, ragged-looking children staring curiously at the rafts from the river bank. Only on one occasion had they been met with hostility from a solitary man, who had shaken his fist at them and hurled abuse at the Romans, from the safety of the river bank.

'Not long now until we reach our disembarkation point,' an accented voice said from close by. 'We will reach Mount Sleza within the next few days. Warm food, good, dry accommodation and friendly faces await you, Roman.'

Warily, Fergus turned to look at Gaiseric. The Vandal Prince was sitting cross-legged on the raft gazing into the distance. Two of the expedition's mules, lashed to the raft by both their heads and rump, stood separating Fergus from Gaiseric and his three warrior companions. Fergus did not reply as he looked away. It was just his luck that Titus had decided to make him look after the gold and silver and had lumped him on the same raft as Gaiseric. In between the two mules, six boxes had been tied to the raft, secured with a tough-looking rope.

'Ballomar will give us a feast when we arrive,' Gaiseric said staring down the river. 'Maybe it will go on for two or three days.'
'Who is Ballomar?' Fergus said sourly.

'He is the Lord of the Vandals,' Gaiseric said idly flicking a twig into the water. 'He is the man with whom Hadrian will negotiate the renewal of his treaty.'

'I thought the Vandals did not just have one leader,' Fergus muttered.

'It is sometimes difficult for a foreigner to understand my people,' Gaiseric said in a calm resigned voice. 'We are not ruled by one man. Each man is free to decide what to do with himself and where to go. We have many leaders, chiefs who rule their own tribes. We simply follow our bravest and most capable warriors. Men must prove themselves in battle and when they do again and again we follow them because they have the favour of Odin, Lord of War and the World. Ballomar is such a man. He has never been defeated in war or beaten in single combat. He is the bravest amongst all of us.'

'Braver than even you?' Fergus replied sarcastically.

On his side of the raft, Gaiseric took a deep breath and for a long moment he stared down into the brown waters of the Oder. 'We got off on the wrong foot,' Gaiseric said at last turning to give Fergus a vain grin, 'I am sorry that you had to see the killing of those villagers. Maybe I was being too harsh on them. If what I did offended you, then please accept my apologies.'
Fergus looked away and did not reply.

'We should be friends, you and I,' Gaiseric said.

Once again Fergus remained silent and in his position on the raft Gaiseric sighed.

'You should know that your friend, Adalwolf is not whom he claims to be,' Gaiseric said in a calm voice.

'What do you mean?' Fergus snapped frowning.

Gaiseric chuckled as he flung another twig into the water. 'Did he tell you that he is a Vandal Prince just like me and that he murdered his brother?'

'He did,' Fergus grunted.

'Did he also tell you that he murdered his brother because he was opposed to a treaty of friendship with Rome?'

Fergus glanced at Gaiseric and nodded silently.

'It was the other way around,' Gaiseric said with a contemptuous shake of his head. 'Adalwolf has never been a friend of Rome. It was he who wanted war with Rome and his brother who wanted an alliance. Hadrian is making a mistake in bringing that piece of shit to the negotiations. Adalwolf is going to be trouble. He is looking for ways in which to win back the favour and support of the Vandal chieftains.'

'How would he be trouble?' Fergus replied with a frown.

Gaiseric turned to look at Fergus, fixing him with a bemused but troubled look.

'Think about it Roman,' Gaiseric said with a cunning gleam in his eye. 'We are carrying a fortune in gold and silver with us. Enough to fund a small, private army. This is Roman wealth. It is meant to be used to buy my people's loyalty, friendship and alliance." Gaiseric paused and flung another twig into the river. 'But in the wrong hands and presented to the wrong chieftains, this gold and silver could also be used to buy their loyalty and support for a war *against* Rome. Do you understand what I am saying? I suspect that Adalwolf may try to take the gold and silver before the negotiations are concluded.' Gaiseric turned to look at Fergus, his face serious. 'Adalwolf is going to be your doom, Roman. That man is going to slaughter you and all your men. You should speak to your Centurion and make sure you take precautions.'

Chapter Thirty-Two – The Feast in the Hall of the Gods

Mount Sleza rose from the flat, forested plains like a great extinct volcano. Its conical summit was hidden in the clouds and along its steep, snow bound and heavily forested slopes, there was nothing to show that this was the sacred mountain of the Vandals, home to the twin Gods Alcis. The solitary mountain, more than two thousand feet high, dominated the land, and as Fergus trudged along staring at it, he felt a strange sense of dread. He knew nothing about the Gods that these Germans worshipped, but he did know that these foreign deities would not be on his side. It was afternoon and a day had passed since they had burned their rafts and left the Oder river behind them. Their long journey was coming to an end. Along the path, the column was winding its way through the trees towards the sacred mountain of the Vandals. They had lost another mule to exhaustion and starvation and the legionaries had been forced to start carrying some of the supplies themselves.

As he strode beside the remaining mules and slaves, Fergus caught a glimpse of Gaiseric up ahead. The Vandal Prince was easily distinguishable due to his height and clothing. Fergus's eyes narrowed suspiciously. He had not forgotten what the young Vandal Prince had told him on the raft. It was though, hard to believe. Could Adalwolf have lied to him? Was he even now planning to betray Hadrian and take the gold and silver for himself? Fergus sighed and shook his head in confusion. He didn't trust Gaiseric an inch, but then again what did he know about Adalwolf? The German merchant could have told him anything. On the journey from the river he'd thought about informing Titus about the conversation with Gaiseric, but had decided against it. Instead he had resolved, at the first opportunity he would confront Adalwolf and force him to reveal the truth.

The expedition was approaching the lower slopes of the mountain, when the mournful noise of a horn echoed away across the snow-covered pine forests. The noise was quickly taken up by another horn. Up ahead Fergus could see that the column had come to a halt amongst the trees. As he peered up the path, trying to see what was going on, one of Gaiseric's warrior's hastened past, heading towards the front of the expedition. Warily Fergus turned to look up at the summit of Mount Sleza but the top of the mountain was still hidden in the clouds. What would they find up there? A temple made of pure gold, naked female priestesses with snakes writhing in their hair? The rumour mill amongst the men had only grown, the closer to their destination they had come.

Then without explanation the column began to move once more. As the expedition began to wind its way up the mountain slopes, the slaves were forced to stay close to the mules, pulling, cursing and threatening the animals, as they struggled to prevent them slipping or getting stuck in the thick, snow-drifts. Stoically Fergus pushed on, pausing now and then to help the slaves force the heavily laden mules up the steep forested slope. It was hard going and Fergus was panting and covered in sweat, when he paused to regain his breath. Along the narrow path that wound its way upwards, the trees closed in on all sides, but a few yards away, standing in what looked like a man made-clearing, was a strange statue carved out of granite. The crude carving looked like that of a man.

For a long moment Fergus nervously stared at the granite figure. There was no doubt that the strange statue was meant as a votive offering but to what and to whom? What strange Gods did these Germans worship? What mysteries were hidden in this mountain? Abruptly Fergus's attention was snatched away by the mournful sound of a German horn. The noise had come from closer by this time. Up the slope and out of sight, a Roman voice suddenly cried out. As he turned to peer up the path, Fergus suddenly caught sight of Furius heading back down the track. The Optio had two scarfs wrapped around his head but his cheeks and nose still seemed to burn with a fierce colour of red.

'What's going on?' Fergus called out, as the Optio came towards the mules.

'We are here,' Furius sniffled in a voice heavily affected by his head-cold. 'We have reached our destination. The Vandal chieftains are here.'

Then he vanished down the path in the direction of the rear guard. Fergus turned to the slaves, who were standing along the path looking utterly exhausted.

'Come on then,' Fergus cried out. 'You heard the man; we have made it. Now let's get these beasts up the mountain and be done with it. Come on, move.'

The slaves did not reply as wearily they turned back to their charges, and once more began leading and cajoling the mules up the steep, slippery, snow-covered mountain path. And the higher they went, the steeper the slope became. Soon Fergus could barely see the legionaries ahead of him, as the forest and path became enveloped in a thick mist that reduced visibility to just a few yards. Just when he was about to despair of the visibility, the foremost slave emerged onto a small flat clearing in the forest and Fergus caught sight of a stone wall that stretched away into the vaporous clouds. And standing on top of the wall were a line of fierce, bearded German warriors, big, tall, ferocious-looking men, with their arms folded across their chests and each of them armed to the teeth. Startled Fergus came to a halt, as he gazed up at the warriors standing on the wall staring down at him, and for a fleeting moment, he was not sure whether they were real or made of stone.

***

On the heavily forested summit of Mount Sleza, a hundred or more camp fires were burning and glowing in the darkness. It was night and from the black moonless heavens snowflakes came slowly drifting down to earth. The hundreds of Germans, men, women and children, who had been waiting for the expedition and who had at first greeted the arrival of the Romans in solemn, curious silence, had at last retreated to their fires and were busy feasting, celebrating, eating and drinking. Their earlier silence had been completely turned on its head. Now the rowdy German singing, laughter, yelling, flute-playing and dancing disturbed the night, but around their own camp fires, the Roman legionaries sat in grim-silence, looking uncomfortable and out of place on this foreign mountain. Fergus sat in the snow in the second row, beside one of the large, crackling fires, just behind Hadrian, Titus and the Legate's advisers. And as he turned to look around at the summit of this sacred mountain, he could not help feeling a tiny bit disappointed. After all the build-up, there was nothing here. No temple, no holy cave, not even a shrine. There was just the thick forest, the tangled undergrowth and the big cloudy sky above their heads. Where then did the Germans go to honour their Gods? Where did they leave their offerings? Where did they come to pray? It was not clear, nothing was, but Fergus had begun to suspect that the Germans did not honour their Gods in the same way as the Romans did. Perhaps for the Germans, their temple was just the open sky and the simple, wild magnificence of the forest grove, and as he thought about it, Fergus felt himself begin to like the idea more and more. The Germans Gods must live free amongst nature itself, not cooped up in a stone temple. They were certainly savage but they were also free and egalitarian. They were the Gods of a fierce, independent warrior people.

Abruptly Fergus's attention was drawn back to the men, sitting around the large fire. The Romans were gathered around one side and facing them, across the crackling, spitting flames, were the Vandal Chieftains, dominated by the huge bulk of Ballomar, first man and leader of the Vandal tribes. From his position in the second row, Fergus had a good, unobstructed view of the Vandal chief. Ballomar looked around fifty. His chin and cheeks were covered by a grey beard and there was a calm, fearlessness and sharp intelligence in his eyes, that Fergus found disconcerting. The Vandal leader was clad in a great, black bearskin-cloak and the strands of his long dark hair were finely braided. The great man was flanked by five other German chieftains, with Gaiseric sitting furthest away from Ballomar. All of them were staring at Hadrian in stoic silence, as the Legate began to speak, choosing his words carefully and slowly, whilst at his side Adalwolf translated the words into German. Beside the fire, six wooden boxes had been set down in the snow, with their contents on show for all to see. In the leaping firelight, the thousands upon thousands of gold and silver coins gleamed and glinted, impossible to ignore.

'The Emperor Trajan,' Hadrian said in a quiet, confident voice, looking across the fire at Ballomar, 'has instructed me to tell you that he wishes for peace between our two great peoples. The Emperor wishes for our old alliance to continue, so he has sent me to present you with these gifts.'

Patiently Hadrian waited for Adalwolf to translate and then the Legate gestured at the six boxes filled with gold and silver coins. 'There is proof of Rome's desire for peace and an alliance with the Vandal peoples,' Hadrian said as he nodded at the chiefs sitting opposite him. 'So what answer shall I take back with me to Trajan?'

For a long moment, no one around the fire spoke. Suddenly Fergus felt his mouth grow dry. If the Vandals rejected the treaty and turned on their guests, he and the whole expedition would be slaughtered like cattle. Tensely Fergus turned to look at Hadrian, but if the Legate was aware of the danger he showed no sign of it. Across the fire from Hadrian, Ballomar finally stirred and slowly ran his fingers across his cheek with a thoughtful gaze.

'Our neighbours to the south,' the Vandal leader growled in broken Latin. 'The Marcomanni and the Quadi came to us a month ago with another proposal. They suggested that we join forces and attack the Danube frontier. They told us that Trajan had reduced his army along the frontier and sent his troops to fight the Dacians. So, it seems that you are in a weak bargaining position, Legate. Tell me then why we should not do as my neighbours propose?'

'War is always an option,' Hadrian replied lifting up his chin and fixing his eyes on Ballomar, 'And one which Rome will never shy away from. Do not forget who we are. Do not underestimate the long reach of Rome. We are perfectly capable of fighting two or three major wars on different fronts. We have beaten the Marcomanni and Quadi before and we will do so again. Make no mistake. Trajan is a great warrior like you. He welcomes war.' Hadrian sighed and looked away as he allowed Adalwolf to catch up with his translation. 'But there is another way,' Hadrian muttered. "Amongst the men I have brought here, I have thirty Batavian warriors, Germans in the service of Rome. They have served us faithfully for many generations and in return, live like free, independent and proud men. We do not rule them nor do we tax them, but each year they give us their finest warriors who we include in our armies.' Hadrian paused again, his eyes on Ballomar. 'The Emperor has also authorised me to offer you this. Give us your young noble born warriors, your second sons and we shall show them the world. We shall show them how the legions fight their wars.'

As Hadrian fell silent, a murmur arose amongst the Vandal chieftains. From his position across the fire, Ballomar was studying Hadrian with a shrewd look.

'Just like Arminius and Flavius of the Cherusci did a hundred years ago,' Ballomar muttered at last, as a faint smile appeared on his lips.

Hadrian nodded. 'Yes,' the Legate replied. 'Just like the brothers Arminius and Flavius of the Cherusci. So, do we have an agreement?'

Ballomar turned to stare into the flames and the men around the fire fell silent as they waited for the great chief to make up his mind.

'Alright, we shall be allies and friends of the Great Senate and People of Rome," Ballomar said looking up at Hadrian. 'Tell your Emperor; tell Trajan that he has nothing to fear from the Vandals.'

In his place beside the fire, Hadrian nodded his gratitude. But hardly had he done so when two of the Vandal chiefs sitting opposite him abruptly rose to their feet, spat into the fire and with an angry scowl, stomped away into the darkness. Unperturbed Ballomar turned to watch his two colleagues vanish into the night. Then with a little gesture he indicated to Gaiseric that he should go after them.

'Is there a problem?' Hadrian said with a frown, as Gaiseric silently rose to his feet and disappeared into the night.

Across from the Legate, Ballomar slowly shook his head. 'They did not wish us to make a treaty of friendship with Rome,' the big man replied sourly. 'They wanted us to join your enemies instead, but the decision has been made.'

Ballomar turned to look around at the tense, Roman faces watching him intently from across the fire. "You have nothing to fear whilst you are here under my protection,' Ballomar exclaimed. 'But the time for talking is over. Let us feast and celebrate our new alliance.'

***

The Roman officers and their Vandal hosts were drunk. There was no shortage of alcohol and cups of beer and mead were flowing freely and around the crackling, spitting fire the men were in a jolly mood, laughing and joking. Only Titus seemed to still be sober. The Centurion sat on the ground, a cup of beer in his hand, staring tiredly into the flames and ignoring the conversation around him. Fergus sat a few paces away in the snow, feeling the heat from the fire on his face. He had hardly touched the beer the Germans had offered him. Some instinct seemed to be telling him that tonight, was not the night to get drunk. The two Vandal chiefs, who'd left in protest at Ballomar's decision to renew the alliance with Rome, had not returned and neither had Gaiseric. Fergus sighed and was about to take a sip of beer, when in the flickering firelight he caught sight of a woman hunkering down amongst the trees a few yards away. It was Titula and she was carefully watching him.

What did the woman want now? Wearily, Fergus stared at the slave girl. She no longer looked angry and there was something resigned in her expression. Abruptly he got up and strode towards her. The girl rose to her feet as he approached. Her large, pale blue eyes examining him cautiously.

'I have a wife,' Fergus said harshly. 'She is expecting my child. I will remain loyal to her because I love her. Do you understand?' Titula's response was not what he had been expecting. Without uttering a sound, she reached out and respectfully touched the iron amulet around Fergus's neck. For a long moment, her eyes were drawn to Galena's amulet as she carefully turned it over in her fingers. Then she blushed and quickly looked away.

'My wife gave it to me,' Fergus said quietly as he looked down at the slave girl. 'She said it would bring me good luck, that it would protect me.'

Titula turned to look down at her feet. Then she took a step towards him and wrapped her arms around his chest, burying her head against him and closing her eyes.

'So you understand,' Fergus said with a relieved sigh, as he wrapped an arm around her. Then slowly he reached out and forced her to look up at him. 'So we are friends again,' he muttered.

Titula was gazing up at him, examining him carefully. Fergus was suddenly aware of an infinite sadness about her. Then the moment passed and loosening her grip, Titula reached up to caress Fergus's unshaven cheeks, and nodded. A little smile appeared on Fergus's rugged features. Without warning, Titula broke away from him and with a sudden, excited smile she began to dance, kicking her legs up into the air as she whirled in and out of the trees, her white winter-cloak and arms swirling through the air. And as he stared at the slave girl, a party of Germans around one of the campfires, seeing Titula dancing, cried out, began to clap and stamp their feet on the ground.

It was late into the night and still the feast went on. Dozily Fergus sat beside the Roman officers around the fire, trying to keep his eyes open. Most of the men had already fallen asleep, overcome by too much beer. Now they lay snoring loudly around the blazing fire. Bleary-eyed Fergus stared into the flames. Just before he had gone to get some rest, Titus had ordered him to stay awake until the Legate called it a night. Under no circumstances, Titus had growled, must Hadrian be left on his own with these Germans, not in his drunken state. At Fergus's side, Titula lay curled up against him, fast asleep, covered in her warm cloak. Around the fire the remaining men, Hadrian, Ballomar and the German chiefs were still awake, occasionally lifting their cups to their lips, as they continued to drink on in stubborn, drunken silence. And around them the snowflakes slowly continued to tumble down out of the heavens. A sudden movement in the darkness, made Fergus raise his head. From the snowy gloom Gaiseric suddenly appeared and smoothly sat down beside the Vandal chiefs. The young prince looked stone-cold sober. He gave the Romans a quick contemptuous glance that Fergus noticed. Then he reached for a cup of beer and flung the contents down his throat in one go.

'You,' Hadrian said suddenly raising his finger to point at Gaiseric. 'You look like a man who likes the taste of cock in his mouth. Well do you?' Hadrian exclaimed, slurring his words as he swayed drunkenly.

'What?' Gaiseric frowned, looking taken aback.

'You heard me,' Hadrian growled, slurring his words again. 'I said you look like a man who would enjoy the company of other men. You look like a homosexual. Did you know that such men are forbidden from serving in the legion's? I could have you sacked for that.'

Across the fire Gaiseric was staring at the Legate with growing anger.

'I like the company of men,' Hadrian grunted drunkenly. 'And I also like women but you. You remind me of someone who just likes cock.'

Slowly Gaiseric rose to his feet, his face seething with rage as he stared at Hadrian. But as he slowly reached for the knife hanging from his belt, Ballomar and the other chiefs suddenly burst out laughing. From his position beside the fire, Hadrian too broke out into a giggling fit as he stared up at Gaiseric.

'Sit down Gaiseric,' Ballomar boomed. 'Don't be so easily offended. Our guest is just jesting with you, man.'

'No I am not,' Hadrian cried out, as he burst out into another giggling fit. 'I meant that as an insult. You were useful but I never liked you. You remind me of a snake, twisting this and that way.'

Quickly Fergus cleared his throat as he saw Gaiseric's silent fury turn to pure hatred.

'Sir, I think it is time for you to retire to your tent,' Fergus said hastily. 'If you follow me I shall show you the way. Please Sir.'

Beside the fire Hadrian's giggling fit slowly passed and he nodded.

'Yes you are right; it's time to sleep,' Hadrian muttered, rising unsteadily to his feet.

Fergus caught the Legate by his arm and steadied him and as he led Hadrian towards his tent, he turned to see Gaiseric watching them in bitter, furious silence.

Chapter Thirty-Three – Homeward Bound

The sky was heavily overcast. It was noon and the small Roman expedition strode onwards through the vast forest, strung out along the snow-covered path. Amongst the trees and deep snow-drifts, all was quiet, peaceful and nothing moved. Fergus, clutching his shield and with his equipment slung over his shoulder on his wooden marching pole, trudged along at the front of the column and just behind Titus, Adalwolf and Hadrian. The men were moving along in a single file, huddled under their thick, hooded white winter-cloaks and no one seemed interested in talking. Two days had passed since the treaty of alliance between Rome and the Vandals had been concluded, and that morning Hadrian, still looking hungover, had finally ordered the company homewards. The long walk back home had begun. Fergus had been present that morning at the 'O group meeting,' when Hadrian, Gaiseric, Adalwolf and Titus had discussed the route home. The officers had agreed that the expedition would head straight for the Moravian Gates, a hundred and fifty-mile trek through the flat, heavily forested plains that lay to the north of the Sudeten mountains. The ten surviving mules were just about able to carry enough food for the expedition to make it home but it would be tight and food would have to be strictly rationed. Once in the mountain pass the expedition would pick up the amber road and head south through the territory of the Marcomanni and Quadi, until they reached the Danube frontier. With a bit of luck the journey would take about a month.

Guardedly, Fergus raised his head to gaze at Hadrian. The Legate had his back to him as he strode on along the path. The man had acted foolishly, when in his drunken state, he had insulted Gaiseric and during the 'O group meeting' that morning both Hadrian and Gaiseric had refused to look at each other. Stupid, stupid, stupid, so unnecessary Fergus thought, as he gazed at Hadrian. It remained to be seen whether those two would be able to bury their quarrel. Wrenching his eyes away from the Legate, Fergus gave Titula a little playful shove. The slave girl responded by darting away into the trees, and a moment later a volley of snow-balls came hurtling towards him. Fergus grinned as he dodged them.

'Enough of that,' Titus's annoyed voice boomed as the Centurion turned around and glared at Fergus. 'You are third in command of this company, act like it.'

'Yes Sir,' Fergus replied hastily as he rearranged the expression on his face. From behind a tree he caught Titula watching him with a mischievous look. Quickly he shot her a warning look and shook his head. The girl's sharp mood swings were hard to understand, but amongst the company her presence seemed to have had a strange calming effect on the men.

From up the path there was a sudden shout and instantly Titus raised his fist above his head and the column of men behind him came to an abrupt halt. A moment later several Batavian horsemen appeared and came trotting down the track. The men looked anxious, and as he caught sight of their faces, Fergus felt a sudden cold, invisible finger of warning touch his temple. Titus was peering at the riders as they came towards him.

'Sir,' one of the Batavian's called out. 'The Vandal guides. They have disappeared. Gaiseric and his men are gone.'

'What?' Titus and Hadrian exclaimed at the same time.

'They have gone Sir,' the Batavian rider repeated. 'Vanished into the forest. All of them.'

'Shit,' Titus muttered in an annoyed voice, turning to face Hadrian. 'Now we have lost our guides. How the hell will we find our way home?'

Hadrian did not reply. Moodily he turned to gaze at the ground as he seemed to be thinking about what to do.

'Alright Centurion,' the Legate muttered at last raising his head.

'Tell the men that we will rest here for a while and gather your officers together. If Gaiseric has deserted us we must come up with a new plan.'

The legionaries were sitting hunkered down in the snow along the forest path when Furius who had been with the rear-guard, came striding towards the small group of officers clustered around Hadrian. The Optio was still suffering from his cold and his head was covered and bound by two scarves and a grey fur Vandal hat. His face looked pale and he was shivering as he hastened to Titus's side.

'What's going on?' Furius muttered.

'Gaiseric has gone and taken his guides with him,' Fergus replied quietly.

'Fuck,' Furius groaned as he sniffed and held his hand up to his nose.

'Alright,' Hadrian growled looking displeased. 'Adalwolf will take over as guide, he knows these lands just as well as Gaiseric. We will keep heading on the same course as before. Nothing has changed. The treaty of alliance between us and the Vandals remains. The alliance will hold so long as Ballomar remains the tribal leader. Gaiseric would have to kill Ballomar to change that and if he does it will cause a civil war.'

At his side Titus nodded in agreement.

'Sir,' Fergus suddenly interrupted, his cheeks suddenly blushing. 'When we were on the river I shared a raft with Gaiseric and his men.' Fergus took a deep breath as he turned to look straight at Adalwolf. 'Gaiseric told me that you were not to be trusted. He said that you murdered your brother because it was you who did not want peace with Rome. Gaiseric said that you were going to betray us and lead us to our doom. If that is so,' Fergus said turning sharply to face Titus. 'Is it wise to allow Adalwolf to be our guide? He could lead us straight into a trap.'

A stunned silence followed.

'They are lies Fergus,' Adalwolf said in a calm voice. 'Gaiseric has filled your head with lies. If I had wanted to sabotage this expedition I could have done it a long time ago. The treaty has been made. We have completed our mission successfully and we are going home.'

'Still, do we trust this man?' Fergus snapped, pointing at Adalwolf.

'I do,' Hadrian replied sharply, 'and that will be enough from you Tesserarius,' the Legate snapped glaring angrily at Fergus. 'I have known Adalwolf for much longer than you have. I trust him. He is my man.'

'I agree,' Titus growled. 'We have no choice. He is the only one who knows this land. The only one who knows the way home.'

Defeated, Fergus lowered his eyes to the ground.

'It's alright young man,' Adalwolf said gazing at Fergus in a conciliatory manner. 'Gaiseric had us all fooled. I suspect he was planning to desert all along. The question is what will he do now?' Calmly Adalwolf turned to Hadrian. 'I would advise you Sir to take precautions. Bring the men in closer together, have the Batavian horsemen screen our flanks and rear. And I would also suggest that we build some rudimentary sledges. The mules can drag them along through the snow and if we lose the mules the men will be able to haul our food supplies along on them.'

The officer's around Hadrian nodded in agreement.

'Alright make it happen, Titus,' Hadrian growled turning to give Fergus a sour look.

***

It was around noon the following day when in between the trees Fergus caught sight of the large frozen lake. The expedition had been heading on a south-easterly course since leaving Mount Sleza and beyond the lake and forest, the heavily- forested slopes and crags of the Sudeten mountains were just about visible on the horizon. The snow-covered ice twisted away into the distance and across the lake he could make out the forest on the far side, some four hundred yards away. Ahead of Fergus, along the path, the ten surviving mules were plodding along, heavily laden with the company's supplies. It was bitterly cold, cold like Fergus had never experienced before and the snow crunched under his boots as he strode along. At his side Titula was keeping pace, her hands buried within her cloak to keep them warm, her breath visible in the crisp, freezing air. The snow that had started to fall from the sky in the morning was beginning to thicken and to the east, dark grey clouds announced an approaching storm.

From the forest to his right, the peace of the afternoon was suddenly shattered by cries and the thud of galloping hooves. Startled, Fergus and the men around him turned to stare in the direction of the noise. Then abruptly a party of Batavian horsemen burst from the trees.

'Gaiseric Sir,' the Batavian Decurion in command of the horsemen yelled as he caught sight of Titus hastening towards him. 'Gaiseric and his men are massing in the forest. We saw him. It's him! They are going to attack. They are right behind us.' For a moment, the Centurion stood staring at the Decurion in stunned indecision. Wildly, Fergus turned to stare into the forest, as from within its depth he suddenly heard wild cries and yells. The noise was rapidly drawing closer.

'How many?' Titus roared.

'Around two or three hundred men,' the Decurion yelled, casting a nervous glance over his shoulder into the forest.

In the forest the screams, wild cries, yells and the sound of running feet were rapidly approaching.

'Fall back onto the lake,' Titus screamed. 'Fall back onto the lake. Fergus get those mules across and onto the far side. Decurion, form your horsemen up on the ice and prepare to charge the enemy when they are exposed and out in the open. The rest of you fall back to the lake. Move, move, move!'

There was no more time. In the forest Fergus suddenly caught sight of armed men running and crashing towards them through the undergrowth. Along the path the Roman column exploded into action as the men bolted through the forest towards the white snow covered and ice bound lake. Instantly all became chaos. Fergus heard himself screaming at the slaves and the mules. Terrified and panic stricken the beats lumbered through the forest bashing into each other and the trees in their haste to get away. Then abruptly they were onto the ice. Fergus slipped and went crashing headlong into the snow dropping his personal equipment. Around him the slaves, mules and Legionaries were spilling out of the forest and onto the open, ice bound lake in a confused fleeing mass.

"Get those beasts across the lake, move, move," Fergus roared as he scrambled to his feet.

There was no time to see whether the slaves were obeying his orders. Dimly Fergus was aware of the Batavian horsemen forming up on the ice, some distance away. Then his attention was drawn to the lake-shore. The forest erupted in a rolling howl and screams as the Germans burst out onto the ice slashing, hacking and stabbing at the fleeing Romans. Wildly Fergus drew his sword and stormed forwards to a knot of Romans around Titus and Furius who were desperately trying to fend off the swarming German attackers. A screaming warrior came at

Fergus, wildly swinging his axe in the air, which thudded straight into Fergus's shield. With a vicious cry, Fergus stabbed the warrior with his sword and kicked him to the ground. On the shore of the lake the small group of legionaries around Titus and Furius seemed to be in desperate straits, nearly surrounded by their attackers. Fergus caught a glimpse of Titus's plumed helmet amongst the yelling, screaming, brawling mass of bodies. All along the lake-shore the Germans were bursting out onto the ice, their dark fur clothes out of place on the pristine, white-snow and ice. But there was no time to take it all in. Two yelling warriors came at Fergus, armed with spears, driving him back and away from the shore. Across the ice all around him the legionaries were scattered and fleeing towards the far shore. There was no question of forming any defence. It was every man for himself. Fergus roared in frustration as the warriors steadily drove him away from where Titus and Furius were fighting for their lives, trapped along the lake shore. He couldn't reach them.

Then the ice under his feet began to tremble and he heard a faint cracking noise. To his right and from across the snow-covered ice, the thirty mounted Batavian horsemen suddenly came charging into the Germans, slashing and stabbing at them with their long cavalry swords and spears.

'Thunder and lashing rain, so Wodan commeth. Thunder and lashing rain, so Wodan commeth.'

The furious cry rose above the tumult, as the Batavians crashed headlong into the enemy. And their magnificent cavalry charge had a devastating impact. In the path of the tight V shaped charge, the Germans everywhere went tumbling to the ground and their shrieks and panicked cries rent the noon air. Nothing could stop the horses' momentum and like a scythe through corn, the Batavian charge cut a bloody path straight through the exposed German ranks sending the survivors fleeing in terror for the safety and cover of the forest. Alarmed the two warriors in front of Fergus turned to see what was going on and instantly

Fergus sprang forwards and buried his sword in one of the men's neck. The other warrior staggered backwards as a fountain of blood went shooting into the air. Then he turned and fled towards the forested shore. Fergus wrenched his sword free and pushed the dying man to the ground with his shield. Then he was bounding across the blood-smeared and corpse-strewn ice towards the small huddle of Roman bodies lying close together on the lakeshore. As he ran forwards across the snow-covered ice, two Roman legionaries came staggering towards him dragging a body behind them through the snow. The soldier's faces were covered in sweat and one of the men was bleeding from a cut to his leg. Fergus's eyes widened in horror, as he saw that the wounded man they were dragging through the snow was Furius. The Optio's eyes were closed and his head lolled from side to side. He'd lost his fur Vandal hat and blood was seeping out from an ugly wound to stomach and leg. 'Titus,' Fergus roared. 'Where is the Centurion?'

'Dead,' one of the legionaries shouted. 'He's dead. You are now in command, Sir.'

Horrified Fergus turned to stare at the mass of dead and dying bodies clustered around the shore of the lake and suddenly, amongst the corpses lying half on-land and half on the ice he recognised Titus's fine red plumed helmet. There was nothing more he could do. Across the ice in the swirling falling snow-flakes, the last of the Roman survivors were racing across the lake towards the far shore. The Batavian charge may have temporarily sent Gaiseric and his men fleeing back into the forest but it would not be long before they regrouped and came back.

'You are in command now, Sir. What should we do Sir?' one of the legionaries dragging Furius across the ice shouted at Fergus.

Fergus stood rooted to the snow, covered ice, unable to take his eyes off the bloody mass of corpses that lay scattered and heaped up around Titus's last stand. Then with a groan, he wrenched his eyes away from the carnage and stooping to grab his equipment pole he hastened after the two men who were dragging Furius across the ice.

'Get your men across the lake and into the forest,' Fergus roared as the Batavian riders came galloping back towards him. 'Let's get the fuck out of here.'

***

The howling, groaning wind blew through the forest, whipping up the snow and moving and swaying the branches of the trees, reducing visibility to a dozen or so yards. From the darkening sky, a blanket of thick snowflakes came tumbling to the ground, coating the men's cloaks, beards and arms. It was nearly dusk and the light was fading rapidly. Stoically, Fergus lowered his head into the blizzard as he tramped stubbornly on through the snow. Behind him the column of plodding, weary, dispirited and silent men came on, winding their way through the forest. Upon reaching the far side of the lake he'd managed to gather the survivors of the attack together, and without delay they had set off into the forest, desperate to put some distance between them and Gaiseric's war band. Ninety-eight men in all had survived and that number included the remaining slaves, civilians, legionaries and Batavians. Nearly a quarter of the men had been lost in the fight on the frozen lake. Tensely Fergus wiped the snow from his face and peered into the forest ahead. There was no path. He was just aimlessly leading his men through the forest without knowing in which direction he was going. There had been no time to think of a plan. But at least the blizzard would help cover their tracks and slow any pursuit. The shock of realising that he was now the most senior remaining officer and in command, had still not fully sunk in. Out of the ninety-eight men now under his command, eighteen were wounded, seven of which seriously and one of the mules had vanished in the confusion. Some of the men had lost their shields and spears and Aledus was missing presumed dead.

Furius was still unconscious and Hadrian too had been badly wounded by a spear and was incapable of walking and delirious with fever. Fergus had ordered the seriously wounded to be lashed to the sledges and now the men were taking it in turn to drag the sledges through the thick and deep snow.

'Sir,' a young frightened looking legionary came hastening through the snow towards Fergus. 'Sir, the Optio is conscious, he is asking for you, Sir.'

Fergus nodded, and turning to the soldier behind him, he gestured for the man to keep heading straight ahead through the forest. Then quickly he began to move down the side of the column of men and plodding mules towards the sledge upon which Furius lay. The Optio looked in a bad way as Fergus reached him and started to walk alongside the men pulling the sledge through the snow.

'It's alright,' Fergus said trying to smile at Furius. 'We have managed to get away for now. You are going to live.'

Upon the crude wooden sledge, nothing more than a few, smooth tree-trunks nailed and bound together with rope, Furius groaned as he turned to stare at Fergus. The Optio's hands were pressed to the wound in his stomach, over which someone had wrapped a white bandage. From his jolting, moving sledge Furius grimaced in sudden pain.

'Titus,' Furius said so softly that Fergus had to lean closer. 'Titus's last instructions to me before they killed him was to make sure that his boys got back home.' Furius groaned and he opened his mouth in sudden agony as he looked up at Fergus. 'He ordered me to get the men safely back home,' Furius whispered. 'Do you understand? Do you understand your orders, Fergus?'

Solemnly Fergus nodded as he reached down and grasped hold of the Optio's hand. 'I will make sure we all get back home,' he said in a determined voice. 'Titus shall rest easy with the Gods and one day we shall salute him again.'

But Furius had already closed his eyes and seemed to be no longer listening. With a weary sigh Fergus patted the wounded man on his shoulder and stomped off back along the line of slow moving men. As he reached the front of the column, Titula came plodding out of the forest and at her side was Adalwolf. Fergus gave both a tense, guarded look, as they fell in beside him.

'Where are we going?' Adalwolf asked quietly, as Fergus led the column on through the snow-covered trees. 'We need a plan, Fergus.'

Fergus sighed as he trudged along through the thick snow.

'We need to put as much distance between us and Gaiseric,' he muttered. 'And we are going home. It's just in this blizzard it is impossible to see where we are.'

'Gaiseric will not give up,' Adalwolf snapped. 'He may have received a bloody nose down on the ice but he will regroup and come after us. I reckon he may only be half a day to a day behind us. If he has hunting dog's, they will pick up our trail and hunt us down. He has the advantage in numbers and he knows this land like the back of his hand. It's only a matter of time. He is going to catch up with us sooner or later. I don't think we can outrun him.'

'Then what would you have me do,' Fergus snapped rounding sharply on the German merchant. 'The men are hardly in any state to put up a fight.'

'I am sorry, I don't know,' Adalwolf said looking away.

Annoyed Fergus shook his head. 'We keep going,' he growled. 'I am not going to give up. We are not going to die out here. Sooner or later this blizzard will pass and then we will able to make a judgement in which way we should head.'

Adalwolf nodded as he kept pace with Fergus as they trudged on through the forest and into the swirling, howling storm.

'If Gaiseric has been planning this for some time,' Adalwolf said in a thoughtful voice, 'he will be anticipating that we are heading towards the Moravian Gates. He may even have placed his scouts in the pass. Remember he was there when we discussed the route back home. He may have another force waiting there to ambush us when we enter the pass.'

Grimly Fergus nodded as he weighed up what Adalwolf had just said. Then slowly he turned to gaze into the forest and the flurry of whirling snowflakes.

'Maybe we should change course,' he growled. 'Maybe we should do something that Gaiseric is not expecting. Maybe we should turn and head due south into the mountains. Maybe we can lose him in the Sudeten.'

'Into the mountains, in this weather,' Adalwolf exclaimed opening his mouth. 'I am not sure.' The amber merchant faltered as he seemed to consider it. Then he frowned and shook his head. 'That would be a gamble, Fergus. There will be little if any food up there and the terrain will be difficult as hell. Our progress will slow and it's a lot colder up there than down here. I am not sure that would be a good idea.'

'And yet that is what we are going to do,' Fergus snapped in a sudden savage voice. 'You asked about a plan. Well our plan is to head into the mountains and try and lose Gaiseric up there. I can't think of anything better, so that is what we are going to do.'

Chapter Thirty-Four – Survival

The large fire crackled and flickered in the entrance to the shallow, forest cave. It was night and the men were packed, crowding around the warmth of the fire, desperately trying to warm their hands, feet and faces. Around them the snow continued to fall. The fierce blizzard had gone on for two days now without respite, and in its wintery grip visibility was severely reduced. Fergus had never experienced anything like it and during the night, the temperature had continued to drop and drop. In the deep snow-drifts and dark, alien, trackless-forest and frozen swamps, the progress of the ragged Roman column had slowed, and despite Fergus's decision to head for the mountains the storm meant he still didn't have a clue if he was heading in the right direction. During the first night after the attack, they had camped out in the forest and he had forbidden the men from starting camp-fires for fear that it would give away their position. The lack of warmth and the chance to prepare a hot meal had weighed heavily on the men's morale and by morning two men had died, one of the wounded succumbing to his wounds and the other had simply frozen to death. There had been no time to bury them in the rock-solid earth and they have been left behind after a brief religious ceremony in which the signifer had said a few words.

But now at least they had found some shelter from the icy wind. The cave was shallow but it's secluded position meant that they could risk a fire. Fergus sat on a rock, a little way off from the fire, his legs drawn up under him, as he huddled under his thick white winter-cloak, his hood drawn over his head. In the forest, a few yards away he could see the sentries moving about trying to keep themselves warm. If Gaiseric were to attack them at this moment, he doubted that many of his men would be able to put up much resistance. The strain of the long journey, their wounds, the lack of a proper rest and the freezing cold were slowly sapping their will to resist. Grimly, Fergus stared into night where the swirling snowflakes kept falling. The only thing he knew for certain was what he didn't want to do. He was not going to give up. He was not going to let his men die out here. Shivering from the cold, he glanced up at the dark night sky. Corbulo would not have given up. His grandfather would have found a way to get his men back to the Danube. But how? He was stranded here, hundreds of miles beyond the frontier about to head into the mountains in the freezing cold with a determined enemy on his tail. How was he going to get himself out of this mess? How would Corbulo have handled that?

From out of the forest a horse and a rider suddenly came walking towards him. Startled, Fergus flung aside his cloak and reached for his sword. Then with an annoyed grunt he relaxed. The rider wearily raised his hand in greeting. A few moments later he was joined by six more riders, their cloaks and hoods covered in fresh snow. The Batavian scouts had returned. The Batavian Decurion slowly dismounted from his horse whilst his men did the same, silently leading their beasts towards the roaring, welcoming warmth of the fire. And as they did, Fergus saw how thin and in bad condition the horses looked.

'Sir,' the Decurion said in a tired voice. 'We did as you instructed. We stayed behind and waited. Gaiseric and his men are on our trail alright. They are perhaps a half-a- day behind. The last we saw of them they were preparing to make a camp for the night.'

'How many men does he have?' Fergus said gazing at the Decurion.

'About two hundred,' the Decurion replied brushing the snow from his cloak. 'We saw no cavalry but he does have a pack of hunting dogs, vicious looking beasts. They didn't pick up our scent because we were up wind but there is no doubt Gaiseric will be able to follow us Sir. We're leaving a massive trail for him to follow, even with all this new snow-fall. I am sorry Sir.'

'Thank you Decurion,' Fergus nodded lowering his head. 'Get some hot food and some rest. We will be setting out again at dawn.'

The Decurion nodded but stayed where he was gazing, instead at the company clustered around the fire at the cave mouth.

'What is it?' Fergus growled as he sensed that the Decurion was not yet finished.

'My horses,' the Decurion said in a gloomy voice. 'They haven't properly eaten for weeks. They are spent Sir. They are going to start dying in the next few days if we don't find any food for them.'

'I don't think we are going to find any fresh food for them, not in the mountains, not in this weather,' Fergus said taking a deep breath.

In the darkness, the Decurion nodded.

'Then with your permission,' the soldier said quietly, 'I would like to allow my men to set their horses free. Maybe they will stand a chance of surviving on their own in the wild. The men feel quite strongly about this Sir.'

But on his rock Fergus slowly shook his head.

'No,' he growled. 'You will do no such thing. I am sorry,' Fergus sighed and wearily looked away into the forest. 'We may need to eat your horses if we run out of food. Your orders are to keep them alive as long as possible. Do you understand?'

In the darkness Fergus was aware of the Decurion staring at him in horror. For a long moment, there was no answer from the gloom.

'Understood Sir,' came the softly spoken reply at last. It was followed by another pause. 'Why did Gaiseric attack us Sir? He was our guide. The men don't understand why he suddenly turned on us?'

Fergus closed his eyes and rubbed his hand across his forehead.

'It's because our esteemed Legate couldn't keep his big mouth shut,' Fergus growled.

***

It was deep into the night when a hand roughly shook Fergus awake. Startled, he reached for his sword but a cold hand and small fingers stopped him. Bleary-eyed he stared straight at Titula. She had drawn her cloak tightly around herself and she was shivering. In her hand, however she was holding up a piece of bread and hard Batavian cheese. Gratefully he took it from her. In the rush to make sure that the company were organised and settled, he had forgotten to eat.

Tiredly he stuffed the food into his mouth and munched away. Then when he had swallowed the last of it he muttered his thanks. Titula was watching him with her large, pale blue eyes as if waiting for something to happen.

'What are you doing here, Valkyrie,' Fergus said wearily reaching out and placing his finger on the tip of her nose. 'What are you doing out here with the likes of me? Come on, talk to me?'

But from the gloom, Titula remained silent. Then slowly and deliberately she raised her fingers to Fergus's face and softly traced the outline of his nose and eyebrows, and as she did, Fergus suddenly had the strangest sense that he was being touched by a goddess. Startled, he drew back and stared at Titula.

'Who are you? What are you really doing here?' he hissed bleary-eyed.

In front of him Titula withdrew her hand and lowered her gaze to the ground. Then abruptly and without making a sound she rose to her feet and vanished into the night.

***

'Come on, move it, move it, we're the finest damn company in the Twentieth Legion, we can do this,' Fergus cried out as the weary column of men, sledges and beasts struggled past him up the forested slope. It was late afternoon and that morning the blizzard had finally died away and the sun had appeared for the first time in two days. Its return had been greeted with excited cries of joy from the men and morale had risen as the fine, blue sky had continued all that morning. The improving weather had also allowed Fergus and Adalwolf to determine their position, and shortly afterwards the company had turned due south and had started climbing up into the foothills of the Sudeten mountains. As he watched the men coming past, Fergus called out to the soldiers, adding words of encouragement to those visibly struggling and reaching out to grasp the hands of the wounded, lying on their sledges and being pulled along by their comrades. It was a display of confidence that he did not feel but it was all he could do. Attitude was the key to survival; old Quintus had once told him when he was still a boy growing up on the farm on Vectis. Attitude and instilling confidence in your men was half the battle, the retired Centurion had explained, even if you don't share it. What is important is that your men see it and believe it, for it will give them strength and courage. And here he was, doing exactly what Quintus had once told him. Slowly Fergus shook his head in disbelief. He was barely twenty years old. He shouldn't be in this position, not at his age, but he was. And suddenly all those old war-stories Quintus had told him, when he was still a boy, were suddenly so relevant. He was glad he had listened.

As the rear-guard came trudging past, Fergus turned to gaze towards the south. In the fine blue skies, the northern slopes of the Sudeten mountains were very close now. The heavily forested slopes, rocky-crags and peaks were not as high and beautiful as the massive, solitary Alpine peaks Fergus had seen on the journey to Carnuntum, but they were nevertheless impressive - some of the peaks rising to over four thousand feet. Along the snow-covered forested route pine trees covered the mountain slopes; weird geological rock formations poked up above the trees; and on top of the mountain peaks, snow gleamed in the sunlight. As Fergus began to follow the company up the slope, he suddenly caught sight of a magnificent Mouflon standing on top of a rocky ledge formation twenty yards away. The red, brown goat- like animal with its fine curled horns was standing motionless up on its rock, staring straight at Fergus.

It had grown dark and the temperature was once more dropping rapidly, when Fergus ordered the company to a halt for the night in a narrow, mountain gorge. As the men started to fan out to collect fire wood, prepare their dinner and build their fires, Fergus stomped off to the top of the gorge. The solid rock walls of the long and narrow gorge towered twenty or thirty yards above the ground, and as he reached the snow-covered summit he knelt in the deep snow and turned to stare northwards. In the night sky above him, were a multitude of twinkling stars. Fergus narrowed his eyes as he peered down into the forested plains to the north. In the darkness, there was little to see. Gaiseric was being careful, he thought, for he could see no sign of fires or light in the gloom. Fergus sighed as he stared into the darkness. The faint outline of the vast pine-forests was just about visible in the dim moonlight. That day he had tried to lead their pursuers onto a false trail, but his Batavian scouts had reported that the enemy had not been fooled. Later that afternoon he had tried to hide their trail but again the Batavians had reported back saying that this trick had not worked either. There seemed no way in which he could shake Gaiseric from their tail. Exhaustedly Fergus rubbed his hand over his tired eyes. He could always leave Hadrian behind he thought. Maybe if Gaiseric was allowed to avenge the insult that had started all this, by killing the Legate, he would give up the chase and let the rest of them go, but as he thought about it Fergus knew the idea was a nonstarter.

'What would you do, grandfather?' Fergus muttered opening his eyes and glancing up at the heavens. 'Please give me a sign that you are with me, please, I beg you. Anything grandfather, anything.'

The night however remained silent and peaceful and in the darkness, nothing moved. In the gloom Fergus suddenly caught sight of a strange-looking rectangular rock-formation that looked definitely man-made. Blinking in surprise he rose to his feet. He was so tired he had not noticed what was right in front of him. With a frown, he took a step forwards and reached out to touch the slab of stone. Slowly he circled the six-feet-long stone mound running his fingers across its snow-covered top. It was a Hunebed, an ancient, stone-tomb and older than all the trees standing in the forest. Adalwolf had talked about the Hunebedden on their journey towards Mount Sleza. He had said they contained the graves of his tribe's distant ancestors, the first men who had made these forests their home. With a surprised grunt, Fergus paused and placed his hand on the hard rock. This grave could easily be three-thousand years old. Whoever had been buried here must have wanted to enjoy the view.

From close by Fergus suddenly sensed movement amongst the trees. Startled he turned to face the forest. Then his eyes widened in terror. Amongst the trees, things were moving, pacing up and down and in the faint light he suddenly caught sight of fur, gleaming eyes and hungry, open jaws. A moment later the night was rent with growls and whining. Wolves. Horrified, Fergus staggered backwards against the rock and then hastily clambered up onto the Hunebed. He was surrounded by a wolf pack. From the trees the growling and whining continued, and then from very close by one of the wolves raised its muzzle into the night sky and howled. The noise, so close by, was utterly terrifying and Fergus nearly pissed himself. Hastily he crouched down on top of the rock and drew his sword and pugio, his army knife from his belt, holding both weapons up in front of him. At the edge of the forest the wolves seemed to be moving up and down in between the trees. Fergus's eyes widened in horror. Had he come this far only to be torn apart and devoured by starving wolves? Was this the fate the gods had in mind for him? At the edge of the forest the whining and growling was growing louder and more urgent.

'Come on then you bastards,' Fergus hissed with sudden fury, as he clutched his two weapons in his hands. 'Who wants to be the first to die? Come on you fucking dogs. I am here. What are you waiting for?'

Then he blinked, blinked again and stared into the night in confusion. Something strange was happening at the edge of the forest. As he gazed into the darkness, his eyes slowly widened in shock and surprise. In the starry darkness, an icy white-blue figure of a woman, clad in brilliant, shining-white clothes and long golden hair had appeared and was calmly striding through the pack of wolves. On her head, she had a crown of icicles and in one of her hands she was holding a knife made of shimmering light. Her face was just a blaze of blueish light. And, as she calmly strode through the milling pack of wolves she slowly turned to face Fergus, crouching on top of the Hunebed, and as she did, she slowly bowed to him. Fergus gasped. Then he closed his eyes. What was the matter with him? What was happening to him? When at last he opened his eyes again the woman had vanished and so had the wolves. Startled, Fergus rose to his feet and peered into the darkness. Had he been so tired that he had started to see things? Was exhaustion playing tricks on him? Had the wolves even been real? Wildly he peered into the night but amongst the trees nothing moved and the night was quiet and peaceful.

Then from down in the gorge below him, he heard a sudden loud commotion. Leaping off the Hunebed, Fergus scrambled down the side of the hill, not caring about the sharp edges and ridges of the rocks. As he made it down onto the floor of the gorge he turned to gaze in the direction of the small Roman camp. Around the blazing fires, snow and towering rock-walls of the gorge, the Romans had risen to their feet and were raising their fists in the air in acts of victory and joy. And as his eyes adjusted to the light, Fergus gasped as he caught sight of Aledus and two other men who had been missing since the attack and who had been presumed to be dead. Aledus was surrounded by his mess-mates, who were hugging him and raising their fists in the air in delight.

With sudden realisation Fergus turned to look up at the star-studded sky. Was this the sign he had asked for? Had Corbulo, his grandfather heard his plea?

'Gods, fuck, thank you, thank you grandfather,' he muttered with wild awe-struck and exhausted looking eyes.

Chapter Thirty-Five – Gallantry in the Face of the Enemy

The rolling hills, sharp rocky walls and cliffs, towering stone-pillars and deep, winding gorges of the Sudeten mountains stretched away to the horizon. The bleak, snowy wilderness was not going to let them go without extracting its toll. Grimly, Fergus paused to catch his breath as the column wound its way across the slope of another heavily forested hill. The ground was growing steeper and more rugged the higher into the mountains they went, and their progress was continuing to slow. It was afternoon and with Adalwolf guiding the expedition they had continued to head southwards. During the night, two more of the wounded had succumbed, and as predicted by the Batavian Decurion, the first of his horses had started to die from exhaustion and starvation. Fergus sighed as he turned to gaze at his men. His face was pale and shrunken and his eyes were red-rimmed from exhaustion and a lack of sleep. The men too, looked in a bad state. That morning Fergus had inquired whether anyone in the company had heard the howl of a wolf in the night but none had. Was he beginning to lose his mind? Tiredly, Fergus rubbed his hand across his forehead and turned to gaze at the men, trudging through the snow, hauling their sledges behind them across the ground. The only positive development had been Aledus's miraculous return. The company had given him up for dead, when he had gone missing during the attack, but after hiding out in the forest for a while Aledus and the two men with him, had somehow managed to find the company's tracks and had followed them onwards and up into the mountains.

'Come on move it, keep moving,' Fergus cried out, trying to smile at the weary, dispirited column and raise their spirits. 'Moving keeps you warm. Moving puts distance between us and the enemy. Moving brings us a step closer home and we are going to get home boys. Do you hear me? We are going to make it back home, all of us.'

In the snow the legionaries, Batavians, slaves and civilians said nothing as they filed past Fergus. Did they not believe him? Fergus lowered his head to the ground. He hardly believed it himself. The company were on the run, fleeing for their lives and with their progress slowing, it would be only a matter of time before Gaiseric and his men overtook them. The Germans would be only a few hours behind them. And when the attack came, his men, weakened through exhaustion, cold and hunger, would only be able to offer a feeble resistance. They would be slaughtered. The situation was growing increasingly desperate. Grimly, Fergus tried to hide his emotions as he turned and started up the slope, plodding through the deep snow alongside the column.

It was growing dark and snow had started to fall once more, when Fergus raised his fist above his head and behind him the column of men and beasts came to a halt. Around them across the flattish land, the forest extended away into the distance but ahead through the trees was a clearing and in the clearing Fergus could see the unmistakeable signs of human habitation. Fergus's hand came to rest on the pommel of his sword, as through the trees, he saw Adalwolf and Aledus hastening back towards him.

'Well,' he snapped, 'is it occupied?'

Adalwolf shook his head.

'The huts are abandoned,' he replied. 'No one has lived here for years. It would make a good spot to make camp for tonight. The shelters are rudimentary but will shield us from the wind and hide the light from our fires and there is plenty of wood.'

Fergus glanced at Aledus who nodded in agreement.

'Then let's go,' he muttered, raising his fist in the air and pumping it up and down.

Cautiously the Romans emerged from the forest and into the clearing. Fergus peered at the small square-settlement. The place seemed to cover about a hundred square yards. A V shaped ditch about a yard deep which ran completely around the outer perimeter, was covered here and there in snowdrifts. Beyond the ditch were the remains of a low wooden-palisade that enclosed the settlement on all four sides, allowing for just one entrance to the south. The palisade however, looked in a high state of disrepair and here and there whole sections were missing or lay rotting in the snow. As he approached, Fergus turned to gaze at the three huts that stood in the middle of the square settlement. The wooden log walls looked sturdy enough but in two of the huts parts of the thatched roof had caved in, leaving gaping holes. The whole bleak looking place was covered with a layer of fresh snow.

'It's old, possibly hundreds of years old,' Adalwolf muttered, glancing around as he and Fergus jumped over the ditch and entered the debris-strewn square enclosure. The ditch and original layout are possibly the work of the Celts. They liked to build their settlements in a square.' Calmly Adalwolf pointed at the three shelters. 'The huts however are newer. They look like the kind that the Marcomanni or Quadi would build. They must have re-used the old settlement.'

Fergus did not reply as he turned to look around the small square settlement. Then with a grunt he made up his mind and turned to Adalwolf.

'Well this is it,' Fergus said. 'I am tired of running. This is where we are going to stay and make our stand.'

'What,' Adalwolf frowned.

'Adalwolf,' Fergus replied in a sudden quiet and resigned voice. 'We are never going to make it back to the Danube without being overtaken by Gaiseric and his warband. You know that just as well as I do. No, it is better if we turn on our pursuers and make a stand. We can fortify this place. Gather our remaining animals within the settlement and await Gaiseric's arrival.'

'And then what?' Adalwolf said in an alarmed voice, as he stared straight at Fergus.

'Then we fight to the death,' Fergus said coldly. 'We either win or we die. But in here the men will at least stand a chance. It is better than being overtaken and massacred in the forest.'

'Some chance,' Adalwolf snorted turning to gaze at the ruined settlement. 'Gaiseric outnumbers us two or three to one and we don't have the time to turn this place into a proper fortress. We are going to get slaughtered.'

'Those are my orders,' Fergus said, harshly rounding on Adalwolf. 'We shall camp here tonight and we shall do what we can to repair the defences. That's what we are going to do. I have made up my mind.' Fergus paused, his chest heaving with sudden emotion. 'As you are not a soldier,' he said in a gentler voice, 'and you haven't sworn an oath of allegiance to the Emperor, you are free to leave us at any time. So, I want you to take Hadrian, his two advisers and the slaves and get the Legate back to Carnuntum. Use one of the sledges. I shall give you our strongest remaining horses and enough supplies to make it back. Do what you must, but get Hadrian back home alive. Do you understand? I, my men and the Batavian's will remain here and we are going to fight. With a bit of luck, we shall delay Gaiseric long enough to allow you to make a clean escape. Hadrian must survive. You are his man. That is the only thing what matters. Gaiseric is after him and if he kills him, the treaty between us and the Vandals will be over and all my men will have lost their lives for nothing.'

Adalwolf was staring at Fergus in stunned silence. Then abruptly he looked away and groaned in dismay.

'So you trust me now, do you?,' Adalwolf said in a strained voice.

'Hadrian trusts you,' Fergus replied. 'And it's his problem if he is wrong.'

'I don't know,' Adalwolf said shaking his head. 'It's a long journey. Things could go wrong.'

'It makes sense,' Fergus hissed, as he took a step towards Adalwolf, grasping him by the shoulder. 'You know the way home and you can do this. You must do this.'

Adalwolf hung his head and gazed down at the snow. Then wearily he nodded in agreement.

'Fine, we will go tonight,' he muttered refusing to look Fergus in the eye.

***

It was night and snowflakes were slowly drifting down to the ground. In the bitter cold Fergus made his way along the perimeter, checking up on the sentries. Beyond the low wooden-palisade, the dark forest was quiet and peaceful. The men had done the best they could to erect crude barriers and obstacles in between the gaps in the low wooden-wall and they had also managed to scoop out the snowdrifts from the ditch that surrounded the small settlement. But there had been no more time to do anything else and the soldiers were already exhausted. As he slowly made his way around the perimeter, Fergus could see that the wooden-stakes, branches and debris were not going to hold back a determined assault. The settlement had not been built with that in purpose. But it was the best they could do with the resources and time they had. He had therefore decided that it was more important that the men got a good night's rest around a fire and out of the icy-cold wind. Blowing on his frozen, fingers Fergus turned and strode towards the three huts where the men and beasts sat and stood huddled-together around their camp fires. Adalwolf had left a few hours earlier, taking Hadrian and four of the strongest horses with him. The Legate had been unconscious, suffering from a fever that his wound had brought on, when Fergus had helped lash him to one of the horses. Then with a quick farewell Adalwolf, accompanied by Hadrian's two civilian advisers and a sledge filled with supplies, had galloped out of the settlement and into the night. And once the small party of horsemen had gone, Fergus had ordered that all Adalwolf's tracks leading into the forest be carefully destroyed. The slaves to-a-man had elected to stay behind and share the fate of the soldiers, and although he admired their courage Fergus did not have any weapons to give to them. Instead the slaves had armed themselves with sticks and stones.

In the hut, some of the men were fast asleep, curled up around the fire whilst others were awake, unable to sleep. Silently they turned to look at Fergus as he knelt and warmed his hands against the crackling fire. Catching sight of Titula sitting on the ground with her back against the wall Fergus smiled at her. The girl was awake and shivering with cold despite her large winter-cloak.

'Sleep,' Fergus muttered, quietly gazing at the slave girl. 'Sleep, you are going to need your strength tomorrow, girl.'

***

It was nearly noon when Fergus heard the barking of the dogs. He stood in the middle of the small square settlement without his shield or spear, which he'd given to a man who had no weapons. At his side stood the company's signifier, clad in his wolfs-skin-head and holding up the proud company banner. The legionaries and Batavians, their armour glinting in the winter sunlight, were down on one knee in their positions along the perimeter facing the forest. The men's large shields were resting against their bodies, and those who still had their spears were resting them on the tops of their shields. Not a man stirred or moved as the noise of the barking dogs drew closer. Calmly Fergus gazed into the forest from where the noise was rapidly coming closer. The men had had a good night's rest and that morning he had allowed them a larger-than-usual ration of food. There was nothing more to do. They were ready. It was time. The enemy was nearly upon them.

'If something happens to me,' Fergus said, turning to the standard bearer, 'you are in command of the company. Titus's last orders were to get the boys home. If the perimeter is overrun, you are to fall back on our last defensive position around the huts. Form two lines and use the huts to secure your flank. You should be able to hold them off like that for a while. And if all is lost it will be every man for himself. But only when all is lost, do you understand?'

'Yes Sir,' the signifer said, ashen faced.

There was no more time for talk. Along the tree-line bordering the forest clearing armed men had appeared. Some of them were holding dogs on leads. Slowly the line of warriors emerging from the forest began to extend right around the clearing. The Vandals seemed in no hurry, as they stared at the Romans pinned down in the derelict settlement. From the forest, came harsh cries and the dogs barked and strained at their leads eager to leap forwards and close with their prey. As Fergus turned he saw the enemy were all around them. From the edge of the trees, the German warriors raised their shields and weapons in the air and cried out, their harsh taunting voices filling the forest with noise. Then Fergus caught sight of Gaiseric. The tall warrior was wearing a horned-helmet on his head and in his hands, he was clutching a battle-axe and a small, round shield. He was striding along the line of his men as the Germans filled the forest with screams, shouts, yells and insults in their preparations to assault the small, square settlement.

'Standard bearer,' Fergus cried out, 'remember what I told you. If the perimeter is over run, fall back on the huts and make your final stand there.'

Then Fergus started walking towards the flimsy barricades, and as he did his hand came to rest on the pommel of his sword.

'What are you doing Sir?' the signifer cried out in alarm.

I am going to end this now,' Fergus roared, his eyes fixed on Gaiseric. 'This is going to end now. My men are not going to be slaughtered out here.'

And before anyone could stop him Fergus clambered over the barricade, leapt over the ditch and stepped out into the snowy clearing and started towards Gaiseric.

'This ends with us,' Fergus cried out as he drew his sword and pointed it at Gaiseric. 'You have come for Hadrian, to avenge an insult. That is what this is all about. But you shall not have him. Instead I challenge you to a duel, man to man, right here. If you want to avenge the insult against you, then fight me.'

Along the tree line, Gaiseric had stopped and was staring at Fergus in silence. Then he took a step forwards and raised his axe in the air and around the edge of the clearing the noise started to die down. Gaiseric was staring at Fergus, his chest heaving with wild emotion and aggression.

'Then to the death, Roman,' Gaiseric roared, in his accented Latin, 'if so I accept. Your men will soon see me raise your severed head in the air.'

'I am here, what are you waiting for,' Fergus roared, as he stood his ground.

And as Fergus fell silent the settlement behind him suddenly erupted with loud shouts and roars as the legionaries and

Batavians rose to their feet and grimly clashed their weapons together.

'Twentieth, Twentieth, Twentieth.' The roar rose.

Contemptuously Gaiseric took another step towards Fergus and spat onto the ground. Then raising his small round shield, he went into a crouch, raising his axe in the air. Warily Fergus watched Gaiseric as he slowly approached. Then he reached for his pugio army-knife and pulled it from his belt so that he was holding both gladius and a knife in both hands. Around the forest and in the settlement, the noise abruptly died down as the two men began to carefully circle each other.

And as Fergus watched his opponent, he reached up to touch Galena's iron amulet hanging around his neck.

Gaiseric was the first to attack. With a deft faint to his left, he suddenly leapt forwards and his axe came slicing through the air aimed at Fergus's neck. Fergus stumbled backwards just in time and the axe cut through the air, inches from his face. Then he lunged forwards but the blade of his sword glanced harmlessly off Gaiseric's shield. Along the edge of the forest the Germans roared in approval. Gaiseric hissed and spat into the snow as he once again swung his axe at Fergus. The attack was followed by a quick, low blow aimed at Fergus's legs. Stumbling backwards, Fergus was suddenly aware that Gaiseric was driving him away from the settlement and towards his men lining the edge of the forest. The man was taller than him and his axe meant his reach was longer, but without a shield he would never be able to get close enough to use his sword. Gaiseric had him at a disadvantage.

In an undignified manner Fergus turned and sprinted away around Gaiseric, and from the German ranks a holler of contemptuous laughter broke out. With his back to the settlement, Fergus turned to face Gaiseric once more. Gaiseric was studying him with an angry, contemptuous look as he slowly advanced towards him, swinging his axe confidently from side to side.

'Why don't you stop running Roman,' he yelled, 'stand still and fight like a man.'

Fergus said nothing as he crouched waiting for the next attack. It came swiftly, as with a yell Gaiseric suddenly charged forwards, his axe once more slicing down towards Fergus's neck. But this time instead of springing backwards, Fergus, judging his moment perfectly, leapt straight at Gaiseric his sword point hammering straight into the young warrior's shield but the pugio, the knife in his left hand, found its mark, and with a vicious slicing-movement, Fergus tore a bloody line across Gaiseric's chest. With a startled painful yelp, Gaiseric dropped his axe and staggered backwards as blood welled up through his clothes. Then he slipped and went tumbling helplessly onto his back in the snow. Fergus leapt forwards and raised his sword to finish off his opponent, but just then an outraged roar rose from the massed Vandal ranks along the edge of the forest. Fergus hesitated as he looked up. A spear came hurtling towards him, missing him by inches. Then the forest erupted as the Vandals came storming towards the settlement.

There was no time to finish off Gaiseric. With a cry, Fergus turned and fled back towards the settlement. Behind him the thud of hundreds of feet chasing him through the snow, closed in. In the square settlement, the squad defending the section of barricades directly ahead of him, raised their spears into a throwing position as Fergus charged straight towards them with dozens and dozens of German warriors hot on his tail. At the last moment Fergus cried out and dived into the ditch as a volley of Roman spears went hurtling straight over his head and into the enemy ranks. Each spear seemed to find its mark and the German line disintegrated into wild shrieks as men went tumbling into the snow. Frantically Fergus clambered out of the ditch and flung himself over the makeshift barricades and into the snow beside his comrades. But there was no time to rest.

The Germans had reached the perimeter and the whole settlement had become a moving, screaming, struggling mass of men, stabbing, hacking and pushing against each other. Leaping to his feet, Fergus had just enough time to see a big warrior come crashing through the barricades mowing down everything in his path with a heavy two-handed axe. Then with a roar the man flung up his arms and his axe went sailing high into the air as a Batavian rammed his sword into the warrior's exposed back, sending him crashing to the ground.

The outnumbered Roman defenders stood no chance in holding back the enemy assault and already Fergus could see that the men were being driven back from the palisade and the makeshift defences they had built in the night.

Stooping to pick up an abandoned axe, Fergus slashed at a German who was clambering over the wall, sending the man falling backwards into the ditch.

'Fall back to the huts,' Fergus roared as he staggered down the thin Roman line, 'Fall back on the huts, form a shield wall. Defend the standard!'

The legionaries needed no further encouragement. Within seconds the men were streaming back towards the space between two huts, where the signifer stood holding up the company banner. Suddenly from the corner of his eye, Fergus caught sight of Titula rushing towards him. The girl's face was pale with terror.

'Get back, get back to the huts,' Fergus screamed as he stumbled towards her. But the girl didn't seem to understand, and as she reached him she grasped hold of his white winter-cloak.

'Get back,' Fergus cried out as a note of desperation entered his voice. Behind him the Vandal warriors were surging unopposed over the palisade and barricades. They would be upon him within seconds.

'Here,' Fergus screamed as he pushed his pugio knife into Titula's hand and began to drag her through the snow towards the solid Roman shield wall that was rapidly forming in the space between two of the huts.

But as he and Titula staggered towards the Roman line, Fergus could see that it was already too late. A party of Vandal warriors had already gotten in between him and the line of Roman shields. They were not going to make it. Desperately Fergus turned to look around for another way of escape but there was none. Smoke was rising from the roof of one of the huts, which had been set on fire. The snow-covered ground around him was littered with corpses, dark red blood-stains, discarded weapons and wounded men, trying to crawl away through the snow. They were trapped, cut off from the rest of the company. Behind him, Fergus suddenly heard a great savage roaring voice coming towards him, and as he turned he saw Gaiseric and a few of his men calmly striding towards him through the black smoke.

Fergus's eyes widened in horror as he and Titula stumbled backwards against the wall of one of the huts. Cut off from the rest of his company, they were not going to stand a chance. Fergus took a desperate step forwards and swung his axe at Gaiseric but the Vandal Prince evaded the blow with contemptuous ease. The man's chest was covered in blood but he still looked capable of fighting. The men with him slowly started to fan out to either side, as they closed in on Fergus and Titula. With his back pressed against the wall, Fergus growled in frustration as he lunged here and there trying to keep the warriors at bay.

'Where is Hadrian? Where is the Legate?' Gaiseric roared as he raised his bloodied axe and pointed it at Fergus.

'He's with the standard,' Fergus bellowed defiantly. 'Like I said you shall not have him. So, fuck off.'

'Brave words for a man who is about to die,' Gaiseric roared.

Then with a speed that took Fergus by surprise Gaiseric lunged and his axe caught Fergus a glancing blow on the side of his torso armour that knocked him to the ground in a howl of pain. Raising his axe in the air with a triumphant yell, Gaiseric was about to bring the weapon down on Fergus's neck when, with a high-pitched scream Titula sprang forwards and buried her knife deep into Gaiseric's neck. A fountain of blood went hurtling into the air and Gaiseric collapsed to the ground without making a sound and his axe tumbled from his lifeless fingers. Fergus grimacing in pain, tried to rise to his feet as the men around Gaiseric charged forwards with a furious, outraged roar. Titula did not stand a chance. As she stood staring down at Gaiseric's corpse she was caught by spear that slammed her hard against the wall of the hut. Without making another sound her body crumpled into the snow. Furiously Fergus hammered his axe into one of the attacker's legs sending the warrior tumbling onto his back. Then with growing fury Fergus staggered to his feet, evaded a clumsy spear-thrust and buried his axe into another man's head, killing him instantly.

'Gaiseric is dead,' Fergus roared, his face stained with blood, his eyes bulging wildly as if he had gone mad. 'The fight is over. The fight is over. Gaiseric is dead.'

In front of him the Vandal warriors seemed to hesitate and waver. Fergus roared and raised his axe in the air as he advanced on them, no longer caring whether he lived or died; his crazy looking eyes bulging in their sockets. From out of the smoke a man came charging at him with a spear but Fergus evaded the thrust and stabbed the man with his sword kicking him to the ground.

'Gaiseric is dead,' Fergus roared. 'The fight is over. Your leader is dead. You have nothing to gain.'

For a moment, nothing changed and the din of battle continued unabated but then suddenly as the smoke cleared, Fergus saw that the Vandals had broken and were streaming back towards the forest in a great disorganised-mass. And as he stared at the fleeing enemy, he slowly sank to his knees in the snow. From the Roman ranks a great victorious cheer rose and as he knelt in the snow, a party of legionaries came rushing past.

'Stay in formation, defend your standard, let the bastards run,' Fergus heard the signifer's voice rising above the din.

In the snow Fergus turned to stare in the direction of the burning huts. They must think I am dead he thought. And why wasn't he? Slowly he turned to look back at the shelter where Titula's body lay crumpled and motionless in the snow. Rising to his feet, he slowly limped towards her and knelt beside her. The girl was dead. Fondly he parted her long, black hair and touched the tip of her nose. Then with a sigh, Fergus closed his eyes and leaned back against the wall of the hut. And as he did so he reached up to touch the circular iron-amulet that Galena had given him. His wife had said the amulet would protect him on his journey across the Empire. She had said it had great magic and maybe it had, he thought. Suddenly he opened his eyes, as a startling thought came to him. Maybe it had been the amulet that had summoned Titula to his side. Maybe that was why she was here? To protect him; and she had done just that. She had killed Gaiseric. A deep blush appeared on Fergus's cheeks as he turned to stare at the dead slave girl. Was this the work of the Gods? Had the Valkyrie after all chosen who was to live and die on the battlefield?

'Thank you,' Fergus whispered as his cheeks burned.

Chapter Thirty-Six – Hadrian

(Late January AD 106, Carnuntum)

The fifty survivors of the Second Company, Second Cohort of the Twentieth Legion stood stiffly to attention in the huge, open legionary parade-ground of Carnuntum. They were the only troops on parade, and around them the fortress seemed deserted. Beyond the long rows of dreary-looking barrack blocks with snow covering their sloping roofs, the walls and watchtowers of the army base were just about visible in the grey, cold and bleak winter weather. Fergus stood in front of his men staring fixedly into space, as Hadrian limped up onto the small podium that had been erected in front of the company. The Legate looked haggard and he had lost a lot of weight but otherwise he was in good shape. At the base of the podium, Adalwolf, two of Hadrian's civilian advisers and the first spear Centurion, the Primus Pilus of the First Legion, stood staring silently at the legionaries.

On the podium, Hadrian, with a thick warm-looking cloak draped over his shoulders, cleared his throat and turned to look at the troops, standing in front of him. For a long moment, he remained silent.

'Men,' he cried out at last, 'I welcome you back. You have had a harrying and most extraordinary journey. We have accomplished our aim. The alliance between Rome and the Vandals will endure. We have achieved much. You have achieved much and you have brought great glory to an already famous Legion. So, I salute you men. You have done well and you shall be rewarded accordingly. Three hundred Denarii for each of you as a special bonus payment.'

Hadrian paused to let the news sink in, but on the parade ground not a soldier moved or made a sound.

'We mourn for our dead,' Hadrian continued. 'We mourn for those we had to leave behind. We mourn the loss of your brave Centurion and the twenty-four others who did not make it back. I have discussed your company's personnel situation with the senior-ranking Centurion in your vexillatio, and we have agreed to the following. Lucullus your Optio, who was forced to remain behind in Britannia, will be taking over as your Centurion. Orders have already been dispatched to summon him to this fortress as soon as he is recovered from his injuries. Furius, your acting Optio will be invalided out of the army, as his wounds mean he is no longer capable of being a soldier. Fergus, you have been promoted to company Optio with immediate effect. I understand that the company took a vote on this and that the promotion was unanimously approved.'

Hadrian paused again, to stare at the legionaries standing stiffly to attention on the parade ground. 'That leaves me just to tell you that come spring our battle group will be heading south east to the Dacian frontier to take part in the campaign that will end King Decebalus's rule and threat to the Empire. Long live the Emperor, Trajan, the Senate and People of Rome!'

'Long live Emperor Trajan,' the men roared.

Satisfied Hadrian turned and nodded at the Primus Pilus of the First Legion as he slowly descended from the podium.

'Company will remain standing to attention,' Fergus shouted as he sensed some of the men behind him start to move.

Silence descended once more across the vast parade ground. Slowly Hadrian turned and came towards Fergus and as he did a frown appeared on the Legate's face. For a moment Hadrian said nothing as he paused to examine Fergus. Then raising his finger, the Legate ticked Fergus lightly on his shoulder.

'I shall be keeping an eye on you,' Hadrian said as a faint smile appeared on his lips.

Characters in Germania and the Veteran of Rome series

Adalwolf: German merchant, guide, adviser and translator for the Roman army.

Ahern: Kyna's son by another man. Dylis and Jowan have adopted him.

Alawa: Hyperborean woman friend of Cunomoltus.

Aledus: Londinium-born friend of Fergus belonging to Fergus's squad.

Alexandros: Greek captain and owner of the Hermes that had sailed to Hyperborea and back.

Arvirargus: Briton fugitive and last of the rebel leaders in AD 105.

Armin: Orphaned child of Lucius.

Ballomar: Leader of the Vandals tribe in Germania

Calista: Daughter of Alexandros.

Catinius: Friend of Fergus and soldier in Fergus's squad.

Claudia: A legate's wife, whom Marcus knew.

Cora: Wife of Alexandros.

Corbulo: Grandfather of Fergus, father of Fergus's father Marcus. Soldier in the Twentieth Legion.

Cunomoltus: Marcus's half-brother.

Decebalus: King of Dacia

Dylis: Younger half-sister of Marcus, adopted by Corbulo.

Efa: Wife of Corbulo, step-mother of Marcus.

Elsa: Orphaned child of Lucius, sister of Armin.

Emogene: The druid who murdered Corbulo.

Fergus: Marcus and Kyna's son, grandson of Corbulo.

Fortuna: The Goddess of Fortune.

Fronto: A squad leader in Fergus's army company.

Furius: Tesserarius and Optio in Fergus's army company

Gaiseric: German Vandal Prince, adviser to Hadrian.

Galena: Newly-wed wife of Fergus, daughter of Taran.

Jodoc: Husband of Calista.

Jowan: Husband of Dylis.

Kyna: Wife of Marcus, mother of Fergus.

Lucullus: Company Optio, at the beginning of Germania.

Lydia: Wife of Titus.

Matunaagd: A Hyperborean native who had volunteered to come back across the ocean.

Petrus: The Christian boy whom Corbulo rescued from certain death in Londinium nearly twenty years earlier.

Priscinus: A wealthy, influential, equestrian Roman aristocrat

Taran: Owner of the Lucky Legionary Tavern, in Deva Victrix.

Titula: A German girl captured by Fergus

Titus: Centurion of Fergus's company.

Trajan: Roman Emperor.

Vittius: Friend of Fergus and soldier in Fergus's squad.

GLOSSARY

Agrimensore: A land surveyor
Aquae Sulis: Bath, UK
Aquilaeia: Roman town near Venice, Italy
Aquilifer: Roman standard bearer carrying the Eagle standard of a Legion
Aquinoctium: Fourteen miles west of Carnuntum, near Vienna
Asturis: Klosterneuburg, Austria, just west of Vienna
Augusta Vindelicorum: Augsburg, Bavaria, Germany
Basilica: A large multi-purpose building for merchants, traders, business people, law courts and for religious ceremonies
Batavia: Area around the big rivers in the middle of The Netherlands
Batavis: Location not now known, but near the Danube
Bonna: Bonn, Germany
Brading: Site of a Roman villa in the south east of the Isle of Wight, UK
Brigantes: A Celtic tribe living in the north of Britain.
Camulodunum: Colchester, UK
Caestus: Leather and metal boxing glove
Carnuntum: Roman Legionary fortress and town, just east of Vienna
Castra: Fortress
Castra Bonnensis: Roman Legionary fortress at Bonn, Germany
Castra Mogontiacum: Mainz, Germany
Castra Regina: Regensburg, Bavaria, Germany
Centurion: Roman officer in charge of a company of about 80 legionaries
Cetium: Location not now known, but near the Danube in Austria
Cherusci: Germanic tribe living in central Germany
Cohort: Roman military unit equivalent to a battalion of around 500 men. Ten cohorts make up a legion
Colonia Agrippina: Cologne, Germany
Contubernium: Eight-man legionary squad. Also known as a barrack room/tent group

Cornicen: Trumpeter
Currach: Celtic boat.
Dacia: The area in Hungary/Romania where the Dacians lived.
Decanus: Soldier in charge of eight-man squad.
Decurion: Roman cavalry officer.
Denarii: Roman money.
Deva Victrix: Chester, UK.
Eburacum: York, UK.
Elysian Fields: The Roman idea of heaven, paradise etc.
Equestrian Order: The Order of Knights – the lower class of Roman aristocracy
Equites: Individual men of the Equestrian Order.
Equus Publicus: A minor noble, from the lower ranks of the aristocracy.
Fibula: A brooch or pin used by the Romans to fasten clothing together.
Focale: Neck scarf, that stops armour from chafing

Funeral societies: The Romans had funeral societies in which they banded together to make sure that their members were given proper funerals.
Garum: Roman fermented fish sauce
Gaul: France
Germania: Germany
Gladius: Standard Roman army short stabbing sword.
Hibernia: Ireland.
Hispania: Spain.
Hunebedden: Ancient stone graves dating back 5,000 years.
Hyperborea: Mythical land beyond the north wind.
Imaginifer: Roman army standard bearer carrying an image of the Emperor.
Iron fire dogs: A Celtic invention. Two iron tripods connected by an iron beam on which one could roast a pig over a fire
Isca: Exeter, UK.
Jupiter: King of the Roman Gods.
Lares: Roman guardian deities.
Legate: Officer in command of a legion
Legionary: Roman soldier.

Libation: An offering to gods or spirits.
Limes: Frontier zone of the Roman Empire.
Lindum: Lincoln, UK.
Londinium: London, UK.
Ludi Magister: The school master.
Lugii: The Vandals were part of the Lugii tribal confederation of central Europe
Luguvalium: Carlisle, UK.
Marcomanni: Germanic tribe living beyond the Danube in northern Austria and Czech Republic
Middle Sea: Mediterranean Sea
Mona Insulis: Anglesey Island, UK.
Mons Graupius: The battlefield in Scotland where Agricola defeated the Caledonian confederation in AD 83.
Mount Sleza: Mount Sleza is a hill south west of the Polish city of Wroclaw in Silesia, Poland
Munifex: Private (non-specialist) Roman Legionary.
Noviomagus Reginorum: Chichester, UK.
Numerii: German irregular Roman allied soldiers.
Odin: Germanic Lord of War and the World
Optio: Roman officer, second in command of a Company
Ovilava: Location not now known, but near the Danube in Austria.
Pannonia: The Roman province in and around Hungary/Slovenia, Serbia, Croatia.
Pilum/pila: Roman Legionary spear(s)
Prefect: Roman officer in command of an auxiliary cohort.
Principia: The HQ building in a Roman army camp/fortress.
Pugio: Roman army dagger.
Quadi: Germanic tribe
Regnenses tribe: Local tribe living around Noviomagus Reginorum.
Rutupiae: Richborough, Kent, UK.
Saturnalia: Roman festival in December.
SPQR: "Senate and People of Rome."
Suevus: The Oder river
Tara: Seat of the High King of Hibernia, north- west of Dublin, Ireland.

Tesserarius: Roman army watch/guard commander, third in line of command in a Roman infantry company

Tessera tile: A small stone carried by the Tesserarius (Watch Commander) on which the daily password was written.

Valkyrie: One of the mythical ladies of the war Lord, Odin

Vebriacum: Charterhouse Roman town, Western England.

Vectis: Isle of Wight, UK.

Vexillatio(n): Temporary Roman army detachment.

Vindobona: Vienna, Austria

Zeus: King of the Greek Gods